HIS WIFE, THE SPY

ENTERPRISING WOMEN, BOOK 4

Peri Maxwell

Dragonblade Publishing, Inc. is an imprint of Kathryn Le Veque Novels, Inc.
P.O. Box 23
Moreno Valley, CA 92556
ceo@dragonbladepublishing.com

Produced in the United States of America

First Edition July 2024
Trade Paperback Edition

ARE YOU SIGNED UP FOR DRAGONBLADE'S BLOG?

You'll get the latest news and information on exclusive giveaways, exclusive excerpts, coming releases, sales, free books, cover reveals and more.

Check out our complete list of authors, too!

No spam, no junk. That's a promise!

Sign Up Here

www.dragonbladepublishing.com

Dearest Reader;

Thank you for your support of a small press. At Dragonblade Publishing, we strive to bring you the highest quality Historical Romance from some of the best authors in the business. Without your support, there is no 'us', so we sincerely hope you adore these stories and find some new favorite authors along the way.

Happy Reading!

CEO, Dragonblade Publishing

For Cheryl, who always tells me the truth.

CHAPTER ONE

"A NNABEL, YOU MUST speak with Father right away."

Annabel Pearce placed her teacup on its saucer and her book in her lap before appraising the young lady she'd been hired to bring into Society. Elizabeth Spencer had the looks valued by the *ton*—suitably tall, appropriately thin, and beautifully fair. Unfortunately, her pale complexion tended to redden when she was in a rush, excited, or angry—and the girl was almost always one of those things. Sometimes several combined.

Today was one of those days. Her bright blue eyes sparkled in her pink face, which made her blonde hair that much brighter.

"Elizabeth, come sit and calm—"

"You're going to tell me to breathe until I'm no longer pink, but we don't have the time." Elizabeth paced from the chair to the door and back at a dizzying pace. "Father will make the wrong decision if we do not act quickly."

Annabel would have—likely *should* have—counseled her charge that fathers made decisions based on more knowledge than daughters understood. However, as Annabel was now working for a living because of her own father's poor choices, it would be a losing argument.

Instead, she poured the girl a cup of tea and placed a *petit four* as bait before the empty chair. "Tell me what has you so agitated."

Elizabeth finally took the chair. She sank her teeth into the cake and chewed much too obviously for a young lady before dumping an alarming amount of sugar into her tea.

Annabel would have to plan more lessons about eating habits. At the present, she was glad the girl's color was fading to normal, and that she hadn't dropped into the chair like a rag doll, which she was inclined to do when behind closed doors.

"Father received a letter from the Marquess of Ramsbury. It must be an invitation to his house party, Annabel. Charlotte Bainbridge received hers two days ago, and I've been watching the post since."

"The letter could be anything," Annabel counseled. "Lord Ramsbury is a member of Parliament, and your father is a courtier. It may be about a vote, or an invitation to White's to discuss business."

"Why would he invite Charlotte and not *me*?" Elizabeth pointed her teacup toward her chest, sloshing the liquid dangerously close to the rim.

Because Charlotte Bainbridge is the diamond of the Season and the daughter of a viscount. Why she considers you part of her social circle is a mystery.

Annabel took a bite of cake and used chewing as an excuse for her silence. Elizabeth took the lack of discussion for agreement.

"Between the two of us, we'll convince him. We'll lay out my wardrobe this afternoon." She looked past Annabel, her smile a match for her calculating gaze. "Imagine the furor if I am to catch him."

Furor, indeed. As far as Annabel knew, there was only one way to catch a man like Jasper Warren, the new Marquess of Ramsbury, and it wasn't with ruffled dresses and croquet.

"Elizabeth—"

A knock on the door announced the arrival of the housekeeper. "Miss Pearce, Mr. Spencer asks that you meet him in the library."

Thanking fate for her rescue from a difficult conversation,

Annabel stood and smoothed her skirt. "Thank you, Mrs. Riordan. I'll follow you down."

As she passed, Elizabeth clasped her hand. Her color had returned to normal. "Please, Annabel. I can't stay in London if everyone else is in Wiltshire. It would be too humiliating."

There were far worse things than missing a party, but as Annabel looked into the girl's large blue eyes and felt the squeeze of her thin fingers, she couldn't say the words. Elizabeth was barely out of the schoolroom, and every slight signaled the end of the world.

"Don't put too much stock in a conversation, dear. This likely has nothing to do with a party." *Not to mention the marquess likely doesn't know your name. I'd be shocked if he remembered mine.*

Mr. Spencer could decide not to send his daughter without input from anyone else. The better guess was that he wanted help designing a suitable distraction. Annabel turned at the door and indicated the easel and canvas at the window. "Please begin drawing. We'll discuss paint choices when I return."

She walked down the empty, quiet hall toward the staircase. Mrs. Riordan ran an efficient household, but she didn't linger to gossip or laugh over tea. All Annabel knew of her was that she reveled in being one of Spencer's trusted staff members, and that she considered it far beneath her station to fetch someone other than a family member.

The wide staircase curved in a long, graceful arc toward the black-and-white-tiled entry hall. It was as grand as any house in Mayfair could be, but Annabel couldn't help comparing it to her family's country home.

She hoped the tenants were enjoying the rivers in Chilworth. They were always best in the spring.

The final step left her aligned with the library door. Her knock echoed through the hall, making it sound less like a polite rap and more like a demanding hammer.

"Enter."

It was unkind to compare this library with the one in Chilworth. The latter was a family library, overstuffed with favorites read until their spines were creased and their covers were tattered at the corners. Not even Father's library here in London could compare with that.

However, even Father's London library smelled of read books. Sir Reginald Spencer's smelled of new leather and tobacco, and the spines glinted in the sunshine like soldiers lined up for review.

"Miss Pearce." Spencer motioned to the chairs in front of his desk. "Sit."

Annabel bristled at the command that made her feel like a prized terrier. At least her employer didn't call her by her Christian name.

She took the chair that claimed the most shadow and waited for Spencer to sit. As he emerged from the sun's glare, his features formed.

As a young man, he'd likely garnered a great deal of attention due to his height. As an older man, everything about him—from his fair skin to his white-blond hair—stretched too thinly over his large bones. He would have been terrifying looming down from a pulpit. Best that he'd given up his parish for a position in the royal household.

"How is Bitty this morning?"

"*Elizabeth* is well." Annabel emphasized the girl's first name. The unfortunate family nickname sounded too much like "Biddy" to be complimentary. Besides that, the girl had inherited her father's height. "She was beginning her art lesson when I left her."

The man nodded, his smile as thin as his eyebrows. His lined face seemed to fight the effort. "She shows some aptitude for it, I believe."

"She does." In truth, Elizabeth sat still for little else. "I would like to challenge her by taking her to the National Museum, where she can study and copy the masters. There are several young ladies who do the same, and it would be good for Elizabeth to try her hand at something unfamiliar."

"Perhaps she should carry her supplies to Wiltshire for new scenery," Spencer said.

Annabel's hopes fell. "She thought she saw an invitation."

"She did, and I have already answered. Elizabeth will leave in four days' time with you as her companion."

"Four days will barely give us time to gather wardrobes, sir."

"She should need no new dresses. Many of the ones purchased for the Season have yet to be worn."

It was true. Elizabeth had all she needed, but Annabel needed…

Nothing. She was a paid companion, hired to step in due to Mrs. Spencer's illness. Two day dresses and something for evening meals were the only requirements. Her days of croquet and ballrooms were over.

But that didn't mean she had no say. She had a job and, to her, part of that was bringing Elizabeth out properly. That meant using her own experiences about which events were better suited to find quality husbands.

The last house party she had attended with Jasper Warren had ended prematurely in a drunken display that left all the ladies in tears and one young man—not a gentleman, despite his upbringing—with a broken nose.

"With respect, sir, are you certain of this? Lord Ramsbury's reputation for bacchanals is no secret, and Elizabeth, frankly, is too impulsive. The environment will most likely—"

"Elizabeth will have the month to grow accustomed to the crowd she will likely mingle with for the rest of her life. As for her impulses, that is why she has you."

"A month?"

A month at the sort of party where Annabel would have been a guest only a year ago. A month with *ton* ladies she knew from ballrooms and rides in the park. They could be horrid to each other in the best of circumstances, and this was not Annabel's best circumstance.

It likely wouldn't be Elizabeth's either. She was better in

shorter events where there was little chance for her manners and temper to wear thin.

"Sir, since we will be near Bath, perhaps a visit to Elizabeth's mother would be in order. Maybe a fortnight there would ease Elizabeth's mind over Mrs. Spencer's health."

The lie was a gamble. Elizabeth was no more worried about her mother than anyone else in the household, including the lady's husband. Annabel wrote to her of Elizabeth's successes in the Season, detailing everything she was missing, but she rarely saw any other letters in the outgoing post.

Spencer looked at her from under his brows. "At month's end, if Elizabeth wishes to see her mother, she may visit for a week, no more. Her mother will not bear the upheaval for a fortnight. But you will spend the month at Kennet Hall. That is plenty of time to accomplish my goal."

His goal? Surely he wasn't title-hunting for his daughter amongst Warren's set. "Sir, Elizabeth has many well-situated suitors in London." Annabel scoured her memory for the standouts amongst Elizabeth's recent dance partners. "Mr. Cameron is heir to the Earl of Whitestone, and Mr.—"

"I do not care to send my daughter husband-hunting more than she already is," Spencer said. "I want to know what goes on in that house."

"You want a scandal." Annabel wasn't a fool. She'd investigated Spencer before entering his employment. The reports had been good, though there were a few whispers of his ability to sniff out secrets and use them to his benefit. There were suspicions that he'd helped bring down Viscount Stratford just a few months earlier.

Spencer shook his head. "I have a well-founded suspicion that Jasper Warren is plotting some sort of upheaval in Wales."

"Surely not." It was one thing for a man to care little for his reputation and his title. It was another thing altogether to hang because of it.

"His man, Yarwood, is a Welsh-born, British-trained soldier.

With his connections both in trade and in the military, and Ramsbury's wealth and political sway, they could create havoc. If Ramsbury includes his French mistress, some bit of fluff with a diplomat father, the interference could cripple London."

The connections were difficult to overlook, but the plan had one flaw. "Sir, Elizabeth will never be able to discover this secret." The girl could barely *keep* a secret.

"Not Elizabeth." Spencer's sharp stare scraped Annabel's skin. "You."

No. Annabel's lot in life had changed, but she would not stoop to sneaking through someone else's house and listening at keyholes. She shook her head. "Sir, this is unwise."

She was risking dismissal, but no one else would speak for her. Learning that had been a bitter lesson. Besides, the Season provided a bit of courage. Elizabeth couldn't go into Society without a chaperone, and unemployed candidates were thin on the ground.

Spencer's eyes narrowed. "It is not. Dressed as you are, with the role you have, no one will notice your moving through the house. Chaperones are unnecessary for rides and games, even balls at the house. You will have time on your hands and fewer eyes on your activity. Plus, you are bright enough to realize what will, or won't, be important."

It was clear from his smile that he'd intended the last to stroke her pride. *Bright enough.*

Enough.

Annabel wanted to throw something at him. Better yet, she could leave his employ altogether. While he might not dismiss her, she could still resign.

But the lack of available chaperones also meant there were no suitable open positions. This job was all that kept Annabel from begging. Or worse.

At least Spencer had a good reputation. His older brother was the Earl of Denton, and his sister was married to the Duke of Somerset. Even his middle brother had retired from the navy as a hero and a wealthy man. Rumor had it that Spencer himself was being considered for a promotion that would give him the ear of the queen.

Perhaps this mission, while distasteful, was valid.

"Find the truth and return with Elizabeth," she said, confirming their agreement.

He nodded. "And to my gratitude."

Annabel stood. "As you wish."

Perhaps Reginald Spencer's gratitude would earn her a letter of reference for her next employer.

JASPER WARREN, THE latest Marquess of Ramsbury, held out his hand to yet another guest and shaped his face into a smile. "Wareham, good of you to come."

The earl's brow was as sweaty as his palm. "Wouldn't miss it. Raines has promised a rousing party."

"Oh, it will be a memorable month." Jasper discreetly wiped his palm against his trousers and focused on the familiar coach lumbering up the lane. "Raines is in the billiards room enjoying my scotch, I believe." Scotch, port, madeira—it made no difference if it kept the gentlemen talking and off their guard.

He stood to the side, encouraging Wareham to clear the way for the next guest. The earl did not take the hint.

"Starnes will show you and your valet to your rooms." Jasper crooked an eyebrow and swept his fingers toward the door. Good Lord, no wonder the man was so horrible at cards.

Without waiting to see if Wareham moved forward, Jasper descended the stairs, waited for the footman to open the door, and stepped forward to offer his hand to the lady inside. For the first time this morning, his smile was genuine. "Welcome, Fi."

Fiona Allen's hat was almost as wide as the door of her coach, and its crown was circled with blue silk flowers exactly matching her day dress. The only thing that spoiled her transformation into a respectable young lady was the twinkle in her dark eyes. "Your lordship."

"I thought I cured you of that years ago," Jasper scolded her as he would one of his sisters. And, like his sisters, Fiona paid no attention. She hadn't since the day they'd met, when he was sixteen and she was the only girl who didn't make calf eyes at him.

"I don't think one can call a marquess Rabbit in polite company." Fiona caught the eye of the older woman descending from the carriage with the help of a footman. "Isn't that correct, Mrs. Linden?"

"Don't tease, miss," the older woman scolded gently. She shook out her skirts before curtsying quickly. "Lord Ramsbury."

Jasper bowed. "Mrs. Linden, it is good to see you again. Welcome to Kennet Hall." He offered his arm to the lady, knowing it would fluster her, and that the good-natured teasing would amuse Fiona. "I've requested that you and Fiona have the rooms overlooking the gardens."

The woman blushed pink under her hat. "That is too kind, your lordship."

"Nonsense. It's the least I can do." He looked over his shoulder at one of his oldest friends. "I know how difficult it is to keep Fiona in line."

Jasper was pleased to see Fiona stick out her tongue. Not that it was unusual—she usually flouted the rules of Society. However, almost a year ago, that rebellious streak had left her in a spot from which he feared she would never emerge.

"Would you prefer I escort you to the conservatory, where the other young ladies and their companions are having tea?" he asked.

The remnants of last year's scandal were evident in Fiona's slight hesitation. "To our rooms, I think. It's been a long journey, and we should rest before dinner. Don't you think, Mrs. Linden?"

The older woman smiled. "As you wish, miss."

Jasper would resent Linden for the change in his friend's demeanor, if he didn't wonder whether she was Fiona's only female friend. That, and Fiona's father had decreed that Fiona's continuation in even limited Society was dependent on Linden's constant presence.

"You don't need to show us up, Jasper." Fiona put her fingers on his arm. "One of your staff can do that while you greet your guests."

As she spoke, horses' hooves announced the arrival of another carriage. As luck would have it, his other trusted friend came down the stairs at the same time.

"Kit," Jasper called. "Please see Fi—Miss Allen and Mrs. Linden to their rooms and ask Starnes to have trays sent up for them."

"Certainly." Kit bowed to both women before taking Mrs. Linden from Jasper. "This way, ladies."

The newest arrival came to a stop as Jasper reached the bottom step and reassembled his smile. The footman handed down a young lady with bright blonde hair, her pink day dress done with just enough embellishment to be tasteful.

"Miss Spencer, welcome to Kennet Hall." He bent over her lace-gloved hand. "It was good of you to come."

"Lord Ramsbury." The girl's blue eyes widened as she curtsied. "Thank you for your kind invitation."

Her cheeks matched her dress, and her voice was breathy. She was overwhelmed, and she wasn't even in the door yet. Jasper suppressed his widening smile. This would be easier than he thought.

He straightened and turned to greet her companion, prepared to give the same bland greeting he'd repeated all afternoon, and stopped. "Miss Pearce?"

The last he'd seen Annabel Pearce, she'd been a guest at his cousin Amelia's disastrous house party. She'd left under the watchful eye of her chaperone.

"Your lordship." She curtsied, and the brim of her hat hid her face.

"I didn't realize you—" He stopped. The gray dress was his first clue that Annabel was not here to support a friend.

She straightened. A blush stained her cheeks, and her eyes were suspiciously bright. "I've been hired to help Miss Spencer with her Season."

Of course. Her father, Baron Chilworth, had a reputation for wild speculation and poor choices. At the time of Amelia's party, he'd suspected those habits were the source of Miss Pearce's odd rhyme.

There once was a man with a daughter, whom he led like a lamb to the slaughter...

Did she consider employment with Spencer akin to an abattoir?

He dipped his head to her, as he'd done to every companion except Mrs. Linden. "Welcome to Kennet Hall. The other ladies are taking tea in the conservatory." Gossiping, most likely. Without Fiona in the room, Jasper could only hope the servants repeated what they overheard. "Starnes can show you the way."

Miss Pearce's lips flattened into a tense line. Jasper was struck by how similar her situation was to Fiona's. She would be between two groups—the young ladies she had danced with last Season, and the paid companions who, unaccustomed to her new position, likely would not trust her.

"If you would prefer to rest in your rooms after you morning's travel, trays can be sent up."

"I'm so excited, I couldn't possibly rest." Elizabeth stormed the steps without a backward glance.

"As you wish, miss." Miss Pearce inclined her head just enough to acknowledge his offer. "Tea sounds lovely, your lordship. Thank you."

Jasper watched her go. Her plain dress was in a shade that did little for her coloring, and an equally drab shawl was draped across her elbows. She removed her hat as she entered the house, giving him a glimpse of light brown braids that led to a neat knot at her nape.

But her spine was straight, and her smile was serene as she greeted his new butler.

Kit came down the steps, and his gaze followed Jasper's. "That's the last of them."

"Is everyone settled?" Jasper asked.

"Their things are in their rooms, and the maids and valets are unpacking now."

"You trust them?"

"As much as we can trust village lads and lasses we hired a week ago." Kit glanced in his direction. "Your new butler is Stapleton, not Starnes."

"Stapleton." Jasper nodded. The man at the door was tall, straight, and fitter than Jasper would have expected of a man his age. "Where did you find him?"

"He's a retired regimental. Good with his fists and a saber. With a gun, too, if we need it." Kit snorted a laugh. "Just get his name right from now on." He, too, kept his eyes on the door. "Who is with Miss Spencer?"

"Annabel Pearce, Baron Chilworth's eldest daughter." Jasper scratched his chin. "I had hoped Spencer would hire some dotty old matron for his daughter's companion."

"Someone who sleeps in the corner and focuses on her knitting?" Kit teased. "Is she going to be a problem?"

An astute guardian would keep Miss Spencer on her best behavior. There would be little chance to baffle her with charm and too much punch and learn more about her father's movements in London.

For years, Jasper had watched the men of Society embark on daring reform, either through legislation or direct action, only to return to stillness and the status quo, their gazes searching the shadows as they spoke. They acted differently. They spoke differently. Their courage died.

After one too many incidents, he began looking where they looked, seeing what they saw. Whom they saw.

Sir Reginald Spencer.

Jasper wanted Spencer off the chessboard. Annabel Pearce was too attentive to let him accomplish it easily.

"Most definitely."

CHAPTER TWO

*I*T IS GOING *to be a long month.*

Annabel strolled through the hedge maze that had likely once been the pride of Kennet Hall's garden. Now, its outer shape was a model of smooth respectability, but its paths were bisected with clumps of weeds. The inner walls were marred with tendrils and sprouts that waved in the breeze like hair escaping its pins.

Despite that, it was the perfect refuge. Its circular shape reminded her of the labyrinth in the courtyard of her village church. Many times she'd walked the worn stones in thought, searching for peace of mind.

Something she desperately needed today.

Sitting in Sir Reginald's library, agreeing to his scheme had seemed the simplest path. Now that she was here, the task he'd set for her seemed enormous. The house was a sprawling mass of staircases and hallways, full of guests and servants. Of which she was neither.

Not for the first time since her father's bankruptcy, Annabel thought it would be easier to be a maid. The work would be difficult, certainly, but she'd be able to leaf through Lord Ramsbury's papers without notice. She'd also have a place far from those who had known her in her past life.

Which made it sound like she had died—faded away with the loss of her dowry.

"I'm still shocked to see Annabel Pearce here—in gray, no less. It's such an unbecoming color on a young lady. She looks as though death will be knocking any moment."

The voice, with its nasal pitch, soaked through the green wall of the maze. It belonged to Belinda Wallace, who had come out the year after Annabel. In a ballroom, clad in silks and lace, butter wouldn't melt in Belinda's mouth. But they weren't in a ballroom, and it was easy to imagine the sly, sharp smile she wore everywhere else.

"Though the gray is at least this year's style," said Charlotte Bainbridge. "Last Season her gowns were all from the year before, if not older." Her hushed tone made it sound as though previously worn dresses were the eighth deadly sin. "It's no wonder that she didn't catch a beau."

"Dresses had nothing to do with it," Belinda said. "She's as poor as a church mouse. Father says Baron Chilworth risked everything in a scheme that came to nothing. They've rented or sold as much as they could. Father's talking of making an offer for their library, though Mother can't understand what he wants with piles of old books."

Despite the warm sun and the spring breeze, a chill went through Annabel. Her family's library would belong to someone else, or to several someones if an auction was required. The *ton* would dismember and distribute it without respect to the family who had curated it with a reverence others reserved for horses.

"Miss Pearce loves her library," Elizabeth said. "She speaks of it often. It will pain her greatly to lose it."

The sadness in the girl's words, her proper use of *Miss Pearce*, gave Annabel's spirit a lift. They would never be true friends, but perhaps she was making an impact on her young charge.

"Aren't you worried about having a companion not much older than you?" Charlotte asked. "I can't imagine why your father chose her."

"Mama was meant to bring me out," Elizabeth explained. "When she grew too ill for London, Father had to find someone quickly. Miss Pearce was the best of those who applied."

Annabel remembered their meeting quite differently. She had been so panicked over being sent to the workhouse that she'd accepted Sir Reginald's offer without questioning the salary. Only after a month did she realize how much she was underpaid.

Still, working for her wages was better than scheming for a wealthy protector.

"It was kind of your family to take her," Belinda said. "But I'd be wary. It would be a shame to have her turn your beau's head while you aren't looking."

In the long pause that followed, Annabel was tempted to break through the hedgerow and tell them all how little she thought of *ton* men and their double lives. How she'd rather spend her days alone than be forced to gossip with empty-headed ladies who sent their children to nannies and their husbands to mistresses without a second thought.

Never mind that the young men queuing up for Elizabeth were barely able to shave.

But it would do no good. No amount of protest would convince these sheltered girls that a different life existed outside their family's walled gardens.

"You shouldn't worry Elizabeth so," Charlotte said. "In that drab color, with her nose in a book and no dowry? No man will ever take notice of Annabel Pearce."

A Season ago, the mean-spirited comments and the malicious giggles that followed would have stung. Now, Annabel's skin was thicker. She had made the difficult choice to pay her own way. She was making—

"Too right, Charlotte," Elizabeth said, laughing. "She'll be lucky to have the blacksmith as a husband. Her children will be born with ashes under their nails."

The girl's jibe sent a pin into Annabel's heart and heat to her ears. She didn't crave a husband, but the thought of never having children woke her in the middle of the night and sent her curling around a pillow. When dawn broke, she consoled herself with the thought of making a difference for others' children. Like Elizabeth.

But she was making no measurable difference at all. She was simply stepping in to ensure another *ton* brat found a better title and a larger house.

"I could tell you that eavesdroppers never hear well of themselves."

Annabel spun to face the speaker, realizing too late that the wild hedges had caught her hair. At least the snare gave her a reason for the tears in her eyes.

"Instead I'll tell you it could be worse." Fiona Allen reached up and helped free her before smoothing the loose strands back into place. Her twisted smile and arched eyebrow gave her words a dark humor. "You could be me."

Every Society matron in London told their daughters, nieces, cousins, and random guests at tea the story of Fiona Allen's fall from grace. It was a twisted fairytale of a beautiful girl with a father so wealthy his lack of title didn't matter, a splash of a first Season, and a quick engagement with the bachelor heir every girl had wanted.

And prematurely anticipating the wedding night, a broken engagement, and a hurried trip to the Continent to avoid the scandal.

She was a walking warning about the results of disobeying the rules.

What Annabel remembered, however, was Amelia Chitester's disastrous house party and Fiona's brazen flirtation with Amelia's fiancé. How scandal shadowed her every step.

Annabel reached to her hair to check the pins. "I'm sorry, Miss Allen."

"Don't be. My life is much less complicated these days." Fiona took Annabel's hand and tucked it into her elbow. "Let's leave these harpies-to-be in our wake. There used to be a lovely statue garden at the end of this path." She stumbled over a flowering vine trailing across the path. "Perhaps the jungle hasn't claimed it yet."

Annabel tried to free herself. Guests could stroll the grounds. She was not a guest. "Miss Allen, I should be—"

"Miss Spencer doesn't need you in the daylight. Besides, all the young men are in the stables, no doubt wagering over whatever race Jasper has planned." Fiona tugged Annabel forward.

"I could return to the house." She should. If Jasper Warren was out planning a race, it was the perfect time to search his office.

"Why waste the sunshine?" Fiona said. "We'll be trapped by rain enough this month." She winked. "Besides that, Linden is resting after our trip, and I need someone to talk to."

They took a turn in the circle, paralleling their earlier path on the other side of the untrimmed hedge.

"How long have you been Miss Spencer's companion?"

"Since January." Annabel had spent one last holiday at Chilworth House before returning to London to look for a placement. "Mrs. Spencer took ill at Christmas and is convalescing in Bath. In her absence, they advertised for someone to help bring Elizabeth into Society." She paused. "How long has Mrs. Linden been with you?"

"Since after the Chitesters' house party." Fiona steered her around another hedge. "I wish I would have had her the Season before." She sighed as they came to another wall and a third turn. "I also wish Jasper would make a shortcut through these dratted hedges."

"The funds must get there somehow." The voice, leaking through the maze's inside wall, was deep and measured. Aristocratic. The man sounded much like Jasper, but Annabel couldn't be certain. She'd only heard him speak when he was bored or poking fun.

Still, her ears perked up.

"What say our friends to the west?" he asked.

"They're being watched too closely to communicate. I don't

blame them after Gareth's disappearance," another man replied. Annabel could place him easily. The very serious Mr. Yarwood had directed her to Elizabeth's rooms upon their arrival. He had supervised the upstairs staff with military precision. "When does Claudette arrive?"

Mr. Spencer said Ramsbury had a French mistress wrapped up in his scheme. Annabel thought it quite bold to include the woman in a house party, not to mention continuing their plot in plain view. But then, Jasper Warren seemed to care little for what Society thought.

She risked a glance at Fiona. After Amelia's party, Annabel would have sworn Fiona was Jasper's latest mistress—or perhaps something more serious. Could the man really intend to have two ladies demanding his attention under the same roof at the same time? Did Fiona not care?

"Within a fortnight. Perhaps a bit later," Jasper mumbled. "Our lady in London will be expecting progress, Kit."

"Then perhaps you shouldn't have invited a house full of strangers for the month. I can't traipse off across Wales and leave you alone."

"I've no need for a mother hen, and I'm hardly alone. Fiona is here."

Yarwood barked a laugh. "Then you have no need of me at all."

Fiona sped their pace and rounded the last corner in a whirl of yellow skirts, pulling Annabel in her wake. "Careful with your next words, Mr. Yarwood. Jasper can vouch for my fighting skills."

Annabel looked between the two men, each dressed well and close in age. Yarwood was the leaner of the two, and he wore his suit with crisp precision.

However, Jasper commanded attention without moving or uttering a word. His dark blond hair, worn at a fashionable length, fell past his broad shoulders and chest. He wore his tailored coat, made of dark blue super-fine, with the casual air of a man accustomed to the best life had to offer.

"Especially when you arrive with reinforcements." He nodded toward Annabel. "Miss Pearce." His slight smile contradicted his sharp, wary gaze. It matched Yarwood's. Both of them reminded her of foxes guarding their kill.

Annabel curtsied. "Your lordship. Mr. Yarwood."

The center of the maze was a wide circle occupied by four female statues facing each direction on the compass and each dressed for a different season. Vines wrapped their feet and dirt stained their faces and streaked their clothing.

"What brings you here, ladies?" Jasper asked.

"Miss Pearce was walking when I took her captive and forced her to accompany me," Fiona said. "I've come to tell you that you promised croquet, and the young ladies need something to occupy their time other than sharpening their tongues."

"Croquet it is, then."

"Excellent. Thank you." Fiona turned to Annabel. "Will you join us, Miss Pearce?"

Annabel shook her head. "Thank you, but no. I should return to the house."

"As you wish," Jasper said. "Kit, please take Miss Allen to the croquet court and help her set out the wickets." He winked at Fiona. "I don't trust her not to cheat."

"Cheat?" Fiona pressed her hand to her chest. "Me? I seem to remember you putting all my wickets uphill."

Jasper's warm and rich laughter rolled like sunshine from behind a cloud. "I did, didn't I?" He walked past her and offered Annabel his arm. "Allow me to accompany you, Miss Pearce."

She resisted the urge to put her hands behind her back. "That's not necessary, your lordship."

He left his arm at a right angle, waiting for her to accept. "Unnecessary, yes, but ungentlemanly otherwise."

The weight of everyone's stares pressed on Annabel's shoulders, forcing her to lift her hand and thread it through Jasper's elbow. Her fingers rested on his thick, solid forearm. His deep blue coat and buff trousers made her gray dress drabber and dowdier than she had believed possible.

"Thank you, your lordship."

❧

JASPER WALKED IN silence beside the woman on his arm. As a general rule, he found the prattling of *ton* ladies annoying. Today, however, was different. In his experience, a quiet woman was rarely a good thing.

"Have you kept in touch with Amelia since the house party?" He hoped his cousin, their one mutual acquaintance, would break the ice. Amelia usually did.

"We correspond, yes."

He waited for more. Amelia's letters were always full of news about the estate and the family. Uncle Augustus was now determined to keep death at bay in order to see his first grand-child upon its arrival, likely in the summer.

Annabel offered nothing further.

Jasper tried again. "She doesn't appear to regret missing the Season."

"No, she doesn't. It is one of the things I admire about her."

Jasper wondered whether Annabel's admiration would be tempered by knowing Amelia eschewed London because her whiskey business demanded much of her attention. "She is an unusual lady."

At that, Annabel glanced up at him. Her furrowed brow enhanced the confusion in her eyes, which were the same color as his favorite chestnut mare.

"What?" he asked.

"You make *unusual* sound like a compliment."

Jasper had met many beautiful women in his life. Annabel Pearce wasn't a traditional beauty, especially with her hair in that severe style and in a dress even a nun would refuse to wear. But her skin was luminous, and she carried herself with a grace that was almost impossible to teach.

"I suppose it is," he replied. "She has a confidence that makes her stand out amongst the other ladies of the *ton*."

Except, perhaps, the young woman in front of him.

Jasper pushed the thought from his mind. Yes, he remembered Miss Pearce's sharp wit and thoughtful stare from Amelia's party, but he wasn't walking with her to test her wits. Not exactly, anyway.

He resumed their stroll through the maze. "You have not been Miss Spencer's companion long."

"No. Mrs. Spencer took ill after the New Year and quit London in favor of Bath. Elizabeth's governess accompanied her."

The New Year. Viscount Stratford's trial had concluded just prior to Christmas. Reginald Spencer had attended it as regularly as a church service, and the gallery had been so crowded that the judge worried it would collapse onto the floor below. Men and women alike had attended as though it were a party at Vauxhall.

"I do not recall seeing you in London over the holiday," he said.

"I do not recall your ever seeing me in London." Her steps faltered. "I apologize, Lord Ramsbury. Apparently being officially invisible has loosened my tongue."

Jasper smiled at the top of her head. "Apology accepted, Miss Pearce."

"Thank you, and you're correct. I was at Chilworth during Christmas. We were packing for the move to London."

The gossip at White's had focused on two topics—Stratford's trial and Baron Chilworth's bankruptcy. Jasper had played cards with the baron on several occasions. He was a gregarious, likable fellow, though always a little too careless with his money.

"You didn't want to live with your family in London?" Jasper asked. He had never been inside the Chilworths' home in the West End, but he knew where it was. It was large enough for several generations of the family.

"I did not." The words had a ring to them, hinting that the topic was closed. Just as well. He didn't wish to discuss her family.

If Miss Pearce wasn't in London during the holiday, then she likely knew little of Stratford's Scandal, as the newspapers had called it. She would know less of Spencer's shadow lurking through the trial of the viscount who had kidnapped, and then murdered, his young mistress.

"At the risk of appearing a mercenary, Mrs. Spencer's illness was my good fortune," Miss Pearce said, almost to herself. "Most reputable companion posts had been filled, or they were for young women I knew from…before."

What Jasper knew of ladies' societies he'd learned either from his sisters or his mistresses. Jane, his youngest sister, had wept for days after some girl or the other had arrived at a ball in a dress that was simply the same color as hers. Viscountess Morton had refused to take him to her bed until she was certain he'd never been her sister's lover.

That conversation must have been awkward.

It would likely have been equally awkward to work as a companion for a young lady you'd recently stood next to in a ballroom.

"Is Mrs. Spencer very ill?" he asked.

"Her letters make no mention of returning."

There was something in her disappearance. Jasper could *feel* it. "Did she not mention it before she left?"

"She was gone before I arrived."

"So Spencer hired you himself?"

Annabel stopped and faced him. "Why are you so concerned about Mr. Spencer?"

Blast. The woman was far too smart. "It's the situation that intrigues me," he said. "My mother has taken ill, and my sisters may need a companion. I have no idea if it is proper for me to do the interviews myself."

Of course he couldn't do them. Any young woman alone

with him in a room would consider it an interview for a wife.

They reached the mouth of the maze. Despite the yawning gap in the hedges and the lawn spreading out before them, Miss Pearce didn't move. The sunlight slanted in to reach them, warming the top of his head. It touched her next, and her hair sparked to life. Gold and warm copper glinted like ore in poor soil.

"Thank you for escorting me, your lordship."

He needed to ask her more questions, not stand here staring at her hair. He definitely didn't need to miss her touch as she separated from him. "We are not to the house yet."

"It's a large house. I'm capable of finding it myself." Her cheeks colored a bright pink, but she didn't apologize.

"Allow me—"

"No," she snapped. Drawing a deep breath, she put more distance between them. "I went into this maze without you. If I exit *with* you, the entire party will be alive with gossip of an assignation."

"I see." Jasper's lips twisted at the irony. He was alone with the one woman he'd met who *didn't* wish to be alone with him.

"Lord Ramsbury, we were hoping…"

The words came as a shadow cast Miss Pearce back into gloomy gray. Jasper turned to greet the intruder.

"Miss Spencer. How may I help you?"

She was blinking at her companion. "Miss Pearce?" She looked between them, her gaze narrowing.

Miss Pearce brushed past Jasper and into the sunlight. "His lordship offered to help me find the way out of his maze. It's become quite overgrown and treacherous over the winter." Her smile was brittle. "Thank you for your assistance, sir."

Jasper dipped his chin. "It was my pleasure to be of assistance, miss."

Rather than stare at her retreating back, he faced his guest and gave her his best smile. "Miss Spencer. How may I assist you?"

"We were hoping you would join us for croquet."

She looked up at him with a wide blue stare that reminded him of his sister Johanna when she'd asked for a puppy. It was difficult not to pat Miss Spencer on the head as he'd done Jo.

"I will shortly." He hated croquet, but he suspected Miss Spencer would wheedle if he refused. Jo wheedled with the best of them. "I use the black mallet with the longest handle. Why don't you ensure that no one else picks it?"

After bouncing a curtsy, she spun on her heel and hurried back in the other direction, barely acknowledging her friends, who fell in behind her. Jasper waited until they were out of sight before lengthening his stride to apprehend Miss Pearce, who was almost to the lowest group of garden steps.

"You are the most exasperating man," she said to his shadow as she avoided his hand. "What if someone saw you run—"

"I hardly ran." He chuckled. It had been more difficult to catch her than he'd expected. She had apparently abandoned the short stride ladies were taught as soon as they could walk. "And no one saw me."

In the silence, their steps ticked off their climb.

"Shouldn't you join us on the lawn? What if I make love to your charge when no one is looking?"

It was a tease he would have made with Fiona, and Miss Pearce's sharp inhale made Jasper wonder if he'd gone too far. However, when she faced him, humor sparked in her eyes. It was the first sign of life he'd seen in them.

"I believe that's too bold, even for you." She arched an eyebrow. "But I'll be keeping an eye on you after sunset."

"Wise woman," he quipped as he opened the door and ushered her into the entry hall.

Jasper intended to leave her at the stairs. However, when he looked down to bid her farewell, she wasn't there.

He found her at the library doorway and returned to her side. She didn't acknowledge his presence.

"I knew it would be lovely," she whispered.

Jasper looked past her to the room that his new staff had spent days dusting so he could work in there without being plagued by sneezing fits. The late morning sun streamed in the windows, highlighting the blossoming shrubs outside and the polished wood within. It was a room full of books and leather, the quietest space in the house.

Miss Pearce stared like it was a sweet shop and she couldn't afford a taste.

"When Fiona visits, Mrs. Linden spends a great deal of time in here," Jasper began. "I believe she naps more than reads, but she is as much of a guest as Fiona."

Joy lit Miss Pearce's eyes for a moment before she shook her head. "It's not proper, but I appreciate your kind offer."

"Anyone can tell you I'm as unkind as I am improper." They probably had already. "Books should be read by someone who can appreciate them." He kept his eyes on hers. "Please make yourself comfortable while you are here, Miss Pearce."

The battle between what she *should* do and what she *wanted* to do was plain. It was equally plain when she decided. Her brilliant smile stole his breath. Though only for a moment.

"Thank you, Lord Ramsbury. I will."

She entered the library and left him standing at the door, watching her peruse the shelves. After a moment, he left to join his guests, lest another young lady search him out and risk Miss Pearce's reputation and employment.

Perhaps croquet would distract him from why that was important.

CHAPTER THREE

ITHOUT LOOKING, ANNABEL was aware of the moment
Jasper left the doorway. It was irritating. But worse, the
echo of the front door closing sent a cloud skittering across her
day. She took a deep breath and exhaled.

He was an incorrigible flirt and a magnet for scandal. He was
also, quite possibly, a traitor.

And she preferred cloudy climates anyway.

Annabel trailed her fingers across the spines at eye level,
focusing on the embossed lettering teasing her fingertips. Worn
spines stood next to new bindings, and she found her favorite
authors easily. However, two shelves down, the alphabet began
again—a section on history, if the titles were any indication.

Closer to the back of the room, and nearer to the desk, fewer
new books were on the shelves. Some of the spines were so
cracked and worn that it was impossible to learn the titles
without squinting.

It was also impossible to ignore the desk. Father kept everything important in his desk.

Just look and be done with it.

Annabel stared warily into the empty hallway as she reached
for the drawer closest to her. The house was so quiet she could
hear the wood creak as she tugged the handle. It didn't budge.

Every drawer along the top row was locked. If this desk was

like her father's, the lower row would be as well. Annabel sighed as she knelt behind the desk. Skullduggery required thoroughness.

"It requires a professional," she muttered. "You were daft to do this in the first place. You should have packed your things and left. Poverty be hanged." She punctuated her sentence with a yeoman's pull on the last—locked—drawer. "Drat."

Taking advantage of her position, Annabel swept her hands along the underside of the desk and down the sides, searching for a key. No matter how far she reached, she found nothing but dust. The thought of spiders lurking in corners sent her sliding back to safety.

One last place to look. She wriggled backward a few inches, lifted the edge of the rug, and folded it backward. There was nothing underneath and nothing tied to the bottom.

He would be daft to leave his secrets unguarded with a house full of guests. "He never struck me as particularly bright anyway," Annabel said as she pushed a loose strand of hair behind her ear.

"Hello? Is anyone in here?" called the butler from the doorway.

She froze, thankful for the large desk and the simple shape of her day dress. Even the hideous gray color helped her become part of the shadows. She might as well be the mouse everyone considered her to be.

The butler lingered in the doorway a moment longer, but it was just enough for Annabel to recall her last words. Guilt singed her ears. As a first son, Jasper Warren would have been well educated at the best schools. Even if he didn't pay close attention, some of it was bound to sink in. He was also well read, given the condition of the books closest to hand. Not to mention, he was the relation of a dear friend, and he'd been kind to her.

Kindness and friendship were difficult to come by these days. When offered, it shouldn't be met by snide assumptions.

He was likely intelligent enough, but careless. That wasn't a crime. Most members of the *ton* believed themselves above reproach or ill fortune.

That was why her family's invitations had all but vanished, taking her sisters' Seasons with them. No one wanted to be reminded that everything they valued could be lost with just one tick in a ledger sheet.

The library door closed. Annabel sat quietly, listening for footfalls against the rug or a creak of a chair, until the silence was a weight on her shoulders. She straightened her posture and looked over the top of the desk, then, finding no one, stood upright. After dusting off her skirt, she glanced at the shelves again, this time focusing on the ones nearest the ceiling. Wooden boxes separated groups of books with unlabeled spines. The size hinted they could be ledgers, possibly journals. The boxes might hold clues as well.

"It would be careless to write anything down," she counseled herself. Still, she found the library ladder and pushed it to the proper shelf. Society men were particularly prone to carelessness, since they were blessed simply by being born.

Annabel climbed the ladder, careful to keep her eyes on the shelf and her boot heels clear of the rungs. Her ribs pressed against her stays in the same quick, shallow rhythm that occurred whenever her feet left the ground.

Father had been born to his title, but she'd never considered him careless. He knew his tenants by name and ensured the family frequented the village shops. They were well loved in Chilworth. But when the fortune dwindled, he'd ignored his man of business, his banker, and his solicitor and gambled everything on a quick solution.

And lost.

Now near the top of the ladder, Annabel kept a white-knuckled grip on the rung at eye level, and reached for the nearest burgundy, leather-clad ledger. It was larger and heavier than she'd expected. There was little hope of descending with it in her arms. That only left one option.

Heart in her throat, she forced her feet to move upward until she could grasp the last rung. She slid the ledger forward, balanced it against her chest, and used the shelf as a reading table.

It was indeed a ledger, which gave Annabel hope. She didn't always write every detail in her journal. There was something unnerving about seeing her innermost thoughts in stark strokes on a white page, and there was always a chance that a nosy interloper, like one of her sisters, would scavenge through her room and find it.

But ledgers… No one ever kept numbers a secret. Even if they tried, the truth eventually emerged in the columns.

Opening the heavy cover and flipping the large pages required her to lean back on her perch. The ladder never wobbled, but Annabel gritted her teeth to help keep her nerves steady. Why on earth had she agreed to do this? She didn't have the constitution required for skulking about.

This particular volume was from several years ago and, given the unsteady handwriting, had been kept by the previous marquess. Still, the rows and columns were neat and easy to follow. The man had been parsimonious when it came to his household and his staff, but it was clear he had weaknesses for three things: art, horses, and his grandson Jasper.

It was also clear that Jasper spent a great deal of money, given the number of payments made to him and the frequency of those payments. "Surely he's not taking funds and putting them in the bank," Annabel whispered as she scanned the rows.

She leaned back again, balancing with one hand while she flipped several pages at once, going further in the marquess's records. The book shifted lower, resting under her breasts, its weight threatening to topple her. It left her no alternative but to use her body to push it back into place. It was unladylike, but there was no one here to call her out or follow her example.

Annabel frowned at the date on the page. She hadn't gone forward in time—she'd gone backward. She lifted the corners of a few other pages to confirm her suspicion and sighed. The old marquess had filled his ledgers from back to front, keeping the most recent accounts at the beginning. That meant going forward in time would require opening another volume.

Which meant moving the ladder and climbing again.

"Drat and damn," Annabel huffed as she wrestled the ledger back into place. It had been easier to pull it out one-handed than it was to put it back.

It was also easier to climb the ladder than it was to descend. Taking a deep breath and keeping a tight grip on the rung above, Annabel lifted one foot and felt for the rung below.

"What the devil are you doing up there?"

Startled, Annabel looked down and into the stern stare of Kit Yarwood. Her head spun, and her boot slipped on the rung. She tightened her hold on her only lifeline and drew a shaky breath. "At the moment, trying not to fall."

He didn't budge from his spot near the door. "Then I suggest you come down. Quickly."

The longer she stayed up here, staring at the floor, the sweatier her palms became. "I'll come down at my own pace. Now stop talking and be patient."

She wiped her palms on her skirt one at a time before stepping down, careful to put both feet on one rung before stepping down again. Yarwood didn't say another word, but he heaved a great sigh with every other step.

Annabel put both feet on solid ground and, ignoring her trembling knees, faced Yarwood. "Lord Ramsbury instructed me to make myself comfortable in the library." She wasn't quite certain of Yarwood's place in the household, but invoking the marquess's name was her best chance of putting him in it.

"And you took that to mean risking your neck on a ladder to see what was kept out of reach?" Yarwood arched an eyebrow.

The jibe was too close to the mark for comfort. "I was making myself familiar with the collection and wondered if the more intriguing works were kept out of reach of careless visitors."

It wasn't necessarily a lie, and Annabel hoped that the heat flushing her cheeks could be put down to irritation rather than embarrassment. His imperious glare was discouraging.

What's the worst he can do, send me back to London in disgrace? It would further ruin her reputation, and it would tarnish Elizabeth's chances. But it would serve Mr. Spencer right for concocting this foolish plot.

She stepped away and pulled the first recognizable title from the shelf. She'd read Currer Bell's novel so often she could recite it without thinking. The weight of the book was comforting. It would be good company over the next few weeks. "If you'll excuse me."

Yarwood stepped forward, blocking the door. "What did you find atop the ladder?"

"Nothing but numbers." Annabel waved the statement away. "Complete gibberish." She hoped her gritted teeth resembled a smile. It was galling to play the role the *ton* demanded of her. Perhaps if she scandalized herself enough, she'd never have to play a simpleton again.

She tilted her head back to look her accuser in the eyes, refusing to be cowed by his height and his stern expression. Poor or not, she was still a baron's daughter.

Yarwood glared back at her and refused to move.

The front door banged open and slammed shut.

"Annabel!"

Elizabeth's wail echoed from the entry hall's stone walls and high ceiling. Had they been home, Annabel would have thought little of it. She'd learned early that Elizabeth wailed at the slightest provocation. But they weren't home, and the girl knew how to behave in public.

Besides that, rushing to her charge's aid was the perfect excuse to avoid further interrogation.

Annabel stepped around Yarwood and strode to the door. "Miss Spencer needs me, sir."

"Gentlemen." Jasper thumped his whiskey tumbler on the table to interrupt the rowdy laughter around the table. "Shall we join the ladies for a respite before billiards?"

In truth, he couldn't wait to vacate a room fogged by cigars. The smoke burned his eyes, and the scent ruined the taste of his whiskey.

"If we must," Viscount Raines grumbled as he pushed himself upright. "Though an evening of music seems damned dull."

"Consider it penance for being banned from the White Rose." Wareham cackled as he stood. "You're doomed to polite ladies, Raines. Might as well grow accustomed to the boredom."

Jasper stood as well, signaling the end of the discussion. "We can't very well leave them to their own devices for the month." He ambled to the sideboard and lifted a decanter of gin. "And at least we won't be required to dance."

Kit opened the door, letting the fresh air in while encouraging the gentlemen into the hall.

Jasper poured a drink from the nearly full decanter, then took a refreshing sip. It was a small blessing that the *ton* considered gin to be beneath them.

As he sipped, he stared into the mirror. What had Raines done to be banned from a brothel, and could it be used against him? Did anyone else know? As luck would have it, the former madam of the White Rose was a recent acquaintance who, Jasper believed, saw the world the same way as he did. If she had banned Raines, she wouldn't balk at sharing the reason.

Kit approached, his reflection grim. "Will you reconsider?"

The man was like a hound on the trail of a fox. "No."

"Jasper, she cannot be trusted." Kit rested his hands on the sideboard, keeping his arms stiff. "She was searching for more than something to read."

"And all she found were my grandfather's five-year-old accounts." All the current ones were locked in the attic for the duration of the party.

"You know as well as I that a determined, intelligent searcher will find *something* if given enough time."

Given his discussion with Annabel in the maze this morning, *determined and intelligent* was an apt description. When she let her guard down and spoke her mind, however, she was intriguing. "And if we march into the music room and confront her? For reading? Everyone in the house will shut their mouths and close ranks. We'll learn nothing." Jasper pointed his glass at Kit. "You know that."

"Then we can bring her in here." Kit's chin was at an angle that reminded him of maths class at Eton.

"Two men alone with an unmarried young lady?" Jasper chuckled. "That will go well."

His pocket watch ticked in his waistcoat. The longer they waited between dinner and billiards, the more sober the men would be. It would make for a long night.

Kit met his gaze in the mirror. "You're going to stand there and tell me you aren't worried?"

Jasper was more concerned about Annabel tumbling from the library ladder and breaking her neck. Those ledgers were unwieldy, even for him. "If we send her home, we'll never know what she was hoping to find."

"Then we keep an eye on her?" Kit stood tall and straightened his coat. "And hope her fruitless searching delivers Spencer into our hands."

Jasper had no doubt that Annabel's employer was behind her unladylike investigating. The challenge was to discover what Reginald Spencer wanted before she gave up looking.

He loved a good challenge.

"Exactly." Jasper refilled his drink before turning toward the door. "Now let's go listen to yet more Mendelssohn and songs meant to make us fall in love."

They crossed the entry hall together, and Kit reached for the latch. Then he dropped his hand and stepped aside, his jaw set and his hand in a fist.

Since his return from the war, Kit had insisted on being first through every door unless Society dictated otherwise.

Jasper clapped him on the shoulder. "I don't think anyone on the other side wants to shoot me. It's only the first week, after all."

Jasper didn't remember ever entering a room unnoticed, but he'd always understood it had little to do with him. He was little more than a title and an estate, wanted for influence and power. Men wanted money, young ladies wanted a husband, older women wanted a lover. The stares grew sharper, hungrier, with every title he inherited.

"My apologies for keeping you waiting," he said as he raised his glass and ignored the irritation crawling across his skin. "Miss Bainbridge, will you honor us with a song?"

Charlotte Bainbridge was a good choice. Jasper had heard her play not long ago when he dined with her family, so he knew she was talented and polished enough to be understated. And, as expected, Viscount Raines stepped to her side with an offer to turn the sheet music.

Jasper sipped his drink to mask his satisfied smirk. Any attention from Charlotte would soften Raines for later. The young fop used any excuse to drink to excess. Celebrating Miss Bainbridge's attention, and the possibility of gaining her sizable dowry, would be good enough.

As the song began, a flutter of activity caught Jasper's attention. Miss Spencer, her face pink under her delicate blonde curls, was agitated. Her companion, again in spectral gray, still faced front, but her head was tilted toward her charge. Despite their postures, their words were quiet.

Jasper ambled through the crowd until he was in earshot, then sat.

"If you must be displeased, you will leave after the performance has concluded," Annabel hissed. She held Miss Spencer's forearm in her grasp. "Without flouncing out in a huff."

"But for him to choose *her*—it's just too much," Elizabeth bit out. "After what she did to me today—"

"She laughed when you missed a wicket, Elizabeth. That is not a crime." Annabel sighed. "It's not even in poor taste."

"She made a fool of me in front of Lord Ramsbury and every other gentleman present." Miss Spencer's fingers twitched in her lap. Social constraint seemed to heighten her irritation. "As I was the wronged party, I should have been asked to open the performances."

"You made a fool of yourself by storming to the house and shouting it down until I arrived."

Annabel's words were so quiet, Jasper found himself leaning forward to catch them.

"And for you to perform musically would only compound that error," she continued.

Jasper rolled his lips inward to keep his laughter bottled up, but it still shook his chair. Miss Spencer's dramatic gasp hid the creaking and kept him unnoticed. However, it also drew the attention of nearby guests.

Annabel nodded to them and kept her gaze focused on Miss Bainbridge. She squeezed Elizabeth's arm to ensure she did the same. They were quiet until all eyes returned to the performance.

"Do not playact, Elizabeth," Annabel whispered. "You know as well as I that the pianoforte isn't your passion. If you wish to display your talents, take your easel into the garden tomorrow and do a watercolor."

"What good will that do? No one can watch me paint."

"But your host will always have a delicate reminder of you and your stay here." Annabel glanced at the girl. "That will outlive any music or missed wicket."

Applause signaled the end of the recital, and Miss Bainbridge stood to curtsy. Viscount Raines stayed at her side, keeping her hand so she could balance into a lower dip. His position gave him the opportunity to glance down her cleavage.

Jasper tightened his grip on his glass as he sipped. The man might have been banned from a brothel, but his thoughts apparently stayed there. He'd need to talk to Kit about the young viscount.

The crowd stood and shifted, allowing new performers to jockey for position and choose their songs. Several approached Charlotte Bainbridge to compliment her playing.

"You may cry off with a headache," Annabel said quietly. "But you should compliment Miss Bainbridge first." She talked over Elizabeth's objection. "It will be a long month full of taunts otherwise."

Miss Spencer walked to the front of the room and spoke to Miss Bainbridge, all under Annabel's watchful eye. When she left the room, her back was straight, her jaw was set, and there was a determined gleam in her eye.

The crowd took their seats again, and Jasper, obeying a perverse impulse, claimed the now-vacant chair beside Annabel. Her eyes widened, and a blush stained her cheeks.

"Your lordship."

"Miss Pearce." Jasper weighed mentioning her conversation but decided against it. Admitting to eavesdropping was a sure way to make sure no one spoke out of turn. "Are you enjoying the music?"

Annabel nodded. The newest performer had chosen a livelier tune. It was a welcome change, but it made it difficult to hear any conversation. Jasper had to lean in to hear what she was saying.

She smelled of clover and apples.

"You should speak to your housekeeper," she said.

He glanced around the room, looking for anything out of place. "Why?"

The look she gave him was the same she'd given the impatient Elizabeth. "Viscount Raines has the stare of a well-trained rogue."

Jasper looked into her expectant gaze. It was clear she was awaiting his response, but he wanted to know how she interpreted what she'd seen.

Her sigh was so deep it moved her shoulders. "The young man is a bounder, but Miss Bainbridge has a sharp-eyed chaperone. He'll not get past her. Your maids will likely not be so safe. They should tend his room in pairs, or with a footman at the door."

Jasper nodded his agreement with a lazy dip of his chin that had taken him months to master. "Thank you."

She turned her attention to the music, leaving him no choice but to sit in silence, watch the people around him, and not wriggle in the too-straight, poorly padded chair. After a moment, the light shifting across her gray silk skirt drew his attention. It was too rhythmic to be a fidget. She was tapping her foot in time with the song.

Jasper didn't remember ever seeing her dance, though, frankly, he didn't remember seeing her in a ballroom at all. Those events were always a crush, and only the peacocks and fools stood out. Annabel was neither of those.

The only small party they had attended had been his cousin's house party, and that had ended before the dance could be had. "It's a shame the floor is crowded. This would be a fine reel."

The tapping stopped. "It would. If one chose to dance."

"Do you not?"

"My dancing days are over."

She'd become a statue in her chair, as though his question had turned her to stone. Agitation skittered over Jasper's skin as he sipped his drink. She liked wordplay and music, but she'd put it all aside. She was observant and forthright, but she carefully measured out her advice. He'd only get answers from her if he could loosen her rigid control.

He thought back over the days of Amelia's house party, of what they'd done and what he recalled of Annabel's attendance. She'd sketched during the hunting party, and she'd read during fishing. They'd ridden, and she'd…

Loved it, if he recalled correctly. She'd cleared every jump and poured enthusiastic praise on her horse. At least, he thought it had been her.

"We're riding tomorrow," he whispered, testing his hypothesis.

Her eyes sparked to life before she could stop them. The fire died slowly. "Elizabeth has discussed painting in the garden. We will likely stay behind."

"Linden always chooses the garden over trailing after Fiona in a carriage. She can keep an eye on Miss Spencer." He applauded as everyone else did and stood to lead the gentlemen to the billiards room. "You can join us for a morning ride."

"Lord Ramsbury, I couldn't possibly."

He stopped halfway to the door and turned. "Miss Pearce, I insist."

CHAPTER FOUR

"THE OLD MARQUESS would have enjoyed seeing the stables and paddocks this full."

"It likely would have reminded him of Tattersalls," Jasper replied to the stable master. He ran his hand over the long, muscled back of his favorite mount, a roan whose black-tinted coat looked blue. "And grandfather loved nothing more than a horse sale."

"Unless it was a race." The servant grunted a laugh as he shoveled fresh hay into a neighboring stall. "His lordship had a damned good eye for a runner."

Let's go for a flutter, boy. Jasper's lips twisted into a wry grin. Grandfather had never been one to merely *flutter*. Days at the track started early, in the stables with the trainers, pacing up and down until the old man pulled a stack of notes from his coat and shoved them at Benchley, his favorite bookmaker. Benchley's frown grew deeper with every win. He likely would have stopped taking Grandfather's wagers if he'd been just another bloke with five quid to spare.

Snorts and stamping feet announced a newcomer. Each horse tossed their mane, either in greeting or as a plea for praise. Even his big blue horse fell victim.

Jasper looked to the door, and a satisfied smile stretched his lips. For all her protests about impropriety, Annabel Pearce had found room in her case for a riding habit.

Like other gentlemen of the *ton*, he knew just enough about women's clothing to realize the dark green skirt and coat had gone out of fashion last Season. However, she'd changed the buttons from bright brass to a more stylish black.

Unlike many gentlemen, Jasper cared little about fashion. He trusted his tailor to keep him in style. He knew what he liked when he saw it.

He liked Annabel in green. He also appreciated what she'd done with her hair. It flowed from under her plain, dark hat and over one shoulder, less a tumble of curls and more a steady stream that was neither fully blonde nor brown.

She dithered in the doorway, tapping her riding cane against her skirt, until she caught his eye. He waited until she'd stepped inside before he approached.

"Good morning, Miss Pearce."

"Good morning, your lordship." She looked past him and into the stable. "I seem to be the first to arrive."

Society women had been known to dawdle in their carriages outside parties, out-waiting one another for the privilege of being last, of having the most eyes on them. Jasper didn't think Annabel's early arrival was accidental.

"The horses don't mind the clock." He offered his arm. "Come see if you approve of your mount."

She took his elbow. Her gloves, from what he could tell by the fingertips, were new and well made. "What if I wish to choose my own?"

"If you disagree with my choice, you are welcome to make your own."

They walked down the row, veering from one side to the other so she could stroke a wide forelock or a velvety nose. "You have a fine stable, Lord Ramsbury."

"To be fair, many of them belong to houseguests. Men rarely travel without their best hunter." He swept his hand along the opposite wall. "And most of the others were purchased by grandfather."

"He did value a well-stocked stable."

Women only knew such things from their fathers or from looking in account books. From what Jasper knew of Baron Chilworth, horses weren't his weakness of choice. Kit was right— Annabel had been reading Grandfather's ledgers. "I suppose he was famous for his excesses."

"Most gentlemen are." Annabel, her ear pink under her hat, led him to the other side of the stable. "Here's a handsome man."

The roan tossed his inky mane and snorted a hello before stretching his neck toward Jasper. More precisely, toward his pocket.

"No you don't, Ceff." Jasper chuckled as he ruffled the big horse's forelock. "You've had your treats already today."

"Ceff?" Annabel glanced up.

"Ceffylglas." The light fell over the stallion's gleaming back. "It's Welsh for 'blue horse.'"

Her laugh took years from her face. "You're joking."

"Not in the least." Jasper relented and reached into his pocket for another carrot. "But, to my credit, I didn't name him. The breeder did." He offered the carrot to Ceff.

"The breeder is Welsh?" Annabel raised her hand to stroke Ceff's neck but dropped it when he shied away.

The tightness in her voice pricked a string in Jasper's gut. If she was suspicious of Wales, then Spencer likely was as well.

"My favorite breeder is outside Cardiff." He kept his eyes on Ceff, holding him steady as the stable hands saddled him. "A wise old gent Kit introduced me to." Jasper slipped the bridle over the horse's ears himself, careful to settle the bit and reins just as Ceff liked them. "Why?"

"I suppose I expect Welsh horses to be ponies," Annabel said in the casual way his mother did when she wanted to gather information without tipping her hand.

"Then you may be disappointed in my choice for you." Jasper turned her to the other wall and led her two stalls down.

The delicate black mare danced patterns in the straw under her feet. Her coat shone like dark silk, and her mane fell in a graceful sweep. Her wide, dark eyes sparkled.

"What's her name?" Annabel propped her cane against the stall's door, then released him to shuck her glove.

Jasper dropped a carrot into her palm. "Ysbryd Du. Dark spirit."

Annabel fed the carrot to the mare with one hand and caught her other glove in her teeth to tug it free.

The honest excitement in her unguarded action tightened Jasper's skin in unexpected places. It worsened when he circled her wrist and pulled her hand closer. "Let me." It was a soft leather, tight enough that he had to pull one finger at a time. They were fully clothed, in the daylight, in the stables, but he'd had the same sensation stripping a woman out of her corset in candlelight. He forced a smile as he released her. "Can't have you ruining them."

"My teeth or the gloves?" Annabel turned back to the horse and stroked her wide forehead. "She is lovely, your lordship. But far too fine for me."

"Nonsense." Jasper waved away her complaint, hoping his irritation would go with it. It shouldn't bother him that she denied herself pleasure in the name of propriety and others' expectations. "She deserves to be ridden by someone who appreciates her."

Laughter filtered in from outside, and the stable hands' boots thudded against the hard-packed earthen floor. The rest of the party was arriving.

The shutters closed over Annabel's eyes, and Jasper caught the nearest servant. "Help Miss Pearce onto the mare." He shot Annabel a glare. "This mare only."

He strode to the door to greet everyone else as the grooms led out their horses. Kit was already swinging into the saddle atop his giant pewter-gray stallion.

"Lord Ramsbury." Charlotte Bainbridge beckoned him to

where she was standing next to a bay mare just her size. "The stable boy said you'd chosen this lovely mount just for me. I'm delighted with her. Thank you."

Every head in the paddock turned to stare, even the horses. "You are quite welcome, Miss Bainbridge. Cricket will give you a pleasant ride this morning."

"Will you do me the honor of riding with me?" she asked. "Your estate is so large, I fear getting lost."

"Would that I could." Jasper sighed to give his words feeling. "However, I'll be near the rear of the party, ensuring everyone stays on the path." He looked past her to the other gentlemen in the party. "Lord Raines or Lord Wareham would be fine partners for you."

Hearing his name, Raines nudged his chestnut gelding in front of Wareham's palomino. "It would be my pleasure, Miss Bainbridge. Perhaps you can keep the ride interesting."

Jasper ground his teeth into a smile. The young viscount had grumbled about hunting all last evening—specifically not doing it. "We'll hunt later in the month, once everyone is accustomed to the fields."

"I, for one, am glad of a gentle ride." Fiona ambled up on the gray she always rode during her visits. The almost silver mare had been christened Fairy by Jasper's sister Jane. Fiona's black habit was severe both in cut and in color. She could have passed for a nun on her way to church if not for her smile. "My bones are still rattling from the carriage."

The women in the group stayed silent and looked anywhere but at Fiona, torn between their own comfort and agreeing with a scandal-ridden miss their mothers had warned them to stay clear of.

Hooves clopped behind them, two distinct patterns. Jasper didn't turn. He knew Ceff's steps in his sleep, and he suspected the source of the others. The young ladies' widened stares told him he was correct. Even the chaperones in the carriage were stunned when they recognized Annabel.

Jasper held his smile until his back was turned, then he strode to his horse and swung into the saddle. He nodded to the horse master who was serving as their guide. "Ready when you are, Martin."

They trailed out of the paddock and into the field. Kit came back to join him, and Fiona flanked his other side. After a few minutes, Jasper looked back to find Annabel trying to keep in step with the carriage, whose occupants were ignoring her. Horse and rider both looked miserable. "She'll do better if you give her her head a bit, Miss Pearce. Come join us."

"Please do!" Fiona called. "I'd be grateful for someone who can talk of fashion and music rather than Parliament and war."

Annabel coaxed Ysbryd Du into a trot and joined Fiona. Jasper fell back with Kit.

"She's had a go at the figures in Grandfather's ledger."

"You don't say." Kit kept his eyes forward.

"Yes, yes. You were right," Jasper grumbled. "She's better with numbers than I considered."

Ahead of them, Fiona nudged her mare into a canter. Annabel followed suit. She sat the horse well, and she handled it easily. "She's a quick learner, too."

"Good for her, bad for us." Kit shifted in his saddle to stare at him. "Are you still for staying the course?"

Fiona leaned toward Annabel, and their heads stayed together for several moments. Fiona's hearty, unguarded laughter floated back to him on the breeze, making him smile. She did that more and more often these days.

"Amelia told me the same story," Fiona said, still chuckling. "I can't say I'm sorry for Mr. Raymond or his nose. I only wish I could have seen it."

"He was dreadful," Annabel said. "It must be reassuring to have Lord Ramsbury's protection."

Her emphasis on the last word caused Jasper's stomach to dip. He'd hoped Fiona would find a kindred soul, or at least a temporary ally in a nest full of vipers. He hadn't expected

Annabel to be another gossipmongering snake.

Fiona's smile curved. "I am grateful every day that Father bought the estate next to the Warrens' country house and gave me the opportunity to have Rabbit as an older brother."

Jasper groaned. That nickname would be all over London before long. He'd never be seen as someone to trust—or fear.

"Rabbit?"

Annabel's smile transformed her face. She should do it more often.

"He has a tendency to scamper away and hide when he senses danger, and he is gifted in finding hiding places," Fiona said. "Given those traits and *Warren*…"

Annabel's laugh, deep and rich, was at odds with her thin frame. It made him think of candlelight and shadows, of champagne and berries.

Ceff tossed his head, and Jasper loosened his grip on the reins. Things were in motion that had nothing to do with his growing curiosity about Annabel Pearce.

"I am," he said to Kit. "This path is the quickest way to our answer."

Though he wasn't sure what, exactly, the path should be. If he asked her intentions, she'd lie, but she was a poor liar. If he exposed her, he'd have to send her packing. That would ruin his opportunity to learn what Spencer wanted—if she knew anything at all.

He could bluff his way through the month and assume she'd find nothing, but she'd already proven herself an astute observer. God only knew what she'd carry back to Spencer and how he would weave the tale.

"Do you think he's used his daughter as an excuse to get Miss Pearce in the door?" Kit asked.

Jasper shook his head. "I think he saw an opportunity and twisted it to his advantage."

Spencer likely thanked Providence when Annabel knocked on his door. At least, he did if he realized how intelligent she was.

How had she ended up spying for him?

"Your lordship," Fiona called over her shoulder. "Please tell me there's luncheon waiting and that you haven't dragged us to the top of the hill simply for the view on the other side."

"An army travels on its stomach," Jasper called back. "Of course there's luncheon waiting. So long as the birds haven't carried it off."

They reached the top of the hill and dismounted in a flurry of helpful stable boys. The ladies near the front of the line craned their necks until they spotted Jasper. Their fluttering fans might have been responsible for the shiver of leaves overhead.

He swung out of the saddle and dropped to the ground. "Once more into the breach."

"Yes. It's such a hardship to have young ladies waiting around every tree," Fiona teased as she beckoned for his help. "I don't know how you'll survive."

Jasper helped her to the ground but kept hold of her a moment longer. "I'm sorry. If I'd known she would think—"

"You are sweet to worry, but it's getting tiresome, Jasper. Men and women can rarely be friends without Society assuming there is more to it. I'm pleased she asked me directly rather than whispering in my wake."

He relaxed and released her. He had been lucky when the Allens arrived in the countryside. Fiona's gregarious nature, while annoying at first, had broken through the reserve he'd been taught from the cradle.

Perhaps she could do the same with Annabel. "Would you please sit with Miss Pearce? I believe she's having trouble navigating between groups."

Fiona raised an eyebrow and glanced from him to Annabel, then back. A slow smile came across her face. "Of course, Rabbit. Anything you'd like."

He nodded his thanks before marching toward Annabel. He arrived as she slid to the ground unaided. Her boots, though not new, were well polished, but they gapped at the ankles.

"You should have waited," he said. "The ground is uneven."

"I've managed worse." She stroked her mare's graceful neck. "Will they look out for her while we rest?"

"Certainly." He stepped forward and lowered his head, enough to be private but not enough to raise eyebrows. "May I ask a favor?" He waited for her to nod. "I must visit with the other guests, but I don't want to leave Fiona on her own. Without Linden here, she has few options for company."

Annabel's eyes softened. "I'll be happy to step in for Linden."

"Thank you, Miss Pearce."

Certain his scheme was going to plan, he joined Raines and Wareham at their table under an ancient oak. "Gentlemen."

"Lovely estate, Ramsbury." Wareham surveyed the length of the ridge and the view of the Hall below. "Almost as large as Faversham's."

The man never let anyone forget he was heir to the Duke of Faversham, who refused to die. Jasper had a suspicion that the duke planned to outlive Wareham and give the title to a grandson who could be overseen by his sons-in-law. Both men had better temperaments and leveler heads than the current heir.

"All you need is a wife," Raines said, his voice pitched to mimic an Almack's matron. "A pretty girl with a good dowry who wants a title."

Wareham's laughter was brief as he glanced to Miss Bainbridge and Miss Wallace. "They seem to be thin on the ground this Season."

None of the ladies in their party gave Wareham much attention, despite the possibility of becoming a duchess. Jasper feigned interest anyway. Talk of women always led to talk of fathers.

"What about Miss Spencer?" he asked.

Wareham leaned back to receive his plate. "She's damned young, don't you think?"

She was far too young, and in ways that had nothing to do with age. "By next Season, I believe her chaperone will have worked her magic."

Wareham looked over his shoulder, back toward the quieter members of the party. "Miss Pearce would be a better choice, I think. A baron's daughter, and she knows how to behave properly."

"No dowry," Raines said. "You'd have a plain—but proper—duchess, and she'd likely have the whole family in tow. I suppose if you kept Chilworth from your treasury…"

Money was always Raines's preferred topic, and it was expected, given his father's position in government. The Marquess of Graydon, treasurer of the Exchequer, had an increasing responsibility due to the new tax collections going into Britain's coffers.

"Miss Allen's dowry caused a stir during her debut." Wareham removed a flask from his coat pocket and offered it first to Raines and then to Jasper. When they refused, he took a gulp large enough for the three of them. "Has her father still settled it on her?"

"Given everything, he may have increased it as an incentive." Raines shrugged. "But I'd prefer not to have the *ton* whispering behind us at every ball."

"Not even for thirty thousand?" Wareham giggled. "And a horse that knows the track?"

"Mind your step, Wareham," Jasper growled. *I will not hit him. I promised Fiona I wouldn't beat every oaf who maligned her.*

"Some bargains are too expensive," Raines said. "The same could be said of Miss Spencer. All the polish in the world could never compensate for her snake of a father." He gathered his plate and moved to another table, immediately distracting both Miss Wallace and Miss Bainbridge from their escorts, who would only inherit modest earldoms.

Just when the conversation was getting interesting.

Jasper left Wareham at the table alone and joined Kit in the shadows.

"You look ready to chew nails," his friend said. "Have you called someone out?"

"Not yet. But I cannot guarantee Wareham will leave in the same condition in which he arrived."

"Wait until he's drunk." Kit barked a laugh. "At least then he won't remember."

As luncheon ended, the only noises were the cries of hawks overhead and the chuffs of horses eager to return to their stalls. It was quiet enough to hear the hum of whispers, and bright enough to see the glances spearing toward Fiona and Annabel walking along the ridge line.

Jasper stood. "Why don't we race downhill back to the hall? If I'm going to spend a lazy afternoon, I'd prefer it be without spiders."

The mention of skittering creatures had Miss Bainbridge and Miss Wallace hurrying for their horses, and the promise of a race had the same effect on Raines and Wareham. Even Kit seemed excited as he escorted the chaperones to their carriage.

Jasper shared a conspiratorial wink with Fiona as he lifted her into the saddle. "Give them a fair shot, Fi."

"Not on your life," she crowed as she maneuvered to the agreed-upon starting line.

Annabel was the only guest not focused on race preparations. Jasper joined her, putting his back to the starting line to watch a pair of hawks soar and dance through the valley below. They called to one another as they followed the silvery-blue river that seemed no wider than a ribbon.

"Can you imagine being that free?" she whispered. He wasn't certain she knew he was at her side.

As the birds vanished from sight, she stepped forward to search them out, but hesitated. In her green habit, she blended into the landscape like a creature afraid to be seen.

Or perhaps afraid to lose her balance.

He put an arm around her waist and coaxed her to the edge. "I won't let you fall."

She trembled with each step, but she took them.

Jasper craned to look over her head and watch the couple

battle and flirt as they skimmed close to the cliffs. "Are any of us free, Miss Pearce?"

Her smile faltered, and the shutters muted the sparkle in her eyes. The wind grew colder around them.

"We're all freer than some, but not as free as others, I suppose." She turned toward her horse, leaving Jasper to follow as he saw fit.

He bent to help her into the saddle. As expected, she balked.

"I can wait for a stable hand."

Jasper didn't relent. "Wareham will cheat and claim his horse was too restless to wait."

"Fine, then." She put her foot in his hands and allowed him to help her mount. Her soft wool skirt teased his wrist, and her simple scent was the perfect complement to a spring picnic.

He watched her until she was settled. "Give the mare her head, Miss Pearce. It's as close as you'll come to flying today. None will catch her."

Jasper was still speaking when Wareham leapt with a whoop meant to startle his opponents in the race. "First to the other side of the lake—by land and not by water!"

Jasper charged from the rear, low over Ceff's neck, the dark mane tickling his cheek. He gave Kit a mocking salute as he sped past.

Only one other rider caught his attention. Annabel had swung wide of the pack. Lying almost flat, she seemed to be floating on her horse's ribs, as though her riding cane was all that was keeping her steady. She'd lost her hat, and her hair streamed behind her like a banner.

Jasper veered to the left to give chase, and his smile widened as the ground leveled beneath Ceff's thudding hooves. Annabel had surveyed the course and found the fastest ground, and the safest for her horse.

He arrived at the finish line half a length behind Annabel. Fiona came third, tied with a swearing Raines.

Jasper didn't know the rest of the rankings. He didn't even

know the basis of the argument that had broken out between Miss Bainbridge and Miss Wallace.

Annabel's eyes were sparkling over her wide, brilliant smile. Her cheeks were pink from the air, and her loose hair framed her face. She draped over her horse's neck in a celebratory embrace as they walked to the stables.

"Did you hear me, Rabbit?" Fiona asked.

"Hmm?" Jasper urged Ceff to follow, which took little encouragement. His nose was in the air, searching for the mare's scent.

Fiona shoved his shoulder. "Did you ask me to take care of Annabel so she'd take care of me?"

He shrugged, and she shoved him again.

"I don't know whether to be angry that you insist on sheltering me or pleased that you trust me enough to befriend a young lady who has turned your head."

Jasper glanced at the woman he loved like a sister. She didn't know everything about his life, and she didn't need to. If she wanted to think he was besotted with Annabel Pearce, so be it. It would make things easier.

"Tell me everything she said."

CHAPTER FIVE

"No." Elizabeth spun from the mirror for Ruth, the maid, to unlace yet another gown. "I need something that will catch the marquess's attention, since I was shunted to the garden this morning."

Annabel took the moment to survey her own reflection, frowning at the gray dinner dress. She'd chosen a fabric with a shadowy pattern to make it seem less institutional and governess-like, but everything seemed drab after spending the morning on horseback in her riding habit—racing, no less.

She'd won that race and Fiona Allen's friendship—and the attention of the man every woman wanted. Annabel could still feel his arm around her waist and see his wild smile as they'd raced side by side.

She paid for her fun all afternoon, whispered about by the young ladies and ostracized by their chaperones. Even the guests who hadn't been there were punishing her, especially Elizabeth. No amount of praise for her painting, and it had been sincere, had stirred her from her sulk.

"You should have known there would be a picnic." Elizabeth twisted one of her curls into place, sparking Annabel's memories of when her hair had been in something other than braids and pins that scraped her scalp.

"As I have told you, the picnic and the race were both surprises." Annabel sighed. "And though you would have enjoyed the picnic and the scenery, you would not have enjoyed the ride, nor the race."

"You keep telling me what I would not enjoy, and it is usually what puts me in Lord Ramsbury's path." Elizabeth swept to the mirror in a swirl of white satin and navy stitching. "I would remind you that I have more to recommend me than a love for horses."

Given Ramsbury's stables and account books, his chosen wife would need to share that passion, or at least understand it. "You have no desire to be nearer to a horse than a carriage ride. And if you'd ridden with the chaperones—"

"Where you should have been." Elizabeth nodded to the maid. "This one."

"It is a lovely choice, Elizabeth." Annabel looked through the jewel chest for the pearls they'd packed specifically for this dress, using the distraction to cool her temper and soften her tongue. "And, as I have told you, Lord Ramsbury chose my mount and insisted I ride." She put up her hand to stop the interruption. "I don't know why, and I don't care to argue about it any longer. He insisted, and I had no polite option but to accept."

And thank goodness. That ride, that horse, would be the highlight of her year. She stepped behind Elizabeth and draped the necklace across her collarbone.

"These earbobs are far too small." Elizabeth made a face in the mirror. "The diamonds catch the eye better."

"The diamonds will look much better under the candles on the dance floor." Annabel met Elizabeth's frown in the mirror. "Ruth can add more curls near your temples and ears to give the illusion of more ornate jewelry."

As the maid worked deftly with the curling rod, Annabel rehung all the discarded dresses in the wardrobe. There had been a time when she'd been careless with her clothing and left messes for others to clean. The behavior had embarrassed her long before this, but being the servant now hammered home a vow that, should she ever escape this fate, she would never take anything for granted again.

Chatter and laughter filled the hallway. "The other young ladies are going down, Elizabeth." It was important to never be first, but one should never be last.

Elizabeth rose to leave, but Annabel kept the door closed and arched an eyebrow as a reminder to thank the young maid, who had earned her wages this evening. Elizabeth was not, as a rule, unkind. However, being surrounded by wealth and gossip this Season, and especially at this party—seeing other young ladies as competitors rather than people, if not friends—had sharpened her edges in an unattractive way.

That was one reason they never should have come.

Another was the quickening pace of Annabel's heart as they descended the stairs. It was foolish. She had been below Jasper's notice even before her father had used her dowry to fund his speculation schemes. Now, as a governess, he was even further from her reach.

There was no need for her heart to pound at the thought of seeing him, and there was certainly no need to take extra care with her appearance. It was a good thing she hadn't packed the gray hair ribbon that matched her dress. It would only serve to make her more foolish and a subject of more hateful gossip.

But it was impossible to deny that her opinion of the marquess changed every time they spoke. He was irreverent, but his offhand manner hid a kindness she hadn't expected.

Like his care over Fiona Allen, born of a lifelong friendship, and unflinching despite the gossip that shadowed her. It echoed, though faintly, in his treatment of Annabel herself.

It was also a lesson about ignoring gossip, because it was widely spread and only *possibly* true.

Or told to her by a man with a respectable position in the royal household.

Spencer's suspicions didn't make Lord Ramsbury a spy, but there was something going on in this house, beginning with the sharp-eyed Mr. Yarwood, who appeared to have no real position in the house. Still, everyone deferred to him. At times, even Lord Ramsbury bent to his friend's will.

And she could not forget the conversation she'd overheard in the maze. Something *was* afoot in Wales, and she didn't believe it had anything to do with buying another horse.

The marquess was intelligent enough to hide his intentions behind his charm and good looks. Not to mention that smile.

"I'm surprised to see you this evening, Miss Pearce. I thought the race might have tired you for the day."

Charlotte Bainbridge wore a lovely maroon dress, no doubt meant to evoke an association with the Ramsbury crest. The lace was delicate, and the opals she wore sparkled like the galaxies Annabel had once seen through a telescope. It was too bad that her snide smile and hard glare ruined the effect.

"You'll find I'm made of sterner stuff, Miss Bainbridge," Annabel replied. Her chin went to the angle she always used with bullies.

"We chaperones must be," said Mrs. Linden as she approached. "Miss Allen tells me you were good company today, Miss Pearce. Thank you for looking after her in my absence."

"It was my pleasure. Thank you for staying in the garden with Miss Spencer." Annabel was certain the older woman had gotten the worst end of the bargain.

"She is a talented artist, and I enjoyed watching her painting take shape—once she focused on where she was rather than where she wasn't." Mrs. Linden sighed as they entered the parlor. "Miss Allen has no patience for sketching and painting. Or needlework, for that matter. She refuses to sit still."

All morning, Annabel had been impressed with Fiona's lively nature and her unfailing resolve to be nothing but herself. She made no excuses for her past behavior, but she also held nothing back from her life. Many young ladies in her situation would have faded into the country and accepted the *ton*'s judgment for the balance of their lives. Fiona had struck back. It was an admirable decision.

"I don't believe sitting is the virtue Society paints it to be." Annabel heard the words in her own voice and felt her cheeks heat with shock. It was one thing to think something so contrary, but another to speak it aloud.

The chaperones turned to face her, eyes wide in their stark faces. Only Mrs. Linden was smiling. Annabel drew a deep breath. *In for a penny…*

"If a gentleman were to sit in the house and wait for the world to come to him, he would be considered a layabout or feeble-minded. But ladies of quality are judged by how little we— they—are heard or seen. We may move the world, or make a mark, but only where no one can see us do it." She stood straighter. "We are led by a queen who is seen and heard every day in law and in custom—even in war. Why must we limit ourselves to silent decoration?"

The older women stared at her as though she'd sprouted horns and a tail. Beyond them, toward the other end of the table, Fiona raised her glass in a silent salute. Annabel wished she'd put that dratted ribbon through her hair after all.

The silence was broken by the marquess's arrival and then the shocked inhale of every lady in the room. On his arm was a thin young lady in a violet gown. The color complemented her pale complexion and auburn hair, which was done simply. She was flanked by Yarwood, his expression hawklike.

"Ladies and gentlemen, may I present Mrs. Hughes, the widow of an old school friend." Jasper smirked as he talked, as though he understood the commotion he was causing. "Claudette could not be here for the beginning of our party because she was in Paris. I hope you will make her welcome."

Everyone bowed, but no one approached. Fiona was the first to breach the divide. "Welcome, Mrs. Hughes. How was your journey? I crossed the channel in the summer and again in the fall, and while I enjoyed the scenery, the ship did pitch violently at times."

The young widow's reply was lost in the sea of whispers from chaperones and English diamonds alike. Charlotte Bainbridge might have had tears in her eyes.

"How dare he bring her here," someone whispered. "To invite eligible, respectable young ladies to his home and raise their hopes about a match, only to flaunt his mistress as a late arrival."

The hiss had a French lilt. There was only one other French lady in attendance—Madame Theodore, a dragon of a companion who had emigrated simply to terrorize young Society ladies with haughty sniffs, arched eyebrows, and lectures on *what the Paris ladies do*. Belinda Wallace was her current pupil.

"That seems an uncharitable assumption about your countrywoman," Mrs. Linden whispered.

"Not all French ladies are reputable." Madame Theodore arched an eyebrow. "Just as all English women cannot claim proper behavior."

Mrs. Linden's mouth hardened into a thin line and color dotted her cheeks, but she remained silent.

Annabel would have admired her restraint if she wasn't focused on Claudette Hughes herself, though for a different reason. The marquess, his Welsh connection, and his Paris mistress were all under the same roof. Was this the opportunity to gather the information Spencer demanded and free herself from their ugly bargain?

You were wrong about Fiona's position in his life. What if you are wrong again?

"I should have worn the blue. I'll never stand out against that Frenchwoman if I look like a meringue."

Annabel pulled Elizabeth away from the crowd. "The blue is for the dance at the end of the week," she said. "And several of the young men in attendance have already cast you admiring glances." She held up a hand to stop the petty argument she could see brewing in Elizabeth's bright eyes and too-rosy cheeks. "There is more to life than a marquess who seems to be declaring what life with him will entail."

It was advice she should heed herself. If Mrs. Hughes was Lord Ramsbury's lover, her inclusion in the party was in poor taste. If she was part of a larger plot, it was treason.

"The best way for you to behave is to do exactly that—behave. Focus on the those to your left and right and keep the conversation away from gossip." She tightened her hold on Elizabeth. "You are better than a man who has no qualms about ridiculing you in public. Remember that."

"Shall we go into dinner?" Lord Ramsbury asked as he turned and led Mrs. Hughes from the room.

Left with no alternative, the party took their seats around the dinner table. Over the first course, the ladies stared daggers at Mrs. Hughes while the men watched her with open curiosity. By the second course, social etiquette prevailed. The dining room was full of conversation.

Since the other chaperones were ignoring Annabel, she stayed focused on the marquess, comparing his behavior with Mrs. Hughes to how he treated Fiona. They spoke quietly, but he didn't ignore the guest to his left. Mrs. Hughes spent a great deal of time in conversation with Yarwood. Her smiles were soft, almost wistful—not the flirtatious masks used in ballrooms and beyond.

After the dessert course had been cleared, the ladies adjourned to the music room. All except Mrs. Hughes, who disappeared into the shadows.

The young ladies gathered teams for whist, and their chaperones retrieved knitting or needlework to occupy their time until the gentlemen arrived. Annabel watched the clock.

After five minutes, she excused herself to no one in particular and entered the great hall. In the daylight, the space loomed overhead as though she were in a cathedral or a courtroom. In the darkness, with creaks and groans permeating the thick, quiet blanket, the space yawned like a mouth that could swallow her whole.

"Will you not come with me?" Mrs. Hughes's English lilted as though she sang the question.

"I have responsibilities here, dearest," Jasper replied. "You will be safe with Kit, and I will join you when I can."

Annabel followed the whispers until she reached a turn in the hallway. The marquess's unique cologne, a mix of fruit and flowers she couldn't identify, scented the still air.

"As you wish." Mrs. Hughes sighed. "But you work too much, Jasper. You should enjoy your new life more."

"I will enjoy it later, once matters are settled." He was smiling. Annabel could hear it in his words. "Rest tomorrow and gather your strength for the journey. You and Kit will sail the day after."

"Will you show me to my room? This house is…*effrayante.*"

"Stapleton will show you up, though you could likely find it on your own by now. If you are worried in the night, simply knock on the door between us. I'll be there."

"*Merci, très cher ami.* Gareth always said…"

"Shh. He would not wish to see you cry. I do not wish to see it either."

Quiet settled between them. Annabel risked a glance around the corner and found herself watching Lord Ramsbury hold his lover in his arms, his cheek against her hair. The moonlight skimmed Mrs. Hughes's dress and dusted Jasper's half with a silvery glow. The rest of him was hidden in shadows.

She retraced her steps to the music room, though the house seemed darker than it had before. It was a tender scene that eased her mind. The young French widow was no more a spy than Annabel was herself.

Though Annabel wished, for the briefest of moments, that she was.

✑

"I SAY, RAMSBURY, having your French treat arrive was a boon to the rest of us." Wareham's declaration sent game birds scattering out of the grass in every direction. "Set the other girls back on their heels, it did."

"Wareham…" Jasper stopped to gather his temper. As much as he wanted to send the man home, losing the worst gambler in the party would put all the other gentlemen in a bad mood. "I'll thank you to be kinder about Mrs. Hughes." After all, he couldn't have the entire party angry at him at the same time.

"I'm simply saying that I had Miss Wallace's attention for most of the evening because she wasn't mooning over you." Somehow, Wareham's whisper was louder than his speaking voice.

"And having the ladies cross with you means a quiet hunting trip." Garret Spaulding shot a gaze at Wareham. "Mostly."

"Yes, yes. Poke fun." Wareham lifted a flask to his lips. "But I'll crow if I like. Miss Wallace has an excellent pedigree and a sizable dowry."

"Which you won't live to spend if you drink while you shoot." Kit had a white-knuckled hold on his rifle. "Do be wise, Lord Wareham."

"Just a nip to cut the chill," Wareham said as he returned his flask to his coat pocket. "Do wish birds slept later."

"Ridiculous man," Raines muttered from his position near Kit.

Or, at least, that was what Jasper believed he'd said. The viscount was one of the few guests who was quieter than Jasper would have liked. He kept a level head while playing cards, ogled the ladies at dinner but did not discuss them otherwise, and drank enough to be a sport but never enough to be sloppy. The only thing he'd lost his head over was Jasper's stables.

All last night, Jasper had paced his room and considered the possibility of bribing the man with a horse if he'd tell what he knew of Spencer and the court. It might be the simplest way of learning the truth.

In the end, he'd dismissed it. He didn't enjoy the idea of one of his horses in Raines's stables, though it was difficult to put his finger on the reason.

They reached the ridge and the hides dotted along it. As the gamekeeper led the hounds down the hill, each man took their position, flanked by their valets as loaders. Jasper claimed the spot at the end, nearest the trees. It had the worst view of the shooting grounds.

"Challenging yourself today?" Kit joked as they half slid into the furrow.

"Must save some of the birds for the guests." Jasper placed his rifle on the low stone wall.

"Not having a loader should slow you down enough for their egos." Kit placed his powder and shot nearby. "Except for me, of course."

Competition zinged through Jasper's blood, much like the race yesterday. He shrugged out of his constricting coat and reached for his weapon. The steel of the barrel chilled his fingers as the hounds sent up their first mournful bay. The rifle bucked against his shoulder, bringing him to life the way few things did.

A volley of shots sent a respectable number of birds to the ground, and the retrievers went to work gathering them into a pile.

"Grouse and pheasants," Kit said as he stared down the hill. "They're only grouse and pheasants."

"Only?" Jasper turned to joke with his friend about their success shooting small targets, but Kit's haunted stare stopped his laughter. "Are you all right, lad?"

The war was continents away now, but it was never far from Kit. Jasper had seen that stare more than once since Kit's final return from Egypt. It didn't always happen while hunting, either. Sometimes it was the weather or a specific smell. Once it was a song in a brothel.

Jasper hated that he could never find, or know, the right words to say. All he could do was wait for his friend to come back to himself.

"Stag!"

The cry brought everyone to their feet, and Jasper had his rifle raised a second before he realized it wasn't loaded. "Blast."

Kit's deep, slow chuckle was the antithesis of his fluid fingers. It became a race to see who could get the first shot. Jasper didn't know why he bothered. Kit always won.

The stag was near the tree line, badgered to and fro by the hounds nipping at his flanks and heels. He was a magnificent creature, with a wide set of antlers, powerful shoulders, and a broad back, all of which he used to his advantage in the fight for his life. Jasper stood watching, silently cheering for the beast to win.

A fly zinged by his ear, or perhaps it was a bee, given the sting to his cheek. Jasper brushed it away but ended up on his back in the hide with Kit towering over him, pointing his rifle in every direction except at the stag below. He put his boot in Jasper's chest to keep him from standing.

"What the bloody hell?" he shouted.

"One of these bastards took a shot at you," Kit shouted back. "Stay down until the firing stops. That bloody beast needs to go back into the woods."

The baying receded as the dogs chased the stag into the forest. When they finally surrendered, the crashing continued. The animal would likely run to Marlborough. The duke could have him.

Jasper pushed Kit's foot. "Let me up, y' bugger."

Kit didn't relent until the shooting stopped. Jasper stood and met Spaulding's wide eyes and raised hands over stones that lined the ridge of his hide.

"The boy couldn't have missed me from there, and he would have hit you first anyway." Jasper redirected Kit's aim down the hill. "It was likely a wild shot with the excitement of following the stag. The dogs had him dithering in every direction."

Kit relented, but the set to his jaw said he didn't believe him.

The cold pool of dread in Jasper's gut said it didn't believe him either.

Jasper used his shirt sleeve to wipe the blood and dirt from his cheekbone. Whoever had done it had been close enough to hit the rock beside him. He scanned the area himself, searching his guests for a guilty stare and then the landscape for a surefooted sniper. He ended staring at the valley, at the gamekeeper surrounded by his hounds.

"Send them again," he shouted to the man. "We've not taken our fill of birds this morning."

"Jasper," Kit whispered. "This is mad."

"It's a party," Jasper replied. "We need them to have a good time." He stretched out in the hide the best he could and used his coat as a pillow. His valet would chide him for days about the state of his clothes. "Keep shooting. I'm going to nap."

He closed his eyes, but every rifle report jarred him alert. Every whoop of success made his feet twitch.

The successful shooting made the return trip to the house much more of a party. Even Raines was happier, given that he'd bagged the largest bird—a pheasant Jasper pledged to serve for dinner during the party. Kit, dour-faced and trudging two steps behind, refused to be drawn into the celebration. Jasper, itchy, filthy, and cold, spent less time talking than he did listening.

It wasn't the words he heard. No one would be daft enough to say something about an errant shot. He listened for the tone of each comment. Did someone sound guilt-ridden over almost killing their host? Worse, could someone's disappointment in the outing be interpreted as failure at meeting another goal?

Stapleton met them at the end of the stairs, and his eyes went wide at Jasper's appearance. "My lord. Should we send for the constable?"

"I'd be better served by a laundress, I believe." Jasper sighed when the man refused to smile at his joke and move from their path. Both would have been satisfying. Either would have been sufficient.

"You can't blame him for asking, Ramsbury," Wareham said. "You look as though you've been through the war."

As though the tipsy blowhard would know anything of war.

"It's not that, my lord." Stapleton leaned forward to whisper, "One of the pistols is missing from the armory. Did you take one?"

"We didn't." The pool of dread re-formed low in Jasper's stomach, filled by the cold trickle running down his spine. "Search the house and the grounds."

"It's being done now. The house has been searched from attic to larder. The young men are in the garden now. I'm going back to direct them."

"Thank you, Stapleton."

Jasper trudged up the stairs and into the house, imagining he could feel Kit's breath on his neck. When they reached the door to his room, Kit stepped around and entered first. For the first time, Jasper didn't mind his friend's overprotective instincts.

"Our plans must change," Kit said once they were alone in the room. "I cannot leave for Cardiff with a killer in the house."

Jasper stripped out of his boots, trousers, and shirt before pouring water in the basin. "We cannot send Claudette to Wales alone, and she must go." He scrubbed the dirt from his face and hands, and the bracing water helped clear his thoughts. "She and Gareth's family have to stop blaming each other and put pressure on the police to investigate his murder."

Travis, his valet, entered the room. "I apologize, my lord. The house is in an uproar, and I wasn't..." He took in Jasper's appearance and the pile of dirt-splotched clothes. "Oh dear."

He went to work then, dressing Jasper in clothing more suited to an afternoon at home. Jasper shook his head when he lifted the coat. "I'd like to be able to move freely, Travis. Thank you."

After all, an assassin might be lurking around every corner, or even at the top of the stairs.

"As you wish." Travis unrolled his shaving kit and used his limited medical supplies to address the cut on Jasper's cheek. "If I may, sir. You should have taken me with you as a loader. You might not have needed me in that position, but it is clear I could have been of help."

After he was finished, the reflection in the mirror looked more like the confident host Jasper needed to be. He let that feeling seep into his bones. "Thank you, Travis. You are right, of course, and I will rely on you, Stapleton, and the others when Kit leaves for Cardiff in the morning with Mrs. Hughes."

He turned to Kit. "You *must* go to Cardiff. Even if the investigation does not move forward, it is what Gareth would have wanted. We owe him that, at the very least."

Jasper left the room without looking back, certain that Kit was giving orders to the valet, who had been a batman for an overly brave officer in Egypt. For the first time, he was glad his home was so full of retired soldiers that it might well be considered a barracks. Not for the first time, he was happy not to see another soul as he entered the library.

His favorite book waited on the shelf across from the fireplace. He'd read it so often in the last three years that the spine was already ragged. It was a good afternoon to sit quietly with an old friend.

He caught the movement in the corner of his eye and whirled, prepared to use the book as a weapon, if only to allow him to gain ground and throttle his opponent himself. It would be a gratifying experience to take revenge on the culprit who had made him afraid in his own home.

Annabel Pearce stood next to the fire, wide-eyed, her hand motionless on her skirt. "My apologies, your lordship. I did not mean to startle you."

Spencer's spy. Or perhaps an assassin sent to do him in. A pistol would have made it easy for anyone to accomplish the task. "I didn't expect a mouse in my library."

It was an apt description for the slight woman who was always in gray, perpetually plain, and so quiet that most of the party failed to see her.

Though last night, her eyes had been bright, and her cheeks had still held the bloom from their ride. Even her gray dress had seemed prettier. He had the impression that the ladies in the party, even her professional compatriots, saw her and chose to look the other way.

"I'll go, then."

Was it possible that Annabel Pearce, the very proper baron's daughter, would steal a pistol, trek across the countryside, and attempt to shoot him in the back? Jasper dismissed the theory with a mental wave of his hand.

If Annabel wanted to kill him, she would do it while facing him.

"Please don't. I apologize for my remarks." He took a chair and motioned to the one she'd vacated. "My failures in shooting this morning have made me cross."

She touched her cheek, marking the spot where his wound appeared. "Did the birds defend themselves?"

He barked a laugh. "A branch caught me unaware."

A fresh-faced maid scurried into the room, carrying a rattling tray of coffee and sweet biscuits. Though it was almost as large as she was, she managed to set it on the table between them without spilling anything or toppling headfirst onto the carpet.

"Thank you," Annabel said to the girl as she departed. She looked to him. "Shall I pour?"

"Please." Jasper waited as she filled his cup. Steam curled over liquid dark enough to match his thoughts. Or, at least, his previous thoughts. In this room, things didn't seem so dismal. "What are you reading?"

"Currer Bell's novel." She divided the biscuits between them. "It's a favorite of mine. And you?"

"Dumas's novel about the musketeers." He wondered over her choice of a book about a governess in love with her secretive employer. It seemed far too romantic for such a practical young lady. "A favorite."

Her smile creased her eyes for a moment before she opened

her book and returned to the pages. Jasper followed suit.

The fire popped and crackled, warming his toes as the coffee banished the chill in his bones. He relaxed against the chair and reached for a biscuit.

"That is my plate, your lordship."

"Apologies," he replied around a mouthful of sweetness. He risked a sideways glance. She was curled into the chair like a cat, her feet tucked under her as she bent over the page. "Have you reached a suspenseful part?"

"There's a fire set to kill Mr. Rochester," she whispered without looking at him.

He returned to his book, and after a moment reached for another biscuit.

Annabel swatted his hand. "Cad." Laughter infused the word.

Jasper chuckled and turned the page.

CHAPTER SIX

"I'M SURE YOU'D rather be on the dance floor, Miss Pearce."

"I've never cared for ballrooms, Madame Theodore." Annabel looked down the row of chaperones. "Though I do enjoy the fashions. Miss Wallace looks particularly lovely this evening."

"Belinda is a beautiful girl, but it is amazing how much the dresses have changed from the last two Seasons." Madame Theodore raised her spectacles to her nose for the briefest moment as she assessed Annabel.

"They have," Mrs. Linden said. "Though I've always found it odd that we dispose of entire wardrobes based on Paris fashions. Especially since we've been at war with France more years than not." She gave Annabel a discreet wink. "Elizabeth looks quite elegant this evening."

Elizabeth wore a dark blue dress that matched her eyes, and the simple lines enhanced her figure. Her blonde curls cascaded from the crown of her head over one shoulder, balancing the teardrop-shaped diamonds dangling from her ears. The matching necklace, one large diamond on a silver chain, stopped at the center of her chest and did not draw the eye to her cleavage.

Madame Theodore flicked her spectacles again. "She is lucky her mother was aware of current fashions and could guide her before she took ill."

The dress's neckline was too low for a girl Elizabeth's age.

Annabel suspected Elizabeth had visited the seamstress for alterations once her mother left for Bath. However, she took pride in the influence she'd been able to wield this evening. Elizabeth looked properly fashionable, as any Society beau would expect. She also danced well, and she'd had two sets with Garret Spaulding, heir to the Earl of Dunraven.

"In Paris, the young ladies benefit from the experience of older women who have had successful Seasons of their own." The Frenchwoman raised an eyebrow as she swept a critical eye over Annabel's dress. "Women who have excelled in Society understand the importance of first impressions."

If they're so successful, why are they not raising daughters of their own? Annabel knew better than to utter the sarcasm-laced question. How many times had her brain alienated her in a ballroom?

"Some ladies will take every opportunity to make their mark, however they can." Mrs. Danforth, the companion to Charlotte Bainbridge, speared a hard-eyed looked down the row toward Annabel. "They certainly don't need dresses to do it." Her smile twisted. "It might help not to have one at all."

Annabel sucked a breath deep into her lungs. It didn't matter if she was dancing or sitting on the sidelines, and the age of her companions made no difference. Women in a ballroom were nasty competitors—even if they were seconds in the duels.

Her cheeks and ears heated. "How dare—"

Mrs. Linden reached for Annabel's fingers. Her grip was warm and firm as she faced the other chaperones. "Ladies, we are above such nastiness. At least we should be."

"Come now, Mary," Miss Danforth said. "You can't ignore that Ramsbury has spent far too much time with Miss Pearce."

"It has damaged Belinda's prospects as well as Charlotte's," Madame Theodore hissed. "The only one not affected is your Miss Allen, but we know she's had her hooks—"

"That is quite enough." Mrs. Linden thumped her cane against the floor. "Miss Allen's relationship with Lord Ramsbury is no one else's concern but mine, and I am convinced of its propriety."

"Mary—"

"I will not hear another word against her or against the marquess. He has always treated me as a guest in his home. I suspect what you've witnessed this past fortnight is nothing but his wicked sense of humor." Mrs. Linden chuckled. "He likes nothing more than taking self-important people down a peg or two."

She released her grip on Annabel's hand but patted it for good measure, as though she was apologizing for dashing a romantic dream.

Annabel gritted her teeth to keep from screeching about Jasper Warren's *kindness* and *wicked sense of humor*. For the past two weeks, he'd had great fun making her a spectacle at every game, ride, or after-dinner musicale. Even a midday visit to the library had become fodder for gossip.

"If you'll excuse me, ladies." She stood and turned on her heel, circling the dance floor on her way to the punchbowl. She wasn't surprised to see the party continuing as if the argument had never happened. No one ever paid attention to chaperones at a ball.

Not even their host. Jasper was dancing with Belinda Wallace. The candlelight cast his hair in a halo-like glow, and his crooked grin made him look as wicked as the devil himself. He cut a fine figure in his black tailcoat and white waistcoat and cravat.

"He's difficult to miss, isn't he?" Fiona asked.

Annabel glanced over her shoulder and at Fiona's doting smile. It was no wonder she and Jasper were friends. They clearly shared the same perverse sense of humor and distaste for social rules.

It was freeing to be surrounded by people who were at ease being themselves.

"Anyone with his height would be difficult to miss."

Fiona tilted her head back in a deep, honest laugh that had several people staring as they left the dance floor. "Oh, I like you," she said.

"You two seem to be enjoying yourselves," Jasper said as he came to Fiona's side. "Did someone miss a step?"

"Miss Pearce was just commenting on your height," Fiona said. Her eyes danced over the rim of her glass.

Jasper accepted the sarcastic compliment with a slow dip of his head and a twisted grin. "I'm glad to see you away from the spectators, Miss Pearce. Are you up for a dance?"

"No, thank you, Lord Ramsbury. I'm not dancing."

"But I insist." The way he leaned forward to whisper, the laughter dripping from his words, sheared the last thread of Annabel's temper.

Every night before she fell asleep, she promised to avoid him and to not rise to the bait. Every day, he never paid her enough attention to be scandalous but just enough to cause whispers, knowing she wouldn't be impolite.

"Insist all you want. I won't be dancing." Annabel struggled to keep her voice low as she glared into Jasper's mocking eyes. "If you wish to prove yourself egalitarian enough to treat paid help as honored guests, go ask Madame Theodore to join you in the next quadrille. I've had quite enough."

She turned her back on both of them, intent on retrieving a drink to calm her nerves and using the darkness past the crowd to mask her escape. However, the break in dancing meant a crowd had gathered for refreshments. Belinda and Charlotte cast cutting glances her way.

It would be like entering a nest of snakes.

"Would you like me to fetch you something?" Jasper's question echoed over the crowd.

She had already been rude to him. Nosing through his house and eavesdropping on conversations was the height of impoliteness. Asking their assigned maid about life in the house, encouraging her to gossip, was improper. One more time wouldn't matter.

Annabel closed the distance so she didn't have to shout. "I

would like for you to leave me alone. I am tired of being shunned simply because you find humor in tweaking everyone else's noses."

Fiona looked between them, her frown deepening. "Annabel…"

She put up a hand to stop the charade. Spencer could go to the devil and take his threats with him. Jasper Warren was nothing more than a bored gentleman skirting scandal for fun.

Elizabeth would throw a tantrum, but if they packed tonight and left first thing in the morning, they could be in Bath by teatime.

Annabel swept her gaze across the crowd, all of whom were being far too obvious about ignoring her. Elizabeth wasn't in the room. "Where is Miss Spencer?" She counted the heads of every man at the party, only relaxing when they were all accounted for.

"I believe she and Charlotte had words. Their heads were together for several minutes before she left the room." Fiona's voice had lost its sparkle. "Elizabeth's color was quite high."

"Thank you." Annabel strode into the hall without looking back to meet the gazes she felt at her back. She ignored the whispers hissing behind her.

At the top of the stairs, she found their maid in the hallway. "Follow me, Ruth."

Wide-eyed, the girl curtsied before hurrying forward. Annabel followed at a quick pace. Perhaps Elizabeth would be more circumspect if there was someone else in the room, especially if she'd had another row with Charlotte.

The maid waited at the door, and Annabel swept in without knocking. "Elizabeth?"

The room was empty. So was the adjoining dressing room. There was no one on the balcony. Annabel's heart hammered against her ribs. Where else would Elizabeth go? Had she arranged an assignation while Annabel had been too busy fighting a battle she'd been lured into? Had that been Jasper's plan all along?

She turned to the maid. "Have you seen Miss Spencer on the upper floors during the dancing?"

The pale young girl bobbed her head in a near fit. "Yes, miss. She was h-heading down the other h-hall."

Jasper's private rooms were in that direction.

"Where?" Annabel grabbed the girl's shoulders and shook her. "Explain."

"She b-begged me not to tell. Sh-she said it was a surprise."

Blast. "Pack everything but our night clothes and traveling dresses for tomorrow. Miss Spencer and I are leaving in the morning."

Annabel raced from the room and across the landing. The candles sputtered in their holders, casting irregular shadows across the dark-paneled walls. The thick carpet muffled her steps.

Her eyes adjusted to the darkness, making it possible to see the glow under the door at the end of the hall. She lengthened her stride and pushed the door open with a *whoosh* that ended with a bang as the latch hit the wall.

Elizabeth stopped wrestling with the ribbons at her back and spun with a shriek.

"Get out of this room." Anger and fear added an unfamiliar gravel to Annabel's voice. "Now."

"I will not." Elizabeth tilted her chin at a stubborn angle. "Charlotte has done nothing but tease me for weeks, that I was too young for Ramsbury to notice me, that he only invited me so you would come. She said he wouldn't even kiss me if he found me naked and waiting. I'm going to prove her wrong."

Annabel couldn't believe her ears. "You are going to ruin yourself to spite Charlotte Bainbridge?" She gathered Elizabeth's slippers and shoved them into her hands. "Are you daft?"

She pushed Elizabeth's shoulder, urging her to the door. The girl dug in her heels.

"You just want Ramsbury for yourself. You've spent the last two weeks turning his head, teasing him, and keeping him from us when *we're* the ones he's meant to choose from. He will never choose you for anything honorable." Her eyes widened. "Is that why you're here?"

"You foolish, *foolish* girl. I am here to keep you from making the worst mistake of your life." Annabel shook Elizabeth until her curls trembled. "Do you really want to marry a man whom you've trapped? To have every woman in Polite Society either cut you directly or whisper behind your back? To walk into a ballroom and wonder how many of the women in attendance have warmed your husband's bed?"

"They wouldn't dare cut a marchioness." Despite the tears in Elizabeth's eyes, her mouth was still set in a stubborn line. "I would be—"

"A laughingstock? Married to a man who only takes you to bed because he needs a legitimate heir and exiles you to the country once you've given him one? Who spends his nights away from home because he doesn't love you, will never love you because of what you forced him to do?"

Tears slid down Elizabeth's cheeks as she shook her head, either in agreement or denial. Annabel wasn't certain of which, but she took advantage of the weakness and shoved the girl toward the door. "Go to our room and have Ruth get you ready for bed. Wash your face. We're leaving as soon as it's light enough to travel."

"No. There's not a reason—"

Charlotte would make sure this tale was well known before breakfast began, and Elizabeth wouldn't be able to fight it. "There is every reason, Elizabeth. Go to our room now. You were never here."

The girl was halfway out the door when her hand flew to her ear. "I've lost an earring, Annabel." Her eyes widened. "I don't know where."

She'd been wearing them both in the ballroom, and Annabel hadn't seen one sparkling on the stairs or in the hallway. Granted, she hadn't been looking. But now she'd have to search this room to make certain it wasn't left behind.

"Go. I'll find it."

Annabel closed the door and dropped to her knees, sweeping her hands over the carpet and looking for the sparkle in the firelight. She found nothing where Elizabeth had been standing, but flattened herself to look under the bed to be certain the diamond hadn't rolled there.

A dark box caught her eye. Her heart thumping in her ears, Annabel pulled it to her and out into the light. The metal was warm against her fingers, and the latch gave easily.

Guilt spread over her skin like ice on the Thames as she lifted a letter from the top of the papers and coins—francs and gold.

Dearest Jasper, Though I am nervous of my role in Cardiff, I will do as you ask and hope it makes a difference. Please tell Kit that his work has reaped rewards in Spain, and I look forward to sharing the tales with him. I hope your mission in London is bearing the fruit you hoped for. With all the love I can spare, Claudette

It was just enough of a love letter to make reading it embarrassing, and it contained enough hints of *work* and *missions* to be concerning.

Annabel rifled through the box. Hand-drawn maps were well creased and heavily marked with notes and runes. Were they really spies?

Tears clouded her vision. She would have wagered money she didn't have that Jasper was more bored than treasonous. She would have lost everything because of a respectable title and a winning smile.

Just like her father had done.

"Kit, I'm not going to get lost going to my room," Jasper grumbled. His voice was muted by the door and the long hallway.

"Lost is the last thing that worries me," Yarwood grumbled back.

Annabel dithered, staring at the letter and the map, knowing they might be the proof Spencer needed, and that Jasper would go to ground if he found them missing. He'd also know who took them. There would be no hiding from him.

The floorboards creaked under their steps, growing louder with each word.

She put everything back the way she'd found them, shoved the box under the bed, and stood facing the door. She locked her trembling knees and straightened her spine as the latch turned.

"Given yesterday's incident, you should have locked your door," Yarwood said.

"I'm not locking my door in my own house." Jasper's voice grew clearer as the door opened. He glanced inside, and the eye she could see widened. "And I don't need you anymore tonight." He looked back for a moment, giving her a glimpse of his tense jaw and the way his hair curled around his ear. "Thank you, Kit."

Annabel held her breath as he entered the room and the latch *snicked* behind him.

"There's a rumor downstairs that a young lady is waiting in my room." He stepped forward. "You aren't who I expected."

Annabel stepped back and gulped as the back of her knees struck the mattress. "I heard the same rumor." She cleared her throat to rid it of the tremor. "I came to make sure Elizabeth wasn't here."

Jasper sipped his drink but kept his eyes on her. "That's the only reason?"

Annabel refused to blink as she held his stare. Her neck ached from looking up at him. "What other reason would there be?"

He set the empty glass on the table near the door before stepping toward her. "Every other young lady in London wants something from me. Why would you be any different?"

He removed his tailcoat and loosened his cravat, his muscles moving under his shirt in a way that warmed her insides as much as the fire in the hearth warmed her skin. "Why are you undressing?" she asked.

A lazy smile spread across his face. "I always undress in my rooms, especially after an evening of being trussed up like a Christmas goose." He removed his cuff links. "But you didn't answer my question. What makes you different than any other lady in London?"

After two weeks of bantering and baiting, he's learned nothing about me. He tormented me for nothing more than sport, and I've received nothing but empty words from a self-important rogue who believes himself special because of a title. Annabel shoved her disappointment and anger aside. Neither would do her any good. They never had. "I'm smart enough to know better."

"Are you?" He loomed over her now, one hand on the bedpost, close enough she could see the shadowy stubble on his jaw and smell the spice of his cologne. For a man who'd had a drink in his hand all evening, his eyes were unusually sharp. His stare pricked her skin.

Or her conscience.

"I'm taking Elizabeth back to London tomorrow." She stepped past him and walked to the door, willing herself not to run.

"That would be wise," he murmured.

The latch gave easily under Annabel's fingers, and the door opened without a sound. She had one foot in the shadows and the other still in the warmth of the room when he caught her from behind and ran his hands from her shoulders to her hips.

She wriggled for freedom, but it was futile. "What are you doing?"

"Making certain my things are still mine." He pushed his fingers through the folds of her skirts.

She spun on him, put her boot in his foot the way her father had taught her, and put her hands flat against his solid, warm chest. "Get your bloody hands off me."

Though he winced in pain, he didn't budge. "Every young lady has a place to hide a handkerchief." He lowered his head until they were nose to nose. "Turn out your pocket."

She did as he asked and glared at him. "Empty as when I

arrived, your lordship."

"I believe I saw someone walking this way." Charlotte's sly words were accompanied by the glow of candles at the head of the hallway.

Annabel pushed herself free but lost her footing when her boot tangled in the carpet. Jasper's hold on her arm, and then her waist, kept her from crashing to the floor.

"Miss Pearce?" called Madame Theodore in a squeal that was too practiced to be shocked. "Is that you?"

"Blast," Annabel whispered as she fought to stand upright.

"Double blast," Jasper muttered as he stepped between her and their audience.

CHAPTER SEVEN

"Y OU WERE SUCH a loving child. I cannot understand when, or why, you grew to be so vexing."

"Don't shout so, Mum." Jasper leaned against the back of the chair he'd been occupying for the last half-hour. "You'll give yourself a megrim."

"It would serve you right if my head caved in." The Countess of Lambourn put her fingers to her temples, careful to keep them out of her perfectly arranged hair. "A *chaperone*, Jasper?"

"Baron Chilworth's oldest daughter." It was a wonder that it took less than one Season for Society to forget a family that had been on everyone's invitation lists. If Chilworth's speculation had been successful, the *ton* would have been lining up at his door.

"Who has no dowry and, if rumor is to be believed, may soon have no home." Mother leaned back against lace pillows that matched her silver-white hair. "They will be an albatross around your neck."

"You are assuming a great deal." Not the least of which was that Annabel Pearce would allow her family to be homeless. "She isn't one to trap a man into marriage."

"Yet she was in your room. In your arms. And you were half undressed." She closed her eyes and heaved a weary sigh. "What possessed you? No, wait, don't answer that."

"I was hardly undressed." And he'd been possessed by the

perverse need to discomfit Miss Pearce as much as she'd done him when she wheeled on him in his own ballroom. "And she was not in my arms until she tripped. Would you have had me watch a young lady tumble to the floor?"

"Don't be obtuse. It doesn't suit you," Mother snapped. "I can understand dalliances with unhappily married women. I don't like it, but I'm aware they happen and are generally safer than…alternatives. And you wouldn't be the first in our family to chase a servant around a bedroom. But this, Jasper. Do you understand the consequences of this gossip?"

He rose from his chair and strode to the fireplace, using his height to feel less like a boy being scolded for stealing sweets. "I did not invite Miss Pearce to my room." *She was there to spy on me.* "I did not mistreat her." *Other than searching her person for anything she might have found.* "And she left for London with her virtue intact."

As had young Miss Spencer, who had been the girl waiting for him, Jasper had no doubt. Though whether it was for her own ruin or as a trap for Annabel, Jasper couldn't tell. Charlotte Bainbridge was a vicious socialite in the making. Heaven help them all when she became Raines's viscountess, which was likely to happen before the end of the Season.

"Which doesn't signify after your involvement with that Stratford mess before the holiday."

Jasper had long kept an eye on Viscount Stratford because he'd believed the man's predilections would make him ripe for blackmail, and therefore a target for Spencer. However, he'd never suspected the man of murder. "Would you rather the Burnleys lost the chance to grieve their daughter?"

"Don't put words in my mouth," his mother said. "I'd rather you hadn't escorted a doxy to a party with the prime minister."

"In the company of two dukes, a viscount, Uncle Augustus's proxy, and Cousin Amelia," Jasper reminded her.

"Amelia's Canadian husband is no more a fit proxy than I am." Mother rolled her eyes. "And then you testified in court that the…woman had been your guest at Ramsbury. It was in all the papers that you'd taken a trollop to the family estate."

"She likely wasn't the first," Jasper muttered.

Mother tossed the bedclothes aside and stood. "Don't be insolent." She pulled on her dressing gown before approaching him. "It was a lucky thing that anyone came to your blasted party, and then you do *this*."

Despite her flair for the dramatic and her penchant for taking to bed whenever she was irritated, the Countess of Lambourn was an imposing figure. Taller than most women, with bright blue eyes that reminded Jasper of lightning in a storm, she was whip-lean and far smarter than most men of his acquaintance. "I didn't do anything, Mum."

Even as he said it, the recollection of Miss Pearce's curves twitched his fingers. She'd been warm and soft, though she'd fought with surprising strength. This morning he'd caught himself smiling at the memory as he struggled to get his bruised foot into a stiff boot.

"The *ton* doesn't care. It will seize on the gossip and the scandal." His mother met his gaze, her mouth in a stern line. As a child, Jasper had been terrified of disappointing her. He had to admit that now, in this darkened room where he couldn't tell her everything, he was still nervous.

"I'll weather it, Mother. After the next ball, the matrons will seize on a new scandal and a new young miss to terrorize." He bent to kiss her cheek and frowned when she avoided him.

"You may, but your sisters will not." She put a finger in his chest. "Jane and Johanna have been insulated from your affairs, but it is their first Season. They need to be invited to the best parties to find good matches."

Jasper's throat tightened. He'd promised his father he'd ensure Jane and Jo's happiness. "They're sisters to a viscount, and they have substantial dowries. They'll be invited to everything."

"They are sisters to a viscount who drags a baron's daughter into his chambers."

"She was a chaperone just a few moments ago," he quipped. He regretted it the moment Mother arched her eyebrow.

"Then you're the man who will seduce young ladies' companions before proposing to them and then chase the servants once you're married. Or you'll bed your sister's friends at *their* parties."

"I'm not marrying to stop malicious gossip. Not even for the girls." This time he did kiss her cheek. She smelled of rosewater. "Not even for you, Mum."

"Jasper."

"I'll be on my best behavior when the *ton* is looking." He left her and walked toward the door. "That's all I'll promise."

Once he was alone in the hallway, Jasper drew a deep breath. He'd been prepared to have a title, to have a voice in Parliament, and to manage estates. No one had prepared him for managing his family.

From adolescence, he'd learned which women were safe for dalliances and which brothels to avoid. Nothing had prepared him for a wide-eyed brunette in gray standing in front of his bed, who was angrier at him than she was worried about getting caught doing whatever she was doing before he arrived.

"Lord Ramsbury?"

"Yes, Charles?" Jasper managed a smile for the family butler who kept his mother's house running like a well-wound clock, no matter the time of day or the events taking place under the roof.

"Miss Allen is in the downstairs drawing room."

He hadn't seen Fiona since Mrs. Linden had shuffled her into a coach the morning after the incident with Annabel. After a week of being lectured by Kit about his safety and scolded by his mother about his choices, the thought of a friendly face made him smile. "Thank you."

The downstairs drawing room was at the front of the house, done in the same wood tones as the other rooms. White satin drapes reflected the light through the windows during the day and candlelight at night, softening the masculine edges and making the room seem larger.

Fiona was at the front window, staring out at the street.

"By God, I'm glad to see you." His smile faded as she turned a stern glare his way. "What?"

"You've talked me into doing a lot of foolish things in our lives, but you've never asked me to be cruel."

"Not you, too." Jasper pushed his hand back through his hair. "Fiona, you don't understand."

"I understand that you encouraged me to make friends with Annabel. You let me believe you might be interested in her, so I would share what she said." Her eyes flashed as she advanced on him. "And then you used that information to torment her and make her a target for every harpy you invited to your house because you thought it would be fun to watch them scheme and connive for the hell of it."

Jasper's back hit the wall by the door, and Fiona got closer—and louder.

"And if that wasn't enough, you've created a scandal and left her to deal with it alone."

"I didn't create a scandal," Jasper said. "She was the one in my room. Without an invitation, by the way."

"So you got half undressed and carried her into the hallway in front of a crowd."

"I took off my coat, and she walked out of my room on her own two feet." Stormed out was more like it. "She even trod on mine on the way out."

"I see," Fiona said in the deadly, quiet voice Jasper had learned to dread. "So that justifies your leaving her to deal with this on her own?"

"Deal with what? She's not without protection—"

"Jasper, she's not a companion because she likes taking entitled brats to parties. You know her family's circumstances, and you know what will happen to her when Spencer dismisses her."

If she hadn't found anything to report to Spencer, he likely *would* dismiss her. It would serve her right for throwing her lot in with a scoundrel and going up against a wiser opponent.

"Jasper, you do know what happens to female servants who are judged to be lacking in virtue, don't you?"

"She isn't a servant, she's a—"

"She'll never be a lady again, never be a companion again. She might be a governess, but every man in the house will consider her fair game." Fiona put her finger to his chest. "You will walk away from this unscathed, but Annabel's life will never be the same. Ever." Tears welled in her eyes. "I thought you were better than this, Rabbit."

Winning was only fun if the fight was fair, if the combatants were equally matched. Spencer was a fair target. Annabel was not. Just as Fiona, eager to prove herself part of the *ton*, hadn't been.

He lifted his friend's finger from his chest and kissed her hand before pulling her into an embrace. "I'll see what I can do."

ANNABEL STOOD IN the center of her father's London library and refused to fidget under Spencer's unrelenting scrutiny.

"Two weeks, and you found nothing?" he asked.

"Nothing." The lie surprised her, both by how easy it was and that she did it at all. The contents of the box under Jasper's bed were suspicious enough to give Spencer a direction for his investigation, and to prove she had completed her assignment. To set her free.

Though freedom was less appealing than it had been two weeks ago.

"I never should have sent you." Spencer prowled the space behind the desk, from bookcase to bookcase and back again.

"Given Elizabeth's behavior, you definitely should have sent me." He should have kept her at home.

"Yet you're the one who was found in his room." He glared

at her. "In his arms."

"Again. Elizabeth was foolish enough to accept an inappropriate dare—"

"So you say."

"So it was," she said through gritted teeth. "Were it not for me, your daughter would be ruined and forced to marry a man who considers her an annoying child."

"Elizabeth says your inappropriate interest in Ramsbury goaded every young woman to misbehave."

"You told me to learn everything about him." It was more difficult to keep her voice level than it had been to lie. "I had to talk to him to do that."

Spencer put his hands flat on the desk. "And in doing so, you fell victim to his charms."

The only thing she'd fallen victim to was this scheme, and possibly one concocted by Charlotte Bainbridge. "I took advantage of your daughter's foolishness and searched his room."

Dearest Jasper… What sort of spy started a letter like that? *Cardiff, Spain, London. Missions.* What sort of spy was that open about their plans?

"And you found nothing?"

"I found ancient account books and love letters from his mistress." Annabel blinked. "Nothing useful."

"I see." Spencer began pacing again, slower this time. "And now, thanks to his behavior while you were in his room, you are no longer free to move in his circles, even on the periphery."

Annabel fought the urge to drop into the chair behind her. She'd explained away Jasper's actions as rash and provocative, and she'd been terrified that he'd see through her bravado and realize what she was doing. She'd never considered that his behavior was purposeful, that he'd ruined her reputation simply to thwart her efforts.

"Unless you marry him."

This time, she did drop into the chair with an unladylike bounce. "What?"

"Lady Lambourn has a reputation for propriety, especially given her family's history."

History? "I've heard nothing scandalous of the Chitester family." Annabel felt the need to defend Amelia, who had remained a true friend despite all that occurred. "And Baron Kilverstone is—"

Spencer waved her protest aside. "She will insist Ramsbury offer for you to save the family from scandal. He will do it, gambling that you'll refuse."

"He would be right." She wouldn't marry Jasper Warren even if he really had compromised her.

A traitorous warmth spread over her chilled skin. It had happened all week whenever she thought of that night in his room, the way he'd handled her.

"And you would be wrong." Spencer sat in her father's chair. "He will not be able to hide everything, all the time, if you are under his roof."

Neither would she. "And when he discovers the truth?"

"You would not be the first, or last, Society couple to live separate lives." Spencer's eyes were wildly bright. "And at least you would not worry for money or a home."

As though Jasper would provide an allowance to any wife who had defrauded him. Not that she would be that wife. This scheme was insane. "No, Mr. Spencer. I won't do it."

"I thought as much." He heaved a great sigh. "Your father had hopes that I could appeal to your more practical nature, but I told him you were far too wise to consider such a scheme. I told him I was sure you already planned to continue on your chosen path despite the gossip and your lack of references."

Annabel had known her failure would doom her future chances. The scandal would follow her through London, if not through all of England.

"I told him you'd likely considered traveling to Scotland, perhaps Ireland." He steepled his fingers together and peered at her over the peak. "Maybe even the Continent. Your French is excellent, and they are more lenient in Paris than they are in London."

She'd been considering the same thing. Perhaps the French, or even the Italians, would pay well for a tutor to teach English, and English manners, to daughters in search of titles. She could send her earnings home to combine with funds gleaned from rents and sales. She wouldn't have to be gone long. In a few years, Ramsbury would be married and the *ton* would have found another scandal.

The only other option was to stay here and watch her family sell their lives piece by piece because, in her attempt to help, she'd only made things worse.

"Your earnings could keep the collectors at bay as long as all his debts are held by different agencies." Spencer's lips shaped into a cruel smile. "But if one agency, one person, bought all his markers, and then called them in…"

Annabel's heart stopped. If all Father's debts were called in at once, they'd be forced to sell everything quickly at a bargain. They'd never have enough, and Father would end up in prison anyway. Mother and the girls would be beside him.

She knew better than to ask if Spencer had them. He didn't talk just to hear himself.

Quick steps in the hallway, punctuated by a cane to form a triplet, signaled Father's approach.

"You will marry Ramsbury and get me the information I need, or your family will be carted through Mayfair on their way to prison," Spencer whispered.

Her father bustled in. "Ramsbury has sent word that he will call within the hour."

"See, Miss Pearce? I told you he would behave like a gentleman eventually." Spencer's jolly announcement sounded very much like a threat. "I'll wait across the hall in case his courage fails."

Once they were alone, her father took the seat facing her. He covered her fingers with his. "Annie, dearest. I want you to know that your mother and I believe your explanation of events. You have always been a good, kind young lady with a stout moral compass and an eye toward protecting those in your care."

Who had looked through a man's room and read his mail. "Thank you, Father." She met his eyes and smiled as much as she could. "I am sorry it has come to this."

"It could be worse. He is a handsome lout who has a kind reputation, and he votes well." A smile curved through his ruddy cheeks. "He's also richer than Croesus."

Which meant he didn't need a wealthy bride. *Aren't I lucky?* "Father—"

"Annie. This is the first bit of luck we've had in the past year. The *ton* won't dare overlook your sisters when you are a marchioness."

While Annabel understood the positive outcome for Rachel and Rebecca, it was also fair to consider the possibilities for her father. Lord Ramsbury would not want to see his father-in-law in debtor's prison. If he bought Father's debts from Spencer, the lout's threat would disappear.

Which meant Spencer wouldn't sell them.

"And if I build on that luck, we could right our ship by the end of the year." His eyes gleamed. "An acquaintance has approached me about a coal mine."

He would never learn. "Let's take one step at a time." She stood and walked to the window, only to turn away when she began searching the street for Lord Ramsbury's carriage. "We assume he wishes to propose. He might have a more unsavory proposition."

He might be bringing a magistrate to arrest her for spying on him in his own home.

Father cleared his throat and refused to meet her eyes. "Even an unsavory proposal would be a relief. You would still have a roof and likely servants of your own. You will have an allowance—a generous one that you could share with your family."

A family who wouldn't be able to acknowledge her on the

street and still have her sisters be respectable. Tears stung her eyes. "Father!"

He used his cane to help him to his feet, then came to her and kissed her cheek. "There are worse things, Annabel. Just think about it before you toss him out on his ear."

She turned away to look out at the weak sunshine that heralded a London spring afternoon. Father's triplet step faded as he crossed the hall to the receiving room where Spencer waited like a greedy specter in the graveyard of her hopes.

Annabel put her head in her hand. She should have simply pushed Elizabeth from the room and followed her down the hall. If she'd never stayed to search for that dratted earring, she never would have looked under the bed. She wouldn't have seen the box, wouldn't have read the letter. None of this would have happened.

The earring hadn't even been in there. Elizabeth had found it in their room, on the floor just over the threshold.

Annabel's life lay before her in two paths. Stay true to herself and spend the rest of her days in service, if she was lucky. She'd have a roof and a chance to make an honest living. If she was lucky, she might find love with a footman or valet. Maybe a shopkeeper. Or she could marry for the sake of her family and live in a cold, gilded cage. She'd never have to worry, but she'd never have love.

She pulled her handkerchief from her pocket and blotted her tears, again and again. It should be an easy choice.

"Miss Pearce?"

She spun to face the door. Jasper stood there, tall and handsome. She'd been so lost in her thoughts that she hadn't heard him arrive. His maroon and blue striped waistcoat was the perfect companion to his blue wool coat. The color was the same shade as his eyes had been that night in the firelight. "I don't wish to marry you," she said.

He blinked for a moment before a wry smile twisted his lips. "Then that is something we have in common."

Despite her declaration, her heart still sank. She stopped it in mid-fall. There was nothing wrong with a life of honest work. "Thank you for coming to—"

He stepped into the room and strode toward her. "Perhaps we could find other things on which we agree."

Annabel forced herself not to run. "We both enjoy riding, I believe." She motioned to a chair in front of the hearth and took the opposite one.

"And books," he said as he sat. "We dislike dancing."

Her toes and fingers stung as the heat penetrated her chilled skin. "And bad music."

He chuckled. "Indeed."

They both quieted as her family's one remaining maid delivered a tea tray. Once she left, Annabel reached for the teapot. "Cream and sugar?"

"Neither, please." Jasper took the cup she offered.

She fixed her tea and sat back in the chair. "I am sorry I was in your room."

"And I am sorry I was an arse about it." He relaxed in his chair. "I also apologize for my behavior while you were a guest in my home. My only excuse is that I enjoy tweaking Society's collective nose, and that I'm frequently thoughtless about it."

"Thank you." She lifted the tea to her lips, anticipating the simple comfort of routine things. Oddly enough, Jasper—with his swearing, easy nature, and blunt honesty—was a unique kind of tonic.

"We should marry, Miss Pearce."

Her cup clattered into the saucer, sloshing tea onto her fingers. He looked the same as he had five minutes ago, but in that time, he had lost his wits. "I beg your pardon, Lord Ramsbury, but are you foxed?"

"I never begin drinking before noon, especially not at my mother's house." He held her gaze. "My behavior has left you with few viable options for your future."

"It wasn't just your behavior, and I don't believe our penance should be a life sentence in a loveless marriage."

He put his teacup back on the table and leaned forward, his elbows on his knees. "Since I inherited my title, my mother has prodded me to choose a wife based on anything but love. I've avoided proposing because every candidate has, quite frankly, bored me senseless. You do not."

Annabel kept a tight grip on her cup but didn't dare drink it. "You know my circumstances."

"I don't need a rich wife," he said. "I need a suitable wife."

She was far from suitable in ways he would never understand. The primary one being that she'd been spying on him, for pity's sake. "You need an heir."

He shrugged. "Not right away." His grin hitched up on one side. "I'm willing to wait and see if we grow more compatible."

The flush on her cheeks had nothing to do with the fire. "And if we don't?"

"Then we'll come to an agreement." His gaze was steady. "Annabel, I believe we will both benefit from marrying, and I think we will find we have many more things in common. Marriages have been built on weaker foundations."

She finally sipped her tea to wet her throat. "I have two sisters who will need a Season, not necessarily this one, but next."

"They can come out with mine this year, and the year after if necessary. We'll see they're matched to decent young men." He paused for a moment, his eyes twinkling. "I'd like your help with that. You are quite the tiger as a chaperone, and the girls are chafing against Mother's decrees."

"Thank you. I'd be happy to help, though my sisters may not listen to *me*." She blinked to clear the tears from her eyes. "I'd like your word that you won't pay my father's debts."

He nodded but frowned. "Why?"

"He won't learn his lesson," she whispered as she stared into the fire. "He's chased schemes for years, and you'll be throwing good money after bad." She met his gaze. "Seasons aren't cheap, and I won't take advantage of your generosity."

"Thank you. But your mother shouldn't suffer. She'll have an allowance my solicitor will manage for her. She'll have enough to keep her in London if she chooses." He caught his bottom lip between his teeth for a moment. "Forgive me, but you'll need a wardrobe. My mother's dressmaker should be willing to fit you quickly."

Although it stung her pride and her conscience, she would have to look like a marchioness, and she couldn't afford that on her own. "I'll be ready."

"No gray, please. You have enough of that."

It was her turn to chuckle. "Agreed." It was easy to do. She hated gray. "One more thing."

He waited, eyebrows arched.

It was difficult to think, much less say. "I am aware you have at least one mistress." She put a hand up to stop his interruption. "I'm not asking you to give them up. I'm just asking that you be discreet. The *ton* will gossip enough as it is."

He offered his hand. "Is that a yes, then, Annabel?"

She slid her fingers into his large, warm palm. "Yes, Lord Ramsbury."

"Jasper." His breath was hot on her skin as he brushed his lips across her knuckles.

"As you wish." Annabel's heart thudded against her ribs. "Jasper."

CHAPTER EIGHT

"Y OU SEND ME to Cardiff and get *married* while I'm gone?"
Kit pushed himself from the mantel and came back to the
desk. "To the woman you caught poking around your bedroom."

"Don't loom over me." Jasper dropped his pen into the ink
pot. "It wasn't my intention."

"The timing or the wedding?"

"Both." Jasper blotted the letter to Claudette before folding it
with as crisp a crease as possible given the ten-pound notes
contained within. "Though I would have waited if I'd known it
would put your nose out of joint."

Kit moved the seal out of reach. "Jasper. Your new wife wants
to see you hang."

"Name a wife in London who doesn't want to see their husband swing."

His best friend stood speechless, his face deepening to purple
with alarming speed. Jasper finally took pity on him.

"I wouldn't have married Annabel if I thought she was a
danger to my life span or my freedom." He dropped bits of blue
sealing wax into the crucible he'd used since his father's death.
"Or to the queen."

"So why *did* you marry her?"

Jasper had been asking himself the same question since he'd
left Annabel in her father's library after their odd betrothal

negotiations. He'd gone there intending to apologize and offer to help find her a place somewhere the gossip wouldn't reach. Then he'd seen Spencer's carriage near the house and decided, instead, to give her a piece of his mind.

But she'd been in tears, which reminded him of Fiona and the muddle she was still trying to climb free of. The difference was that Fiona's scandal was based on fact, and her family had money the *ton* couldn't ignore. Annabel didn't. "Fiona tore a strip off me for being a careless, heartless lout."

"Fiona." Kit rolled his eyes. "Her redemption is becoming a pain in the arse."

The phrase took Jasper back to the library, where he'd sworn without thinking and Annabel hadn't reprimanded him for his manners. Surprisingly, it seemed to put her at ease. There had been something about her honesty and wry humor that had done the same for him, despite her association with Spencer.

"Annabel is the best path toward learning Spencer's game."

"You could have simply asked her," Kit said.

"She wouldn't have told me." Jasper didn't believe she knew. Spencer had proven to be wily prey because he kept his own counsel.

"Everyone has a price, Jasper."

Annabel's had been the chance for her sisters to find suitable husbands and an allowance for her mother. He put the wax over the candle. "Her loyalty is not for sale."

"Goddammit, Jasper." Kit pushed himself from the chair and ambled to the liquor cabinet. After filling a glass, he stood at the window. The afternoon light spilled over his shoulders and onto his back. "You've yoked yourself to someone who depends on your enemy for safety."

Jasper was wagering that Annabel didn't depend on Spencer for anything. She was smarter than that. He was hoping vows in a church and keeping his word would buy him the time to win her to his side.

Or his ego was getting the better of him. "Perhaps."

"You say that the way you did at Eton when you were convinced of your answer, even if it didn't match the lecture."

The indigo wax pooled in the crucible. "What did you find in Cardiff?"

"The miners are all whispering about a new company, fronted by Abel Collins."

"What do we know about him?"

"Da's known him for years. He's strong as an ox and as determined as a man has to be to go down a shaft every day and come out black inside and out. And the word is that you'd rather have him on your side in a fight. But Da has never trusted him. *He* definitely has a price."

"Do you know what he's doing?"

"Not yet," Kit said. "Everyone whispers, but there's nothing solid. What I do know is that he's got a pub he favors and a table in the corner that's always full of foremen and shift leaders. He always picks up the tab."

"Not his money?"

Kit shook his head. "No way in hell. He's always paid his own way, but *just* his own way. Someone is bankrolling him for something."

Jasper poured the wax over the envelope and placed his seal in the center.

I have Some exploSive goSSip to Share when I arrive in London, Gareth had written.

The letter had arrived, but he hadn't. He also hadn't returned to his wife in Paris. No one had seen him riding in a coach or aboard a ship. Their friend had vanished. More likely, his body was yet to be found. "Could Gareth and Collins have crossed paths?"

"The pub is near the docks and is attached to a reputable inn. There's also a post service across the street." The ice rattled in Kit's glass. "It's why I started there."

Jasper lifted the seal from the envelope. The ram's head with curved horns that was part of his family crest stared back at him.

"The S's in Gareth's letter could simply mean he was in a hurry to make the post."

"Claudette can produce numerous letters, written in battle, where he never made that error," Kit argued. "He meant Spencer. I'm certain of it."

I never should have told him anything about Sir Reginald Spencer and why he needed to be stopped. His involvement—his death—lies squarely with me.

"And even if he didn't, he still discovered something that *someone* killed him to hide," Kit said.

The front door opened, and the hall echoed with the chatter and giggling of four young women all rushing to speak at once.

Kit scooped the letter from the desk and slipped it into his coat pocket. "We'll talk more later."

"As you wish." Jasper rose from the desk. Given the noise in the hallway, he could have shouted their plot and not been heard. That was one of the problems with sharing his mother's home while Ramsbury House was under repair.

The benefit, however, was that the presence of his family helped ease the awkwardness of newlywed life as he and Annabel got better acquainted.

He stopped at the door. His new wife was flanked by his mother and surrounded by his sisters and hers in their colorful day dresses and large-brimmed bonnets, but her wide smile and sparkling eyes made her stand out. Her alto-pitched laugh harmonized with the girls' shrill giggles.

If Jasper had ever seen her like this near the ferns in a ballroom, he wouldn't have forgotten it. And, predictably, it faded when she saw him.

"Do it again, Annie. Do it again!"

The family name made her seem younger, but her cheeks flushed in a way that Jasper recognized from experience. The shortened name agitated her.

"Here now." He waded into the fray to reach Annabel's side, leaving Kit behind. "Lady Ramsbury, if you please, Miss Pearce."

Rebecca, Annabel's next oldest sister, bobbed a quick curtsy, but her eyes flashed. "Yes, your lordship." Her frown made the end of her sentence pop like a pebble against a window.

"Behave, Rebecca." Annabel's words were quiet, but they caught and held her sister's attention.

Unwilling to let the exchange ruin the gaiety or his quest to learn more, Jasper widened his smile as he looked down at his wife. "What must you *do again?*"

The laughter had gone from her eyes. "The girls are simply easy to entertain."

"No," Johanna said, her giggles erupting again. "Jasper, you should have heard Annie—Lady Ramsbury—in the coach. She perfectly mimics Madame Theodore, right down to the tilt of her pointy chin."

"I would swear her nose grew as we bounced along the cobbles," Rachel added, with a wide smile that resembled Annabel's.

"Don't swear, Rachel." Annabel looked past them. "Especially not in front of our visitor. It is a pleasure to see you again, Mr. Yarwood."

Kit stepped forward, and Jasper held his breath in dreadful anticipation.

"Lady Ramsbury." Kit's bow was stiff and shallow, but it was enough to be polite. "May I congratulate you on your wedding?"

"Thank you." Annabel's curtsy was quick, and her cheeks flushed cherry red. "That is very kind. I regret that you were not in London and able to attend." She turned to the younger ladies. "May I present my sisters, Miss Rachel Pearce and Miss Rebecca Pearce?"

"Miss Pearce, Rebecca." Kit's smile widened as he shifted his attention to the rest of the party. "Janie. Jo-Jo. It is good to see you again."

Jasper's sisters ran squealing to the man they'd known since they were in the nursery. They'd learned to knit so they could send him lopsided scarves and mismatched socks while he was fighting in Egypt—though Jasper had told them woolens and sand were a poor combination.

Annabel's sisters stayed rooted to the floor. Rachel's mouth fell open. A quick elbow from the new marchioness reminded her to close it.

"That's quite enough," Mother declared, clapping loudly to call her daughters back to proper behavior and a proper distance. Jane and Johanna reluctantly obeyed.

"It is a pleasure to see you again, Lady Lambourn." Kit bowed with the same military precision he'd given Annabel. "Forgive me, but I must be on my way."

Jasper saw him to the door. Behind them, Mother and Annabel directed the girls upstairs to change clothes for an afternoon of art practice at home.

"Stay aware, Jasper. She is more dangerous—"

"I may not be a soldier, but I'm perfectly capable of looking after my interests." Jasper put a hand on his friend's shoulder. Given Kit's wince, it landed harder than he had intended. "Stay focused on the connection, Kit. Not the distraction."

He closed the door and went to the upstairs drawing room, where his mother preferred to take tea.

"My apologies for the outburst earlier, Lady Lambourn." Annabel's quiet words carried into the hallway. "I should not have encouraged the girls with that unkind impersonation."

"Your behavior had nothing to do with theirs. Jane and Johanna have always been hoydens. They inherited it from the Chitester side of the family."

Jasper smiled. Cousin Amelia was the epitome of a hoyden, but it was difficult to imagine his mother as anything but prim and proper.

"And your impersonation was flawless." Humor warmed Mother's words. "That horrible woman deserves your unkindness and much more."

Then again, Mother always surprised him. He rapped on the door before entering. "I take it the French terror and Belinda Wallace were at Lady Carmichael's luncheon?" He chose a seat near enough to Annabel to see her reactions.

"They were, though their remarks were mild thanks to Lady Lambourn's presence." She poured him a cup of tea the way he liked it and delivered it. Their fingers brushed, and she snatched hers away as though he were made of thorns.

Was she nervous or frightened of him? What had Spencer told her to gain her involvement in his plot?

"Nonsense," Mother said as she lifted a biscuit from the neat stack on the tray. "The way you carried yourself reminded everyone of your station without my saying a word or lifting a finger."

Jasper raised his ridiculously delicate teacup. "To the new Marchioness of Ramsbury." He didn't have any justification for the pride that surged through his chest. Annabel had done all the work before she ever agreed to their odd bargain. Still, he was proud to have a wife who could hold her own in Society.

As long as she doesn't want to see me hang.

"It helped that I've known Ellen, Viscountess Carmichael, for years. Her family has an estate near Chilworth. Summers at country dances form friendships almost as well as battle."

So she hadn't always avoided dancing. What had changed her mind?

Trevor Harrow, Viscount Carmichael, was an honest man with a level head. In a city full of men with secrets, he seemed to have few, and his word in Lords carried more weight than men half his age. His viscountess was known both for her beauty and her good sense. It shouldn't be a surprise that Annabel had sensible friends.

Except for Spencer. Was she so loyal to the man that she would have married someone she thought was a traitor?

Mother stood. "I'm going to rest before preparing for the Haverstocks' ball this evening. It will be a crush."

She left the room, and Jasper counted silently. It was a new game that was more ironic than entertaining.

He reached three. Annabel placed her cup on the tray without the slightest rattle. "I should as well."

"Stay."

The sharpness in his voice had her dropping back to her spot on the settee with a frown. "I'm not a hunting dog, your lordship."

At least that proved she wasn't a mouse either. He moved to join her, sitting close enough that he could touch her. "Jasper." He smiled to soften the reminder. "And I apologize for barking at you as though *I* was the dog."

The corners of her mouth lifted in the beginnings of a grin. That was an encouraging sign.

"Are you regretting our bargain already?" he asked.

"What?"

He should be concerned about whether she'd been listening at keyholes and misinterpreted something, or whether she'd followed him when he left the house. Those would be the logical questions when living with a spy. Instead, he was entranced by the shape of her eyebrows when she frowned and relieved that she didn't burst into tears.

"You..." *Smile at everyone but me.* "We..." *Are never alone together.* "It..." *Isn't what I had hoped.*

Jasper raked his hand through his hair. He hadn't had this much difficulty speaking to a woman since he'd emerged from puberty. "Are you unhappy?"

She drew a deep breath and let it out with a whoosh. "No, Jasper, and I apologize for leaving you with that impression. It has been overwhelming—learning how to be a marchioness, and new staff, and being in Society with your mother. I'm so busy making sure I don't embarrass your mother, not to mention my sisters, that I'm barely able to keep up with the conversations. We're accustomed to much more informal gatherings, or to never having attention on us, you see."

"I do." The rush of words made him smile. She hadn't spoken to him this much since they'd met, unless she was scolding him. "Frankly, I enjoy the informality of being a family. I suspect

Mother is playing the countess because she believes it's what *you* expect."

He relaxed against the back of the settee. His knee touched hers, but she didn't move away.

"Oh." She looked at him and blinked. "I hadn't thought of that. Are you pretending, too?"

Right now, he was acting as though the scent of her perfume wasn't tempting him to move closer, that he wasn't doing it for fear of sending her scurrying out of the room. "I am often pretending." He winked at her. "But never at home, and not with you. I am simply…trying to adjust to having you here."

She was quiet for a long moment. "What do you expect of me, Jasper?"

It was his turn to fall silent. Since he'd learned to walk, he'd been lectured on what others would expect from him. No one had ever turned the question around.

"I enjoy talking with you, even if you're scolding me." He relished the smile she gave him—sharing the teasing moment. "I like seeing you in a room, even if we're quiet together." He wanted to see her curled into a chair in his library, her nose in a book. "I want you to be honest with me." He took her hand and waited until he had her attention.

This young woman was kind, intelligent, and caring. Her deep brown eyes and sweet scent reminded him of rambling through gardens. Her calmness seeped into his bones, and her laughter brought sunshine with it.

Jasper's mouth went dry. He wanted a proper wife as much as he didn't want to hang. "I want us to be friends, Annabel."

"I can do those things—minus the scoldings. Thank you, Jasper." She squeezed his fingers, just enough to leave an impression.

Just enough to hope.

✍

"YOU LOOK LOVELY, my lady."

Annabel forced herself to smile into the mirror. "Thank you, Barnes."

Her new lady's maid, who was only a few years older than Annabel herself, put a warm hand on her shoulder. "I believe every new lady is nervous at the first ball after her wedding." She moved away, her apron rustling against her starched skirts. "Perhaps what the marquess left you will help."

The lady in the mirror had perfectly styled hair, studded with the pearl pins Annabel's mother had given her on her wedding day. She wore a deep blue dress with a maroon bodice—Ramsbury family colors. Her skin was lovely, and her cosmetics subtly framed her deep brown eyes.

She was an impostor.

"Oh, these are beautiful." Barnes returned to the dressing table with an open jewelry box. She lifted a ruby necklace from its velvet bed. "They're a perfect match for your dress."

The necklace was an intricate web of diamonds and topaz surrounding teardrop rubies of varying sizes. The earrings were large enough to be noticed, but small enough to be tasteful.

Annabel held her breath, expecting the stones to be cold. They weren't. They were as warm as Jasper's hand on hers today in the drawing room.

The floor creaked, drawing Annabel's attention to the door on the opposite wall, the same as her bed. It went to Jasper's room. He was there now, with his valet, preparing for their first social engagement as a married couple.

It was expected for them to share a suite of rooms. It was customary for husbands to use those doors to protect their wives' sensibilities. Everyone expected newlywed brides to be awkward in front of others while they learned their private responsibilities.

If Barnes noticed the key in the lock, she didn't remark on it.

If Jasper suspected she was a spy, he didn't act like it.

The *ton* never remarked on anything, at least in public.

Annabel drew her spine straight and her neck tall. She was a baron's daughter, trained to mix at events like this. She might dread them, but she'd learned to hide her feelings and emotions years ago. The rubies and diamonds caught the light, adding sparkle to her eyes.

"There are ruby-headed pins here as well—we could replace the pearls." Barnes reached for her hair.

"Just a few." Annabel evaded her maid's fingers. "Mix them sparingly with the pearls."

"As you wish, my lady." Barnes worked quickly, smiling as she finished. "You were right. The effect is lovely."

Annabel was half her old self and half her new. Satisfied with the preparations, she stood and accepted her wrap. "Thank you, Barnes."

"Have a wonderful time, my lady."

Annabel walked to the stairs, paused for a deep breath, and began her way down. As she made the first turn, the ground floor came into view. Jasper stood with his hand on the baluster, watching her descend. A smile spread over his face as he offered his hand to guide her the last few steps.

"You look beautiful, Annabel," he said. "I knew those jewels would be perfect with that dress."

"How did you know—" She paused. Had he followed her to the dressmaker? Or had he searched the boxes to make sure they held only dresses?

Jasper leaned forward with a guilty grin. "I bribed Barnes with a sticky bun."

He was a handsome man, her husband. There was no denying his looks or his charm. His kindness and humor had surprised her, however. His family doted on him, and he on them. He'd welcomed her sisters with genuine warmth and generosity.

This afternoon, in this very hall, it had been easy to imagine them becoming a real family.

But they weren't, and likely would never be. She would expose him to Spencer, or he would catch her in her deception. Their marriage would wither under layers of hatred and distrust.

"Are you certain it's wise to go?" she asked.

"The longer we wait, the worse the whispers will be." Jasper tucked her hand into his elbow and led her to the doors and the waiting footmen. "We'll face this together. Gossip be damned."

At the bottom of the steps, the groom opened the carriage door. Annabel could not dismiss the feeling that she was going to the gallows rather than a party.

"I believe the Carmichaels will be in attendance this evening," Jasper said as he sat. "As will Amelia and Richard. Friends will help."

Is he trying to convince me or himself?

Annabel sat across from him, careful to keep the upholstery from ruining her hair. "It is a shame that Mr. Yarwood had to leave so soon after his arrival."

She suspected Yarwood's quick departure, and dour expression, had everything to do with his opinion of her and her marriage. He had watched her like an eagle did a mouse during the house party.

"Kit always has somewhere else to be." Jasper watched the shadows of London as they passed through the city. "He says it comes from his time in the military, when they were always on the move."

"He believes our marriage to be unwise," she said.

He cast her a sideways glance. "I believe your honesty will always set me on my heels. But you are partly right. Kit's experience in war makes him a fine protector but can sometimes close his mind."

Sometimes. Not always. "Only partly right?"

Though he chuckled, his smile was sad. "My mother has never been welcoming, likely because Kit is lowborn. He attended Eton and gained his commission with the help of a sponsor."

That didn't sound like the countess who had welcomed Annabel as her son's wife despite their scandalous beginning. However, beginning an argument before a party was not wise. "It is a shame they cannot overcome their reservations."

"I keep hoping for that." The carriage slowed to a stop, and he looked out the window. "We are in line. It will be a few minutes."

They'd been in the carriage long enough for Annabel's nerves to settle. Now they flared back to life. "We could have walked here."

"Your skirts would have gotten dirty." Jasper combed his fingers through his hair and squared his waistcoat, then his coat, and finally his cuffs. "And we wouldn't have had a chance to talk."

"Your cravat is crooked." Her smile widened as he worked to fix it, but only made it worse. "Come here. Let me fix it."

He joined her on her seat and stretched one arm across the back so she would have access to his clothes. "Cravats are akin to wearing nooses. I can't imagine anything less comfortable."

His cravat had been the first thing he removed in his room that evening.

"You should try a corset, my lord." Annabel unpinned his tie to straighten and refold the fabric. However, to re-pin it, she would have to slide her fingers beneath his shirt.

"Perhaps I will," he quipped. "I'll ask Madame Genest for a fitting." Jasper slid her fingers between his buttons but kept his gaze level with hers. "Would you recommend lace trim?"

"Lace can be itchy, and it would ruin the line of your shirt." His body warmed the back of her hand, even through her gloves. "If you wanted frippery, you might consider stitching. Flowers, perhaps." Madame Genest had stitched flowers into the corset she was wearing tonight.

The pin passed over her gloves without snagging the fabric, which was a miracle considering the tremble in her fingers. "Though madame would likely swallow her tongue, and half of Society would blame you for the death of their favorite modiste."

"I'm willing to risk it if you'll go to my tailor for a cravat." He flashed a bone-melting smile. "A red one to match the roses on my corset."

"What if I prefer pink?"

He tilted his head back and laughed, full and long. "I look better in red."

The carriage door opened. "Lord and Lady Ramsbury, if you please."

Jasper climbed down first and brushed the footman aside to hand Annabel down himself. She looked up at him as she took the arm he offered. "You did that on purpose to distract me from where we are."

"I like it when you forget to be proper." He lifted her knuckles to his lips and winked before he escorted her into the Haverstocks' ball.

"The Marquess and Marchioness of Ramsbury," the doorman announced.

Every head in the room turned to stare. Ladies snapped open their fans to hide their whispers, as though Annabel couldn't imagine them anyway. *Annabel Pearce, with no looks and no dowry, had at least been smart enough to trap a wealthy husband.*

A warm hand covered hers.

I don't need a rich wife. I need a suitable one.

She was more than suitable. And she was smarter than most. She glared into every glittering stare. She was smarter than all of *them.*

"Shall we go find our hosts, Lady Ramsbury?"

The crowd began to swirl again, and Annabel snorted an unladylike laugh.

"What's funny?" Jasper's breath heated her temple and stirred the dainty curls Barnes had expertly twirled around the curling rod.

"I attended a Zoological Society lecture last year." It had been a final treat to herself before she began looking for a position, while her time was still her own. "The topic was the sea life in the Caribbean, specifically the predatory ones." She kept her voice low so the couples waiting ahead of them in the receiving line could not overhear. "If sharks stop moving, stop hunting, they die."

He squeezed her hand. "But I believe he also said they are solitary creatures."

"Mostly, but some travel in schools. I wonder if they learn useful things like arranging—" She looked up into his eyes, which were much closer to hers than she expected. "You were there?"

His smile widened. "So you either didn't see me or didn't consider me to be interested in things past my own nose. I don't know whether to be amused or insulted."

"You keep telling me you have no feelings to hurt," she said, mimicking his breezy tone. "Besides, you didn't notice me either."

They stepped forward in the line.

"Men aren't allowed in the upper galleries with the single ladies. Fear of orgies, you know."

The couple in front of them turned to give them both disapproving stares. Annabel rapped Jasper's knuckles with her fan, which only made his laughter worse.

"Married ladies, however, can sit with their husbands," he said. "It's a little-known rule, likely because most men attend the lectures to avoid their wives."

Annabel couldn't stop giggling, which only drew more attention. "If you don't behave, we're going to be eaten alive."

"Can't have that just yet." He cleared his throat and straightened to his full height as they greeted the Earl and Countess of Haverstock and moved into the crowd. Annabel could see nothing but dresses and curls, so she was left to trust Jasper as he searched for friends.

"There's Carmichael." His hand was warm at her back and his fingers shaped to her waist to guide her. "This month's lecture is on the tigers in India. Would you like to attend?"

"Very much, thank you." She refused to be embarrassed by the eagerness in her voice. He'd offered her something better than any dress or glittering jewelry, and she wouldn't lie about her excitement.

"I must say, Ramsbury, I expected you to still be on your wedding trip," Lord Carmichael said when they reached the couple. Their table was far from the dance floor.

"We discussed it but decided to wait until the session had concluded for the summer."

"And you agreed to postpone Paris for London, Lady Ramsbury?"

"Do not tease her, Trevor," Lady Carmichael said. "Annabel is far more levelheaded than most of us."

Though the compliment made her sound as interesting as a table, Annabel smiled her thanks to her friend. "My husband's work in Parliament is far more important than visiting Mr. Worth, Lord Carmichael." She sipped her champagne and did her best not to wrinkle her nose before setting it aside. She had never developed a taste for the drink's sharp, sweet taste.

"Thank you, darling." Jasper looked over the rim of his glass, his blue eyes warm.

Tingles shot from Annabel's scalp to her toes, and her breasts pressed against her corset until her nipples rubbed against the fabric. It was an alarming, but not distressing, reaction.

The orchestra took their seats, and the floor cleared. Jasper set his glass on a nearby tray. "Shall we dance, my lady?"

She blinked at his outstretched hand before following his arm to his face. His smile held a challenge.

"The highest-ranking gentleman dances with the hostess to open the ball." Even as she said it, she placed her hand in his.

"There's always a duke lying about somewhere at these things, especially this time of year."

As he spoke, a gentleman in a kilt led the countess to the floor. Annabel craned to get a better look. "Is that the Duke of Argyll?"

"It is," Jasper whispered, warming her ear as he put a hand to her waist. "He addressed Parliament this morning on the subject of liquor taxes."

He urged her to the floor when it was their turn in line. Rather than staying near the edges, as men had always done when dancing with her, Jasper led her under the chandelier and took her in his arms for a waltz. "Don't be nervous. I want everyone to see how proud I am of my new wife."

It was exactly what he would do to thumb his nose at the persistent gossip regarding their marriage. It didn't mean that was what he truly thought. Still, warmth surged through her until she relaxed in his strong embrace. "Thank you, Jasper."

CHAPTER NINE

H E WAS BECOMING addicted to making his wife smile.

Jasper spun Annabel under the lights in the ballroom, enjoying the brush of her skirts against his trousers and the way her hand grasped his. Rather than a vine clinging to him and waiting for him to move, she had strength and agility that challenged him to improve his footwork.

"I wasn't aware that you followed my parliamentary career," he said. He'd been surprised both by her knowledge and the ring of pride in her voice.

"Don't most wives?"

He didn't believe his mother had ever discussed politics with his father. "I don't know. I've never had one before."

"A wife, or a career?"

"Touché, Annabel." He looked past her to the other dancers.

When he entered Lords as the Earl of Lambourn he had stayed at his grandfather's shoulder. For the first few sessions, he'd voted in lockstep with the old man, learning as he went. All it had taken was one argument, one thump of a cane, for Jasper to step out on his own. After that, he'd carried his tenants' concerns with him and learned to negotiate to meet their expectations.

Now Grandfather was gone. *He* was the marquess, and on his way to becoming an effective statesman. He had formed alliances with men who wielded their power wisely.

At the beginning, it had been more of a chore than a privilege. Now something thrummed in him every time he entered the chamber. He wanted to make a difference in the country, not just the counties where his property lay.

But he had no idea what that looked like.

"Jasper?"

A shiver of pleasure went down his spine. Annabel never used his name in public. It brought all sorts of private places to his mind, helped along by her breath on his neck and her body under his hands. She was staring up at him, concern written across her face. He'd spent weeks teasing her until she laughed with him. Now she'd teased first, and he'd not lived up to her expectations.

"I'm fine." He dropped a kiss on her forehead. "Every lady in the *ton* will race to tell you I have no feelings to hurt."

He missed a step in their dance and narrowly avoided treading on her foot. He'd kissed her. In the middle of a dance floor. And, given the amused stares from several of his friends, it hadn't gone unnoticed.

"Everyone is staring," she whispered. "We must be near Lord Argyll. Every lady in the room has been admiring his legs in his kilt."

"They're likely wondering what he's wearing underneath." He grinned down at her. "There's a rumor that Scotsmen wear naught but fresh air."

She blushed to her hairline. "That would be inconvenient in a waltz."

Cad that he was, he was considering how convenient it would be in other ways. "Do you know what I'm thinking?"

"That you should have a kilt to go with your corset?"

And how many ways he could use a pink cravat. Jasper leaned close to her ear. "Do you have pink roses against your skin, Lady Ramsbury?"

A shiver went down her spine, teasing his fingers and his imagination. Dear God, she smelled like a spring field in the Wiltshire sunshine. How many times had he lain in those fields, staring up at the sky, and let the grass tickle his ears?

Her eyes sparkled wickedly. "Peonies, my lord."

He should have known. Roses were far too delicate and fragile for her. Peonies, on the other hand, were sweet and hardy, and they worked hard to be upstanding and straight, even if their stems betrayed them.

The waltz ended, and Jasper bowed to Annabel before ushering her from the floor and back to the chair beside Lady Carmichael. The walk helped rein in his thoughts and ease the tightness in his trousers.

Cousin Amelia and her husband Richard were at the table, chatting with Lord and Lady Carmichael. Jasper bent double to kiss her cheek. She returned it and squeezed his shoulder on her way to Annabel.

"Ferrand." He shook Richard's hand. "Good to see you in London."

He liked Amelia's husband. He had a level head, a keen business sense, and a fortune he'd earned through hard work. He also voted well as Uncle Augustus's proxy.

"You as well." Richard looked past Jasper to the ladies. "But be prepared. Amelia's talked of little else but cornering Annabel for a *long talk.*"

They returned quicker than expected, both smiling. Amelia returned to Richard's side like a magnet. "I'm stealing your wife tomorrow, Cousin."

Annabel's eyes sparkled brighter than when they'd been on the dance floor. "She's invited me to tea with her charity circle."

"I always find it wise to yield to the worthier opponent." Jasper's tease was only a half measure. He knew from personal experience that his young cousin was formidable.

Richard's crooked smile and raised eyebrow gave him a moment's pause, however. Apparently *tea* meant *whiskey* in some way.

"What exactly—"

"Lord Ramsbury, Lady Ramsbury?" Garret Spaulding joined

their circle. "May I congratulate you on your wedding."

Jasper took the young man's hand and then his measure. His gaze was direct and sincere, his grasp strong. "Thank you, Spaulding."

"May I have the next dance with the bride?"

When Annabel nodded, Jasper swallowed his pride and watched her go. He'd had to marry Annabel to dance with her. All Spaulding had to was ask.

Pull yourself together, man. He's being kind, and she's doing her job—and having fun while doing it. You need to do yours.

"Into the breach, Cousin." He kissed Amelia's cheek. "Thank you for inviting her to join you."

"You say that now." Richard chuckled as they shook hands.

Amelia discreetly punched her husband in the arm and led him away, laughing. "As though you mind."

Jasper watched them go, sharing their laughter alone. He'd need to warn his wife about his cousin's odd, and lucrative, pastime before tomorrow.

For now, he focused on the row of young ladies on the far side of the ballroom, watching the party pass them by. Society required that he make sure as many as possible had a pleasant memory from the evening.

"Jasper?" The feminine squeal was accompanied by thin, long fingers on his arm and a cloud of perfume. "Have you grown bored of married life already? I was telling Grace just this afternoon over tea that I didn't expect home and hearth to hold your interest long."

Gwendolyn Harris, Viscountess Granville, had long enjoyed being the most beautiful lady in the *ton*. She used her husband's money to bolster that impression, though it wasn't for his benefit. Tonight her red silk dress was trimmed with a cloud of lace that kept her respectable until she and one of her many partners were on the dance floor or outside in the garden.

"It's lovely to see you, Gwennie." Jasper lifted her almost boneless hand to his lips. He knew better than to consider her weak, especially given the brittleness of her smile, which made her clinging to him that much more annoying. He curved his lips into a smile. "But I hope you didn't wager on my happiness."

"I wouldn't be so gauche as to revel in your unfortunate circumstances," Gwen said as she smirked at the ladies flanking her.

The hell she wouldn't. She'd screamed the house down when he called off their affair. It was difficult to sleep with a woman if you admired her husband.

"Not unfortunate at all. Lady Ramsbury and I have been enjoying life in London a great deal." He stepped back and bowed to the lady and her companions. "If you'll excuse me."

"Are you going to leave me on the edge of the dance floor awaiting a partner?"

A young man stood just behind her, staring at Jasper with raised eyebrows. Jasper nodded to him as he increased the distance between himself and Gwen. "I believe you have a more eager gentleman in the wings, Lady Granville."

Annabel was still on the floor, this time with the Duke of Chippenham, and she looked far from pleased about it. The man had a reputation for drinking heavily and a love of cigars.

Just as Jasper reached the row of ferns and the young ladies guarded by their chaperones, a commotion drew all eyes to the dancers. He turned just in time to see Annabel march from her partner, leaving him to limp from the floor alone.

She kept moving, leaving the room with Lady Carmichael hurrying behind. All Jasper could do was stand and watch. "Spaulding should have known better than to hand her over to Chippenham."

"And you should know better than to think he had a choice," Lord Carmichael said as he walked away. "I'll get you a drink. We may be here awhile."

They were on their second round when Lady Carmichael returned, her eyes flashing lightning. "She'll be down in a moment, once she's calm."

"What happened?" Jasper asked. It had to be something the duke had done. Annabel was far too proper to leave the floor in the middle of a dance.

The lady glared across the room. "He made her an offer that a lady should never hear, much less repeat."

"I see." Jasper stood. "If you'll excuse me, I'll wait for her at the stairs." He'd replaced Chippenham in Gwendolyn Harris's bed. It was a fair wager than Chippenham wanted some of his own back.

"You can't throttle a duke in public, Ramsbury."

He nodded to Carmichael. "Given his limp, I believe Annabel defended herself quite well."

He couldn't understand, much less explain, the need to ensure she was well or, if not, to whisk her away without the stares and gossip that dogged them both.

There were many things he'd expected from their marriage. The most obvious was that there were more people in the house. New maids, his sisters-in-law, his wife at the breakfast table. The creak in the floor as she moved through her adjoining suite. He'd even expected the locked door.

He hadn't reckoned with being comforted by it. If Annabel had been willing to share his bed from the first night, he would have suspected her protestations to be a fraud. Worse, he'd have wondered how far she would be willing to go to gain the information Spencer had sent her to learn.

Jasper gave up waiting and began climbing the stairs toward the ladies' retiring room. He hadn't expected the compulsion to tell her every detail of his day, as though it would prove to her that he was not visiting whichever mistress he was rumored to have. He found himself smiling as he listened to her guide the younger girls through their lessons or when she asked his mother for advice.

At the top of the stairs, he looked for the best place to hide, certain she would be there. A flash of blue caught his eye, and the pearls in her hair caught the candlelight.

The same light bounced from Reginald Spencer's almost-bald head.

"What do you mean you've found nothing?" Spencer bit out in a whisper. "My man in Cardiff says Yarwood was there just last week with so many coins it was a wonder he could walk."

"Between fittings, social calls with Lady Lambourn, and learning how to run the household, I am not in a position to lurk outside doors and listen at keyholes," Annabel replied with just as much venom.

Despite the circumstances, Jasper was proud of her for holding her own. Still, he slipped into the shadows and approached on quiet feet.

She drew a deep breath. "If you would care to know, there is a speculation scheme afoot to cheat foolish gentlemen by—"

"Unless the *gentleman* is Ramsbury, I care nothing for *ton* gossip." Spencer's eyes narrowed. "Have you fallen for your husband's appeal as well as his pocketbook?"

Jasper tightened his fingers into a fist. Annabel's wardrobe bills had been meager in comparison with Mother's and the girls'—and they already had updated closets. Her frugality spoke of some sort of loyalty.

Didn't it?

She snapped her closed fan against her skirts. "How dare you ask that when you are well aware of why and how I came to be in this position." Even from his hiding place, Jasper could see her knuckles whiten. "If I am a poor and useless wife, he will not trust me. If Jas—Lord Ramsbury has no faith in me, I will not find the answers you seek."

Spencer pulled his tailcoat straight. "So long as you remember the stakes should you fail."

"As though I could forget them."

He walked around her but stopped at her shoulder. "Find me my answers, *Lady* Ramsbury."

"I will find the truth." Annabel's spine was straight, and the tilt of her head reminded Jasper of the night she'd scolded him at his own dance.

Her bravery lasted until Spencer left the hallway, then she sagged against the wall and put her head in her hand.

Were Kit here, he would insist on storming from the shadows and demanding answers. It likely wouldn't take much to make Annabel confess. Jasper would know what Spencer wanted. From there, it would be easy to guess the man's scheme. The marriage could be quietly annulled with the flourish of a pen.

He stepped from the shadows. "There you are."

She turned on him, her deep brown eyes wide and sparkling too brightly. "I'm sorry."

It would be so easy…

"Chippenham is a sheep's arse. Always has been. I'm certain you're not the first lady to leave him stranded at a ball." The quirk of her lips gave him permission to smile as he offered his arm. "Shall we go home?"

❧

FOR THE SECOND time in a few short hours, the Ramsbury carriage loomed before Annabel like a prison cart.

Foolish girl. You dreaded a dance and gossip. And now fate has dropped you in a much worse dilemma.

How long had Jasper been in the hallway? How much had he overheard? And why, oh why, hadn't she told Reginald Spencer to go jump in the narrowest part of the Thames?

The footman held the door. At least the ride home would be short.

"Take us through the park please, Larrabee," Jasper called to their coachman as he followed her inside.

A detour through Hyde Park would add at least half an hour to their evening. Dread and fear mixed in Annabel's stomach, sending a chill through her limbs.

It didn't matter that the carriage was lit by small oil lamps and a hot brick lay wrapped near her feet. Jasper sat on the opposite bench, on the other end, so he could peer out through the curtain at the passing houses. He put his free arm around his waist and shifted in his place. Annabel thought she saw a shiver.

"There is enough heat from this brick for the both of us," she whispered, fearful of his reaction. It was one thing to leave all the heat for her. It was another, dreadful, thing if he didn't want to be close to her.

He regarded her for a long moment before moving to face her. He stretched his long legs forward and crossed his feet at the ankles with a sigh. "Thank you, Annabel."

The lamplight gilded his hair and the planes of his face. The shadows and sharpness should have been frightening, especially with his uncharacteristic silence. Perhaps it was the exhaustion from the dance, or maybe the heat from the brick, but Annabel wasn't afraid of him.

What bothered her most was not having the answers he'd want. She didn't know what Spencer had found, or his aims. Her husband would be another in the line of people she was disappointing.

"You don't have to wait for an invitation to be warm, Jasper."

His stare was a tangible thing, and his smile flashed in the dark. "My mother taught me it was a gentleman's duty to be uncomfortable."

She disagreed with Lady Lambourn on that point. "I see. What did she say about remembering staff names?" His comical glance made her chuckle. "Your driver's name is Lawrence, not Larrabee."

"Ah." He unpinned his cravat and slid his finger into the knot. "Kit hired him, so I...didn't pay much attention."

"Did he also hire Stapleton?" If she remembered correctly, Jasper had gotten the butler's name wrong several times during the house party.

He nodded. "After my grandfather's death, his younger staff left without notice. The remaining, older, ones were...not suited for the activity of a more active house."

The younger staff had likely preferred the activity, and better pay, found in London. "What happened to the older ones?"

"The ones who wished to remain in service moved to Lambourn Manor—Mother likes quiet in the country—or to my uncles' country properties. The cook joined Cousin Amelia's household. The ones who wished to retire in Wiltshire were given tenancies on the estate."

Somehow, she hadn't expected him to do anything less. "None of them came to the London house?"

"I prefer to be surrounded by familiar faces."

"And loyal ones." The moment the words came out of her mouth, Annabel wanted to dive from the carriage. She had given him the perfect opening to question her.

"Loyalty is underrated in Society. Wouldn't you agree, Annabel?"

Annabel met his stare and evened her breathing. It was important, for more than one reason, that he believed her. "I would, Jasper."

She'd left Wiltshire more than half convinced that he was a decent man. A rake, perhaps, but not a traitor. Nothing since their wedding had provided evidence to the contrary. He had kept to his end of their odd contract. Her sisters had been launched into Society and had introductions to the *ton*'s most respectable matrons. Their post was full of invitations to the best balls, and they had renewed acquaintances that had fallen away with the family's misfortune.

Though Annabel wished they would make other friends, she could not fault her husband for her sisters' choices.

The noise from the city faded as they entered Hyde Park. The curtains swung, giving glimpses of paths lit by gaslights. The trees, their limbs fuzzy with spring leaves, loomed overhead, reaching into the fog that was rolling in from the river.

Annabel chafed her gloved hands against her arms, imagining being cast out into that fog with nothing but an impractical dress and dancing slippers.

Without warning, Jasper swung to her side of the carriage, close enough to touch her. Annabel scrambled into the corner, panicked that he'd read her thoughts and decided to do that.

His fine blond brows knitted together over blue eyes that reminded her of the spring birds that flitted from branch to branch in her garden at home. "You've had a difficult night, I think."

"I…" The squeak in that one word had her clearing her throat to try again. "I had a much better time than I anticipated, until Chippenham."

The fun had leached from the evening when she saw Jasper talking with Gwendolyn Harris, but she'd never admit it. Her part of their bargain was that she'd not interfere in his dalliances. Though she did wonder if he knew Gwennie was a viper in curls.

"George and I have competed over any number of things since Eton. The last was the…attention of a certain lady."

"And you won." No woman would choose Chippenham over Jasper. It would also help explain the duke's vulgar suggestion.

He nodded. "Though it wasn't much of a prize."

But he'd still claimed it.

"And I no longer hold it." He took her hand in his and coaxed her closer. "It is important to me for you know that."

"Thank you." Her tongue was coated with the bitter taste of a confession she didn't dare make. Though her fear of retaliation faded a little more each day, she refused to lay her sins, and her father's debts, at her husband's feet. It was too much to ask of anyone.

"Would you tell me what he said?" He lowered his head to meet her gaze. "It might be embarrassing, but it will better than my wondering for weeks."

She wanted to ask why he'd spend an extra minute wondering about her, but she expected it had to do with Society's expectations and the respect she was due. He'd already reprimanded Rachel for calling her Annie—a name Annabel hated because it made her sound like a scullery maid.

She drew in a deep breath and closed her eyes. "He complimented me on the necklace but said if I was willing to ruin myself for stones that size, perhaps I would be interested in his, since they were larger."

Jasper's laugh had a bitter, hard sound to it, like hail against a window.

"I see." His hold on her tightened. "I expected better from Chippenham, which I will explain to him when—"

"If you fight the *ton* for every insult, we'll never be invited anywhere respectable again." It touched her that he would be concerned over her feelings, but there were more practical considerations, such as the effect of their behavior on their sisters. "We expected this, though not quite so blatant."

Truthfully, she suspected Chippenham was foxed and wouldn't remember the conversation tomorrow. Though his foot would likely be swollen. Her heel still throbbed. Dancing slippers were not made for self-protection.

"That's why you stomped on his foot, then? To protect your honor?" He dipped his head to meet her eyes again, and his lopsided smile made her heart stutter. "Because that is a husband's duty, Annabel."

It would be so easy to get accustomed to him, to the feelings he stirred in her, to the life that would be possible with him. However, once he learned her purpose in his household, it would all disappear. All she could hope was that her sisters were married and that he'd keep an annulment quiet for the sake of his family.

"But who protects you?" Annabel asked. "He stood there and implied that you took advantage of me in your home, while I was there as less than a guest and entirely dependent upon you. I will not have that." She kept her eyes on his. "If that is not a wife's duty, then it should be."

"Thank you." He raised her knuckles to his lips, and his breath skimmed her skin. "I shall do my best to avoid the duke at the club tomorrow. Which reminds me, your father sent a letter asking me to meet with him tomorrow, but he wants it to be us alone. Is there something I should know?"

Her father wanted money. He wouldn't ask for it outright, but he would call it a loan and promise to repay it once his luck had changed, which it was certain to do this time. "Before we married, he mentioned speculating on a mine." Annabel found it easier to talk in the shadows with Jasper's warm, strong hand in hers. He had negotiated their marriage with her alone. Perhaps he would listen to her again. "Tonight in the retiring room, I heard a young lady, Miss Thorn, I believe, discuss how her chosen beau was not her family's choice because of his lack of fortune, but that was about to change because he was about to make his fortune in coal."

"It has been the talk of White's," Jasper said. "Why does this scheme bother you?"

"Would you offer an interest to a spendthrift baron and a young man with no fortune? Especially when there are rumors of renewed unrest amongst the Welsh miners?"

Her husband shook his head, staring at her like she'd sprouted another eye. "How do you know that?"

"I read it in the newspaper." Annabel sighed. She was tired of having men think she was odd for reading. "Whoever is involved is using greed and desperation to dig yet another, likely useless, hole in Wales."

"Someone should look to the slate they shift for the holes," Jasper said. "If he was trying for a stake in a slate pile, I'd be tempted."

"Slate would be wise. If you could produce shingles inexpensively, they would be a prime building material. But buy your own stake." It was Annabel's turn to search out his gaze, to make sure he understood her. "My father will never be happy with a small profit or a modest success, and he will not repay you." They had lost just as many friends from his empty promises as they had from poverty itself.

"You are the most unusual woman I have ever met," Jasper whispered as he drew closer.

His lips touched her forehead before his breath fanned her eyelids, coaxing them to close. He kept one hand in a gentle prison while he cradled her jaw with the other. All the while his lips traced the length of her nose to reach her mouth. The warmth of his kiss shaped her lips until they were clinging to his, which gave her a chance to feel his smile.

Jasper's thumb swept from her ear to her chin and back at a seductive pace that warmed her tongue until it was heavy in her mouth and opening for him was a relief. He licked his way into her mouth, stealing her breath and replacing it with his own. The touch of his tongue was a shock, and he allowed her a moment of withdrawal before he pursued her again, teasing hers to dance.

His deep, shuddering groan heated her through until she was panting against the stays of her corset and the fabric was touching her where she wanted his hands to be.

The carriage rocked to a stop, and the cold evening rushed through the open door. "Your lordsh—Oh, I'm…I'm…so-sorry."

Jasper rested his forehead against hers, and his harsh breath fanned her skin. "It's fine… Frederick?" He whispered the footman's name and, when Annabel nodded, repeated it louder. "Give us a moment, please."

Once they were alone, he kissed her softly before moving away. His eyes were glassy, and his lips were wet, but otherwise he was untouched as he stepped from the coach and reached back for her.

His hand left hers only to curve against her back as they climbed the shallow steps to the front door. Annabel's heart pounded in time with her feet.

Stapleton opened the door and offered an envelope to Jasper. "This was left for you, your lordship."

Jasper frowned as he took it, and the expression remained, possibly darkened, as he read the letter inside. When he raised his eyes, they were a deep blue that hinted at secrets and shadows. "I have to go out." He kissed her fingers, but her gloves put the first sliver of distance between them. "Don't wait up."

Annabel felt the loss of him keenly, but she wasn't going to cling to him on the threshold. "Please be safe."

His smile was as brief as his nod as he reversed direction, leaving her standing in the doorway. She watched until the carriage rocked around the bend crowded with trees and rosebushes.

Her lips still tasted of him as she entered the hall. Stapleton shoved the lock home, and the sound echoed through the quiet house as she climbed the stairs.

Barnes was waiting just inside her door. The maid urged her to the dressing table and removed the rubies before unfastening the dress. "Tell me everything, your ladyship."

Annabel stared into the mirror as she recited the events of the evening. She left out smashing the Duke of Chippenham's foot. She also didn't mention the kiss in the coach.

As Barnes undressed her and combed her hair, Annabel considered that kiss and the note that had sent Jasper back out into the night. He hadn't seemed reluctant to leave her, so perhaps she'd done something wrong. The kiss had been wonderful for her, even better than she'd imagined, but it didn't necessarily follow that he felt the same. He had kissed many more women with more experience.

She slipped between the sheets and lay back on a mountain of pillows as Barnes pulled the sheets tight.

The other consideration was that the note was not from a lover but from a traitor to the Crown hoping to meet in the shadows to discuss a plot or provide information.

"Goodnight, my lady," Barnes called as she carried the candles from the room and shut the door.

The firelight danced on the canopy overhead. Jasper's rooms were quiet. The door between them remained locked.

"Please, God," Annabel whispered, "let him be with a mistress."

CHAPTER TEN

"IN THAT WHITE waistcoat, you might as well be a light-house," Kit said as he pulled open the coach's door. "And you came with livery?"

"Your note said it was urgent." Jasper stripped to his shirt sleeves. After rolling them to his elbows, he snatched the lap blanket Annabel had used on their trip home and wound it around his shoulders, hoping to hide the glare of his starched shirt and keep the fog from soaking through his clothes. "I didn't think to change for a visit to the dockyard."

Kit cast an eye over the hasty disguise. "That will work so long as the gaslight doesn't glint off your shoes."

Jasper wasn't scuffing his shoes for anyone. "What's the game?"

Kit looked up at the driver, Lawrence. "Meet us in Hyde Park at the end of Upper Grosvenor, please."

The mention of Spencer's street made the walk from the docks to the park more appealing. Still, it was a lonely feeling to watch the easiest way home clatter over the cobblestones and into the shadows.

Home. Until a fortnight ago, Jasper had never thought twice about visiting sources under cover of darkness. Tonight, for a half-second, he'd considered shirking his duty to queen and country—and to Kit—to stay home with his wife. To continue kissing her until she unlocked the door between them and let him into her bed.

"Why are we on the docks in the middle of the night?" Jasper shoved his hands into his coat pockets, seeking what warmth he could find in clothes meant for indoors.

"Abel Collins came ashore from Cardiff a few hours ago." Kit led the way across the rough streets and made their way to a shabby, but busy, pub. "He's stopped in here, and as far as I know he hasn't left."

"Waiting for the party crowd to clear the streets, no doubt." Balls went on into the wee hours, mostly because everyone in attendance could sleep until noon.

For years Jasper had teased his grandfather about leaving dances before midnight supper. But the longer he worked in Parliament, the more difficult it had become to keep up with things if he slept the day away. It was a fine balance between what he needed to do in the daylight and what he could learn by lurking in ballrooms.

Tonight, he'd been happy to ignore gathering useful intelligence to ride in Hyde Park alone with Annabel. She'd given him a piece of gossip in return—a mining scheme. Was it a coincidence that Kit was investigating a mine as well?

One of the things he respected the most about her was her mind. She'd proven it tonight with her ability to connect random conversations with something from the newspaper and make a clear decision.

Perhaps her review of his grandfather's old journals hadn't been as fruitless as he'd originally thought.

It was an uncomfortable thought, because he wasn't used to misjudging people and because he didn't want to misjudge her. Despite their beginnings, despite what he knew of her employer, he didn't want Annabel to be a spy.

The most redeeming evidence he could point to was her honesty, which was brutal at times. He'd rarely heard a woman be so harsh about her own father.

He and Kit entered the pub and waded through the rowdy crowd to the bar. Whiskeys in hand, they found a table in the corner that gave them a view of the room. Collins was easy to find. He was a large man with a square jaw and a well-tailored but cheap suit.

Jasper fiddled with his glass, spinning it first one way and then the other. He didn't want to drink it. If he touched his tongue to the correct place on this bottom lip, he could still taste Annabel's kiss. It had been years since he'd sampled a woman who tasted of innocence and sin at the same time.

"If you don't drink that, he's going to get suspicious," Kit said from behind a smile.

Two young women who were more undressed than not, and who didn't seem to mind, approached in a practiced amble. Recognizing an opportunity, Jasper gave them his most welcoming smile.

"Hello there, handsome." The blonde woman dropped into Kit's lap, causing the table to screech against the floor. "You gents are far too fine for the docks."

Her red-headed companion tumbled into Jasper, knocking him and his chair against the wall. "That's a right smart shirt, duck. Looks like Savile Row."

There was no way to lie his way out of it. Jasper tipped his glass and let the liquor burn a path down his throat. "You have a good eye, my girl."

"I wasn't always this." She winked, and the painted mole near her eye wrinkled. "I'm Sally. This here is Bridget."

Bridget was already ordering a second round of drinks for the table.

"I'm Edgar," Jasper said, offering one of his many names. It also belonged to his second favorite, and only exiled, uncle.

"Why's a toff like you on the docks dressed for a dance, Eddie?"

"My pal Cecil just put his feet on dry land after three years at sea. We made for the first pub we could find."

It was an easy story to fall back on. They'd done exactly that after Kit returned from the war.

Kit put a sharp elbow in his ribs. "Eddie here got married while I was gone, and his wife is driving him mad. Home life doesn't suit him."

It seemed traitorous to laugh the drunk guffaw that was expected, especially in a wrap that still smelled of Annabel's cologne if he burrowed deep enough, but Jasper did it anyway. He'd been committed to Kit far longer. "She's got the sharpest wit and the hardest boots I've ever seen." He wiggled his foot, jostling Sally on his lap.

Her heat leached through his trousers and into his knee. The scent of roses and lavender clung to her like a week-old bouquet.

"So you're down at the docks hiding from a nagging wife and a brood of whiny dukelings?"

Jasper took a sip of his second drink. He needed to keep his wits about him. "I'm not a duke."

The girl shrugged her thin shoulder. "If you say so."

"I do." He lifted the girl and turned her to face him. The position hid his offer of a gold double sovereign and Sally's wide eyes. "Tell me about the man on the opposite wall, please."

"The lantern-jawed fella?"

Jasper touched her cheek, coaxing her gaze back to him. Annabel was softer and more delicate. He wanted to be home. "Is he a regular customer?"

Sally nodded. "Every month. Two visits. Once when he docks and again when he leaves the next morning. He gets drunker the second time, but he's still a cheap bastard." She rubbed her elbow. "And he's none too gentle."

Jasper looked over her shoulder, taking the measure of Collins's companion. The man was dressed as a dock worker, but he was too clean to have put in a day's work. "Who is he with?"

"Never seen him before." This time Sally didn't turn to stare. "Irish, I think."

A round of harsh laughter went through the bar as the pretend wharfie slid from his stool and into Collins, spilling both their drinks.

"Thank you." Jasper took her hand and pressed the coin into it, along with his calling card. "Keep both of these as our secret."

Kit rapped the table before he stood, practically dumping Bridget onto the floor. Sally scrambled from Jasper so he could do the same. Collins was on the move.

Adopting the loose joints and rubbery limbs of a drunk, Jasper leaned heavily against Kit, and they parted the crowd like a plow through wet soil.

Once outside and away from the pub's windows, Jasper stood straighter but kept his shoulder to Kit's. "This seems a rather direct path."

"Regardless of how he's going, we suspect where he'll end up," Kit whispered. "This way will get you out of the cold more quickly."

Jasper sighed. "You know, when I look in the mirror every morning, I'd swear I see a full-grown man."

"Who isn't dressed for the weather."

"Because I was in a carriage for less than fifteen minutes with a brick for my feet." And a warm woman in his arms. "And I had a coat that made you frown not half an hour ago because it couldn't be disguised." They dodged a wobbly couple using the wall to make their way home. "Truman would have—"

"Your valet's name is Travis."

Dammit. Why did he have such trouble with this? "*Travis* would have built me a better disguise if you had told him to or written more than the pub name on your note."

"There are too many eyes and ears in your house."

Two too many. "She's not lurking at doors and reading my mail."

"That you know of."

"She's too busy with the Season." Jasper smiled. He'd always thought he preferred a quiet house, where life revolved around him. Turned out, the house was more alive when it was full of giggly girls and a wife who read the newspaper after he left for Parliament.

"Speaking of." Kit pulled him to one side of the street to avoid another couple so far in the shadows it was impossible to tell their intentions. "I've been called north tomorrow on business. You'll be fine on your own?"

Jasper was always impressed at how seriously Kit took the job he'd given himself, but it chafed that he questioned Jasper's instincts. He wasn't a daft git with a death wish. "I promise not to get myself hanged while you're away."

Gaslights flickered ahead. They veered right to skirt the park and stay unseen. The cobbles smoothed out, allowing them to walk faster. Jasper straightened his posture but kept the blanket over his shoulders.

"Cold?" Kit smirked.

"The fog is clinging," Jasper replied.

Admitting he was uncomfortable was better than confessing that the wool across his chin reminded him of how it scratched the back of his hand as he'd kissed his wife. She'd squeezed his fingers tightly, as though she were afraid of falling from a cliff—or running toward the edge and taking him with her.

Kit grabbed his elbow and pulled him behind a tree. "The *chill* has reached your brain."

They were across from Spencer's house, where a low light flickered in the window. Sir Reginald was working far into the night for a ceremonial chaplain who had only a handful of parishioners.

They didn't have to wait long. Collins strolled down the street as though it was the middle of the day and he was headed to market. He rapped on Spencer's door and was admitted without delay.

I have Some exploSive goSSip to Share...

Kit was right. Wales, Collins, the pub, the odd capitalization in Gareth's letter—everything pointed to an alliance with Spencer. A plot Gareth should have never been aware of, much less involved in.

"We have him," Jasper whispered as he watched the light in the window. A thrill shot through him, akin to aiming at his prey at the end of a hunt. If he couldn't guarantee a completely honest Parliament, at least one rotter would be gone.

"We have him drinking with a business acquaintance after the gentleman arrived on the last ship from Wales," Kit said. "We have a good start, but we need more answers."

Minutes ticked by before Collins left the house, patting his vest pocket before he turned back toward the docks, his shoulders back and his chin high, tipping his hat to every passing carriage.

The house went dark.

Jasper met Kit's steady stare. "Why the hell is Spencer sending money to Cardiff?"

The glint in Kit's eyes was lethal. "And where is it coming from?"

"FREDDIE SAID HIS lordship came home at dawn, smelling of cheap women and cheaper rum."

Annabel dropped against her pillows. It was one thing to hope her husband visited another woman rather than plotted to bring down the government, but it was quite another to hear the maids giggling over it. And yet another still to realize he'd chosen the docks for his dalliance.

"Perhaps you should wonder how young Frederick knows the scent of either," Barnes snapped in time with her heels on the floorboards. "And if you insist on gossiping like girls in school, move away from her ladyship's door."

The latch rattled, and Annabel slipped her fingers beneath her eyes to make sure there were no misguided tears. She'd told Jasper to carry on as he had been. There was no reason to weep when he did it.

The girls scurried away before Barnes opened the bedroom door and entered, carrying a breakfast tray. "You're awake, then."

"It's difficult to lie about with music lessons going on down-stairs." As if to prove her point, the battle between Jane and the piano began anew. Annabel forced a smile and swung her legs over the bed. "I'm perfectly capable of sitting at a table."

"I thought you might want stay upstairs after last night." Barnes blinked, and color stained her cheeks. "Your feet must ache—"

"I know you mean well, Barnes, but please don't coddle me. His lordship..." Annabel paused with one arm in her favorite dressing gown, made of jade-green silk. She could either ease her maid's mind or keep her agreement with her husband. "His lordship and I are both satisfied with our marriage."

She sat at the table, and Barnes squeezed her hand before she poured coffee. "Are you certain you wouldn't prefer tea, my lady?"

I'm certain I wish you would call me Annabel. "I am." She poured a liberal amount of cream over the coffee and then dropped a cube of sugar into the cup. The square disappeared with a plop that sent the lighter color swirling toward the rim. Just the scent of it made her relax. "It was wonderful to sleep later than normal, though. Last night was exhausting."

She'd woken with every creak in the floor, wondering if Jasper had returned. At dawn, she'd vowed to never spend another night like that again. She was not going to mope about the house and add kindling to the gossipy fire. She had a job to do.

More than one.

"I need to get started with my day. Mrs. Ferrand expects me for her charity luncheon." Her social correspondence lay next to a plate of toast, eggs, and bacon. Annabel set the invitations aside in favor of the newspaper. "His lordship has left for Parliament, then?"

"He has, my lady."

She ignored Barnes's pity-filled glance as she opened the

newspaper. It was only available to her once Stapleton determined it was no longer useful to Jasper. Still, reading about Parliament made Annabel believe she was learning something about the man she'd worried over all night. Even if it was only that he would be out of the house for the day.

"Thank you, Barnes."

"Of course, my lady." Barnes backed toward the door and left the room.

"I'm not the bloody queen," Annabel mumbled as she scanned the headlines. She wasn't even a real marchioness. It was only a title—a job—and a temporary one at that.

She ate while reading, gathering information about London and beyond, seeing familiar names and events, and reading complaints about the collection and allocation of the taxes. There was one story about how one poorer area of the city wasn't seeing the improvements they'd been promised.

Another headline hinted at new unrest in Wales, tying it to mining wages and safety. Many miners, widows of miners, and mine owners felt overlooked in recent policy decisions.

Could it be that Jasper was behind the mining scheme meant to snare London's greediest and most desperate investors? Had her father approached him, or had it been the other way around? And had she shown her hand when she explained her reasoning for it being a bad investment?

Perhaps he'd kissed her as a distraction, and his pleasure in it had been an act.

Annabel turned the page. She'd spent most of the night tossing and turning, pondering the meaning of that kiss. She had wasted a good sleep, and she wasn't about to ruin a lovely day.

It was just a kiss. It had meant little to Jasper, so it should mean nothing to her.

She'd find the truth for Spencer, and he could either accept it or choke on it. It was time to accept that truth herself. She wouldn't spend any more time here than necessary. It would be painful to leave, she already knew that, but it would be less painful if she hurried.

Society's most scandalous marchioness made a cracking debut...

Annabel folded the paper, careful to put the gossip on the inside. No matter what had happened after the ball, or in the future, she'd meant what she'd told Jasper. He and his family had been kind to her when they didn't have to be. Chippenham had insulted them, and she'd made him pay for it. She'd never be upset about how their dance had ended.

For sale, library of well-established collector. Varied titles include geography, science, and world history as well as popular novels. Several first editions available. Well curated and in impeccable condition. Buyers for the entire collection preferred, but a piecemeal sale will be considered. Inquire: Patton Booksellers, 14 Charlton Street, London.

She flipped the paper over to hide the announcement. She'd known her father would be forced to sell their library. Other than the entailed property, and the home the family now lived in, it was their largest asset. Still, seeing the advertisement was like reading the obituary of a dear friend. The only consolation was that she'd known Cleo Patton at school, and she knew the library was in safe hands.

For the second time that morning, Annabel dried her tears before they could make her eyes red. The best way to recover from grief was to face her responsibilities.

The stack of correspondence had grown every day since her wedding. It was taller today than yesterday, which was surprising, given last night. Even more stunning were the letters from women who applauded her reaction, women whose names she recognized, who had watched her leave the dance floor.

After accepting their invitations and a few others that interested her, she chose a visiting dress from the wardrobe and rang the bell for Barnes's help in dressing and pinning her braids in the style she preferred.

As she slipped into her coat, the piano lessons had changed from a fight to a duet. Johanna was at the keyboard now.

Annabel stopped in the music room, where Jane was sitting

with Rachel and Rebecca, who were yet to begin their lessons. The girls' furtive whispers stopped when they saw her, and Annabel's suspicions flared. She recognized a plot when she saw one, but she had no time to discover it this morning.

"Good morning, Lady Ramsbury." Rebecca's lips twisted around the words.

Rachel stood and enveloped her in a hug that made it seem they'd been separated for years instead of hours. "Pay her no mind, Annabel. She's always sour lately."

Annabel closed her hand over Jane's shoulder. "How were your lessons, Jane?" Perhaps if she acted as though she had enjoyed the morning's off-kilter serenade, the girl would gain some confidence.

"Awful." Jane stared across the room as her sister played an intricate melody next to their smiling instructor. "He never smiles when I play."

Oh dear. Annabel looked again. As focused as Johanna was on the keys, Jane was focused on the man turning the pages. He was young, and handsome enough to turn a lady's eye, but Countess Lambourn wouldn't take to a piano teacher as a son-in-law.

It was something else to solve. "I'll return after luncheon. Enjoy your lessons." She knew the routine for the day. Music, then dancing while the piano master was here to provide the accompaniment. After that, luncheon would include comportment and ballroom etiquette, followed by French.

It had been tiring to plan. It would be exhausting to do. But Rebecca and Rachel had much to learn, especially since a second Season wasn't guaranteed.

CHAPTER ELEVEN

I T WAS A short walk from Lambourn House to the address Amelia had provided the previous evening.

The footman opened the door, revealing a dashing older man with a brilliant smile and in butler's black. Laughter floated into the hall behind him. Annabel's spirits brightened without her forcing them to. "Good morning. Annabel P—the Marchioness of Ramsbury. Mrs. Ferrand invited me."

"Of course, your ladyship." He helped her from her coat, waited for her hat, and surrendered both to the footman with a kindness that was rare to see between senior and junior staff. "I am Martin. Mrs. Ferrand is with the duchess and her aunt, in the boardroom. To your left."

Boardroom? Annabel looked to her left, where many ball-rooms were located in houses this large. Perhaps she'd misheard, given the chatter echoing from the high ceilings. She definitely hadn't misheard *duchess.*

It seemed she hadn't misheard *boardroom,* either. The only item remaining from the large room's previous use was the ornate chandelier that resembled a tiered cake tilted on its head. It sat above the hollow center of a round table, which was circled by a double row of dark red chairs.

Amelia swept along the arc of the furnishings, a smile on her face and her hands outstretched. "I am so glad you came,

Annabel. Let me introduce you to our hostess."

The two women at the top of the circle looked enough alike to be mother and daughter. One she recognized—Thea Fowler, the Duchess of Rushford. The duke and duchess had an estate in Norfolk bordering Amelia's family home.

"Your Grace." Annabel tucked one foot behind the other, prepared to curtsy. Thea stopped her by offering her hand.

"None of that here, please. I was Thea in this room long before I was a duchess." She turned to the older lady, whose elegant indigo dress complemented both her thin frame and her almost peach-colored hair. "Aunt Tavie, may I present Annabel Warren, the Marchioness of Ramsbury," Thea said. "Annabel, this is my aunt, Octavia Foster, the leader of our outlaw band."

The twinkle in the woman's eye softened her regal bearing. "May I call you Annabel?"

"Please do." Annabel liked this woman, this place. For the first time in weeks, she felt more like herself. "It will be much easier."

"Then you must call me Tavie. Welcome to the London Ladies Charity Circle."

"Thank you."

The noise from the hall flowed into the boardroom, and Annabel marked familiar faces. She'd seen these women in ballrooms, some on the matron's row but others on the arms of escorts or husbands, or at teas where the conversation was much more subdued.

Now they were on the arms of unfamiliar men, dressed for business rather than for dancing. The women took the chairs at the table, the men the ones behind.

Annabel's dressmaker caught her eye and nodded with a wary smile. Others were openly curious.

Thea and Tavie took their seats, in front of a man who reminded Annabel of a raven in a navy and silver waistcoat, and beside a regal woman in a simple day dress the color of bluebells.

"Sit here." Amelia indicated a chair. "I have to join Tavie and

Thea, but you'll be fine." She nibbled her bottom lip. "Don't flee at the conclusion. You'll have all sorts of questions, and we'll answer them. I promise."

She turned with a swish of skirts and hurried to the head of the table, where she greeted the raven and the bluebell with warm embraces before taking her seat.

Tavie tapped a gavel on its sounding block. "The Circle will come to order." She waited for silence. "We're continuing our efforts to raise funds for the children's hospital. Last month's ball, hosted by Lady Ambrose, raised almost one hundred pounds."

Polite applause filled the room.

"We add that to the total from the other events, and we've reached a total near three hundred pounds." Tavie paused for more celebration. "Mrs. Fletcher has offered to host the next event."

"A carnival," the bluebell said. "A combination of a village fete and a traveling circus."

"Won't the costs be prohibitive?" an older lady in green asked from the far end of the table. "Prizes can be costly."

"I've secured a venue and have already begun a drive for donated raffle prizes," Mrs. Fletcher replied with a sweet smile. "Several food vendors are also interested in purchasing booth space. Any other expenses will be divided equally between the Circle and myself, which was the same agreement between the group and Lady Ambrose."

She took her seat, and Tavie's gaze swept the room. "All in favor?"

The vote was unanimous. Mrs. Fletcher and the raven exchanged winks and wide smiles.

Annabel wasn't certain what had made Amelia so nervous about this meeting. Hosting balls and circuses seemed quite in line with what Society women did all the time, usually for their own amusement. These ladies were helping ill children.

She wished she'd known about them sooner.

"Moving on to the next item, business reports," Tavie said.

"Mrs. Ferrand, would you begin, please?"

"Certainly." Amelia's gaze flicked to Annabel as she cleared her throat. "I'm pleased to announce that Eamon Brewer has secured four new distributors and new storage space for the barrels that are aging. Mr. Fletcher and I are also finalizing plans for expansion of the distillery in Norfolk."

"You each should have copies in front of you," the raven said without looking up from his notes.

Eamon Brewer. Annabel recognized the name. Father owned a bottle of Brewer's whiskey that he only brought out for special occasions. Jasper owned several.

"With this growth, we anticipate an increase in profits of ten percent in the next year," Amelia said.

"Mrs. Ferrand has also paid double the monthly amount due to the Circle for her initial advance." Tavie smiled at her niece. "Your Grace?"

Thea shook her head and smiled. "The Galloping Goat continues to make a profit. Despite concern over the train cutting travel time to London, we've been fortunate that travelers debark in Thetford near teatime. I've secured a coach and driver to take advantage. And the Thetford Women's Preparatory School will welcome its first class this autumn. Lillian Graves, the headmistress, will join us next month to give a more detailed report."

Annabel dropped back in her chair and snapped her lips closed, listening as Thea concluded and the next woman began her report.

"ALL THOSE WOMEN own businesses." Annabel sat in Tavie's drawing room in the now-empty house. Their hostess had retired upstairs for a rest.

"Yes," Thea said. "They've either continued the family business after the deaths of their husbands or fathers, or have begun their own."

Women can't own property. "How?"

"The Circle has operated for years, helping each other and selected newcomers take control of their own futures," Thea said. "We work behind straw men who accept a salary to be the faces of the businesses. We loan capital for a modest return and provide advice and expertise when needed."

"And the men never steal the businesses?" Annabel asked. No contract with a woman would be valid in court.

"The salary is very good," Jocelyn Fletcher said as she plucked a biscuit from the tea tray. "And the women involved are more powerful than you think. A man who crossed them would likely pray for prison."

"Jocelyn's husband, Drake, represents Tavie, me, and Amelia." Thea sipped her lemonade. "It's a good thing he had the sense to marry Jocelyn and bring her in as a partner."

"So your business is a business?" Annabel asked.

"Of a sort," Jocelyn said. "I'm involved with Drake's transportation enterprises on a daily basis. I also help the Circle members with discreet inquiries and introductions. My previous business provided me with useful connections." She drew a deep breath. "I was the madam of the White Rose."

"You're Jocelyn Kirk?" Annabel had followed Viscount Stratford's lurid trial in the paper, even though she'd had to sneak it out of her father's office and read under a tree in the back garden. She'd found herself envying the daring madam with the courage to fight for justice. "You're incredible."

The woman blushed. "I was incredibly reckless, but thank you."

Annabel turned to Amelia, who was curled into the corner of the sofa, her shoes on the floor and her feet tucked under her skirt. "And you are a distiller?"

Amelia sat straighter. "I am. And I'm Richard's partner in his winery. The family knows, and you're family now. This is the best way I could find to tell you before Jasper gossiped over breakfast." She blinked. "He didn't tell you, did he?"

"I'm not certain I would have believed him."

"How are you finding life with my charming cousin?" Amelia asked.

They had trusted her with their secrets, but Annabel wasn't yet comfortable trusting them with hers. "It is an adjustment."

"Annabel was working for Sir Reginald Spencer before she married Jasper," Amelia said to the others. "She accompanied his daughter Elizabeth to Jasper's house party, and… Oh dear. That sounded so much better in my head."

Annabel blushed. The story was the truth, but there was so much more to it that she couldn't explain. These women had shared damning secrets with her, and she could tell them nothing.

"We have all remade ourselves in some way," Jocelyn whispered. "You are among friends."

Annabel looked at each of them in turn. "Thank you for trusting me, but I'm not certain what I can offer."

"Our charitable efforts are legitimate, so if you do nothing but lend your support to those, you'll be welcome," Thea said.

"However, if you find a cause or an enterprise that interests you, you have friends." Amelia dropped her feet to the floor so she could reach the tea tray. "How is *numero tres*, Thea?"

The duchess curved her hand over her stomach. "Growing at an alarming rate, though he hasn't started kicking yet."

"He?"

"Oliver is hoping for another boy, as is Simon." Her smile softened. "I have no preference, but I think they're in for a surprise."

"A girl?" Jocelyn asked.

"Twins." Thea's eyes twinkled. "We'd be tied with you and Drake."

"You have *four* children?" Annabel blushed at the indelicacy of her question. "Forgive me, but you do not look old enough."

"Clean living," Jocelyn quipped with a twinkle in her eye. Amelia struggled to swallow her drink as Thea shook with laughter.

Annabel wasn't certain if she was the reason for the joke or the subject of it.

"Forgive me. Drake says my humor can be poorly timed." Jocelyn put a hand near Annabel's, but not on it. "He took the boys in from the streets over the past few years, before I came along. They're ours by agreement, but not by birth."

"How noble," Annabel said.

"You wouldn't think that if you heard him thunder about *not running down the bloody stairs*." She deepened her voice, likely imitating her husband. The other ladies broke into peals of laughter.

This time, Annabel joined them. She lifted a square of lemon drizzle cake from the tray. "Do any of you have advice about how to distract a young lady with a *tendre* for her piano teacher?"

CHAPTER TWELVE

JASPER WALKED INTO White's and handed his hat and gloves to the porter, who stored them on the shelf above his name plate. "Welcome back, Lord Ramsbury."

You would think I've been gone a month instead of just a few hours. "Thank you, Sellers."

He entered the mahogany-paneled great room, which contained so many members of Parliament that he expected a vote at any moment. He scanned the familiar faces, noting that several small groups stopped talking to stare.

Spencer was in one of them, noticeable both by his height and the way his hair reflected the sunlight. The young men surrounding him only made him look more like an aging clergyman.

He met Jasper's stare and lifted his glass in a mocking salute.

A whisper campaign was afoot, and Jasper was the target.

Viscount Granville caught his attention and raised his glass. Jasper took it as an invitation and joined the older man at the corner of the bar. His preferred drink arrived with admirable speed. He let the cool liquid clear his throat while he gathered his thoughts.

Spencer had to be a guest, likely invited by one of the young bucks surrounding him. Jasper recognized one of them, a new earl angling for support of a bill that would benefit no county but his own, and meagerly at that.

"It looks like Standridge would rather curry favor than re-write his proposal," Granville said.

"He won't realize the price until it's too late." Jasper glanced down at the bar, ignoring the prickling at the back of his neck. The betting book was open. "Making a wager, Granville?"

"Made it last night, after the ball." The other man held his drink in one hand and spun the book with the other. "I believe it is a safe one."

The line was short, but it had a long list of takers. Viscount Raines was one of them. The young man could never resist a wager. Neither could his father, the Marquess of Graydon, which made him an odd choice to hold the empire's purse strings. Rumor had it, the man had some powerful backers in his bid for the job.

"Have I offended you or put an idea in your head?" Granville asked.

Jasper forced his attention from his thoughts to the ledger he'd been staring at for too long. "What makes you think I'll do it?"

"Because I've seen you dance with your wife, and I've seen you dance with mine." Granville's smile was tinged with sadness. "The difference is impossible to ignore."

The statement stopped Jasper short. He treated Annabel differently than he'd treated Gwennie, but he also cared about them in different ways.

His conscience twinged at the lie. He hadn't cared about Gwennie at all, nor she for him. He'd slept with Granville's wife simply because he could. He'd taken something from the man for no reason but sheer boredom.

The Duke of Chippenham was across the room laughing with his cronies. The man didn't care about Gwennie either—he'd just hated to lose.

Worse, the long list of gentlemen willing to take Granville's money knew Jasper cared nothing for her either. He had a well-earned reputation for flirting and fleeing. There was likely a wager somewhere about how long it would be before he took another mistress and sent his wife to the country.

Jasper downed his drink in one long gulp, thumped his glass on the bar, and strode across the room.

The duke watched him approach, one eyebrow raised. A smile slid over his angled features. "Interesting reading in the paper this morning, wouldn't you say, Ramsbury?"

Chippenham had made an indecent proposal as revenge. Though Annabel had decisively refused it, gossip would ignore his behavior and excoriate her for hers.

Jasper threw the punch from his waist so as not to telegraph his reaction. The resulting haymaker snapped Chippenham's head back and sent him crashing to the floor like a marionette with its strings cut.

"Stay well clear of my wife," Jasper said as he turned on his heel. The management might fine him for his behavior, or perhaps suspend his privileges, but it was a price worth paying. He wished Kit had been here to see it rather than skulking about in the country on some mysterious errand.

He returned to the bar, where members were tossing ten-pound notes over Granville's shoulders. It was a modest pile. And it was the least he could do.

"Thank you for giving me an excuse to do that." Jasper took up his refilled glass and forced his trembling hand to steady. His knuckles ached in the best possible way, but they would bruise before the night was out, and it would be impossible to explain with anything but the truth.

There were a few more truths that needed to be said.

"*I'm sorry* is inadequate, Granville, but I am." He met the man's stare. "Deeply."

"And that is enough," the other man said. "Thank you."

A door opened across the way, and Annabel's father exited a private meeting room just in front of Amos Patton, one of the most trusted booksellers in London, if not in all of Britain. He was even a fair hand at valuing antiquities.

Baron Chilworth was selling the family library. It was a wise decision, given the amount of his debt, but Jasper had seen the wonder in Annabel's eyes anytime she entered a room with books in it. Even his mother's small collection here in London had made her smile.

Chilworth spotted him, bade Patton farewell, and then navigated the crowd to the bar. Granville had pocketed his winnings and was marking the wager from the books.

"What's all the commotion? What did we miss?"

"A minor entertainment," Jasper said as he shepherded his father-in-law to a table on the edge of the room. "What did you want to discuss, sir?"

"I've been offered a chance to buy into a new coal mine. Since the pit has not yet been dug, shares are a bargain. I can buy twice as many and recoup a profit twice as fast." Chilworth searched the crowd and motioned for another man to join them.

The well-dressed newcomer stuck out his hand. "Charles Christian, your lordship. Thank you for agreeing to meet with me."

Jasper didn't trust Christian's easy manner, and he didn't like the attention they were attracting. "I agreed to meet with my wife's father, Mr. Christian. You are a surprise."

Christian's smile faltered for a moment. "I see. Well, I won't take much of your time." He took the chair next to Chilworth. "My partners and I are looking for investors in a new mine in Wales."

"You mean there is a still land in Wales without a hole in it?" Jasper stretched his arm across the empty chair beside him.

Christian's lips quirked at the joke, but his eyes stayed predatory. It was like watching a snake hunt its prey. "We have taken samples, and the coal deposits are impressive. Our hope is to begin excavating within a month."

Jasper would wager next year's rents that Charles Christian and Abel Collins were two sides of the same coin.

"And how are you planning to find miners? Most in Wales

already have jobs, do they not?" Jasper watched the man's eyes, waiting for the strike. If Kit was right, he already knew what was coming.

"Our company learned a great deal from the previous unrest in Wales. We are investing in every modern measure to ensure our workers' safety, and given the interest, we will be able to pay a much better hourly wage."

"See, Ramsbury?" Chilworth leaned forward like a supplicant at the communion rail. "This investment promises to make its shareholders a fortune for years to come. With a few hundred pounds, I could earn enough to…to keep the family coffers full for several generations."

Jasper didn't think Chilworth needed to be discreet about his finances. Christian would have done his research and chosen his victims carefully. He would know the man was in debt up to his daughter's mink-brown eyeballs. Just as Jasper knew that once the money from the family's library landed in Chilworth's hands, it would go into a worthless hole in the ground.

"I know a mining inspector. I will want him to review your plans," Jasper said. "I will also want my man of business to review your investments and your payroll plan."

Christian blinked. "He would be welcome once the excavation has begun. These funds will help begin that process."

"I see." Jasper finished his drink and stood, eager to be free of the stench of greed and desperation. "Good afternoon, gentlemen."

Chilworth followed him out. "But the money, Ramsbury? This discounted offer will not last."

"If Christian wants my money, he can submit to audit and inspection. Once I am satisfied, you can buy your shares. No sooner." Jasper collected his hat and gloves before meeting his father-in-law's pleading stare. "You have asked for a great deal of money in addition to what I have already willingly spent."

"But you agreed, and it is your responsibility to—"

"No, baron. It is *your* responsibility, and you will be patient if you want my help."

Jasper left before his irritation overcame his mother's lessons on politeness. Annabel had been willing to barter herself into marriage, to someone she might consider a traitor, for the sake of her sisters' futures and her mother's comfort. None of that should have fallen to her.

He held his hat to his head to combat the wind. Chilworth's obsession in rebuilding his fortune was understandable, but his desperation was dangerous. As each scheme inevitably failed, he sought riskier ventures. His debts were multiplying like wild boars, and the destruction would be catastrophic.

It likely had been already. Someone in London owned Baron Chilworth's debts.

Remember the stakes should you fail, Spencer had told Annabel.

The man collected secrets and scandal as currency. It would not be a far stretch for him to collect vowels as well. Was that his price for her intelligence and her loyalty?

Jasper stepped into the street, eager to get home to see Annabel, to tell her she had been right about her father's plans. To find a way to broach her connection to Spencer.

Years around horses had taught him the sound of an animal's breath when it was racing, when it was laboring under a heavy load, or both. He also knew the chorus of a team and the creak of springs, the crack of a whip as they were forced forward.

Jasper looked to his left and saw nothing save the wild eyes of a team of four and the hulking black carriage behind them. A woman may have screamed.

He lost his hat to the wind and rushed forward, out of the path, only to dodge fleeing pedestrians and plodding draft carts that narrowly missed his toes. Breathless, his heart pounding, he turned to get a look at the coach. No crest on the door, no identifiable livery, no one other than a driver.

No surprise.

His hat was mangled in the street.

Jasper found the nearest alley and slouched against the wall.

That had been no runaway team. If his legs were shorter, he'd be in a broken pile in the mud next to his hat. He slid back in the shadows and forced himself to take slow, deep breaths until his heartbeat no longer deafened him. He had to get moving in case the driver doubled back for another attempt.

He stripped to his shirt and suspenders, then rolled his shirt sleeves to his elbows and gathered his coats in the crook of his arm. The last step was to tousle his hair. Then he entered the flow of people in the street, head down and shoulders stooped, hands in his pockets.

Just another working lad making his way home after a difficult day, eager to see the woman he'd missed since last night.

ANNABEL BALANCED HER needlework basket against her hip while she knocked on Lady Lambourn's door.

"Come in," the countess called.

Annabel liked her mother-in-law. She had an even temper and a good sense of humor, and she had raised children with the same. Her kindness extended from the servants to the inconvenient daughter-in-law she was teaching to be a marchioness. "Good afternoon, Lady Lambourn."

"I do wish you would call me Sylvia." The lady looked up from her knitting. "After all, *you* are Lady Lambourn now."

Annabel took a seat in the sunshine and lifted her sewing into her lap. "You will always be Lady Lambourn." She noticed the open correspondence at Sylvia's elbow. "News from Warwick?"

It had become their routine to spend the afternoon with their hands busy while Sylvia told stories of their family—including her brother Edgar, the Earl of Warwick, who shared his nephew's irreverence and inappropriate humor.

"Edgar's condition has worsened, but he refuses to come to London. He says he will die where he was exiled." Sylvia sighed.

"Just to spite a man who is already dead."

"Exiled?" Annabel's family had never had a black sheep, or even a slightly gray one, until her father's recent behavior. Jasper's family reminded her of a novel or a stage play.

"My father lost his patience with Edgar's antics and tiny acts of rebellion." Sylvia's smile was sad. "He was always good for a laugh, but he never knew when to stop. So Father packed him off to the countryside, never to return."

"Never?"

"He could have, if he'd apologized and agreed to behave, but Edgar refused." She stared out the window as though looking into the past. "It was easy to believe that Edgar cared for nothing but himself, but he had his own set of principles that he would not forsake. Not even for his family. We always thought Father lived so long simply because he didn't want Edgar to have the title." The countess came back to herself in several rapid blinks. "Enough about that for now. What have you learned today?"

That Edgar sounds very much like his nephew.

"I believe Jane should take up another instrument. Perhaps the violin or the cello?"

Sylvia's knitting needles clicked at an enviable pace. "I know she's not a talented pianist, but perhaps with time she'll at least be passable."

"She'll never be as good as Johanna, which will always discourage her." Rachel had been the same as a child, refusing to read because she couldn't do it as well as Annabel, even though several years separated them. "A string instrument would complement the piano."

"The cello is such an unladylike instrument." The countess glanced up as she turned the row.

"It's far more acceptable than having a pianist as a son-in-law."

The needles clacked together as the knitting landed in a pile. "Oh dear. I'd never have guessed."

"The symphony's cellist is a lovely young lady just a few

years older than Jane herself," Annabel said. "She's taking private pupils, all young girls."

"How resourceful of you."

The other woman's laugh rang to the rafters. It sounded so like Jasper's that Annabel's heart twinged. "Thank you, my lady."

"He's done something thoughtless, hasn't he?" Sylvia reached for her and tightened her grip when Annabel would have denied it. "I know my son, dearest girl. He doesn't mean to be cruel, but he's a creature of the company he's forced to keep."

"It's quite all right, Lady Lambourn. We were both very clear about our expectations before we married."

"Pish. You two should have gone to the Continent, Parliament be hanged." Her eyes gleamed. "Which is why I'm taking the girls to the Alfords' house party. You two need time alone."

Annabel's insides quivered at the thought of being alone with Jasper for more than time in a carriage or with less than the length of the table between them. Worse, the scheme ran the risk of her simply being on her own.

Worse still, they could be alone together, and she would begin to believe she was going to be a true part of his life. "About the party. I think Rachel and Rebecca should stay home."

"Whatever for? The young ladies in their set are quite fond of them, and the Alfords will be excellent hosts. It will be a grand event full of people their own age."

"And they will be haunted by the ghost of what their sister did at her last house party," Annabel said quietly. "Jane and Johanna will escape it because we're not related by blood, and Jasper's behavior has always been…rebellious. But my sisters will be whispered about every time they leave the room. We'll undo all your generosity. Or, worse, one of them—likely Rebecca—will misbehave, and we'll disgrace your family as well."

"No wonder he likes you." After a long sip of tea, Sylvia nodded. "So be it. I'll take Jane and Johanna, but we'll send your mother and sisters to Bath for a holiday." She held up her hand to stop Annabel's protest. "That's my price, Annabel. Rachel and

Rebecca need a treat, as does your mother—as do you. We will go to the Alfords, they will go to Bath, and you and Jasper will go somewhere altogether different. Alone."

Alone. With Jasper.

Annabel put her needlepoint aside for fear of poking her finger and bleeding all over the sofa cushions.

"You do like him, don't you?" the countess asked. "I know things didn't start on solid footing, but you both seemed to be adjusting well. Am I wrong?"

That was the rub, wasn't it? Despite his teasing—or maybe because of it—Annabel liked Jasper. His manner relaxed her, perhaps too much, and when they were alone, it was easy to believe he might like her as well.

Then there was last night's kiss. It might have been her first, but she'd heard other girls talk about their experiences and knew that most of them had been unenjoyable. Hers had been something she'd remember when she was old and gray.

She'd remember her time in this house fondly, but Lady Lambourn and her children wouldn't feel the same. Especially if Reginald Spencer was able to convince those in power that Jasper was conspiring against the Crown.

"Lady Lambourn—"

A knock on the door preceded Stapleton's arrival. "Lady Ramsbury, I apologize for the interruption, but your assistance is required in the kitchen."

"Certainly." Annabel smiled a goodbye to her mother-in-law before walking into the hallway and waiting for Stapleton to close the door behind her.

"Thank you, my lady." He kept just behind her shoulder as they descended the stairs, and his long stride urged Annabel to quicken her pace. "Facing the French at Waterloo was easier than standing between Cook and Mrs. Wright."

"Come now. Mrs. Wright wouldn't hurt a fly." And Mrs. Elliot, the family cook, was well loved by all the staff, though she did have a sharp tongue when her reputation was on the line.

However, as they reached the hall and went through the staff entrance, screeching floated up the back stairs. Now Stapleton took the lead.

"All of you, back to work." His command sent wide-eyed maids and houseboys scurrying.

The cook and the housekeeper stood on opposing sides of the table, but their duel stuttered to a stop as Annabel entered the kitchen. "What seems to be the trouble?"

The housekeeper shot a shaking finger at her opponent. "She has accused me of skimping on the food budget and pocketing the difference."

"I never said you'd pocketed the difference, but you *have* been skimping on the budget." Cook lifted a limp, spotted bunch of greens. "I wouldn't feed these to hogs."

"They weren't spotted when I put them in the larder. You shouldn't have kept them for so long."

"They were wilted when the grocer brought them," Cook shouted. "Not to mention the berries. Flats of them that went soft within two days."

Annabel remembered the berries. They'd been served with every meal during her first week in the house. Jasper had grumbled that his hair was changing color.

"You have the purse and the key to the larder, and I have to make do with what you bring me." Mrs. Elliot shook the greens to punctuate her sentence, and one ruined leaf landed on the floor with a sickening slap.

Annabel bit the inside of her cheek to keep from smiling, though it was difficult when Stapleton coughed to hide his laughter. It would be easy to fall back on her experience with Jasper as a generous husband, to suspect the housekeeper of skimming. Except for the tears shining in her eyes and what Annabel remembered from the old marquess's journals in the Kennet Hall library.

"Mrs. Elliot, please make an inventory of the larder. Mrs. Wright, please gather your records and bring them to his lordship's office." She nodded to the butler. "Come with me, Stapleton."

They returned upstairs, and Annabel led the way to Jasper's study. "Where does Lord Ramsbury keep his ledgers?"

"Your ladyship, I'm not certain—"

She wasn't either. "I am certain that his lordship would prefer his marchioness handle matters of the household so he can focus on matters in Parliament."

After a moment's hesitation, he pulled a key from his pocket and opened the bottom desk drawer. It housed nothing but a heavy red leather ledger identical to the ones in Wiltshire. Annabel lifted it to the desk and flipped to the most recent pages, careful not to topple the pile of unopened correspondence on the corner of the desk.

Mrs. Wright joined them with her records, which she surrendered to Annabel.

Annabel ran her finger down the entries, made in Jasper's hand, until she found the latest amounts for the kitchen.

"His lordship has marked down thirty pounds for food this month. Up from twenty, which is to be expected with our marriage and the expectations of the Season." It was also plenty to provide fresh, prime food.

"Thirty pounds?" The housekeeper dropped into the nearest chair. "My lady, I was given twenty. And on the months he had allotted twenty, I was lucky to get fifteen. I give you my word."

"And I trust that word, Mrs. Wright. Leave it to me to decipher." Annabel gave her what she hoped was a reassuring smile. "His lordship and I will resolve this matter when he returns home this evening."

If he returned home while she was awake.

"Thank you, your ladyship." Mrs. Wright left in a whisper of skirts, her back straight and her shoulders square.

Once alone, Annabel swept back to the beginning of the ledger, looking for the point when Jasper had inherited. His stark, straight figures were easy to decipher. The strokes reminded her of her husband himself, and it doubled her focus. Jasper's open manner often masked something he wanted to hide.

The only new expense was a regular payment to Kit Yarwood—not much more than Stapleton's salary. Annabel had thought he and Jasper were merely friends, but who paid their friends a salary?

Stapleton cleared his throat. "I don't believe Mrs. Wright to be a thief."

"Neither do I, but I want the evidence to submit to his lordship." Annabel reviewed the housekeeper's ledger and receipts, noting the dates and amounts. Always five to ten pounds less than the amounts in the ledger, but always exact. "Do you have receipts for other expenses?

"Yes, your ladyship." Stapleton left, only to return with a ledger of his own.

They worked together then, comparing the amounts spent on the household to the amounts in Jasper's ledgers. The shortages were obvious. "There is no reason for him to steal from himself," she whispered.

He also couldn't finance a rebellion on twenty pounds a month.

"Does his lordship give you the funds directly, Stapleton?"

"I do not. My man of business manages payments." Jasper dropped his coat on the chair nearest the door. His waistcoat had a wide patch of gold splayed across it like a flag. "But I would like to know why my wife is reviewing my finances."

CHAPTER THIRTEEN

HIS WIFE WAS at his desk reading his ledgers while his butler looked over her shoulder. The chair loomed behind her like a throne, and she had an ink smudge across the bridge of her nose.

Her day dress was stitched with daisies, and the green ribbon beneath her breasts matched the flowers' stems. It was a lovely distraction from the task at hand.

"You need a new man of business."

Of all the things she could have said, he hadn't expected that. "What?"

"Your man of business is skimming from the budget before he delivers the funds to your staff."

Jasper strode behind the desk to stand over her shoulder, opposite Stapleton. This couldn't be possible. Gerald Jones had been the family's man of business for years. He was older than King Arthur. "Show me."

As Annabel and Stapleton laid out their discoveries, Jasper drew up a chair and pushed his hand through his hair. "How long?"

"I've only reached the point when you inherited," Annabel said.

Manners dictated that Jasper tell her about the ink on her nose, but he liked it there. Just as he liked imagining the scent of her perfume soaking into the fabric of his chair. "Did you find anything else?"

Kit would have his head if he didn't ask that question. Though he wasn't certain why Kit thought he'd be daft enough to keep a running tally of the money they'd spent in Cardiff mixed in with the household accounts.

Annabel smiled up at the butler. "Thank you, Stapleton. His lordship will let you know how to move forward."

Once they were alone, she faced Jasper, elbows on the chair and fingers steepled in front of her. "I haven't noticed anything here, but…" Her cheeks colored as she chewed on her bottom lip. "While we were in Ramsbury, I accidentally saw one of your grandfather's old ledgers."

After scaling twice his height to haul it from the topmost shelf.

The color in her cheeks deepened. "Forgive me, Jasper, but your grandfather didn't invest a great deal in the tenants' holdings or in improvements."

Irritation burbled under his skin. He hadn't always agreed with his grandfather, but the old man had managed his estates well. "He believed tenants took more pride in their homes if they worked for things rather than being given them."

"That works well for children, but your tenants aren't children. They are trying to manage their farms and raise their families. If Mr. Jones was skimming from your grandfather, they were doing it on a pittance while still trying to pay rent."

"We should audit those accounts as well." Jasper raked his hand back through his hair and winced at the bruises he had anticipated. "And I'll terminate Jones's firm right away."

If Jones couldn't be trusted, and Kit wasn't here, there were damned few choices for a replacement. Parliament, Society, and spying left him precious little time to find one, and next to no time to do it himself.

He stared at his wife. Ink on her nose, practically buried in bookkeeping and figures, she'd never looked more at home. It was an unorthodox situation, but…

"Until I find a new firm, would you mind stepping forward to help?"

"I'm here, and you're busy with other things. It makes sense." Annabel corked the ink pot. "Though most husbands would balk at having their wives in their accounts. Not to mention in their chair." She pushed backward, intending to stand, and the correspondence he'd ignored since before their wedding tumbled to the floor. "Jasper, many of these are unopened."

He knelt to scrape the notes from the carpet. "There's been no time to hire a secretary." Kit had brought several for interviews, but Jasper hadn't liked any of them.

"Isn't that Mr. Yarwood's position?"

"No. He would loathe spending all day at a desk. He'd rather be moving about gathering information." Jasper gulped. "About London. He didn't spend much time in town before the war, so he's making up for lost time."

It was difficult to keep his head around her, to remember what he shouldn't say. Perhaps she wouldn't notice if he kept talking.

"Kit's more a retainer than anything." That seemed a better explanation than *bodyguard*, which Jasper felt made him sound either self-important or afraid of his own shadow. It also risked piquing Annabel's interest about why he needed a protector or, worse, frightening her. "He's fun to have around."

"So definitely not a secretary."

That impish grin of hers would be his undoing. Not to mention how her eyes sparkled when she teased him. It was difficult to imagine anyone who looked at him like that wanted him to hang.

I will find the truth, she'd told Spencer. It occurred to him that this was a perfect opportunity to help her do just that. "Could you help with that as well? Just until Kit can find someone more suitable."

When Kit learned what Jasper had done, he would drag the

first young man off the street and teach him to read, if necessary.

Annabel's smile wobbled, and Jasper worried he'd over-stepped.

"Suitable?" she whispered.

"Most wives would rather not spend their time reading their husband's correspondence." Jasper's will failed him. He pulled his handkerchief from his pocket before gently grasping her chin. "But you aren't like other wives." He wiped the ink from her nose and chuckled as her cheeks reddened.

"I'll be happy to help keep you honest," she whispered.

His mouth watered to the point of embarrassment, and his tongue was so heavy it was difficult to speak. "Honest is both the first and last thing I want to be around you." He lowered his head toward hers.

She met him halfway, and her warm, sweet mouth was both a relief and a torment. Jasper tasted her, searching for her secrets in the flavor of her tongue, and then teased it into his mouth so she could do the same. She was a quick and eager pupil, his wife.

Annabel's touch on his arm, warm through his cotton shirt, sent a jolt through him that stopped his breath. She seemed content to leave it there, her fingers toying with the fabric as she starved him of air. It made him think of her hands on his skin, his hands on hers.

Jasper gathered her to him and left her mouth in favor of her jaw. Her dress did little to hide the warmth of her and the way her breath shivered with every swipe of his tongue. When he reached her ear, he felt her gasp as well as heard it. It rippled through him like a pebble skipping over a pond.

She swept her hand up his arm, and her fingers brushed his neck before burrowing into his hair. It was the most innocent caress he'd had in years, likely since his first kiss, and it inspired every indecent impulse.

He cupped her breast, relishing the weight of it. Annabel rewarded him by arching into his hand, driving her hardened nipple into his palm.

Jasper teased it with his thumb until she was squirming closer and whimpering with each breath. She made him hungry in a way few others had. Not young wives bored of their older husbands or practiced flirts in Paris brothels.

One tug had Annabel in his lap, her knees on either side of his hips. Jasper resumed kissing her, stroking his tongue into her mouth as he rocked her against his length, asking for what he wanted in the basest way possible.

Her hips shivered against his fingers, and her breath caught as she placed her palm against his chest. Jasper stilled, though he needed her like he needed air. It was always important to him for his partner to be willing, that she understood the choice she was making. It was doubly true with his wife.

The movement under his hands might have been his imagination, but the second one was a definite flex. Slow, as though she was learning the feel of him—or trying to kill him. The third was a strong, certain rock.

Thank God, thank God, thank God.

Jasper pulled her mouth to his and tangled their tongues together until he could close his lips around hers and suck. Annabel's nails scraped his chest through his shirt. Jasper did it again, knowing she'd learn the trick. Her groan rattled through him, stoking his hunger until he ached.

Her lips closed over his tongue and drew it into her mouth.

She deserved better than rutting half-dressed on the floor in his office. He deserved to see her naked with her hair in knots and her skin flushed pink all over. They weren't going to get that—at least not this time. He curled his fingers around her skirt.

Pain lanced through his hand from his fingertips to his forearm. "Damn."

Annabel leapt from his lap, her eyes wide. "What did I do?"

Jasper grasped her fingers for fear she'd run from the room. "Everything right, I swear. It's not you."

"Your hand." Her gasp had nothing to do with sex. It was just as well; the pain had distracted them both.

She freed herself and tugged the bellpull. Stapleton's double-time march up the stairs was as comforting as it was comical. He entered without knocking and rushed forward when he saw Jasper prone on the floor. The color drained from his face. "My lord?"

Jasper wasn't certain if his concern was born from years of military training or if Kit had told him to keep an eye on Annabel. One was understandable; the other was becoming an irritation. "I'm fine, Stapleton. It's nothing."

"It is not nothing," Annabel said. "Stapleton, his lordship came home with an injury to his hand. Please send for the doctor and have a maid bring up ice from the icebox."

"Travis has medical training, my lady. Might I suggest…"

"Of course." Annabel nodded. "That is a much better solution, thank you."

Jasper pushed himself up from the floor, wincing, and dropped into his chair.

"Are you certain you should move?"

"I've injured my hand, dearest, not my back." He snorted a laugh. His libido and pride were wounded as well, but Travis wouldn't have a remedy for them.

Travis came into the room and took the ice from the maid when she arrived. His examination was quick and relatively painless. "Just a bruise, I believe, but a bad one." His grin was that of a soldier used to skirmishes and victories. "The other man, however, may be the worse for wear." He stood. "Keep ice on it, my lady. It will help ease the swelling."

He left them alone, closing the door behind him. Annabel rested against the desk, standing half stooped to keep the towel-wrapped ice on his knuckles. Her eyes were full of questions.

Jasper pulled her to his knee and kept her hand in his good one, twining their fingers. "Chippenham was at White's." He thought it best to leave out Granville and his wager.

"Is that why you came home in your shirt sleeves?"

"No." He glanced at his discarded coat and waistcoat. Would

she believe he had removed them at the door? "There wasn't a boxing match. I ambushed him in the bar."

Her lips quirked, sparking a light in her eyes. "I wish I could have seen that."

His laughter shook them both. "I'll do a command performance at the next ball, just for you."

"With your other hand, please." Her giggle revived his flagging cock.

"Yes, dear." He pressed a kiss to her temple and let his nose rest against her hair. She smelled of spring, though he thought he could smell something of himself on her now. "He won't be asking you to dance—or anything else—again."

She brushed her lips across his cheek. "Thank you, Jasper."

The house was alive with noise, piano practice and servants on the stairs. Carriages rattled past outside, and the downstairs clock chimed the half-hour. The dressing gong would be next. Their lives were not their own.

A month-long honeymoon on the Continent had always seemed frivolous and unnecessary. New wives returned with wardrobes, and new husbands replenished their stables. When they attended balls, they seemed as distant as they'd been before the wedding.

Given the nature of their engagement and wedding, Jasper had considered it a waste of time and money. Annabel had agreed.

Her kisses hinted that perhaps she'd changed her mind. They had certainly changed his.

But they'd lost the opportunity for a long trip to anywhere private. However, a break in Parliament's schedule and a traveling coach could be a decent substitute.

"We should visit the country while Parliament is in recess," he said, hoping he sounded decisive. She was no longer in the throes of passion and might have changed her mind. "Just the two of us."

"I would like that," she said in a whisper. After a moment, she straightened her spine. "We could do our audit while we're there." Her businesslike tone made him smile. "And visit with the tenants and—"

He put his finger on her lips. "We can do *anything*."

The dressing gong rang through the house. Annabel, her cheeks pink, stood. "I'll make preparations for the end of the month."

Two weeks? He was supposed to be under the same roof with her, sharing a wall but not touching her, for a fortnight?

Fuck privacy.

Her skirts swayed as she walked away from him. She didn't need to know that he'd knock on her door tonight, did she? Honesty didn't equal no surprises at all, did it?

She paused at the door. "Where's your hat?"

"The wind caught it while I was crossing the street, and a carriage trod it into the mud."

After all, there was a fine line between honest and *honest*.

CHAPTER FOURTEEN

ANNABEL COULDN'T STOP watching her husband. Less than two hours ago, they'd been locked together on the floor of his office, their lips swollen, and their eyes glazed with passion. Now he was across the room, teasing his sisters and talking to his mother about his Uncle Edgar's health.

We can do anything.

The growl in his voice, the spark in his eyes, had been full of a promise she didn't quite understand, but she wanted to know. Dinner had only heightened her curiosity. Every time he savored his food or his wine, she felt his lips on her skin. His laughter was like his hands on her body, warming her until it was difficult to concentrate.

Which was why she had removed the same five stitches from her embroidery for the last half-hour. When she closed her eyes, she was back in his arms. When she opened them, he was staring at her like she was a rabbit, and he was a hound.

She was likely the only rabbit in Britain who hoped she was devoured. But was that wise, given her purpose in his house?

Was he a spy?

She'd found nothing to indicate it, and Jasper didn't appear to be hiding anything from her. No door was locked, no question unanswered. He'd even given her free access to his finances and his correspondence.

No Society husband did that, did he?

Of course, he wouldn't write his schemes in his ledgers, and he could have his private mail sent to his office at Parliament or to White's. And if he wasn't a spy, then he'd spent all last evening with another woman after promising, in church, to be faithful to *her*.

Most Society husbands did that.

But then again, she'd made promises, in church, while working as a spy. She'd turned their marriage contract into a negotiation to benefit her family, and she kept the door locked between their bedrooms. She'd even *told* him he could have a mistress.

With a disgusted snort, Annabel tossed the fabric aside.

"Are you all right, dearest?"

She met her husband's gaze. Perhaps she should just ask him. *Are you betraying your country for the love of a French widow I want you to reject for me?*

Jasper would answer, but it would also open the door for him to ask her the same question, and Annabel wouldn't be dishonest. Not the best trait for a spy, she knew, but she was a horrible liar. Her eyes always betrayed her.

He winked at her.

She didn't want to tell him the truth tonight.

"I find myself out of sorts this evening." She returned her embroidery to the basket at her feet and stood. "If you'll excuse me."

Barnes was already waiting for her upstairs, and Annabel wondered if they taught lady's maids some sort of translocation spell.

Annabel watched herself in the mirror as propriety was removed layer by layer, leaving her naked for only a moment before her nightdress, made of cotton as fine as silk, floated over her head.

She didn't want to be hidden her whole life, naked for only a moment and only when it was someone's job or when she was alone. Never touched as Jasper had done this afternoon.

But what if—

Enough.

Barnes reached for her hairpins, and irritation shivered down Annabel's spine. "Thank you, Barnes. I'll finish from here." She met the maid's wide-eyed stare in the mirror. "It's nothing. I'd just like to be alone."

The older woman squeezed her shoulder, her smile full of pity. "I understand, my lady."

The door closed and Annabel risked another look at her reflection, finding a woman who wanted to be anything but alone. Her eyes always gave her away.

She unpinned her hair and unwound her braids.

"You have never listened to anyone other than yourself," she said to the woman in the mirror. "Your instincts have never betrayed you." She'd known Chippenham was a cad the moment he touched her on the dance floor. In a sea of gossip full of silk-clad sharks, she'd found true and loyal friends. "What do *you* think of him?"

Jasper's irreverence was contagious. She had laughed more since the house party than she had in months. It was freeing, like racing down the hill with her heart thudding in time to her horse's hooves. She lacked for nothing, but she was also valued. He didn't love her, but he acted as though he liked her. He certainly *wanted* her.

Her nipples drew tight against her nightdress. She definitely wanted him.

Was he dangerous? Yes, he was. He was intelligent, observant, and disarming. But, more than that, the pleasure he offered required her to reach for it, and she believed freedom waited on the other side of it. Finding that, only to lose it, would be devastating. Never reaching for it, however, would be tragic.

She smacked the brush to her dressing table, making the hairpins jump. "Your husband is not a traitor."

The words soaked through her, and they felt right. True.

They brought along an emotion that also felt true, one she didn't dare acknowledge.

A breath of air fluttered the hem of her nightdress against her ankles. Annabel turned to find Jasper in the open doorway between their rooms, staring at his hand on the knob.

"How long has this been unlocked?"

"Since last night." She rose from the chair on shaky knees and walked toward him at what she hoped was a normal pace.

"Annabel, I—"

She didn't want to talk about last night. She didn't want to know where he'd been or what he'd done. "Why did you try it?"

His blue dressing grown was tied at the waist, resulting in a vee that displayed dark gold hair swirling over the center of his chest. The hem stopped just above his feet. Seeing his bare toes made him seem as vulnerable as she felt. It made this easier.

"Wishful thinking, I suppose." He took her hand and tugged her over the threshold.

Where her room was painted a color that reminded her of fresh cream, his was a blue as dark as the night sky. What wasn't painted was covered by mahogany panels.

There were probably other differences. She knew there was other furniture because he guided her around it as he walked backward toward the bed. Where her drapes were trimmed with fringe, his had ribbon. Her sheets were edged with lace. His were plain and square.

"I like your room better than mine."

"Change yours if you wish."

He lowered his mouth to hers and kissed her until she was dizzy from it. The only thing anchoring her to the ground was his hand covering her breast as it had been in the library, as she'd wanted all through dinner.

"Do you have an idea of what to expect?" he asked before sweeping his tongue along her jaw to her ear.

All Annabel could do was nod. Her mother's explanation had been hurried and likely incomplete because, as Jasper circled his thumb around her nipple, she believed there was nothing she'd have to *endure*.

His other hand loosened her gown, and the laces slithered against her skin as they gave way. "If I make you uncomfortable, we'll slow down." Heat pooled in places that were only warm with him. "If I hurt you, we'll stop."

There was a breath of warm air against her shoulder as he covered her breast with his hand. She thought his fingers might have been shaking, but that was impossible, especially when he rolled her nipple between those same fingers. Zings of pleasure ricocheted through her core to her knees, then her toes.

"Otherwise, anything we do to one another, all pleasure we give each other, is allowed."

Her gown slithered from her shoulders, past her hips, to her feet. His gaze flicked over her like firelight. Her breath sped as though she'd run for years to get here.

"Christ. You are stunning."

Any woman would be beautiful in shadow.

"Don't, Annabel." He swept his hand through her hair. "Topaz." Down her back. "Silk." Around her ribs. "Strength." He brushed his lips over her forehead. "Wisdom." Over her eyes. "Kindness." Across her lips. "Sweetness."

Tears flooded her eyes as she wound her fingers through his thick hair. "Jasper..."

"You are my wife," he whispered against her mouth. "And you are the loveliest woman in London. And if you don't put your hands on me, I'm going to shake to pieces." He tugged her fingers from his hair and slid them under his robe. "Please, Annabel."

The hair on his chest reminded her of sheep after shearing— short, soft curls clung to her fingers, coaxing her to explore his broad chest and hard muscles. His bones were thick, but she still felt his heart thudding against her palm.

The tie at his waist gave easily under her fingers, and then he was naked in front of her.

During her mother's explanation of *wifely duties*, Annabel had been tempted to confess that she'd found Father's illustrated anatomy encyclopedia on the top shelf of the library years earlier. She wasn't sure whether Mother would be scandalized or relieved.

Annabel felt…cheated. The flagging manhood in the drawings had little relation to the erect specimen in front of her that was almost as wide as her wrist.

Butterflies went through her stomach as she swept her tongue over her much-kissed lips. Men and women did this all the time. No one died from it. "It will be fine."

Jasper curved his fingers around her waist and pulled her close. His stiff shaft was hot against her stomach. His eyes glittered like a satyr's. "If it's not better than *fine*, I'll chew off my tongue."

Her laughter ended on a gasp as he avoided kissing her, but then he closed his lips over her nipple and sucked it deep into his mouth. Annabel's knees buckled as a deep moan rushed over her tongue.

Embarrassment heated her skin. "I'm sorry."

Jasper lifted his face from her body but didn't release her. "For?"

"That noise was—"

"Darling, I'm praying that's the most ladylike noise you make for the rest of the night." To prove his point, he returned his attention to her breasts, twirling his tongue around one nipple while his fingers teased the other.

Her moans became a litany that sharpened whenever he switched his attention. Soon she was twisting in his arms, demanding his mouth on her skin, needing the tug she felt go through her with every pull of his lips.

It wasn't enough now. She tangled her hand in his hair and grasped his solid shoulder, urging him closer. When that didn't work, she wrapped her ankle around his calf and pulled. "Please, Jasper."

The sheets were cool against her heated skin, and his hand was solid against her back. She pushed against his chest, lifting his lips from hers. "Your hand."

He freed it with ease and ran it along her hip until it rested between her legs. "This is the only reason I want to you worry over my hand."

Sparks pricked her skin as he stroked her there, tracing her folds as he nudged her knees wider. Cool air brushed over her wet skin, but Annabel didn't have time to worry over it. He brushed the spot that had been aching since he'd kissed her last night, and the sparks doubled.

Jasper tormented that spot, caressing it, flicking it, rotating his thumb over it, catching it between his fingers as he'd done with her nipples, which were now aching with jealousy. Annabel slid her hands over his sweaty shoulders as her heels scraped the sheets. Every breath chafed her dry throat.

Warm air was her only warning before his mouth closed over her center and his tongue delved inside to drink her in. Fireworks exploded against the back of her eyes and her body tried to expand and contract at the same time, ripping a cry from her as she clung to Jasper to keep from flying apart. It was terrifying.

And the minute it shivered to a stop, she wanted it again.

"You are going to kill me," he breathed against her skin as he kissed the inside of her thigh, his tongue drawing sinful circles. "But it beats the hell out of hanging."

He moved up her body then, forcing her to release her grip on his hair, which she didn't remember doing. His kisses had always tasted of him, but now his tongue had a different flavor. Sweeter, darker.

She closed her hand over his shaft. Hot and heavy against her palm, it was difficult to wrap her fingers around it. Her mouth would be a challenge as well, but it was soft enough that perhaps... If she tasted him, would the flavor of their kisses change again?

Jasper lifted his mouth from hers. "I can hear you thinking."

She stroked him and watched his eyes darken. Heat bloomed in her chest, threatening to choke her words. But it was just them, and he'd never laughed at her. "May I do that to you? Is it the same?"

"Dear God, you *are* going to kill me." He lifted her hand from his body and kissed her knuckles. "Yes, I'm fairly certain it feels the same, but no, you can't right now. I don't want to be distracted, and I won't be responsible for my actions."

Annabel contented herself with putting an open-mouth kiss to the side of his throat, adding a swipe of her tongue for good measure. His salty flavor made her hungry, and the tease of his chest hair made her nipples ache.

He dragged his hand down her body and slid one finger inside her, then two, then three. Annabel closed her eyes and rocked against them as she'd done his tongue.

Then his fingers were gone, and Jasper was between her legs, his strong ribs against her thighs. He slid inside her, stretching her, filling her with heat.

"Look at me, Annabel." He traced her cheek with a sex-scented finger until she obeyed. His jaw was tight, and his smile looked more like he was gritting his teeth. "Breathe."

She drew a deep breath, exhaled, and felt him go deeper. Another breath, deeper still. Then he withdrew, leaving her emptier than she could remember. He returned with a groan that made her smile.

The next time he left her, his fingers returned. Just as tempting, but not as satisfying. Still, the fireworks built again, only to sputter when he filled her again, pushing deep and withdrawing until her muscles shivered, only for his fingers to return.

Growling, Annabel pushed to her elbows to glare at her husband. Jasper sat on his heels, covered in sweat, his blond hair dark around his face. His grin hitched at one corner, matching the question in his eyes as he withdrew his hand and positioned his manhood at her entrance. Feeling him inside her was delicious; watching him get there was decadent. It put them nose to nose.

"This?" Jasper asked as he drove his hips forward. "Or that?"

Desire flooded through Annabel, making words impossible, but she knew the rhythm of the game. When he went to withdraw, she grasped his muscled behind and held him to her. "This."

He stayed, but the strokes changed. Shallow circles and short thrusts alternated with deeper ones that stole her breath and banged the headboard against the wall. After one round of torment, Annabel knew what she needed, and she put her heels on Jasper's thighs to keep him there. "This. God, Jasper, please. Give me this."

"Yes." The word ground out of him as he lifted her hips from the mattress and slammed into her again and again. Annabel's world narrowed to hearing her body accept him, feeling him hold her in a grip like iron, as he claimed her. Her heart felt ready to explode as she raced toward the sun.

Jasper dropped his forehead to hers. His breath sawed out of him like he'd climbed a mountain. "Fly, sweetheart. Fly."

And she did, keening his name as she tumbled, only to rise again and again, until he was with her, racing to get closer as his muscles twisted under her hands and his shouts filled the air.

She floated back to earth, but kept her eyes closed as her breathing returned to normal and her senses returned. When she opened them, Jasper was propped on one elbow, watching her with a satisfied gleam in his eyes. He pulled the bedclothes over them. "Better than fine?"

Annabel chucked the nearest pillow at him and squirmed across the bed when he threatened to do the same. He caught her, only to pin her to the mattress for a lingering kiss.

"The sheets are warm over here," she whispered.

"Travis has warmed the whole bed every night since we married. Hope springs eternal, I suppose."

"Barnes does the same." The words were a reminder. She had a bed, a room, on the other side of the wall. Her mother had always been alone in bed in the mornings.

Annabel tossed the covers aside.

Jasper kept hold of her hand. "Where are you going?"

"I thought I should gather my nightdress and—"

"You should stay in this room, which you prefer to the other, and stay naked, which I prefer to your nightdress." He pulled her back to bed.

"Sleep naked?" Annabel slid back under the bedclothes. "Here?"

His grin was wicked. "I only wore the dressing gown so I wouldn't frighten you." He kissed her slowly, but the heat between them built quickly. Boneless as she was, Annabel didn't realize her ankle was on his shoulder until he was nudging inside her. "Besides, it saves time."

He was as hard as he'd been when she'd undressed him. "Hope is not the only thing that springs eternal." Her giggle ended on a lustful moan as he went deeper and she melted around him.

CHAPTER FIFTEEN

S HE WOKE EXPECTING Jasper's head on the pillow. A pink camellia stared at her instead. When she lifted it, a note slid to the mattress. Jasper's bold handwriting left grooves in the paper.

Too early for peonies. Please don't scorn the substitute. Duty demands I leave you. There is a hot bath waiting in the other room, assuming you haven't slept the day away. –J

PS You have delightfully warm feet.

Annabel read the note again as she lifted the flower to her nose. The petals were strong, but surprisingly soft, and they smelled of peaches and violets.

It smelled like Jasper. So did the pillow next to her, and the sheets tangled around her bare legs.

So did she.

A smile split her face as she wriggled against the mattress. He'd been right about sleeping naked. The sheets caressed her skin, reminding her of his hands on her body. The pillow curved against her like he had in the night. Annabel had always thought it would be awkward to sleep with another person, but it had felt natural to drift off in Jasper's arms and feel his breath on her shoulder.

The floor squeaked a moment before a knock sounded at the

door. "Er, my lady?" Travis cleared his throat. "Should, er, the maid—"

Everyone in the house had responsibilities. So did she. "No, Travis." The words squeaked out in a most un-marchioness-like way. She drew a deep breath. "I'll step to my room. Just a moment, please."

Annabel threw back the covers and scrambled across Jasper's side of the bed, the sheets cold against her knees and palms. She swept up her nightdress before hurrying to the door, the rug muffling her flight.

You don't need to run. You didn't break in this time.

"Thank you, Travis." She closed the door behind her.

Her room was too bright, but it was warm. A copper tub sat in front of a fire stoked high enough to keep the water warm. There was a lot of water, clouded with milk. Rose petals floated on the surface. She trailed her fingers through the water, which was almost hot, and watched the pink petals bob across the ripples.

It was a decadent bath that had taken the staff a great deal of time. If she dawdled until it was cold, it would be a waste of that effort. She slipped into the water one leg at a time before sitting slowly enough not to make puddles on the floor. She soaped a sponge and stroked her skin with the spruce and floral soap that reminded her of home.

Afterward, her spine curved to the back of the tub without effort, and her arms floated in the sweet, cloudy water.

"My lady?" Barnes called as she knocked on the door.

"Yes?" Even Annabel's voice was softer.

The maid entered, bringing cooler air with her. "What would you—" She put her hand over her mouth, but not quick enough to hide her smile, and not hard enough to mask her laughter. "Your hair."

Annabel put her wet hands to her head. Her normally straight, boring hair was a mass of tangles. Heat curled through her insides that had nothing to do with embarrassment. "Drat."

"It will be easy to repair." Barnes strode across the room. The nearer she came, the easier it was to see the crinkles at the corners of her eyes. She gathered Annabel's hair in her hands and lifted it over the edge of the tub. "I'll brush while you soak."

Annabel closed her eyes and let the heat seep through her. Though her joints were loose already, she ached in unfamiliar, but not unpleasant, places. Barnes worked carefully on her hair, but every gentle tug was a reminder of how they got there in the first place. A knot formed low in her stomach, making her squirm until her feet stirred the water.

"My lady?" Barnes pulled the brush through the now-smooth strands, roots to ends, section by section. "If you don't mind my saying, it's about bloody time."

"Barnes!" Annabel covered her face with her damp hands to muffle her laughter. Barnes's giggle was muffled as well.

After a moment, she closed one hand on Annabel's shoulder and retrieved the sponge with the other. "The water will cool soon. Let's get you into dry clothes."

Barnes helped her from the tub and into a dry towel, and then into a velvet dressing gown the color of butter. It was so lovely that Annabel had never felt worthy of wearing it. "Could we do something different with my hair?"

"Of course. Why not a chignon?"

The maid was so excited. Annabel felt guilty for making her do braids every morning for the last few weeks. "Whatever you'd like, Barnes. Thank you."

The result, a low bun with wisps of curls at her ears, was soft and simple. Annabel loved it. "Perfect. I think the red dress today. I'll be going out for a bit after I resolve some household business."

"Lovely choice, my lady."

Annabel left her room feeling like a marchioness for the first time. The maids scurried from Jasper's room under Stapleton's watchful gaze, hiding their smiles.

"Breakfast, Lady Ramsbury?"

Given the reactions of the staff, Annabel wasn't certain she could face Jasper's mother and sisters over eggs and toast. After all, she wasn't sure how much noise had escaped their room, and the house wasn't that large.

"Lady Lambourn hasn't come down yet, and the young ladies are with their French tutor."

"In that case, please have a tray sent to his lordship's study. I would like to start work."

The butler dipped his head. "As you wish. Tea or coffee?"

"Coffee, please." Today, of all days, she was glad for the man's unswerving, stoic nature. "Thank you, Stapleton."

She entered the office and took the chair behind the desk, steadfastly ignoring the spot on the floor where last night had begun. There had been enough relishing the events of the night, and now she needed to get on with the tasks ahead of her.

Breakfast arrived as she was making a list of the household receipts, and she sipped her coffee as she checked her math. Her evidence had to be perfect when Jasper confronted Mr. Jones. Otherwise, the careless man of business would explain it away as Jasper putting too much faith in his wife, whose sex made her incapable of rational thinking.

As she chewed her toast, she scanned the newspaper headlines. Talk of London's continued growth and hunger for goods occupied one column, while reports of unrest and complaints about working conditions filled the other.

On the inside, the announcement of Charlotte Bainbridge's betrothal to Philip Melton, Viscount Raines, led the social calendar.

Ramming his way into Wales? The headline caught her eyes, coaxing her to read further.

We have word that Lord R may be exchanging his love of Welsh horses for a vein of Welsh coal. Could he have some inside knowledge, or perhaps a frank friend has given him an advantage…

Annabel sighed as she laid the paper aside. Logic dictated that the gossip would fade, but was it a coincidence that every move they made was broadcast and dissected?

Jasper's correspondence consisted of invitations for events that had already occurred, requests for patronage or donations, and investment speculations. The more detailed the letter, the more tempting the profit, the more her suspicions were raised. She put the reasonable offers aside to discuss with Jasper.

There were letters from the vicars in both Ramsbury and Lambourn, updating him on the state of affairs in both villages, which Annabel used to begin a list of concerns they could address on their visits. She opened the last letter and looked at the signature first—*Uncle Edgar*. Reading no further, she put it back in the envelope and on the top of the pile.

The newspaper waited for her, and she needed to meet with the senior staff to discuss budgets, menus, and social engagements. She could also—

"You could stop delaying what you need to do," she scolded herself, and slouched back against the chair.

She had to see Reginald Spencer, and the quicker she did it, the better. It was also better if she didn't ask for an appointment or wait for him to catch her in another ballroom.

On her way to the door, she paused at the liquor cabinet. The cut glass decanters caught the sunlight and cast dozens of rainbows across the cabinet walls. Their contents glimmered. Liquid courage. Wasn't that what Father had called it? Perhaps she could do with some of that herself.

Annabel dithered over the decanters before choosing the clear one. Jasper always drank a clear whiskey. She poured a small amount in the glass and sipped, expecting her nose to burn from fumes. It didn't. She sipped again. No bitter taste coated her tongue. It tasted like water. Another sip had her giggling.

The Marquess of Ramsbury, known for his devil-may-care drunkenness, drank *water*.

She scoured and smelled the bottles on the other shelves until she found the gin. Then she poured the water into the nearest plant and refilled the decanter. Imagining his reaction gave her an extra bounce as she descended the stairs.

Barnes, ever efficient, had left her coat, hat, and reticule near the front door. The hat, which had always perched atop her braids like a seabird on a boulder, slid on easily and slanted at an intriguing angle once pinned, giving her a new appreciation for the chignon.

"Shall I have the carriage brought up, my lady?"

The last thing she wanted was a coach and a driver who could report where she'd gone. The household already knew far too much about how she'd spent her time. Besides that, she liked walking in London and seeing things easily overlooked or hidden by curtains. "I'll walk, Stapleton. Thank you. It's not far."

It was early enough in the day that the streets, though crowded, were relatively clean. Visiting hours had not yet begun, since most young ladies were recovering from the latest ball and midnight dinner.

Annabel had never been more grateful to be excluded from social activities, either because the hostess believed gossip or had not invited the newlywed couple out of practicality. Why waste the invitation when the marquess and his new wife would be enjoying each other's company at home?

She hadn't lied to Stapleton. The walk to Spencer's home was brief, for which Annabel was grateful. Too long of a trip would give her time to lose her confidence. And men let their gazes linger a bit too long after they'd tipped their hats. That had never happened when she'd been in gray. Was it the gossip, or did she seem different after last night?

The door opened almost before she could remove her fingers from the knocker. The old butler raised his overgrown white eyebrows. "Miss Pearce?" He blinked, before bowing slightly. "Forgive me. Lady Ramsbury."

Annabel summoned every lesson she'd learned by watching Jasper's mother. "Good morning, Henderson. Please tell Mr. Spencer that I wi—am here to speak with him." It had not been so long that she'd forgotten Spencer's routine. He wouldn't visit the palace until after luncheon, when the family was ready to do business.

"He is already in meetings." Mrs. Riordan emerged from the shadows. "If you will leave your card, Miss Pearce?"

Annabel stepped into the hall, keeping her eye on the housekeeper as she removed her hat. She ignored Henderson's request for it. She would not delay her departure from this house once her errand was finished. "When his business is concluded, you can tell him the Marchioness of Ramsbury is waiting."

The housekeeper motioned to a bench near the stairs. "As you wish."

Annabel ground her molars together and drew a deep breath through her nose. "Please have coffee brought to the drawing room."

Once alone in the room, with the door closed, Annabel gave in to pacing as she considered her speech. It should be short and to the point. He should be given no opening for argument or innuendo. She was in the right, and her husband's title now gave her the power to dictate terms.

Once that was settled, she had little else to do. She wondered which door Spencer would use. The one from the hall was the most direct, but he preferred ambush and surprise.

They had added new drapes to the windows, but the rich brocade only highlighted the faded wallpaper and worn rugs. Even the art was uninspiring. Spencer should take the opportunity to hang some of Elizabeth's artwork where her suitors could see it when they called.

The coffee had not yet arrived. Annabel had expected the slight. Mrs. Riordan had never been kind, and Elizabeth's perceived failure at the house party wouldn't have improved her mood. Still, Annabel had a perverse compulsion to make the older woman comply. Her husband, it seemed, was rubbing off on her in more ways than one.

She opened the door and stepped into the hallway, intent on finding the housekeeper in her favorite hiding place—the shadows behind the stairs, in the hallway that led to the kitchen.

"Do you realize what you've done?" Spencer's voice seeped through the library door. "I have spent months whispering in titled ears and planting stories in the newspaper, and your actions in one night have endangered the entire scheme."

"Saved it, you mean?" another man asked. His familiar accent tickled her brain. "The man saw me with the Irishman, and he had the connections to make sure your little plan would blow up in *our* faces."

"Which it still might, since you have garnered unwanted attention by your decisions and your arrival here off schedule."

"I had no choice. Christian has several blokes on the hook and needed a sample to seal the deals. I can be back in Cardiff by—"

Wales. The man was Welsh, like Yarwood.

"You are supposed to be focused on hiring crew and finding an—"

"I have your man already." The stranger's dismissive tone gave the impression that murder and scheming were second nature. "Best powder man in Cork, but he isn't cheap."

"I'll have the funds when they're needed," Spencer said.

"Bollocks! The man's gonna want—"

"Fine, I'll get half before your return in two weeks. Let's just hope no one finds the results of your last decision."

"The body will never be found without me, which I have no reason to disclose. At present."

Even through the door, Annabel could discern the threat. She kept a wary eye out for household staff as she all but pressed her ear to the door.

"Focus, Collins," Spencer snapped. "No more of your own decisions. I have told you what I expect. Veer from that again, and my action will be swift."

"As will mine, *Sir* Reginald."

The floorboards creaked as someone stood. A cane thumped heavily against the thin carpet.

Annabel returned to the drawing room on quick, quiet feet and eased the door closed without even a click. The hall grew noisy with activity as she dithered between sitting and standing. Standing would be best. She would not be subservient to Spencer, and it would be easier to run if the murderer followed him through the door.

Sir Reginald entered the room alone through the most direct route. "Lady Ramsbury. This is a pleasant surprise."

He clearly found it no more pleasant that she did. Annabel squared her shoulders. Her announcement was never going to be received well, but his last conversation had ensured it. "Our business is at an end, Mr. Spencer. The Marquess of Ramsbury is not a traitor, and no amount of skulking about will prove otherwise."

"I see." Spencer stepped toward her, his eyes narrow. "This is what I get for sending a woman to do a man's job. Even one I considered bright enough to see through flash and charm."

"I promised you the truth." She would not plead for reason, and she would not run like a frightened deer. One was out of the question, and the other would make her prey. "You have it."

"And your father? Have you *guaranteed* his security?"

Annabel's gut twisted. She hated the heat that rose to her cheeks at the insinuation that she had bargained her body in exchange for her father's vowels. "My father has the ability to rescue himself, should he choose to do so. I will not tell a lie to save him."

"But to save yourself? If Ramsbury were to learn of your purpose in his house, his…generosity would end."

Annabel ignored the skip in her heart and tore a page from Mr. Collins's book. "If you expose me, you expose yourself. You will not take that risk."

Mrs. Riordan finally arrived with a tray, providing an avenue for escape. Annabel took it, sweeping past Spencer and into the hall, toward the door. Henderson already held it open.

Annabel was to the end of the block before she slowed her pace. The sunshine warmed her hair through her hat, and, though the air carried the acrid scents of town, it helped clear the dread and fear from her lungs. Though her skin still crawled as though someone was watching her.

She suspected this discovery somehow tied to her original, horrible assignment, and her first impulse was to tell Jasper everything. However, the risk was not just to her. She would be placing him in the path of a murderer. She needed to learn more before she confessed.

"Lady Ramsbury!"

She quickened her pace, not looking to see who was behind her.

"Lady Ramsbury! Annabel!"

Fiona Allen. Annabel shaped her mouth into a smile and forced her feet to stay in one place. Turning to wait for Fiona to join her, she had a chance to scan the crowd. Though she had no idea what Collins looked like, she paid close attention to any man walking alone with a cane.

"It is a pleasure to see you out this morning," Fiona said. "What is your next destination?"

"Home." Annabel slowed her pace to match Fiona's, who kept a watchful eye on Mrs. Linden's position in the crowd. "I've had quite enough of town this morning."

"Nonsense." Fiona looped her arm through Annabel's and opened her parasol. "Let's take a turn in the park and enjoy the flowers. I have so many questions about what I'm missing in ballrooms this Season, and Jasper will tell me nothing. It's up to you, I'm afraid."

Despite herself, Annabel grinned. Fiona's good humor and spring flowers might be the best cure for the drama from the morning. She was also fairly certain Mrs. Linden could fend off a murderer with her glare alone. She turned with Fiona toward the park. "Very well, and then I insist you both come for tea."

"Please, no tea. There's only so much one lady can drink when it's her only social outlet," Fiona said. "Let's stop at Gunter's for ices instead."

CHAPTER SIXTEEN

"I FOUND THE tigers fascinating, didn't you?"

Not nearly as fascinating as her new hairstyle.

"A nine-foot-long, thirty-five-stone cat who loves water. What's not to love?" Jasper teased. "The illustrations of its habitat were intriguing as well."

"Hacking through a thick forest full of snakes and spiders and having my blood sucked by insects I can't see?" Annabel asked. "I can't wait to go."

She'd hung on every word of the lecture, judging by the way she'd squeezed his hand throughout. He couldn't blame her. Five minutes after the speaker had begun, Jasper had forgotten to glare at the stodgy attendees who were staring at his wife either in outrage or with frank interest.

Not that he could blame the latter ones. Two weeks of waking with Annabel in his arms had done nothing but make him hungrier for her. Even now, on the road toward Ramsbury, every rock and sway made him think about sex in a carriage.

He swung across to sit beside her and smiled when she made room for him, but just enough that their bodies touched. He draped his arm around her shoulders, and her head fell to his shoulder.

"Have you been?" she asked.

"To India? No." He'd never been farther than Paris, because

heirs were packed with feathers and straw. "Kit is better traveled than me." Stapleton and Travis were better traveled than he was. "One meager benefit of serving queen and country."

"Memories of the jungle are poor substitutions for the losses they risk."

"I agree." Jasper pressed a kiss to the top of her head. "The country should treat them better."

"You are the country, you know?"

The landscape rocked past the window, dusted in silver moonlight and topped with stars. The quiet gave her words weight. Giving Kit a home, helping Gareth's widow, solving the young man's murder—these were all small steps. He had the capability and the connections to do more.

But not tonight. He was on holiday, and his wife was warm in his arms.

"How go your redecorating plans?" he whispered in her ear, and enjoyed the shiver that went through her.

"Are you anxious to be rid of me?" Annabel tilted her head, not to escape him, but to give him access to her neck.

He was happy to take advantage. Her skin was soft, but strong muscles flexed against his tongue. "Never. You can leave it pink, frilly, and vacant for all I care."

"Now that I've begun, I should finish."

"Mm-hmm." He slid his hand along the curve of her knee and the inside of her thigh. "You definitely should."

She put a firm hand on his wrist. "No, Jasper. Not now."

"I owe you something for refilling my gin." He nipped her earlobe. "I damn near coughed myself to death."

Now, as then, her giggle unraveled him. He tangled his fingers in her skirts and pulled. She insisted on pushing them back to the floor.

"I've finally realized *your mother* cannot hear us, but I draw the line at male staff in the quiet countryside."

"Fine." Not to be completely deterred, he kissed her and groaned in relief when she opened for him eagerly. Her hum of anticipation tickled his tongue. "If you're certain."

"I am," Annabel panted as she tangled her fingers in his hair.

Her collarbone gave him a path to the hollow in her throat and down her sternum. She arched into the caress, putting her breast in his hand. Jasper could swear his world was speeding to match the hammering of her heart.

"Highwaymen!"

Lawrence's cry pulled Jasper back to reality, but it took a moment to clear his head. All he could see was a lantern, but the longer he stared, the clearer the shapes became. One rider in a dark coat on a black horse—a fast one.

"Blast."

"There's one on this side as well," Annabel said. Her words were rushed, but her voice was steady. "Closing fast."

He pulled her from the window as he extinguished the lantern. "Get on the floor."

He lifted the vacant seat and retrieved a pistol. Five delicate fingers beckoned for it. He looked over his shoulder and into her defiant stare. She was nowhere near the floor.

"No, Annabel."

"I will not cower while you hang out the window shooting at people."

"It's not that dramatic." A shot rang out from behind them, proving him wrong at the worst possible time. The carriage lurched forward at Lawrence's urging, and Frederick returned fire.

"You have more than one weapon, and I am not helpless." Her face was pale, but her hand was still out.

"Do you know how to shoot?" He put the gun in her hand and watched her nod a little too fast for comfort. He pushed her into the corner of the bench and lifted her feet so her knees were bent. "Balance your arm on your knees and brace your back against the corner." He shoved her down. "Keep your head clear of the window."

He'd groused to no end when Kit had given him this lecture—as though he'd never considered dueling or having to defend himself.

"Both barrels are loaded. If you fire them at the same time, you'll either scare the hell out of your target or break your elbow. Either way, you'll ruin your chance for a second shot." He lifted the pistol and her hand with it. "Pull the rear trigger first. If you need it, pull the front. They will have to be close, darling. Don't close your eyes, and don't hesitate."

Once she nodded, he retrieved the other pistol and practically fell into his seat as the coach hit a rut in the road. He doused the lantern over his head, braced himself against the motion, and waited.

The world narrowed to pounding footsteps and shadows stretching across the floor. Frederick's rifle came at regular intervals. He was trying, and failing, to spook the robbers before they reached the coach.

"Remember to breathe," he said to Annabel as much as himself.

The lanterns grew brighter, gold replacing silver moonlight inside the coach. A shadow loomed over his head, while a hulking figure filled the window nearest Annabel.

Jasper aimed and fired, and the blast deafened him. Annabel's shot set her wide-eyed face into stark relief. Moonlight flooded the coach as the riders fell back. Before he could move, she scrambled across the seat, braced her arm against the door, and fired again. She flew back against the velvet cushions with a yelp as the pistol fell from her hand.

Her target shouted and fell back out of sight.

"Annabel!" Heedless of the windows and whether the highwaymen were still in range, Jasper leapt across to her and pulled her into his arms. Ragged breaths sawed through her, warming his suddenly cold skin.

Jasper ran his hands over her, praying for nothing wet or sticky. "Are you injured?"

She blinked up at him, frowning.

"Hurt, Annabel," he shouted. "Are you hurt?"

She shook her head slowly, then with more force. Her smile was almost feral. "I'm fine. Though I should have listened more closely about how the pistol would kick."

Jasper handed her his weapon and retrieved the other from the floor. "I'll reload. Use that if you need it."

A wild turn sent them toppling into each other, and trees shrouded them in darkness. Lawrence slowed the coach to a stop. In the quiet, every breath was distinguishable. But no one found them.

"Are you all right down there, my lord?" Lawrence whispered.

"Yes," Jasper replied. "You?"

"Fine, sir. There is an inn up ahead. Off the route, but out of the way. Thought it would be best to rest the horses."

"Excellent thinking. Thank you."

Silence stretched as they wound deeper into the trees on a road that twisted back on itself multiple times. Jasper didn't dare light the lanterns, and he gave up staring into the darkness trying to make sense of the shapes surrounding them.

He took the almost-useless pistol from Annabel. "I told you to stay out of the windows."

She curved against him, lifting his arm over her shoulders. "Forgive me, but he had a sword, and I like your head where it is."

Her arm draped across his waist, and her breathing evened out, deepened. Still, she trembled against him. Or perhaps it was his shaking. Jasper closed his eyes and listened to the sounds of travel and the cries of night birds.

He jolted awake when they came to a halt. The pistol was level with the window and cocked before he recognized Frederick. "My apologies." He lowered the weapon. "Have we arrived?" Beside him, Annabel swung her feet to the floor.

"Yes, your lordship. Lawrence has arranged the room with Mr. and Mrs. Holt, the innkeepers. If you'll follow me."

"Fine shooting back there," Jasper said as he helped Annabel down. "Rifle regiment?"

"Yes, sir. Served with Major Yarwood in Egypt." The footman led the way up the stairs. "I'll stand guard downstairs. Lawrence will patrol outside." His eyes shone over his wide grin. "Stapleton and Travis will be sorry they had to go ahead."

The innkeeper and his wife waited just inside the room. Their smiles contradicted their bleary stares. "It's our pleasure to welcome you, your lordship," the man said. His wife's curtsy embarrassed Jasper. Had he been in their shoes, he would not have been so good-natured. And, he suspected, if he and Annabel had been any other traveler, they might have had a different reception.

"Thank you for your hospitality and your kindness, Mr. and Mrs. Holt." Jasper took in their surroundings. The fire was beating the chill from the room at a rapid pace, and two rather exhausted servants were struggling to pour buckets of water into a giant tub. It would take them most of the night.

"Please," Annabel said. "The bath is very kind, but unnecessary. We are imposing quite enough at this late hour. What you've provided here is fine."

The relief on everyone's faces was almost laughable.

"As you wish, my lady." Mrs. Holt curtsied again. "We served stew this evening with a nice, thick bread and fresh butter." She motioned toward the small table, where the food was already waiting. "It's only simple fare, but—"

"It will be perfect," Jasper said. "Thank you."

Once they were alone, Annabel turned in his arms and stood on her tiptoes to pull his lips to hers for a kiss that was anything but shy. Jasper recovered from his surprise and caught her lips between his. "Now?"

"Now," she whispered. "Please."

They undressed without separating for any longer than necessary, and Jasper ran his hands over her skin, letting her wholeness and warmth reassure him. Her touch singed him, carving his muscles into iron and hardening his cock to stone.

He sat on the bed and pulled her between his knees, still kissing her as he lifted her breasts in his hands and stroked her nipples until she was pulling away and pushing his head down, demanding attention that he was eager to give.

Her taste recalled sweets and cream, and she smelled of flowers and spruce. But her nails scraped his scalp as she shuddered against him. Jasper trailed his fingers down her back to her hips and around to her thighs. He pulled away to watch as he slid his fingers inside her.

Annabel's eyes drifted closed as her teeth dug into her bottom lip, but she rocked forward, taking him deeper into her slick heat. He knew then what he wanted. He nudged her knee with his free hand. "Come up here." She stepped back with a confused frown, and he tightened his knees and added his now-free hand to the encouragement. "Astride."

Her sharp inhale made him pause and wait for her to make up her mind. After a long moment, she did as he'd asked. The question in her eyes dissolved as he curved his hands under her hips, letting his fingers trail through her wetness to the spot that drove her wild. "Take your hair down, please."

One thing he loved about her new hairstyle was how easy it was to disassemble. A few pins, and it coiled down her back. One shake of her head, and it was loose over her shoulders.

Keeping hold of her, Jasper reclined on the bed. His shaft was throbbing between them. "Take me in your hand." She'd done that before, and it had nearly driven him mad. Today was no different, but he forced himself to follow through with his plan.

"Put me inside you." He gulped against the instinct to do it himself. "Rise up and come down." She'd felt him—watched him—do it enough times that he knew she could.

Her heat spread over him slowly until he was fully engulfed. "Bloody hell."

"Am I hurting you?" She lifted away, and he grasped her hips to pull her back. Her squeal made him smile.

"The only way you'll hurt me is if you stop—or perhaps twist in an unexpected direction." He pushed through his heels and pulled her toward him, rocking her as he drove deeper, showing her what he needed from her. "Ride, Annabel." He rocked against her again. "Ride."

She moved on him then, meeting him as he surged beneath her, again and again, until he was panting and slick with sweat and her hand was planted on his chest for balance as she raced with him toward oblivion. Her hair shrouded him from everything but the look on her face as they reached it. He pulled her mouth to his to muffle her screams as he found her center and stroked it until she was limp against him.

Jasper rolled her to her back and kissed her damp forehead before rising from the bed. The water in the tub was warm enough for him to wet a cloth and clean himself before returning to the bed and doing the same for Annabel, who was sloe-eyed and smiling. "Jasper?"

His heart pounded in his ears. If she said she loved him, he'd say it back. And he'd mean it.

"I'm starving," she mumbled.

"Me too." He fished her shift from the floor and handed it to her before going in search of his trousers. "Let's eat."

CHAPTER SEVENTEEN

JASPER PUSHED AWAY from the desk and Annabel's thorough list of necessary repairs, ignored tenant requests, and shoddy workmanship. All his life, his grandfather had lectured him to pay attention to what mattered. It wasn't that Jasper hadn't listened. There was just so much that required his management, and there was only one of him.

Until now.

It had taken every ounce of his persuasive charm to convince his tenants to talk to him honestly. *I don't have a complaint, your lordship. Your grandfather was a fine man, your lordship. We've been doing well, your lordship. Your rents will be on time, your lordship.*

Annabel had done better with their wives. Apparently, they needed little encouragement to be brutally honest.

Jasper left the library and found Stapleton standing sentry at the door. "Where is Frederick?"

"With her ladyship in the garden," the older man said. "I thought it best, since his eyes are sharper."

"And she likely had her gardening tools." Jasper chuckled. The staff had learned quickly that gardening with Annabel was neither a short nor passive task. "I'll go relieve him."

"She mentioned something about the maze, sir."

He nodded his thanks as he opened the door. Once outside, it was easier to breathe. The air held scents he'd known since childhood. Roses at the front of the house, lavender nearer the laundry sheds, newly turned earth by the kitchen door. Yesterday, when they rode to visit the tenants, the world had consisted of hay, recent rains, and mud. Barnyards and sheep pastures had added a solid reminder on how he made his living and who depended on his care.

The sunshine warmed his hair, banishing his brewing headache as he entered the maze in search of his wife.

The towering hedges had terrified him into stillness as a child. He'd hidden, fighting tears, until Bottoms, grandfather's gardener, taught him to use a string to retrace his steps to the exit. Now, newly trimmed growth littered the path at every turn, pulling him forward but reassuring him of the path out again.

Voices drifted to meet him. Annabel's measured tones mixed with another, more excited one. Familiar, but not, and definitely not Frederick. Jasper lengthened his stride and took the corners shorter, snagging his shirt on sharp-ended branches.

He stopped at the edge of the circle. Annabel was in an apron and a hat with a brim large enough to keep two of her shaded. Hands on her hips, her gloves clenched in one fist, she nodded along as the man beside her waved his hands as though conducting a green orchestra.

"Camellias will do better against the hedges, on trellises," the man said. "We could find other shrubs for the centerpiece.

"Peonies." Jasper walked forward, his grin widening as he stretched out his hand. "It's good to see you again, Bottoms."

"It is, your lordship." Bottoms returned the greeting, his smile just as wide. "Word spread that old Jones was no longer in charge of the purse, and I thought I'd come see if we could put the garden in proper shape. Her ladyship happened to be out here working on her own." He cast a glare at Frederick.

"It's good to have you back, Bottoms. Start an accounting for what you will need." Jasper put his hand at his wife's waist. "I need to borrow Lady Ramsbury for a moment."

They walked away from the gardener and their rifleman

guard to the statues that stood as the centerpiece. The muses gleamed white from head to foot, making the larger cracks easier to see.

"We'll need a plasterer to repair these," Jasper said. "Otherwise, we'll lose them altogether." He bent to her ear. "Thank you for hiring Bottoms. I had no idea he'd left because of Jones's greed."

"Your grandfather's earlier ledgers showed a larger expenditure on the gardens than in later years. Was that down to your grandmother?"

Jasper nodded. "She spent as much time outdoors as she did in ballrooms. She and Bottoms were thick as thieves."

The old gardener walked the circle, tilting his head to stare at the shrubbery and empty beds much as an artist stared at a canvas.

"This place will be in good hands." Jasper twined his fingers through Annabel's. "And yours will be saved from all this weeding."

"A little gardening now and then helps me think." She thumped his shoulder with her thick work gloves. "Which is what you've asked me to do."

"You'll likely have plenty of things to think about at Lambourn. Father disliked bookkeeping and put his faith in Jones much earlier than Grandfather." The old man had managed his own accounts until he could no longer see to write straight. "But Mother has likely rid it of weeds already."

"I seem to remember your telling me your mother was ill, and you were looking for a companion for your sisters. Almost in this very spot." Annabel's eyes danced.

Being caught in a lie had never been this much fun. "It was thirty paces north." He kissed her nose. "But yes, I lied to keep you talking."

Unspoken questions lay heavy on his tongue. Further ones flitted across her eyes. She blinked, and they vanished.

"I can write ahead to Lambourn and let them know to open

the house for next week," Annabel said. "If you'd like."

She was bolder in many areas, and she spoke her mind more freely—mostly when they were alone. However, answering his correspondence had concerned her. It wasn't her decisions that gave her pause, it was her handwriting. She didn't want it to look like a woman was writing his letters. She needn't have worried. Her penmanship was as straightforward as she was.

How had Spencer ever considered her a suitable spy?

"We'll have to visit Warwick Manor first. Uncle Edgar's invitation mentioned something he's left too long." He sighed. "The house is likely a pile."

"It must be a weight," she said. "My father found one estate a chore."

Jasper had two if he didn't count the estate in Norfolk, which he didn't because Uncle Augustus wasn't dead yet. And even after he was, Cousin Amelia and Richard would be looking after it. He'd have three after Edgar died.

What am I going to do with more houses?

"Is that how you came to understand ledgers?" he asked.

"Numbers always made sense to me. Though we weren't taught much more than how not to overspend what husbands would allow us, the principles for budgets are the same. The sums may be larger, but the mathematics involved don't change." She walked away from him to snip an errant sprout. "It's easy to find truth in numbers."

Jasper followed her. He'd learned long ago that he discovered more when he was quiet. People said things without saying them, or when they were saying something else. The way they held their bodies or spoke their word choices were telling. Annabel's choice of *truth* spoke volumes.

"You're the one who discovered your father's debts?"

She nodded. "It took time, tracking down things he'd sold at bargains, and invoices that were paid late. There were improvements he'd listed but never made, and investments he'd purchased from fraudsters and thieves." She pulled a weed with such vehemence that she beheaded it.

Perhaps she *would* have made a good spy. "What did you do?"

"I confronted him with the differences between his ledger and the one I'd translated using his records. He'd become so wrapped up in his schemes, he didn't even know how broke we were." She dropped to her knees to dig out the remainder of the intruder. "Why would he do that? It never made sense that he would lie to himself."

"Lenders review our accounts before they loan money," Jasper said. "It's usually a formality, especially if you have a title and an estate. No one would investigate past the last few pages."

No one but a daughter who was determined to learn the truth. Jasper lifted her to her feet and took her trowel. She had done enough work today.

"He said reading through ledgers and doing sums wasn't a *suitable* pastime for a lady."

Jasper's ears twitched. "You don't like that word, do you? Suitable."

Annabel's steps slowed. "Almost as much as you like *your lordship*."

He understood *his* aversion. He wanted to understand hers. "Why?"

"It means I've met a mark but not exceeded it. I'm good *enough*, smart *enough*, pretty *enough*." Her tone sharpened. "You buy a cart horse because *she'll do*. You buy a racehorse because she captivates you, and you consider her valuable."

I need a suitable wife. He'd meant it as a compliment. She'd heard *cart horse*. And now he had her managing his household and handling his correspondence. And cuddling against him in the middle of the night.

Does she consider everything I ask of her a job?

A houseboy appeared at the gap to the hedges. He whipped off his hat and gave a bow that reminded Jasper of a broken toy. "Visitors, your lordship."

Assassins likely wouldn't show themselves in the middle of

the day. Still, Jasper kept Annabel close as they walked toward the house. Frederick walked at a safe but respectful distance, his rifle at the ready.

This was their current truth, and none of them had to say a word about it. However, the longer the silence stretched, the more Jasper's skin crawled with the impression someone other than Frederick was watching his back. If he felt that way, Annabel certainly must.

Stapleton met them at the door. "Lady Lambourn and Mr. Yarwood are in the library, Lord Ramsbury."

Mother would never leave the girls unattended at a house party unless something had happened, and Kit would have never let her travel alone. This was bad news. "Thank you, Stapleton."

It was only a few steps to the library, but Annabel took his hand before they reached the door. Her fingers warmed his icy ones, but the warmth crept deeper still. At every other critical point in his life, he'd been alone. Even when there were other people in the room, they were not the ones to bear the responsibilities that followed.

He wasn't alone any longer.

They entered the library together. Mother, in black, had taken the chair farthest from the windows. She held a crumpled handkerchief to the corner of one red-rimmed eye. Kit, on the other end of the room, paced from wall to wall, head down and deep in thought.

Jasper went to his mother first and curved his free hand around her shoulder. "The girls are fine, yes?" The words almost choked him. Having Annabel in the path of assassins had brought home how dangerous his foes could be to those around him. A house party wouldn't have a rifleman on the roof.

"They're fine." She patted his hand. "Having a wonderful time. Mrs. Linden was kind enough to step in so I could leave." Her tears began anew. "Edgar has died."

Jasper hadn't spent much time with his uncle as an adult, not after his exile to the countryside and his stubborn refusal to repent and reform. What he remembered most was a man with a laugh that was too large for his body, his mother's favorite sibling in a family she loved to a fault. "I'm sorry, Mum."

Annabel set a cup of tea on the nearest table.

"Thank you, dear girl," his mother said. "I am so glad you're here."

So was he. Just as he'd been glad to have Annabel across from him in the coach last night and meeting with tenants this morning.

"Are we planning the funeral for here?" Jasper asked. "Or did he make arrangements for a crypt at Warwick?"

Mother looked past him toward the other end of the room, to Kit. It took Jasper back to his father's death, when Mother had looked over the girls' bowed heads and sought his input, when he'd navigated the swamp of grief to give the answers everyone expected. Six months ago, after Grandfather's death, everyone had stood in this room and waited for him to do it again.

Kit had stopped pacing and now stood in front of the desk, facing them, his hands behind his back and his chin held high, as though he was meeting a firing squad. Mother, her mouth in a firm line and her blue eyes like ice, could easily pull the trigger.

"Edgar wanted to be buried in Warwick's churchyard." Kit pulled an envelope from his coat pocket. "No crypt, simple stone."

Jasper's father had kept a similar envelope in his safe. So had Grandfather. They'd shown him where to find it and what it meant.

Heirs were told those things.

Heirs...

Kit's nod was short and quick.

"Leave us." Jasper cast a glance at his mother and his wife. Sending Annabel from the room was like losing a lifeline through the maze in his head, but he needed to ask some very rude, very direct, questions.

The door clicked closed.

"Jasper."

Ignoring Kit, he walked to the liquor cabinet and poured two shots of Cousin Amelia's best whiskey. He delivered one to the man he'd considered a brother, if not by blood then by experience. The boy he'd fought beside in the schoolyard. The friend he'd worried over during the war. The man he'd trusted with his secrets and his life. "Cousin."

Kit's stare was wary over the rim of his glass. Ever vigilant, his friend. No one read a situation better, whether it was a rowdy crowd in a pub or one man in a library. He could always find the easiest way out, the surest plan of attack, the information that was needed.

"How long have you known?" Jasper asked.

"Since Mum's death." Kit stepped back so he could lean against the desk.

Kit had lost his mother during their third year at Eton. "That long?"

"Da told me, but only because he was foxed and miserable." Kit pulled his body into the shape of a man who spent far too much time stooped in a mine and then slouched on a stool in his favorite pub. "*You will always be my boy, even if in the eyes of the law you're a bastard.*" He straightened his spine and sighed. "As though I needed to be told either thing. It was plain the old man loved me, and just as obvious that I looked nothing like him."

"That's hardly proof that—"

"Mum had a letter from Edgar in the trunk at the end of her bed, agreeing to pay for my education but nothing else."

The boys at Eton had teased Kit mercilessly over two things: his Welsh accent and the identity of his benefactor. The larger the crowd, the wilder the guesses, until Kit lashed out. Jasper had fought next to him every time. "Why didn't you tell me?"

"Honestly?" Kit shrugged. "I thought you knew."

"You thought I *knew*?" Jasper raked his hand through his hair, struggling to keep his temper in check and his brain clear enough to follow Kit's reasoning. "And simply didn't mention it for twenty years."

Kit tilted his glass, first to one side and then the other, as he stared over his shoulder and out the window. "I know how Society is about bastard children."

Jasper ground his back teeth together to silence his protest. This story was not about him. "How did you get from *nothing else* to knowing where Edgar kept his will?"

"I never expected to hear from him, but when I enlisted, he sent an invitation to Warwick. I was curious, so I went."

Edgar had never invited anyone to the country house he'd once referred to as his own personal Elba.

"Big house, garden full of flowers I couldn't pronounce. Awkward silences. He did say he'd been sad to learn of Mum's death, which was kind, and then he offered to pay for my commission. Said he thought Mum would want him to do whatever it took to keep me safe, which was true. I took it for her."

Edgar could have kept his heir in Britain altogether. "Nothing else?"

"I didn't want to be the Earl of fucking Warwick, and there was still a possibility for him to father a legitimate heir."

Stranger things had happened.

"That changed after Egypt." Kit refilled his glass and carried the decanter to Jasper, who shook his head. He needed his wits about him. "I went to see him after I returned—once I saw Da." He returned the whiskey to the cabinet and kept walking. He reached the door before he reversed direction. "I wanted him to know he'd invested wisely, I suppose."

Jasper understood that compulsion. He'd often wondered whether his father would be proud of what he was accomplishing. Since Grandfather's death, the curiosity had doubled.

"It was clear he was ill." Kit's jaw kicked sideways. "Very ill. We went on a carriage ride around the village and the estate, and then we went back to the hall. Edgar warned me he'd written a new will, claiming me. He wanted to keep Warwick safe."

"Safe?" Jasper thumped his glass to his desk. "From me?"

"That was a poor choice—"

"Get out." Jasper heard his knuckles crack before he felt them. His heartbeat deafened him to anything other than his breathing. "Leave."

Kit placed his glass on the nearest table and walked to the door.

"Wait." Jasper didn't turn, but he knew Kit would stop. He always did. "We were set upon by highwaymen on the way here. We may be getting too close, either in London or in Cardiff. Be careful."

"Thank you for the warning."

The door closed with a *snick*. Jasper refilled his drink, his back to the empty room. The latch clicked again.

"Jasper?"

"Mother." He had so many questions, but he didn't dare face her until he had better control of his emotions.

Instead, she put herself in his line of vision. "There is a way to fight this. Mr. Burks says we can argue that Edgar's illness rendered him incompetent. That a devious man took advantage of a previous kindness, and—"

"You knew, didn't you?" She had to have known. She and the family lawyer hadn't arrived at this plan of action surrounded by strangers at a house party. It explained also her cold civility every time Kit visited. "All this time, you knew and you said nothing."

"We thought it best."

Best. To keep the secret that his best friend, the man he thought of as a brother, was actually related to him.

"Burks is ready with the paperwork—"

"I will not lie about Kit's paternity. Edgar did the right thing, finally, and we will honor it."

He lifted the decanter and carried it with him to a chair that faced the gardens. "Leave me." The glass was half full when he remembered his manners. "Please."

She did.

Jasper drank until the garden resembled the impressionist painting hanging over the mantel in the dining room.

His life was full of secrets and lies, the ones he'd perpetuated as a façade to hunt other liars and thieves and the ones others told him. His mother, his best friend, his family—even his wife.

Darkness fell as he finished the whiskey and moved on to the gin.

Was Annabel a spy, using everything at her disposal to get close to him? Or was her interest, her affection, authentic? Had he let her into his life only so she could tell Spencer everything and ruin his plans? Or worse, given the attack on the road? He couldn't be sure of anything any longer.

Stapleton was a shadow against the firelight as he set a tray on the desk. "Lady Ramsbury insists you eat, your lordship."

Jasper nodded but didn't leave his chair. There was every possibility she'd poisoned it. Or, since Kit had hired Stapleton, they were working in concert. Perhaps the assassination attempts weren't related to his progress in the embezzlement case or Gareth's death, but instead led to his newly discovered cousin's darker motives.

His stomach rumbled and gurgled as the scent from roast beef and herbed potatoes curled through his nose and downward. Using the desk for balance, he moved to his chair and sat. After choking down the first few bites, eating became easier. The room was brighter and warmer than he'd thought, though he'd never heard anyone stoke the fire or bring in candles.

Annabel. It had to be her doing. Mother would have fussed, and the servants would have never breached the door of their own accord. Would a woman who wished him dead care whether he sat starving and cold in the dark?

Jasper finished his dinner and stood. He left the room and several of his doubts behind, though he listed to the right as he crossed the hall. He clung to the banister and watched his feet as he climbed the stairs. It would never do to evade being trampled and shot only to tumble backward and bash in his head on his own stairs.

His bed was turned down, but empty. His eyes adjusted to the dim light. Annabel's door was ajar, a sliver of firelight tempting him to go through it.

A bleary-eyed Travis entered the room a few moments later. "Your lordship. Do you need—"

"Thank you, Travis, but return to bed," Jasper whispered, hoping to avoid waking his wife. "I can do this myself."

He did just that, stripping off his clothes before filling the basin and scrubbing clean. He cleaned his teeth last, hoping to rid himself of the smell of alcohol, if not the effects.

He opened the door to a room he'd never entered as an adult, other than during the tour the previous butler had insisted on conducting before his departure. Likely to prove he hadn't stolen anything.

All Jasper cared for was the woman in the bed, facing the door. Everything he wanted to ask her, every word he wanted to say, jumbled together in his brain and stayed there. "My feet are cold."

A slow smile crept over Annabel's face as she pulled the bed-clothes back in invitation. Jasper slid beneath them and into her arms. Her warm cheek rested against his chest. "Your mother told me everything."

Likely not everything. He didn't even *want* to tell her everything. Not tonight.

"She believes you are angry over Edgar's slight." Her breath heated and tickled his skin.

Her hair was silk against his fingers. "What do you believe?"

"That you want a fourth estate like you want a third arm."

"A third arm might be useful now and then." He stroked her spine, and she arched closer, pressing her breasts against his ribs. "They lied to me, Annabel."

"Do you tell the truth all the time?"

He forced himself not to squirm away from her question. "This isn't water in my gin glass. He's my *cousin*, and he couldn't find a good time over the last twenty years to tell me. Neither could Mother."

"Sometimes the longer you've kept a secret, the more difficult it is to reveal," she whispered. "Especially if you care about the person."

Her words pricked his conscience, but he pushed the impulse aside as he pressed a kiss to her forehead. The peace she gave him was addictive, and he didn't wish to lose it. Perhaps, though, he could explain the reasons for his decisions and it would help later. When he was sober. And clothed, without her knee resting near vital bits of his anatomy.

"Society wraps heirs in soft cloth until we're needed," he said. "We're all shipped off to school, safe from any drama of home and family. We're groomed to manage estates, but not work them; to create children, but not raise them; to declare wars, but not fight in them."

He drew a deep breath. "For years I wished for an older brother."

"Maybe two." Annabel's smile teased his skin. "You could have been third."

"God, no." Jasper's laughter shook the bed. "Can you imagine me in the pulpit every Sunday?" He kissed the top of her head. "Besides, I don't think I could manage being *that* poor." He sighed. "But soldiering…"

Her knee grazed his thigh, but she stayed quiet. Only her uneven breath told him she was still awake, listening to him ramble as the gin wore off.

"Rather than declaring Kit his heir and saving him from war, Edgar paid for his commission."

"Did Kit wish to be saved?"

"He says no. That he told Edgar he didn't want to be an earl, and Edgar went along with it."

"I see." She raised her head and rested her chin on the back of her hand. "Who are you angry with, then?"

Her deep brown eyes held his. The mattress was soft against his back, and the fire warmed the room. Her body was warmer still, soft and yielding.

"Both," he whispered. "I had to stay behind and watch Kit and Gareth sail for Egypt."

"Gareth?"

"Claudette's husband." He twined a lock of her thick hair around his finger, then unfurled it, only to repeat the action.

"He died in the war?"

He shook his head against the pillow. "Afterward. He and Kit came home whole and safe. I would have, too."

Her sharp inhale shifted her ribs away from his. "You wanted to go?"

"I thought it was only fair."

"Jasper," she scolded him quietly for the lie.

"Fine." He met her arched eyebrow with one of his own. "My titles, which I have simply because I am the only male of my generation on my father's side of the family, give me every luxury but adventure." He put a finger to her lips to stop her protest. "And, before you say it, I know war is not an adventure. However, I'm allowed to go to the Continent to shop, or for sex, but I'm forced to stay in England while young men without the benefit of birth or fortune go fight for something vastly more important. Something their government, of which I am a part, has ordered them to do."

Annabel shifted against him, rising just enough to press a soft kiss against his lips. Her palm cradled his jaw. "I, for one, am glad you didn't go to war, whatever the reason."

There was nothing but sincerity in her eyes and her words. It was the same every time he looked at her, every time he held her. Whatever misguided belief had brought her into his life, she offered something he'd never expected to find—a place to be himself. He couldn't imagine being anywhere else.

"So am I." He drew another deep breath. Once he put this wish in the air, he was committed. "But I want to do something to help them."

She yawned and snuggled closer. "Then that's what you'll do."

CHAPTER EIGHTEEN

"**B**ATH WAS BUSIER than I'd expected it to be during the Season," Mother said as she poured more tea. "I suppose everyone took the opportunity to leave London during the break."

"I'm relieved to hear it." Annabel took the cup and shifted her attention to her sisters. "Did you enjoy yourselves?"

Rachel bounced against the sofa cushions the way she'd done last Christmas when she received her first piece of jewelry—a delicate diamond bracelet. "The Lambourn townhouse is lovely, and so many of the young ladies accepted our invitation for tea." Her eyes went wide. "You don't think the countess will mind that we entertained, do you? She did tell us to treat it as though it was ours."

"She will be happy that you heeded her instructions." *As long as Father didn't follow them and steal the silver.* "Were there very many parties?"

"We had a stack of invitations waiting when we arrived." Mother was almost as excited as Rachel. "The girls danced almost every night. Peter Drew, the heir to the Earl of Makepeace, danced with Rachel at each opportunity. The last night we were there he asked for two sets."

"Then Madame Fleur's hours of lessons have been worth the torture." Annabel winked at her sister and put her still-full, cooling teacup on the table.

It wasn't the tea's fault. It was a higher quality than they'd been drinking when she'd left, and they had cubes of sugar now rather than honey.

The tea service unnerved her. Her mother had two. The family service was heavy, plain pottery made by a tenant years before Annabel had been born, likely several barons ago. The inside of the pot was mud brown from years of use, and the large cups fit to your hand to warm your palm and provide comfort on cold days. The guest service was fine porcelain, hand-painted and gilt-edged. It was lovely, but the cups were too small to be satisfying. They were also difficult to hold. Mother only pulled them from the pantry when she wanted to impress a visitor.

This was the guest service.

A painting opposite her caught Annabel's eye. It had always hung upstairs in Mother's room. It was her favorite. It was Annabel's, too. She'd spent hours staring into the rolling green landscape, imagining the soft grass against her feet and the rain-scented wind in her loose hair.

It looked very much like Wiltshire and the Ramsbury estate.

"You've moved this from upstairs?"

Mother nodded. "Rebecca suggested that it would add something to this room, and I believe she was right. It's like doing my needlework with an old friend." She smiled up at the artwork. "It looks so much brighter since we've had it cleaned."

Annabel turned her attention to her middle sister, who had yet to say anything other than hello. Rebecca wasn't as bubbly as Rachel, and her temper matched Annabel's—as did her wit. But she was a lovely girl, especially when she smiled, which wasn't often of late. "And you, Rebecca?" Annabel teased. "Did you leave a smitten suitor behind."

"No."

"Rebecca preferred the soldiers in attendance," Rachel said in the gossipy tone preferred by the *ton*. "I will say their uniforms added a bit of flash in amongst all the evening suits."

"Their conversations were more interesting as well," Rebecca said. "They could talk about more than horses and dance steps and how much they'd lost at cards."

"I'm sure they were interesting, and those we met were polite and treated all the ladies well." Mother looked over the rim of her teacup. "Many navy officers have done quite well for themselves, but I'm not certain a military man is suitable. Wouldn't you agree?"

As the eldest, Annabel had been in this position many times before. Mother never wanted to be the one who said no, at least not on her own. Usually, her requests were small.

This one wasn't. Given Rebecca's rising color, she was ready for a fight. And now Annabel knew men like Yarwood. He didn't like her, but he had always been loyal to Jasper.

"I don't, Mother. Yes, some military men can be rogues and scoundrels, but not all of them are. Just like all young men in Society aren't gentlemen." Annabel nodded to her sister. "I'm glad you weren't bored, Rebecca."

"We saw Colonel Spencer at several events," Rachel said. "He cuts quite a dashing figure."

Nothing like his younger brother, then. "Sir Reginald spoke often of him and his successes. The family is quite proud of him."

Annabel always though Sir Reginald sounded a bit like Rebecca when she thought Rachel got a prettier hat.

The clock in the hallway chimed, signaling the hour. "I must be going. Jasper will be home soon, and I need to prepare for the Bainbridges' ball." Father would be home soon as well.

"I'm so looking forward to it." Rachel's smile glittered. "Isn't it romantic?"

"Oh yes." Rebecca's sharp stare fastened on to Annabel. "Romantic."

A familiar irritation simmered under her skin. It didn't matter that she shared Rebecca's opinion about the evening. Neither of them should ruin Rachel's excitement. Annabel stood and kissed her mother's cheek. "I do wish you'd change your mind and attend."

"London parties can be trying." Mother blinked, and the clouds in her eyes cleared. "Besides, I danced quite enough in Bath." She squeezed Annabel's fingers. "Enjoy the evening, dear. Give my best to Lord Ramsbury."

Annabel was in the hallway securing her hat when the reflection in the mirror distracted her. "What is it, Rebecca?"

"Why did you send us to Bath rather than the Alfords' house party?" The words were hard, but Rebecca knew better than to yell. A loud argument would do nothing but upset Mother and Rachel.

Annabel pulled her sister into the dining room and closed the door. "You have to ask that?"

"So you catch a marquess at a house party, and Rachel chooses between barons and earls in Bath?"

"Rachel *gets* to choose," Annabel snapped. "As do you."

"I certainly do." Rebecca sounded anything but grateful—or happy.

"What do you want, Rebecca?" Annabel's fists struck her hips. "Bad tea and no art or silver in the house? Nights listening to other families' carriages rock by on their way to parties we weren't invited to attend? A lifetime of being in the shadows?"

"When you left us at the first of the year, you claimed you would rather be in the shadows than trapped in Papa's schemes." Rebecca mirrored her pose, putting them nose to nose. "And you changed your mind."

Burning words climbed Annabel's throat. "I gave you and Rachel a chance for life you would have never—"

"You told us you were going to prove to Father that his scheming was worthless and that you could care for yourself. Instead you did exactly what he'd planned in the first place." Rebecca's eyes glittered. "And don't say it was for us, to give us what we wanted, because you never asked."

Taken aback by the unshed tears, Annabel drew a deep breath and straightened. "Then tell me."

Rebecca blinked.

"Would you have preferred to go the house party?" Annabel worked to banish the sarcasm of her question. She thought she could guess the answer, but this was about more than being right.

"Rachel was disappointed, I think, but we didn't have much time to talk about it. She was busy packing while I was hiding anything Father could sell while we were gone."

Which was why the painting had been cleaned. "Smart girl."

"Good of you to notice." Rebecca snorted a laugh. "I wanted to go to the country to be out in the air, but Bath was almost as good. Plus there were lectures on all sorts of topics. A botanist spent an entire afternoon discussing and displaying the orchids he'd gathered from the jungle."

"You always did like flowers." Annabel walked away from the door and propped her hip against the table, much like Jasper did when they were talking. She was grateful when her sister followed.

"Plants, Annie. I like plants."

"And I despise *Annie*."

"Because Father always shortens our names when he wants something," Rebecca said. Her lips twisted. "But I draw the line at Lady Ramsbury."

"Unless we're in public." Annabel winked. "Speaking of which, we received an invitation to an upcoming Botanical Society lecture. Would you like to attend with me? Jasper will be in Lords." She would miss sitting next to him on the main floor while they tried not to laugh at the gray-bearded men who were shocked by her presence.

"I would, thank you." Rebecca nibbled her bottom lip for a moment. "Do you think we could find a Latin tutor as well?"

"I'll do my best." It would be difficult to find one who wouldn't be scandalized by teaching a young lady.

Annabel blinked. For the first time in years, she didn't worry about the expense. She knew Jasper's accounts like she knew her favorite novel. She also didn't worry about whether Jasper would agree. He was generous to a fault with his family.

"The next time we visit Ramsbury, we'll take you with us. The gardens there are being redone, and the man leading the project is a wonderful teacher."

Rebecca pulled her into a quick, tight embrace. "Thank you." When she pulled away, her smile was bright. "You are happy, aren't you?"

"What?"

"Rachel and I wondered, at first. But he seems to be kind, and he's almost always in good humor. He is, isn't he? He's not one way when we're there and then another when you're alone?"

The knot in her throat kept Annabel from speaking. All she could do was shake her head.

"You smile more, and you say his name very often in conversation." Rebecca's eyes gleamed as she leaned forward, the same as when they'd shared sisterly secrets. "Jane and Johanna say he's quite besotted."

He had also quite thoroughly convinced the *ton* he was a drunkard while sipping on water. Heat climbed Annabel's neck. "You four shouldn't gossip."

"As though we have anything else to do during piano lessons." Rebecca rolled her eyes. "And you know Rachel. *It's so romantic.*"

"Don't tease her so." Annabel led the way from the dining room to the front door.

After one last tight embrace with her sister, she left the house in a better mood than when she had arrived. Her improving relationship with Rebecca was one reason. The other was that Jasper would be waiting at the other end of her journey.

And, yes, despite everything, it was rather romantic.

"Pardon me. So sorry." Jasper tipped his hat to yet another lady, this one because he'd plowed into the other end of her pram.

The baby wailed in his wake as he refocused on the pedestrians in front of him. It was easier to find Raines now that the sea of hats had thinned to a trickle, but it was just as difficult to keep up with him.

"Mind your feet, sir."

"My apologies." Jasper tipped his hat without looking before skirting around another slow-moving couple.

A woman's sturdy, simple cane caught his eye at the last possible moment. He stepped right to avoid kicking it away from her and jostled someone else. Someone much shorter.

"Paper, sir?"

Jasper pulled a coin from his pocket and took the paper with a quick nod and an even briefer smile. It still smelled of ink and would stain his gloves, but it might be a useful disguise. If Raines had spotted him earlier, the paper could throw him off at a second glance.

The young viscount turned the corner, heading away from Mayfair and deeper into town.

Damnation. That was the wrong way. Perhaps he should admit defeat and go home. It was where he wanted to be anyway. He slowed his steps and watched his quarry escape, second-guessing his decision to follow the man in the first place.

"I say! This is a coincidence. How are you, Ramsbury?"

Jasper glanced first to his father-in-law and then up the street to make certain Raines hadn't heard the enthusiastic greeting.

"Baron Chilworth. How are you?" He renewed his pursuit.

All day, something had itched at the back of his brain. It had begun in Lords, where he'd caught Raines staring a few times too often.

"I've just come from Patton's, and he's given me the good news," Chilworth said. He was quieter now that he had to keep up with Jasper's purposeful stride. "It's an odd wedding gift, though. Most husbands give jewelry. I gave my lady wife a set that…"

Annabel's eyes don't light up over jewelry.

Jasper had followed Raines to White's, where the younger man had joined a game of cards and Jasper chose a table with his back to the room, his face to a mirror. He'd reviewed his notes from the day and welcomed anyone who wished to speak with him, but the back of his neck prickled the entire time.

"And it's just in time, as well—the mine stock offer is closing soon," Chilworth said as he fell into step.

"The money will go to your creditors," Jasper said as he checked his pace. It wouldn't do to pass the young viscount on the street simply because he wished to be rid of Annabel's father. If he had to double back, Raines would grow suspicious. He wasn't daft.

"I'm sure many of them would be satisfied with a bulk payment and a note for the rest," Chilworth said. He was huffing in his attempt to keep pace.

"Patton will make the payments to them personally," Jasper snapped. "The money will not go into your hands."

Having played cards with Raines on several occasions, Jasper respected his skill and his strategy. Today he'd watched him do it. His wagers were smaller than normal, and, though always taciturn, he'd spoken few words. He also stared at his cards too long on rounds where he folded. There was a secret there, but Jasper would have to catch him to find it.

"Oh, well then. At least it will free up capital for—"

Jasper stopped his pursuit and faced the baron, heedless of the crowd moving past them and who might hear. He wasn't certain if the man was hapless or stubborn. Perhaps he was addled in some way. Surely no man this stupid could have a daughter as brilliant as Annabel.

Regardless, it was vital that Chilworth hear this conversation and grasp its meaning. "I have written to every banker in London, threatening to remove *my* money should they loan a penny to you without my approval. Which you will not have."

The man's eyes widened in his red, sweaty face. "See here!

That's overstepping."

It likely was, but this man's carelessness had pushed his daughter into more than one devil's bargain. "Dear God, Chilworth. Will you not be happy until all your daughters are in service?"

"I did not send Annabel into service. She chose it to spite me." The baron's eyes flashed. "I told her to take one more Season and do everything she could to make a match."

In Society, with outdated fashions and no dowry, throwing herself at any man who would have her like a bird flailing against a cage. Jasper had seen too many young ladies like that in ballrooms. He knew what men said about them, and he knew the offers they made. Chilworth did, too. It was there in the words he chose. Not a husband—a match.

"And look at her now. A marchioness."

But not of her own free will. Not really. And—dear God—the man seemed to believe the gossip about his own daughter. "Do you realize how badly this could have gone for her? Or do you simply not care?"

"Look here, lad. You've no right to look down your nose at me for trying to better my lot."

"I don't look down on you for that, Chilworth." Raines was almost to the end of the block, where he'd be lost in the shopping crowds. Jasper had wasted enough time on this foolish man who only thought of himself. "I look down on you because you were blind to what you already had."

He left the man standing and threaded his way through the crowd. If Raines looked back, it would be impossible to hide his purpose.

The viscount reached his destination and removed his hat before entering Gunter's.

Jasper had damn near broken his neck to follow a man who was going for ices. Kit would be laughing his arse off. If he were here.

Jasper again weighed proceeding against catching a cab and

heading for home.

In for a penny…

He strolled by the window and glanced inside. Raines was escorting Charlotte Bainbridge to a table. Sometimes men said unguarded things to the women in their lives. Perhaps their conversation could be useful.

Men did not go into Gunter's alone.

A tap on the window caught his attention. Fiona waved from her table in the sunshine.

Jasper strode into the shop and dropped his paper and hat to the table before bowing over her hand. "Thank you for waiting. I ran into a distraction on the street."

She blinked for a moment before catching his game. "You're lucky Mrs. Linden has the day off, or she would have pushed me out the door after five minutes in fear I'd look desperate for company." She thrust his belongings at him and stood. "Let's move to the back. This sun is warmer than I expected."

Jasper led her to a table near enough to watch Raines but far enough to have an alibi.

"You got newsprint on my gloves," Fiona groused. "Mrs. Linden will have to scrub them twice as hard."

"You could wash them yourself." He swept his eyes down the menu. "The sunshine was pleasant, I thought."

"I'd rather not see *Scandalized Socialite Seduces Marquess* as tomorrow's gossip headline." She flicked a glance toward Charlotte. "I quite like Annabel, you know."

Jasper winked at her. "So do I."

The server came to take their order. Lemon for Fiona, and vanilla for Jasper.

"I'm glad to hear it, but your domestic bliss is cheating me out of ballroom gossip. Do you two do nothing but stay at home?"

"We just returned from Ramsbury."

Fiona paused for a moment, nibbling her lip. "How are things?"

"You've spoken with Mother?" Her nod gave him permission to drop his guard. "Nothing much has changed since."

He'd received one letter from Kit, but the message had only been about the progress in Wales. Claudette had charmed Gareth's family, and their reconciliation had unified the Welsh constabulary's pursuit of Collins.

Annabel had stopped paying Kit's wages.

The pay had begun as a salve to his conscience. Kit hadn't wanted it, but Jasper could think of nothing else to do for a man who insisted on walking through every door first, who dropped everything on a whim, and spent his time in unsavory crowds doing little but hiding in the dark.

Their ices arrived, and Jasper tucked into his. He didn't particularly like vanilla, but there had been too many other choices, and his head was beginning to ache.

"This can't be easy for him either," Fiona said.

Jasper had been overwhelmed when he took his father's title, and he'd been prepared for it since birth. Kit had been at his side, watching everything as an outsider, keeping his inheritance a secret while being employed by his cousin. "I'm sure it isn't, but he hasn't asked for help."

Jasper had been paying his cousin to be his friend.

"I'm glad we could see each other today," Fiona said. "Father is sending me to Paris again."

What scrape had she gotten into now? "I thought Mrs. Linden was keeping you out of trouble."

"I am keeping myself out of trouble, thank you. She is there as my guardian angel." Though Fiona's tone was light, she was fiddling with her ice as it melted. "He's decided I should go back out next Season. A visit with Mr. Worth is the first step."

"Fi." He resisted covering her hand with his. Charlotte would be too happy to spread a rumor neither Fiona nor Annabel needed. Instead, he waited for her gaze to meet his.

The doubt he saw there touched the same spot Jane and Johanna found. He wanted to do more to the man that had hurt her than simply break his nose. "You'll be the star of every ball."

Her eyes twinkled. "Not a diamond?"

"Diamonds are overrated." He said it loud enough for Charlotte to hear. "Annabel says so."

His skin prickled. He glanced from Fiona to Raines and caught the young man staring again. Just like he stared at his cards before folding.

When he had something to hide.

CHAPTER NINETEEN

"THANK YOU FOR accepting my invitation." Annabel felt nothing like a marchioness while entertaining her first guest, but she did her best to channel Lady Lambourn as she served coffee.

"I was pleased to receive it." Jocelyn Fletcher added cream and sugar to her cup. "How was your visit to the country?"

Annabel tapped her biscuit against her saucer, debating how to begin, or whether to begin at all. She and Jasper had agreed not to share the details of their visit, but several things concerned her, and she suspected Jocelyn could help.

"We encountered highwaymen on the road to Ramsbury." Just saying the words made her bones shake at the memory of firing the pistol.

"Drake and I had something similar happen, but they were sent to kill us." Jocelyn's brows gathered as she frowned. "Do you think there's a similarity?"

"Our histories share the same man." Annabel's words came out in a rush, and relief washed in to fill the void.

"Tell me everything."

Annabel recounted the story, pouring in every detail that she had rolled over in her brain since that night on the road. She had hoped to make better sense of events, but something still bothered her.

Jocelyn set her coffee aside. "You don't believe this was a simple robbery, do you?"

Annabel saw the moonlight glinting off the narrow sword in every nightmare. Sometimes she didn't have to be asleep. "No."

"And Jasper agrees with you?"

Given that their armed footman had followed behind them at a discreet pace throughout their stay in Ramsbury, and that Jasper had insisted she take carriages rather than walk in London... "Yes."

"Wise man." Jocelyn looked away, staring out the window as she toyed with her necklace. "Is it safe to assume you have fully broken with Spencer?"

The odd choice of words made Annabel pause mid-sip. She put the coffee and treats aside. "How did you know?"

"He doesn't like to be crossed. He and Stratford have that in common." She turned back and refilled her coffee.

Her pebble-hard gaze stole Annabel's breath. It was very much like Yarwood's. A soldier who had faced danger and come out the other side.

"He convinced you of something about your new husband, likely using your family's situation as an incentive. Am I correct?"

Tears pricked Annabel's eyes as she nodded.

"It isn't your fault." The words should have been comforting, but there was little softness in them. "It's what he does, and he has practiced it for years."

Annabel leapt from the sofa and walked to the fireplace, putting distance between them. How could she have been so stupid? "Why didn't you tell me this the first time we met?"

"Because, in my experience, no one changes just because someone tells them to." Jocelyn kept her seat. "And because, from that same experience, I know strength comes as much from bravery as from knowledge." She gave a dry chuckle. "Plus, *Hello, nice to meet you, your employer is a lying prat,* is not the way to make new friends."

It felt good to laugh. Annabel returned to the sofa and lifted a biscuit from her saucer. "New friends are nice to have."

In the companionable silence that stretched between them, she wondered how much to tell her new friend. "He told me Jasper was conspiring against the Crown." Saying it aloud was liberating. "Which is total rubbish." That felt even better.

"It is. But there *is* more to Lord Ramsbury than meets the eye."

"What do you—"

Jocelyn put up a hand. "That's for him to tell you. What *I* can tell you is that Spencer's stories are never far from the truth and, at times, are twisted to mirror his own motives." She shifted in the corner of the sofa and drew her feet up under her. "However, I'm more interested in what you saw during your daring encounter."

"I told you."

"No. You told the story, but something else is bothering you. Something only you saw," Jocelyn said. "Close your eyes."

Annabel did as she asked. The first part she had no problem recalling. "He had a sword, but not..." She drew a deep breath and let her thoughts unwind, like watching a play. "It was an epee, like he was expecting a duel rather than an ambush." *Highwaymen don't duel, do they?*

"Good. What else?" Jocelyn asked. "Was it his horse? Perhaps the color?"

Annabel had been so focused on the man's movements, she'd barely noticed he was riding at all. But color...

"His hair curled out from under the scarf he used as a mask. It glowed in the moonlight like his blade." She followed that hair to the rest of him. Broad shoulders, determined jaw, gritted teeth. She'd seen him before, closing in on her. In a horse race.

"Viscount Raines." Her eyes flew open, and she was shocked to see the world was exactly as she'd left it a moment earlier. "It was Viscount Raines, I'm certain of it."

Jocelyn nodded, though her eyes were sad. "That makes sense. Spencer would want to use someone the *ton* would never suspect, much less accuse."

"What information could Sir Reginald possibly have on Viscount Raines?" The young man was rather a snob and too fond of horses. He never refused a game of cards. But a murderer?

"Raines attacked a young girl at the Rose—my housekeeper's daughter—though I came along before the worst of the damage could be done. Spencer was at my elbow when I had Raines evicted and banned. Half clothed, I might add."

The situation was too common in households, and it was one of the largest reasons Annabel had dreaded going into service. "Is the young lady all right?"

"She is. Once the new school begins in Thetford, she'll be moving in with us," Jocelyn said. "But Miss Bainbridge's well-connected father might not want his daughter—or her dowry—going to a rapist in the making."

So Spencer had convinced him to kill Jasper? It seemed a bit far-fetched on its face, but he'd used a less potent reason to convince Annabel to become a spy.

"I do not know how Spencer is connected to Jasper otherwise, but I can hazard a guess that Raines's behavior is only one layer of secrets." Jocelyn chose a cake from the tray. "I also suspect your safety, and your husband's, depends on your trusting one another."

"If I tell him, I'm afraid I'll lose him." Annabel wasn't certain which would be worse, being sent away or being kept on hand for appearances.

"He may surprise you." Jocelyn finished her coffee and stood. Her smile was warm. "You have certainly surprised me."

Annabel saw her to the door and swept her into a quick embrace. "Thank you."

"Call on me anytime. It's rare that my skills can be used in Society."

Jocelyn was going down the steps as the family carriage pulled to the door. Stapleton's march echoed through the hall.

"Lady Ramsbury?" He already had her coat and hat. "His

lordship has asked that we bring you to him."

Jocelyn's words made Annabel less resentful of her Frederick-shaped shadow and the carriage that kept her out of the sunshine. She rode in the middle of the seat, her fingers clenched into a fist to fight the urge to stare out the window and see if anyone was following. The quiet pressed on her like a winter cloak.

There is more to Lord Ramsbury than meets the eye. Annabel gave an unladylike snort. There was more to everyone in this scheme than met the eye. It was a maze that made her head spin until she didn't know up from down. All she knew was she needed to find a way out, through her father's debts, her sisters' futures, and past a killer viscount only she could identify—someone who was a threat to the man she loved.

She'd felt it for weeks, though she'd originally marked it down to the intimacies she and Jasper shared. Making love with a handsome man turned every woman's head, didn't it? But every day gave her a glimpse of the man behind the face that sent every Society lady into a swoon. And when Raines had aimed his sword at Jasper's neck, the cold anger that flooded her spoke of something deeper than attraction.

"I have to tell him the truth," Annabel whispered. She wouldn't be another person in his life who loved him too much to be honest. Besides that, if Spencer had been desperate enough to send Raines as an assassin, Jasper was somehow a threat to a larger plot. He needed to know everything.

If she lost him because of it, at least he would be safe.

Outside the window, the crowds and noise faded. Rather than the creamy-white uniformity of houses in Belgravia and Mayfair, the homes here had their own personalities, and they faced the Green Park. If Annabel squinted, she could just make out the spires of Buckingham Palace.

The coach slowed to a stop, and the door opened. Rather than Frederick with his serious stare, Jasper stuck his head into the coach. "Welcome home, Lady Ramsbury."

His wide smile was irresistible as he helped her from the

carriage and led her forward.

Rather than imposing steps, the red-doored entrance was simple, and the front windows were skirted with flower boxes. Once inside, the hall was generous, but not grand, and the stairwell coiled along the walls. Scaling three stories. A large glass window, set in the roof, flooded the space with light.

"Welcome to Ramsbury House," Jasper said, still keeping hold of her hand. "I wanted to ensure the roof was sound before we visited."

"It's beautiful." If they stood on the top floor at night, they might be able to see the stars. Annabel slid free of him and pulled her pin from her hat.

"While I'm glad you're free of those ridiculous ribbons, I'm worried that pin will puncture your brain."

She fingered the lovely onyx and ruby-headed pin that reached from her fingertips to her wrist. "I thought that was the reason you bought it."

He put his lips to hers in a warm kiss, and she felt him smile before he withdrew. "Your brain is one of my favorite things about you, darling."

Eager to explore, Annabel walked into the drawing room, where the rugs were rolled against the walls and the furnishings were shrouded. Jasper lifted a cover to reveal a green sofa that had been in style several years earlier.

"Grandfather wasn't much for entertaining." Jasper grimaced. "There's not even a ballroom. If you'd prefer, we could stay—"

"I love it here," Annabel said, meaning every word. Ramsbury House was a home. She could imagine raising a family here—a rowdy gang of laughing, tow-headed boys.

"You can decorate however you'd like." Jasper took her hand and led her from the room, talking as he pulled her along. "Paint, wallpaper, whatever furnishings you want—but there's one last room I want you to see."

They walked to the back of the house, away from the street. The door opened to an empty library. At the far end of the narrow room, a large bay window with a deep seat overlooked a small, private garden—or what would be one eventually. The scent of new paint hung in the air. The green walls would match the view.

"Do you like it?" he asked.

"I do." She ran her fingers across the top of a crate, wondering what was inside. "Are these your grandfather's books?"

Rather than answering her, Jasper lifted the lid. A beloved marble face, shrouded in straw, stared back at her.

"Plato?" Annabel ran her finger along the base, finding the divot Rachel and Rebecca had caused while playing tag. Mother had heard the crash and flown through the house, terrified the immortalized philosopher had killed one of her daughters. Novels filled the remainder of the box, their titles like the names of old friends.

Aristotle was in the second box with the geography books. Annabel's vision blurred so that she couldn't read the titles. Tears filled her eyes as she looked up at her husband.

He was to her in two long steps. Annabel leaned into his arms.

"I remembered your face when you were in the library at Ramsbury." He pulled her closer. "And thinking you must have loved the library at Chilworth—this library. It belongs with you."

"You are a constant surprise." She cradled his heavy jaw in her palm and let his soft hair tickle her fingers. "Thank you, Jasper."

"That look makes me wish the bed upstairs wasn't in pieces."

She stood on her tiptoes to reach his ear. "Then perhaps we should go back to Lambourn House."

"In the middle of the afternoon?" Jasper gave a mock gasp. "Lady Ramsbury, you shock me."

Annabel evaded his grasp and stepped to the third crate. "Far be it from me to scandalize such an upstanding—"

Jasper snatched her hand and dragged her to the door. "I'll show you upstanding." His laughter tumbled up the stairs. "Get your hat."

At the coach, she turned back to look at the gracious, unique home which now held something other than tempting promises. She missed it already.

"Ramsbury?"

She turned but got only a glimpse of a tall man in a black coat with his hat pulled low over his eyes before Jasper stepped in front of her. The man brushed past at a brisk pace, pushing Jasper aside.

Trapped between his back and the coach, Annabel reached to steady him before he crushed her. He doubled over with a gasp.

"Get in the coach," he said. "Now."

Annabel reached for the door and stopped. Her glove was soaked in blood.

She spun to stare at Jasper. His lips were set in a firm line, matching the hard curve of his jaw. Blood seeped across his side, staining his waistcoat with alarming speed.

"Frederick!" She'd meant the word to come out as a command. It was more a shriek.

The footman came to help, but Annabel pushed him away. "Find that man. Dark coat, dark cap. He went into the park."

He followed her instructions without pause or a backward glance.

"Lawrence, take us to hosp—"

"Home," Jasper rasped as he urged her into the coach. "We'll be safer at home."

Annabel's arguments died on her lips. His blond hair was dark against his pallid, sweaty face. "Home, Lawrence," she barked. "As fast as you can go."

Jasper fell into the seat, eyes closed. His every wheezing breath twisted Annabel's own lungs. She pushed her shawl against the wound, but the useless fabric was more a sieve than a bandage.

"It will be fine." Jasper's fingers slipped from hers. "Don't let Mother worry." His eyes drifted closed.

Tears blurred her vision. "Hurry," she whispered, willing the horses to go faster, though the motion of the carriage added to her sick stomach and spinning head. At the next turn, Jasper slid against her like a rag doll. His forehead was cool against her lips.

"Faster, Lawrence," she screamed. "Hurry!"

CHAPTER TWENTY

THE HOUSE WAS too quiet.

Annabel wanted nothing more than to run through the halls and wake everyone just so she wouldn't be alone in her worry, but Jasper's last words—his last *coherent* words—had stuck in her head as Travis and Lawrence had wrestled him up the back stairs and to his room, after Stapleton had rushed the female staff into the front of the house for hastily invented tasks.

Only Barnes knew anything, as she had stripped off Annabel's bloody clothes, and she'd been as tight-lipped as the grave.

Annabel shivered. She would not even *think* that word in this room.

Jasper's color had returned while he slept, and his third set of bandages remained clean. Travis's stitches had finally done their work.

Just as there was more to her husband than met the eye, there was more to the men surrounding him. Frederick and Lawrence had already proven their mettle under fire; now Travis was exposed as a medic, if not a surgeon. Even Stapleton was standing guard at the door, a rifle within reach, since slinging it over his shoulder would cause alarm.

She'd stopped bathing Jasper when his skin had warmed. His bandages didn't need to be changed, and his bedding was dry. There was nothing to do but sit here and watch him breathe while she considered the attack.

Ramsbury House had been under repair for months. There would be no reason for anyone to lie in wait for them there, which meant they had been followed. Jasper had either arrived on foot or in a cab, which meant he'd been one of a crowd or in a carriage that looked very much like any other. It would have made him difficult to find. She had been in the more conspicuous conveyance, and leaving the family home.

The assassin-the *would-be* assassin—had followed her to find Jasper. She had crossed Spencer by refusing to spy for him, and then Jasper had crossed him again by paying off her father's debts and loosening the strings that bound her to his malicious will.

But it had also untied her tongue. There would be no repercussions for her family, at least for the foreseeable future, if she confided in her husband.

The consequences would be hers alone.

A knock sounded a moment before the door opened. Frederick entered, smoothing his dark hair. "My apologies, your ladyship, but Stapleton said to come up without him." His gaze went to the bed and to his master.

"He'll be fine." Annabel had repeated the phrase like an incantation all evening. "Were you able to find the cowardly bastard who did this?"

The young man's wide eyes flew back to hers, and his cheeks reddened. Annabel ignored the heat creeping up her neck. There was no shame in letting the world know what she thought of the man who had tried to kill her husband.

"I was able to catch up to him, but he slithered away before I could get a solid hold." He returned to his usual color. "If I hadn't been in a crowd, I'd have shot him, but…"

Blast. Annabel nodded. "You were right, of course."

"I did give his right arm a good wrench. I'd imagine he'll be in pain from either his shoulder or his elbow."

A man favoring his right arm in a town full of laborers. It would be as useless to search as it had been to give chase in the first place.

Annabel made herself smile as she put a hand on his solid shoulder. Worry and exhaustion clouded his eyes. "Thank you, Frederick. I'm glad you're back safely." She opened the door. "Mrs. Elliot should have a warm plate for you in the kitchen."

"I'll be happy to spell Stapleton on watch, my lady."

Once a soldier, always a soldier. "Take that up with Stapleton after you've eaten."

She closed the door and rested her head against it. *Safer at home,* Jasper had said. No wonder. There was a small private army between them and the street, and Yarwood had hired them all.

He should be here as well.

"Cowardly bastard?" Jasper croaked in a whisper.

Annabel rushed to the bed and to the hard chair that had tortured her almost as much as her guilt. "You've been a bad influence." Tears clogged her throat, garbling the last word. She swallowed them down. He didn't need to see her cry.

"Help me sit." He pushed against the mattress to no avail. "I don't want to stare at the canopy all night."

"Stop fidgeting before you tear your stitches." Rather than tugging him upright, Annabel slid pillows under his shoulders until he was reclining. "Better?"

He nodded and reached for her. His fingers were almost as cold as the sheet, but they were always chilled. It was normal.

He's going to be fine.

The tears she'd been keeping at bay all evening now flooded down her cheeks.

"Come here."

Rather than obeying him, she stood and pulled her handkerchief from her pocket. If she crawled onto the bed, she might tear his stitches herself. And if she was in his arms, she would never tell him the truth.

She walked to the fireplace and let the warmth give her courage. "This was my fault."

"Annabel—"

"Let me finish." She made herself face him. He deserved to see her as she confessed. "Reginald Spencer hired me to prove you were a spy."

His lazy grin was not what she'd expected. Perhaps he wasn't fully himself.

"I know," he whispered.

What? "How?"

"No one climbs a ladder to read ledgers, darling. No matter how boring a party might be." He pushed himself straighter and grimaced with the effort. "And there was no other reason for you to be in my room."

Annabel was glued to the floor. He'd known, and he'd married her anyway. "I don't understand."

"I don't either, not really." Jasper sagged against the pillows and, despite his earlier complaint, stared at the ceiling. "I didn't intend things to go this way, but I saw you in tears and knew it was my doing. And the way you said *I don't want to marry you…* It was clear someone else wanted you to, someone you couldn't ignore—and you'd already proven you could disobey your father's wishes." His dry laugh ended in a cough. "I thought that, if Spencer was pushing you, then maybe I could learn what he wanted."

Annabel's pulse echoed in her hollow chest. *Keep your friends close.* "Keep your enemies closer," she whispered. Her fingers found the twists in the belt of her hastily tied dressing gown.

"You aren't my enemy." Jasper raised his head. His blue eyes were bright and clear. "And I'm not yours."

There is more to Lord Ramsbury than meets the eye. "What are you, then?"

He shrugged, but his stare remained level. "A spy, but not how you think."

"How, then?" she whispered. Questions begat more questions. Right now it was best to focus on the ones that wouldn't break her heart.

"The queen has asked Kit and me to uncover an embezzler, but we think the money is part of a larger scheme."

"I see." She didn't. All she could see was that Kit wasn't here, and Jasper was wounded. "Spencer is involved."

It wasn't a question. She was certain of it, though she didn't yet know how a chaplain in the royal household could breach the treasury or why he would do it.

Jasper's nod wobbled as he covered a yawn. "You told him you'd find the truth. *That's* the truth."

She'd told Spencer that the night Jasper first kissed her. When he'd confessed to things much more trivial than a mission for the queen, and she had let him closer than anyone had ever been yet told him nothing.

The night she'd unlocked her door.

"What happens now?" she asked.

There wasn't an answer. Jasper was asleep, his broad chest rising and falling in a reassuring rhythm. The bandages peeked out above the blankets with every inhale.

Annabel made sure he wasn't bleeding and tucked the blankets tighter to keep him warm, then returned to the torturous chair to keep watch. It would be just like him to open his wounds in a fit of stubborn independence and bleed to death while she slept in the other room.

The fire popped and sizzled, and the candles sputtered. Darkness danced along the walls in random patterns that grew more menacing the longer she stared. It was easy to see their ending. Arguments. Isolation. Loneliness.

Annabel drew a deep breath. If she didn't rein herself in, she'd be mad by morning.

She knew the shadows. She'd lived in them before. The light was more difficult to see. She'd had glimpses of it, so brief it was difficult to believe it was permanent. Anything could happen.

Anything. She gritted her teeth and stared at her fears.

There was more to her than met the eye.

CHAPTER TWENTY-ONE

JASPER SHIFTED, AND pain sent him curling around the pillow—which was helpful, since he didn't want Annabel to hear him scream. He'd had muscle pains and stitches before. He'd even woken with cramps from sleeping in odd positions.

He'd never had them all at the same time.

The cool sheets should have been soothing. Instead, they reminded him he was alone in bed for the first time in weeks.

He hadn't slept alone, though. Time had passed in fitful gaps, but Annabel had been there whenever he woke, dozing beside him in a chair that looked like it had been used in the Inquisition. She had fussed over him in in her quiet way, as silent as the gray ghost he'd once teased her of being.

Jasper had considered joking with her, just to see her smile. He'd thought better of it when he saw the questions swirling in her eyes.

The door between their rooms gaped open like an empty mouth.

"Annabel?" Hating the tremble in his voice, he cleared his throat. "Annabel?"

The only answer he received was an echo.

He'd botched it. Half out of his mind on laudanum and weak from blood loss, he'd believed she would welcome no longer having secrets between them. Instead, she looked as though he was going to lock her in the Tower of London.

Gritting his teeth, Jasper reached to the bell rope and fell back against the pillows, swearing against the pain.

The door flew open, shocking in both the force of it and how quickly Travis answered the call.

"What the bloody hell did you do?" Kit roared. "And why the deuce didn't you wait for me?"

Travis pushed past him like he wasn't there. "What do you need, your lordship?"

"Where is my wife?" Jasper demanded. "And why is no one at the door?"

"Lady Ramsbury is in the garden with your mother and sisters explaining your…illness and necessary quarantine. Frederick is with her, at a distance that will not worry Lady Lambourn, so Stapleton—"

"Stapleton is at the door and didn't receive word that I shouldn't be let up." Kit strode in the room. "Thank you, Travis. If you'll leave—"

"Don't order my staff about. This is not your house." Jasper tossed the covers back and gratefully accepted Travis's arm to stand. "What day is it?"

"Thursday, sir."

Two days. He'd been asleep for *two days*. Annabel was likely wandering the house stooped in the shape of that blasted chair.

The medic-cum-valet helped him into his dressing gown but, thankfully, left it for him to tie himself. Even that simple act was exhausting. "Thank you for your help, Travis."

"I'll send a maid up with a tray. Some good coffee, scones, and eggs will serve you well. Both of you." Travis left the room without a backward glance.

Kit glowered from his place near the hearth. "Still wishing you'd gone to war?"

"Still hating being an earl?" Laughing sent needles to Jasper's fingertips. "Because you seem to be adjusting well."

The maid arrived with a rattling tray that had been prepared so promptly it was likely waiting for him to wake. He'd have Annabel to thank for that. Sitting was a combination of relief and torture, but he managed. Just.

Kit sat in the opposite chair. After filling a coffee cup, he helped himself to a scone—devouring half of it in one bite. "I'm tired."

"And hungry, apparently." Jasper sipped his coffee and nibbled on his eggs, waiting to see if his hunger would reap the consequences of being drugged during minor surgery. "Don't you have a cook?"

"I did when I left." Kit lifted a piece of streaky bacon from the tray. "But I've been in Wales, fetching Claudette."

"You didn't tell me you were going to Cardiff." Jasper buttered a scone.

"You didn't tell me you were going to get into a knife fight."

When he'd had to protect himself or someone else, he'd always been armed and prepared. Last night he'd done nothing but step in front of Annabel and offer himself as a sacrifice to stupidity. He'd known better than to let down his guard. "It was less fight and more ambush."

"Where?"

"Outside Ramsbury House. Repairs are finished, so I wanted to show it to Annabel. She met me there after the session ended." He shook his head, cursing himself a fool for putting her in danger. "We left, someone approached us, and I don't remember much after that."

Except Annabel telling him everything he already knew but not sharing his relief in the knowing.

"Was it one of your highwaymen?"

"Possibly, but it was dark during the first attack, and this one was too fast." He'd always thought he'd be better at details. "How are things in Cardiff?"

"Claudette has worked her magic. Gareth's father is falling all over himself to make up for lost time." Kit swallowed a gulp of coffee and grimaced at the burn. "And you know how the major gets when the bit's between his teeth."

In the months after Gareth's death, his father had been ready to rouse a mob and storm Paris in a search for his son's *murderous bitch of a wife.* "They've mended fences, then?"

"It's delicate, but I think bringing Collins to justice will solidify it."

Gareth would be pleased, and so was Kit, given the look on his face. "There's progress?"

"Put a widow in a room full of women who waited for men to come home from war, or doting pensioners who see a pretty, sad young lady alone?" Kit snorted a laugh. "We should have done it earlier. They're lining up to talk to her. Some of it has helped our investigation, but much of it has done wonders for her. They've given her a full sketch of the Gareth they knew before the war. She's happier, and the major is putting pressure on the constable, who is drawing the circle tighter."

"Why did you bring her back to London, then?"

"She needs a break from death and reminiscing, Jasper." He cleaned his mouth and chin with a serviette. "And I'd like her away from Cardiff if Collins panics. I don't want her alone."

"She'll have to stay here." Jasper grinned at his newest cousin's confused frown. "You're an earl, Kit. And there are already rumors that Claudette is *my* mistress. A night in your house will have the *ton* spinning tales that we're sharing her. You'd have to marry her." He raised an eyebrow. "Do you *want* to marry her?"

"One forced marriage is enough." Kit rolled his eyes. "It will look like a family epidemic."

Which would reflect poorly on the girls. "You're right. One of us is bad enough."

"I'll ask the maids to make up a room."

Jasper twisted to the door—the one he hadn't closed—and swore as his stitches caught and stretched. Wetness seeped over his skin. Annabel was standing there, but the light behind her made her a silhouette. A thin one.

He always forgot how slight she was.

She stood at the threshold as though she were waiting on an invitation she had never needed.

"Thank you." He didn't dare invite her closer. She would see the blood. He couldn't stand for the same reason. "Would you put her across the hall, please? She has—"

"Of course." She bowed to him. It was a mere dip of her chin as she clutched her skirts, but it was a bloody *bow*. His bandage was squishy and warm against his skin.

"Annabel, it isn't—"

"My mother has sent a card, asking me to call on family business. Since you won't be alone in the house, I'll go now." Her words were level, but her voice was lifeless.

There was no possibility of her listening to reason now.

"Take the coach and Frederick." He didn't say please. It wasn't a request. If he couldn't keep her safe, he'd make damn sure someone did.

"Lord Warwick?" she called without entering the room. "Will you stay until we return? I don't want...the household unprotected."

Kit arched an eyebrow, likely hearing the same hesitation in her statement. Her concern had become the people in the house, not just her husband. Perhaps not her husband at all. "As long as Lord Ramsbury doesn't toss me out on my ear, my lady."

"Thank you." She stood for a moment. "Goodbye."

Those words, in her flat voice, sent a chill through Jasper. Ignoring his wet bandages, he kept his eyes on her blank face. "I will see you when you come home, Annabel."

He blinked and she was gone.

"Shall we play chess or poker?" Kit asked. "I can finally make the ante—"

"Get Travis." The room began to tilt. "Now."

He left without question and without a backward glance. Everyone in Jasper's life seemed to do that. He pressed his hand to his side and gritted his teeth.

Don't pity yourself. Only your wife ran away from you.

Quick, light steps in the hallway curved his lips into a smile. Annabel was worried about him after all.

"Jasper! Wait until you—" Claudette stuttered to a stop, her eyes widening, when she saw the state of him. "I don't understand. Your wife said you were expecting me."

Jasper's disappointment doubled. Not only had Annabel misinterpreted his humor and ignored his attempts to explain, but she'd also fallen back to *ton* gossip over his connection to Claudette. Because a man would be expected to meet his mistress in his dressing gown.

"I am very happy to see you." Jasper made himself smile, though sweat trickled down his spine. "But I'm sure you're exhausted. Your room is across the hall."

Travis hurried into the room with Kit on his heels.

"Leave us please, Claudette." Jasper struggled to his feet. "We'll visit—" His knees buckled without warning. "Damn."

his whiskey-soaked breath. "They'll be your age or better, and they'll treat Rachel like property because that's what you'll make her. You'll sell her into marriage for the price of worthless stocks and then look the other way when they take their losses out on her." She was lucky that—or worse—hadn't happened to her.

"You'll give your mother tea and sisters dresses, but you won't spare me an investment that will put me back—"

"I will give the girls a chance at a better life, which is the same as you have now. Your debts are paid. Your rents are yours again."

"Rents are a pittance." It was his turn to snort. "It would take years to finance an investment that would make any difference."

This was not the father she knew. He'd spent hours tromping through the fields surveying fence lines and livestock, laughing with the farmers who depended on him. Some of her fondest memories were of him rowing across the small lake as she listened to stories from his childhood.

"When did our home, our family, stop being enough for you?" she asked. "When did it become all or nothing, and this grasping desperation?"

"You know nothing of what it takes to make a success."

He was wrong. She'd watched Jasper since their marriage. He worked diligently at both building his reputation and protecting his family. He was honorable and kind, intelligent and patient.

He was also an arse who had just put his mistress in the room across the hall.

"I know it's not being blind to what you've done to the people who loved you." Annabel blinked away her tears. She would not cry in front of him. "It's not drinking in a shell of a house and bemoaning the luck you made for yourself. And it isn't selling your nineteen-year-old daughter to a man old enough to be her father."

"In time she will realize how this decision benefits her family."

The man she'd loved would have never treated his daughters

like commodities to be bartered for his own benefit. If he had, she never would have left them alone with him. She wasn't going to abandon them again. "I have risked more than you will ever know," she said. "And I will lose more than you will ever understand." She drew a deep breath. "But my sisters will marry men who love them."

"You have no say on this matter." He reached for the copy of *Debrett's*.

She pushed it away. "I have no say, but I have a voice. If you barter Rebecca and Rachel for foolish schemes, everyone in the *ton* will know." She knew better than anyone how one whisper would become a chorus. "All of London will learn that you would see your wife in the poorhouse and your daughters sold as broodmares and mistresses so long as your pockets are lined."

"You wouldn't court a scandal like that."

She had married a man to spy on him and ended up in his bed. She had shot at highwaymen and held that same husband's bleeding body in her arms. She'd confessed her mission but withheld her heart, and he'd installed his mistress under her nose. "I am already scandalous. It won't make a difference."

Especially if she was never seen in London again.

"Annie—"

She ignored his wheedling tone and lifted a page from the sheaf of paper he always kept nearby. "Go upstairs and do something about your appearance." She took his pen. "I'll summon Mr. Drew here immediately. When he arrives, you will apologize for being out of sorts and give your permission for this marriage."

If he didn't, she'd loan Rachel the Ramsbury carriage for a run toward Scotland.

He remained in his chair, daring Annabel to move him like a child. Unlike the last time they'd argued, when she'd let him continue driving them toward poverty, she stared him down. Relief only came when realization dawned, and he pushed himself upright and walked toward the door with a straight spine but wobbly legs.

Once alone, Annabel finished the letter before ringing the bell. She was blotting the ink on the envelope when Symes, their beloved butler, appeared. His face was lined with concern.

"You rang, Lady Ann—Lady Ramsbury?"

She wasn't sure what kept him with a family who couldn't pay him, but she was forever grateful for his steadying presence. "Please have this letter delivered to the Drew household immediately, and ask Cook to prepare for visitors." She stopped. "Father will require a strong pot of coffee."

"A maid just took up a tray." The old butler smiled. "We thought it would be wise to have on hand."

"Thank you." She stood on tiptoe to kiss his rough cheek as she left the room. "And Lady Annabel is fine, Symes."

There were times, like today, where she missed being *Lady Annabel*. She would forever be tied to the Ramsbury name now, whether or not she and Jasper lived together. Unless, of course, he divorced her, which he might do.

She'd always known divorce was possible, even likely, given her reasons for entering the marriage and her ties to the man who wanted to see him hang. It was even more possible now that Claudette was in the house. There was no reason to hide behind a charade, was there?

Pain lanced through her at the thought of all she'd never get to do again, and none of it had anything to do with ball gowns, teas, or grand houses—unless you counted the gardens.

Misery filled the gap that regret had created, but Annabel forced it to flow through her before she wept rivers that would shock even her romantic youngest sister.

Admit it. You fell in love with a man for the best and worst of reasons, and he sat in his room laughing about his poor decisions. You knew this was a possibility.

She had been through worse, and those experiences had taught her how to survive.

Putting one foot in front of the other, she walked down the

hall, past the staircase, and to the drawing room. By the time she arrived at the door, her back was straight and her smile was wide.

"Rachel, dearest, Peter is returning to speak with Father. Let's get some cold cloths for your eyes so he doesn't second-guess his decision."

⁓

"Where the bloody hell is she?"

Jasper looked at the book in his lap as though it could answer his question. It couldn't even hold his attention past the first line.

He wasn't worried. Lawrence and Frederick would look out for her—unless she convinced them to help her make a run for it. Given her state when she'd left, he wouldn't be surprised. Though more likely she'd send them home without her to avoid witnesses and to get a running start.

He *wasn't* worried. Family matters, he knew, could get complicated. Dressmaker appointments took hours; packing for travel took weeks. Jane and Johanna always ended up sniping over who had more lace on their sleeves, or the larger trunk.

"She'll be back, and you can talk. She knows the consequences of Claudette staying in Kit's home alone better than anyone."

It's how she got into this marriage in the first place.

Jasper swung his feet over the edge of the mattress and let his feet take his weight, ensuring he wouldn't fall if he stood. He was lightheaded, true, but the room didn't spin and his knees stayed firm. All he had to do was not twist.

If he'd been more careful this afternoon, he could have explained things to Annabel while looking her in the eye. He also could have avoided passing out—though at least that had spared him the torture of new stitches.

I don't wish to marry you.

She'd told him that the day he'd proposed. And, in the name of his mission and his family name, he had convinced her to do it

244

anyway. He'd promised her everything but love. She'd told him she didn't even expect loyalty. Was it any wonder that she had assumed the worst of him?

How did he begin to convince her—

A muffled scream had him moving toward the door as quickly as he could manage. Once through, another noise from across the hall, a sharp wail that would have proven to Annabel how well their room muffled sound.

Jasper entered Claudette's room without knocking—it wouldn't have mattered anyway—and went to her bedside. She was bolt upright, eyes open but unseeing.

"Claudette." He took her hand. *"Très chère, réveille-toi."* French always worked best to rouse her. *"Réveille-toi. Tu es en sécurité."* She had quieted, but her stare was still vacant. Her short, panting breaths sounded as though she'd run a foot race in her sleep. *"Tout est bien."*

Her shoulders sagged, taking her chin with them. Jasper perched on the edge of the bed and braced himself as she fell against him. He kept a steady stream of comforting French platitudes until her breaths grew longer and more even.

"Je suis désolé," Claudette mumbled. "I had hoped my…*cauchemars* would not reappear."

She said the same thing every time she visited. Nightmares would likely hound her until they found Gareth. Seeing Jasper weak and bloody this afternoon likely hadn't helped. He shifted, working to relieve the pressure on his stitches so it didn't happen again. "Would you like to tell me?"

She shook her head. "They are always the same. I can hear him but not find him, and the longer I search, the more desperate he becomes." She gave a watery sniffle. "I miss him, Jasper."

They all did. The man's laugh, his sense of adventure, had been impossible to ignore. "He was a special man." If they were right, if Collins had taken Gareth from them, the man would pay. One way or another, they would all have peace.

"I hope I did not disturb your wife." Claudette sat straighter and wiped her eyes with the sleeve of her ridiculously frilly nightdress.

Jasper shook his head. "She is still with her family."

"You are worried," Claudette said. "I can hear it in what you do not say."

Annabel shouldn't have to deal with things alone, but Jasper couldn't have gone even if she'd asked. Which she hadn't done. That was almost more worrisome than what might have been waiting for her.

"Her father is very challenging, and she is very determined." He wasn't certain what else he could say. Annabel had left without a word or even a backward glance.

"That can be a difficult combination," Claudette said. "She seemed *plein d'émotions* when she left."

Full of emotions. With the French, that could mean she was weeping hysterically or carrying a gun. "She can handle herself." He said it as much as for his own reassurance as for an explanation to Claudette. Whatever her family's problem, Annabel had the strength and intelligence to manage it.

"Even strong women need their husbands," Claudette whispered. "Sometimes more than others. Perhaps even more than they may realize." She pushed his arm. "Go wait for her return. She will need you more than I."

Jasper waited until she was settled against the pillows and then left the room.

He felt Annabel's presence before he saw her at the top of the stairs.

Bollocks. Would he never learn to check the hallway before he stumbled from a room in a compromising position?

For a moment he considered explaining Claudette's terrible nightmares, but one look at his wife's stiff shoulders and white knuckles hinted she wouldn't believe him anyway. "Welcome home."

"Thank you." She didn't move from her place, halfway between the stairs and her door. Too far to reach, but close enough he could see her struggle for what to say next.

"Annabel," he began. "I—"

"You're pale." She was strangling her gloves as she stared at him with eyes that were too bright. "Are you well?"

"I overdid it while you were gone." Jasper kicked himself when her eyes went to the door behind him. "How did you leave your family?" he asked as he stepped toward her.

"Peter Drew offered for Rachel."

He knew Drew's family. His uncle was an honest man who ran his estates well. He was also a formidable proponent in Lords for agricultural protections. From what Jasper knew of Peter, he was a levelheaded chap who would do credit to the title when he inherited it. "It would be a good match, if she's agreeable."

"She's over the moon." Annabel walked to her door, away from him so that all he could see was her simply styled hair. "They are madly in love."

She should have sounded happier, and, if all she'd been doing was celebrating a happy match, she should have been home hours ago. He followed her. "What happened?"

"Father." She sighed. "He decided if Rachel was ready to marry, he could match her to someone with a larger purse, someone so grateful for a young wife that he'd support any scheme her father suggested."

Any goodwill would end the moment the investment soured, and Rachel would likely suffer the consequences. "You fought him."

It wasn't a question. He didn't need it to be. Annabel would do anything for her sisters, even marry the devil himself.

"I blackmailed him into agreeing and then stayed until the contracts were signed. They are downstairs in your safe, along with his copy of *Debrett's*." She looked at him then, and the disappointment dulling her eyes and muting her happiness made Jasper ache to hold her.

"I also promised to help them elope if he became a problem, so we might need to borrow the carriage." She sighed. "But you'll be relieved of sponsoring Rebecca. She'd rather go to college than have another Season."

She hadn't moved from her dressing table, but the distance between them was widening. "We should host a party for Rachel and Peter," Jasper said. "A proper engagement ball." Every young woman in love deserved that.

Annabel hadn't had one. She'd never asked.

Her smile was too quick and too thin. "Thank you, but we agreed to a Season and a match, if possible. We didn't negotiate a party. We didn't even say anything about lessons or house parties, which you've already provided." She looked around the room as though she were trying to memorize it, but she wouldn't look at him. "You've been far too generous already."

"Dammit, Annabel." She was turning their life into a balance sheet, and though all the numbers were in his column, he was still losing. "Don't do this."

"You were coming out of her room, Jasper."

It was on the tip of his tongue to rail at her for sending a vulnerable young widow to his room when he was a bloody mess and then judging him for settling that same woman's nightmares, for walking away from him when he'd needed her to hold his hand. But she hadn't been aware of any of that. If she had been, she would have stayed with him.

He knew that because he *knew* her. He'd felt it at Amelia's blasted house party and that silly limerick contest, where she had skewered everything Society held dear with one simple rhyme.

There once was a man with a daughter,
Whom he led like a lamb to the slaughter.
And though she did bleat,
He swore she was sweet;
But pity the young man who caught her.

The woman in front of him was no lamb to be led anywhere, but she also wasn't aware of how magnificent she was. And she didn't know him at all.

"After everything that has passed between us, that's what you think of me?" He kept his tone quiet. He didn't want to fight with her, but he wouldn't let her assumptions stand. "That I would be callous enough to do that to you?" He walked to the door between their rooms, careful not to shuffle, though he felt ancient and frail. Today had drained him of everything he had.

On his side of the threshold, he turned back to face her. It felt wrong to see her this way, to leave her alone. "I'm sorry that your father has disappointed you, Annabel, but I'm not him." His fingers tightened on the latch. "Not everyone in your life wants to hurt you."

He made himself close the door, and he made himself stay quiet when the floorboard creaked as she approached—only to twist the key in the lock.

And later, as he lay in the dark in his cold bed and stared at his boring ceiling, he balled his fingers into fists as his wife cried herself to sleep.

❦

CHAPTER TWENTY-THREE

THE LONDON GARDEN was too small to provide much of a distraction, so Annabel took her time in examining each stalk before pruning it and second-guessing whether a weed was actually a weed. However, pondering every decision allowed her to consider *every* decision.

Not everyone in your life wants to hurt you.

Yet he'd still been in Claudette's room. The look on his face, like a child caught sneaking a forbidden treat, had flayed her heart to pieces.

"It's your own fault," she muttered as she uprooted a weed, ferreting out all the sprawling tendrils to prevent its return. "You told him to keep going as he had been, and he has."

She stripped off her gloves to dig her fingers in the dirt. It was easier to follow the roots' paths and determine if they'd tangled with useful plantings. "And his enjoying you in bed doesn't prevent him from enjoying other women." She dug under the errant plant and lifted it away, shaking the usable dirt back into the hole. "Or vice versa."

The weed landed in the bucket with a soft *whump*. "If peers with mistresses ceased sleeping with their wives, there would be no one in Lords by now."

Jasper's pale face had been grooved with pain, and he'd held himself awkwardly. She'd had a doll once that, if twisted, lost its head. She'd treated it with care, cradling it in her arms. She'd wanted to do the same with her husband.

I overdid it while you were gone.

He and Claudette had been apart for months.

Not everyone sought to hurt people, but they were hurt all the same.

She moved to the next rosebush, dead-heading the faded blooms and checking for pests. They had been honest about their reasons for marriage, and he'd lived up to his side of their bargain. Fairness demanded she do the same.

But she loved him too much to knowingly share him with someone else. She would have to make plans to leave. Annabel blinked to clear her vision before she lifted her clippers to a stray stem.

"Lady Ramsbury?"

Annabel dropped her tool, and the stem whipped forward, driving the thorn into her thumb. The tears she'd been ignoring trickled down the edge of her nose. "Blast."

"I am sorry to interrupt," Claudette said in her soft voice with its musical lilt. "If you would prefer, I can wait inside until you are finished."

I would prefer you go back to bloody Paris and wait until hell freezes over. Annabel paused. None of her etiquette lessons had taught her to how to behave when having her husband's mistress as a houseguest. Spiteful and hateful would be easy, but looking herself in the mirror would be difficult.

The Warren family was always kind to others, and she was a Warren for a little while yet.

"It's too lovely this morning to stay inside." Annabel looked up to the sky, noticing the sunshine for the first time. "There is coffee on the table." She motioned toward the tree where Barnes had insisted on setting the service.

"Will you join me?" Claudette asked. She sounded impossibly young.

"I believe I will." Annabel stopped short of thanking her for the invitation. This was still *her* home. Instead, she washed her hands in the nearby basin and used a cloth to clean her nails.

She joined Claudette at the table. "How do you prefer it?"

"Two creams and three sugars." Claudette grinned. "Jasper teases that I like it so my spoon stands up on its own."

"That sounds like something he would say." Annabel handed the cup to her guest without tipping it into her stupid French lap. "Did you sleep well?"

"Eventually." Claudette sipped her coffee. "I can never sleep aboard ship for fear we will sink, but the exhaustion worsens my *cauchemars*. Sleep is elusive most days."

"Why not come over land, then? Surely Lord Warwick—"

"Kit says the sea is safer because there are fewer people and narrowed avenues for attack, but I believe he simply likes it." She smiled, but her eyes were sad. "I tease that he and Gareth would have been happier in the navy, though we likely never would have met."

"They were stationed in Paris?"

"Oh no. My father represented the French government in Egypt. I met them in Cairo during the Ottoman War."

"It must have been frightening." Annabel had been in danger only a handful of times. She couldn't imagine living in a country where death was a constant threat. No wonder the young lady had nightmares.

"At times." Claudette gave her a sideways glance. "But it also had its thrilling moments."

Annabel's fingers tingled with the memory of firing the pistol and the thrill of watching her prey retreat. Nothing had prepared her for that feeling, or for how alive she'd felt when they were out of danger. "Most things in life have two sides."

"That is true." Claudette refilled her coffee. "My friends in Paris are always shocked when I tell them Egypt was the happiest time of my life."

"Because of Gareth?"

The other woman nodded. "I had traveled Europe with Father for several years, so each post had begun to resemble the others. Gareth had never been farther from Wales than London, so he was eager to see everything as his time allowed. In between, he and Kit told me stories of growing up in Cardiff surrounded by his father's horses and the fun they'd had with Jasper." She was quiet for several moments, lost in her memories. "*En chemin, je suis tombé amoureux.*"

Love did happen when it was least expected, for better or worse. "You married after the war?"

"No, during. My father was...*livide*, but he eventually gave us his blessing. I believe he didn't want any harshness between us when I followed the regiment to stay near Gareth."

"You followed him onto the battlefield?"

"As close as I could be. He insisted I stay at the rear, but I wanted to do my part. I volunteered in the hospital, helping with surgeries and praying I would never see Gareth—or Kit—on the surgeon's table."

Jasper had said Gareth survived the war. Despite her better judgment, Annabel wanted to know how Claudette had gone from happy bride to widowed mistress. "You came back to Wales after the war ended?"

"We settled in Paris. Gareth's family was not happy with him for marrying a French girl." She stared at her folded hands. "For five years, they returned every letter he wrote to them. And so he decided to go to Cardiff and confront them. He never returned."

Annabel put herself in Claudette's place. What would she have done if Jasper left and never returned? What if he'd been attacked while he was alone and bled to death in the street? "You came looking for him."

Claudette nodded. "Kit met me on the docks in his very solemn way and brought me here to meet Jasper." A small, quick smile flitted across her face. "He is so like Gareth. He thinks more than he says, and his body races to keep up with his mind."

A knife pierced Annabel's heart. That was one characteristic she loved as well. She'd couldn't bear this story any longer. "I should return to my weeding."

"You are worried for Jasper? Is he worse again?"

Again?

The word, combined with the concern in Claudette's eyes, pricked Annabel's conscience. "He is too stubborn to get worse. He's likely prowling his room like a tiger in a cage."

"He does that when he thinks," Claudette said. "And the faster his feet, the faster his thoughts. *Cela me donne le vertige.*" She fastened her gaze on Annabel. "We all have our ways. I bake. You garden."

And yet nothing was solved. Everything was still as confusing, as dizzying, as watching Jasper wear a path in the rug. "Mrs. Hughes, what is your relationship with my husband?"

Claudette inhaled deeply, held the breath for a moment, and then released it. "I am grateful that you asked." She frowned. "That is the wrong word. *Reconnaissante.* Do you understand that word?"

Thankful. Annabel nodded, her heart thudding.

"Society sees a Frenchwoman who is dependent on a handsome man and assumes many things that are untrue. The more the *hypothèse* is repeated, the easier it is to believe. Even if it is painful." Claudette briefly squeezed Annabel's fingers. "There is more to our story than the superficial."

Biting her tongue, Annabel forced herself to wait for the rest of the tale.

"All I have of Gareth is the letter he sent me from Cardiff, saying his family was still angry, and he was sailing for home. I don't even have a grave where I can grieve." Her fists tightened until her knuckles were white. "For the past year, they have accused me of killing him when he returned to Paris empty-handed. I, in turn, have been foolish enough to retaliate—accusing them of harming him when he refused to abandon me."

Tears gathered at the corners of her eyes. "Jasper and Kit have been *infatigable* in finding the truth, in convincing all of us that we were stronger together if we focused on the same goal.

Without them, I would have lost my will to fight for Gareth. And for myself."

Again, Annabel put herself in Claudette's place. She had slept very little last night, and Jasper was still alive on the other side of the wall. How much would it torture her to know he was lost and might never be found? That she would never see him again, even if it was only to argue?

"That is the cause of your nightmares?"

Claudette shivered. "They are terrible. Jasper says I scream the house down, though I never remember it. All I know is his kindness when I wake."

Is that what you think of me?

"I have misjudged you," Annabel said, meaning every word. "I am sorry."

"It is already forgiven." Claudette dabbed her eyes and smiled. "I was often jealous of Gareth. When you find someone you love, it is easy to believe that everyone loves them in the same way. I am happy that Jasper has you."

"Yes, well…" Annabel floundered for a topic that was not her marriage or the husband she had disappointed. "Have you been in Cardiff since we first met at Kennet Hall?"

Claudette nodded. "Jasper and Kit convinced me to stay, to see if villagers might talk to a widow more easily. That worked in two ways. The women were more willing to talk to me, but Gareth's family also observed from a distance. I wrote them an apology, and we have met. Our friendship is fragile, though, and they look for any reason to doubt me."

Which was why she couldn't stay at Kit's new home. A newlywed marquess and his wife were the perfect hosts. "Are you closer to finding the truth?"

"We have a name and a collection of stories, but we don't know how anything ties to Gareth. It couldn't have been his military service, not in Wales. He'd been gone so long that any grudges would have likely faded. That only leaves his father's stables, but the family has no records of dealing with Mr. Collins."

Annabel lost her breath. Mr. Collins from Wales. A body that would never be found. A scheme in danger of failing.

Spencer.

She pushed away from the table and fought to keep her chair upright. "Excuse me. I must speak with Jasper right away."

❧

"WHY DIDN'T YOU tell me this earlier?" Jasper demanded.

"I was distracted by your collapsing in my arms in a bloody heap," Kit said around a mouthful of scone.

He made it sound far worse than it had been. "And after that?"

"You were unconscious for a good bit. I had to choose between watching you sleep or catching up on things at Warwick House."

"You mean *home*, Cousin?"

It was odd to call Kit that, but it felt good to do so. And now that he was privy to the family secret, Jasper could see the resemblance between his best friend and the uncle he'd known all those years ago.

"Is that what it is?" Kit filled his coffee cup. "My staff hates me, the reading from Lords puts me to sleep, and there are calling cards piling up at the door. And tenants? Jasper, I have *tenants*."

Jasper understood the feeling. Sometimes it seemed as though the only real *privilege* of a title was waiting to get it. Once you had it, the responsibilities fell heavily. Especially the care for those who had no privilege at all.

"You will be an excellent landlord." He meant it. There was no one better at logical decisions than Kit.

"Thank you," Kit said. "It will help that I have you to ask." He drew a deep breath. "But to the matter at hand…"

Finally. Jasper rocked forward and put his elbows on his knees, only to straighten when his body protested.

"Collins is making the rounds to every mine. He goes to the nearest pub, finds the biggest groups, and feeds them money and alcohol while bragging about his new job as a foreman at a new concern. Better pay, better conditions, more opportunities." Kit shifted in his chair. "The authorities there haven't given him much thought. Bragging, even lying, isn't a crime."

"But murder is," Jasper said.

"Which is where Claudette has helped. We know for certain where Gareth was, and at what time. We know Collins and some of his cronies crossed his path. We just don't have a motive."

Without that, they'd fail to give solace to Claudette and to Gareth's family.

And if Spencer wasn't tied to the scheme, they'd likely fail the queen.

The key in the lock turned, and Annabel stepped from her room to his. "We need to talk, right away."

"Your husband and I are discussing matters not for public knowledge, Lady Ramsbury," Kit barked. "Kindly leave—"

Annabel squared off to face him. "Do you mean trying to find an embezzler in the palace? Or finding a murderer in Cardiff?"

"Christ, Jasper. Do you ever stop and think?" Kit pushed himself upright. "Isn't it convenient that you've never been set upon by highwaymen until you were traveling with her? And now your attacker was waiting outside a house that has been vacant for months?" He thrust a finger toward Annabel. "Perhaps she told him—"

"Oh yes, perhaps I told them so I could try to kill one of them in the dark. Or so I could have the joy of a dress covered in my husband's blood while we raced home," Annabel parried.

"It would be a wise move to thwart an assassination as part of your role—"

"Enough." Jasper resisted the impulse to tighten the belt on his dressing gown. It was difficult to issue commands while dressed in silk, but perhaps if he acted like he was wearing trousers, he could bluff his way through it. "She is my wife, Kit. I trust her."

There was a difference between that and disappointment that she suspected him of things far worse than being a traitor.

"Why?" Kit demanded.

Jasper held up his hand and ticked off his reasoning with each raised finger. "I told her of the embezzlement but not the murder. The visit to Ramsbury House was a surprise. I was on foot, so it would have been easier to follow me." He drew a deep breath and raised his pinkie. "I wasn't the target."

It haunted him every time he was still. A thin man all in black, a cap pulled low over his eyes, a scarf pulled to his nose as he strode toward Annabel. The knife glinting in the sunlight.

"I apologize, dearest. I didn't mean for you to find out that way." He extended his hand and was relieved when she took it.

Despite her paler-than-normal complexion, she wore a predictable frown. "You're wrong, Jasper. He called for you, not for me."

"I am not wrong." The stranger called *Lady Ramsbury* in his nightmares. "But we can argue over it later." He indicated the chair nearest him, even though her sitting meant releasing his hand. "What did you need to tell me?"

"I can tie Reginald Spencer to Mr. Collins," she said. A ghost of a smile flitted across her lips, but her eyes held questions that broke his heart anew. She didn't doubt her conclusion. She feared what he would do with it.

"How?" Kit snapped. "How do you know Mr. Collins?"

"I don't know him, exactly." Her fingers writhed in her gardening apron, twisting the fabric first one way and then the other. "It's more that I know *of* him."

Kit snorted, and Jasper shot him a quelling look before refocusing on Annabel's story. "Tell me."

"The last time I was in Spencer's home, he was there."

"Before your wedding?" Kit's sharp question would have been welcome any other time, with any other witness.

Annabel ignored him. Her deep brown eyes focused on Jasper

as her color heightened. "Two days after the Haverstocks' ball."

"Why that day?" Kit asked. "What did you—"

Annabel's eyes flashed before she turned to face her inquisitor. "Lord Warwick, you will have your answers if you allow me to finish my explanation without interruption."

Given their midnight activities after the ball, Jasper could understand Kit's concern over the timing of her visit. That didn't keep him from laughing. "Just so. Please continue, my marchioness."

It wouldn't hurt to remind Kit that he wasn't the ranking member of their party. It also wouldn't hurt—at all—to hold her hand. If nothing else, it would be a show of unity. It would also save her apron.

"I went to tell Spencer that I was through, and he could do his worst." Her hands stilled, reminding Jasper of her midnight confession. Annabel took confessing very seriously. "He held my father's debts."

"The sale of the library satisfied them, and I made certain Patton paid him directly." Jasper glanced at Kit. This distinction was important for his point. There was no longer a reason for Annabel to keep Spencer's secrets. It made her a threat. A target. "But back to Collins. He was there?"

Annabel nodded. "He and Sir Reginald were in the library. I heard them when I went in search of his dreadful housekeeper. Collins confessed to a murder, and I believe it was Gareth's." She glanced from Jasper to Kit and back again. "He said the man had heard too much of their scheme."

And now she's heard too much. Jasper resisted the urge to draw the curtains and move her into a corner of the room. "What else?"

"Collins was here to meet with someone named Christian—"

"The man I met with your father." A thrill went through him as his instincts were confirmed.

"And there was talk of someone from Cork and something about…powder?"

"Holy God," Kit breathed from his chair.

Jasper had forgotten he was in the room. "Are you certain, dearest? Was there anything else?"

"Their partnership is not an easy one," Annabel said. "Collins seems to have as much sway over Spencer as Spencer has over him."

"Not a position Spencer would enjoy," Kit murmured.

He also doesn't like people telling him no. Jasper turned back to Annabel and hoped his fingers weren't as cold as the rest of him. "Do they know you overheard them?"

"The door stayed closed." Her brows knitted together. "But there is a chance that his housekeeper saw me listening. She's a dreadful busybody."

Jasper fought the urge to laugh, but only until he saw the sparkle in her eye.

"It won't hold up in court." Kit prowled the other end of the room. "All she can say is that she heard Spencer call someone Collins while discussing a murder in Wales. Collins is a common enough name that it could have been anyone."

"He walked with a cane," Annabel said. "If that helps."

"Slightly." Jasper squeezed her fingers. "And though it may not hold up in court, which I'd prefer you not be involved in anyway, it gives us a wedge to put between them. If Collins thought Spencer was about to betray him..."

"And Spencer thought Collins was about to do the same..." Kit dropped into the nearest chair.

They were quiet for a long few moments. "It could work," Jasper said.

"It has to." Kit's jaw was tight. "A new mine with outlandish promises, staffed by men who are already disgruntled, and an Irish bomber who already has half his money?" Blowing up a mine wouldn't be cheap. "How did Spencer get it?"

"He has new curtains in his drawing room," Annabel whispered.

"What does that matter?" Kit's question, though abrupt, was

not dismissive.

Jasper was accustomed to Kit's brusque debating style, but it had chafed at first. He was relieved to see Annabel's reaction limited to a slight frown and a deep inhale.

"He has several new expenses tied to Elizabeth's Season. The house here is leased, and Mrs. Spencer is in Bath. Even though she's in the family home there, her upkeep is not free." She shifted in her chair to face Kit. "While I lived with the family, the furnishings weren't sparse, but they weren't lavish. We ate well enough, but not sumptuously. Elizabeth went out, but he rarely went anywhere but his club."

Jasper thought back over his social outings, considering where he'd seen Spencer outside of Parliament. The last was when he'd met Gwennie Harris at the latest stage comedy. "He has a box at the theatre."

Jasper had thought it odd. Spencer always seemed too dour to enjoy dramatics.

"And?" Kit motioned for them to get to their point.

"He's third." Jasper smiled as Annabel's voice chimed with his. A glance her way revealed her impish grin and set his heart racing.

But he needed to focus.

"His role as chaplain doesn't command a lavish salary, and even before that, his earnings as a clergyman would have been adequate, at best." Jasper stood, driven by his whirring brain to pace the floor. "His eldest brother, Lord Benton, is parsimonious, even with his own family." The man never went anywhere, and his daughters were so seldom seen that there were frequent rumors they'd been shuffled off to nunneries. "He's not going to waste money on his youngest brother's new drapes."

"So you believe he's stealing it from the queen for *furniture*?" Kit cast him a dubious look. "That seems rather shortsighted. Perhaps he's just blackmailing someone for the coin."

"No."

Annabel's decisive contradiction drew Jasper up short. "Explain."

"Someone recently told me that Spencer's schemes are never far from the truth." She looked from him to Kit, then back. "He told me you two were plotting upheaval in Wales. Which he is doing."

"He is tying you to the investment," Kit said.

Jasper snorted a laugh. "He's not going to use gunpowder to ruin my reputation."

Kit rolled his eyes. "You haven't been to Cardiff in a while, Jasper. *Unrest* is a mild term. Those men are tired of risking their lives to heat all of England for only shillings a day. Another unsafe hole in the ground will lead to a strike. The queen won't let them hold the country hostage."

"And Spencer gets to be the hero," Jasper said. He'd spun his role in Stratford's scandal in a similar fashion, benefitting from Drake and Jocelyn Fletcher's desire for anonymity. "He already has Collins and Christian to make the introductions so he can smooth things over. The queen will give him anything he asks."

"Like the promotion he's been chasing," Annabel added. "He also sees your reputation ruined. You'll be tied to the mine by gossip, and you will lose your influence in Parliament and with the prime minister."

Kit uttered the curse that Jasper's mind couldn't yet form. No wonder Spencer wanted Annabel dead.

"Graydon's giving him the money, Jasper. It's the only way he'd have enough to pay for something this large this quickly." Kit had the look of a pointer on the trail of a fox. "And Graydon owes him his help in securing the Exchequer position."

Jasper didn't want to believe that Charles Melton, the Marquess of Graydon, had any role in this scheme. The man had a reputation for horse racing, yes, but it was a long way from gambling debts to treason. And he was never in Spencer's company.

Not that anyone had seen—or at least noticed. But the Graydon family also had a box at the theatre. It was near Jasper's.

"*Much Ado About Nothing* is on stage in two days' time." He walked to Annabel and smiled at her curious frown. Her shoulder was firm against his palm, but her collarbones were delicate. It would be too easy to injure her. Or worse. He should send her to Ramsbury until this was over. "Would you like to go to the theatre?"

"I love Shakespeare." Realization lit her eyes, and she curved her warm, strong hand over his. "Thank you."

CHAPTER TWENTY-FOUR

ANNABEL HAD NEVER understood why her mother considered the theatre scandalous. For her, it was a book come to life. Time both stood still and passed too quickly as she'd watched her favorite characters repeat oft-read words in front of intricately painted scenes.

While the canvas backgrounds had always been disappointing, the actors rarely let her down. Tonight was no exception. Watching Beatrice and Benedick's reluctant romance grow provided a pleasant distraction after the drama from the past week.

Even Jasper seemed to forget himself as the play unfolded beneath their box. His deep laughter rolled over her as the couple bantered their way into love, and he paid rapt attention to Don John's plot to ruin the happiness of every party.

Hero's funeral signaled the intermission, and the lights came up in a wave. Jasper turned to her with a smile on his face. "Fitting that we should both enjoy a play about gossip."

"You never fail to surprise me," Annabel said. "I wouldn't have imagined you, willingly, at the theatre."

He shrugged, though his grin turned wicked. "Perhaps I'm enjoying being out of the house and in something other than my dressing gown."

It was nice to forget their concerns, if only for a few hours.

However, they were likely the only box with an armed guard in the shadows. "And to have something to eat other than soup?"

"God, yes." Jasper looked longingly at the empty refreshment tray. "I wonder if I could bribe an attendant for another visit."

Annabel stood. "I should visit Lady Carmichael while we have time, and I believe I saw the Duchess of Rushford."

"I'll go with you. Though we should avoid being seen with the duke and duchess." He winked at her. "After Stratford's arrest, we draw attention when we're seen together."

She nodded, though she shot a glance across the theatre at the Rushfords' box. As much as she wanted to visit with Thea, they needed to avoid the attention tonight of all nights.

Once in the hallway, and in the crush of people wishing to be seen and heard, Annabel regretted their decision to leave their seats. She went to move to the outside, meaning to protect Jasper, but only succeeded in stepping on his toes.

He draped his arm around her waist. "Relax, dearest. We're fine."

The weight of his hand shifted with every step, tightening when he swung his left leg. Annabel looked over her shoulder, fearing an attacker masked as a friend.

"The secret is to not look afraid," Jasper whispered. "We're just another couple at a play."

"Lady Ramsbury," Ellen Harrow cried as she approached with a smile. "I was just coming to your box."

"Lady Carmichael." Annabel reached for her friend, grateful to see someone she knew wasn't a threat. "I'm lucky you found us in this crush. I was just coming to you."

The crowd jostled them, and Jasper's hissed curse sent a ripple of fear through her.

"Are you well?" Ellen asked.

"I'm fine, but we should get out of this hallway."

"You both look worn through," Ellen said as she took Annabel's arm. "We'll go to the retiring room for some quiet. My husband is at the bar, Lord Ramsbury."

Annabel looked over her shoulder as she left Jasper behind. His height kept him visible longer than most would be, and his smile gave her the courage she needed to keep up with Ellen's quick pace and steady stream of gossip.

The retiring room was at the end of two hallways, the shorter of which connected the wings of the building. Annabel looked into the shadows to ensure their safety and saw a flash of light blue silk fly around the corner. A muffled cry followed.

The hair on Annabel's neck rose. "I'll be right in, Ellen. Excuse me a moment."

Halfway down the hall, it was clear there was a struggle at the other end. One a lady was losing. Armed with nothing but her fan, Annabel wasn't certain how she could help.

"Annabel." Ellen reached her in two strides. "Where are you going?"

Thank God. "The Rushfords' box is on the other side of the theatre," Annabel all but shouted. "I'd like to pay my respects."

Heavy footsteps thudded down the adjoining hall, just as they made the turn. All that remained was a shuddering girl in a lovely dress.

Annabel reached for her shoulder, meaning to offer comfort, but the girl flinched away with a gasp. Annabel mirrored it when she recognized the victim.

"Miss Bainbridge?"

Charlotte gathered her shawl to her shoulders, but not quick enough to hide the finger-shaped bruises on her arms.

"Shall I fetch someone? Perhaps the viscount—"

"No!" Charlotte drew a deep breath. "No, thank you. I'll be fine in a moment." She bobbed a curtsy. "Thank you for your concern, Lady Ramsbury."

It was the proper thing to say, but it wasn't what Annabel had expected to hear from Charlotte. Nothing about this terrified girl resembled the young lady who had celebrated her engagement just last week.

Jocelyn Fletcher's tales of Viscount Raines tumbled into Annabel's brain and combined with what Annabel now suspected of him. The result put her in front of the young lady, blocking her escape. "Charlotte, do not marry a man who hurts you."

The girl blinked. "I'm sorry?"

Annabel touched the bruises as gently as possible. "No man—no title—is worth this."

New tears pooled in Charlotte's eyes. "You don't understand. It's too late. The party, and the announcements, my dress. The settlements have been drawn up."

"Surely your father would not want you married to brute simply to save paperwork," Ellen said from her side of the hallway.

Charlotte used her handkerchief to dab the tears before they fell, but her lips still trembled. "No one else will have me after…" She put her hand over her mouth to muffle her sob. "Please. I can't…"

"You *can*, Charlotte," Annabel insisted. "It will not be easy, and it will require a great deal of bravery. Your friends—"

"My *friends* would step over my ruined body to get to him. They would feign support over tea and then spread the gossip across London before dinner." Charlotte sniffed. "I know because I've done the same."

Annabel imagined Rachel in this same situation and knew what she would want her sister to have. "Then you make new friends, more powerful ones." She tilted the girl's chin and helped blot her tears. "You know where Lady Carmichael or I can be found when you need us. Knock on the door or send word, day or night."

"Charlotte? What is taking so long?" Belinda Wallace called from the other, brighter, end of the hallway. "You don't want to keep Melton waiting."

"Just a moment." Charlotte's cheerful answer belied her shaking fingers as she grasped Annabel's hand. "Thank you," she whispered before stepping past and around the corner.

Annabel and Ellen followed after the girls' voices faded, and walked in silent solidarity toward their husbands, who were waiting near the Ramsbury box.

Though she was in no mood for social conversation, Annabel managed a brief interchange with Lord Carmichael. All the while, she was conscious of Jasper's fingers on her waist and his steady gaze.

Once they were alone, he escorted her back to their seats, nodding to Frederick as they passed his post at the door.

"What has happened?" he whispered once they were settled. "You look angrier than I've seen you in a while." He snorted a laugh. "At least in the last two days."

She tapped his knee with her fan. "You can be a very vexing man."

"I wasn't vexing in the retiring room." He took her hand and waited for her to meet his eyes. "Are you frightened?"

"No." She was never frightened for herself when she was with him, yet she was terrified of life without him. Since her marriage, her days had been full of laughter, warmth that had nothing to do with fireplaces, and color that was more than furnishings and the dressmaker's. Even London had been brighter. With the exception of the last week, she didn't know how long it had been since she'd seen a cloudy day.

"Why didn't you just tell me about Claudette?" she asked.

"Because you were in no mood to believe me." He watched the activity on the floor below them as he shrugged. "You needed to discover it for yourself."

Annabel wanted to protest, to tell him he was wrong, that she was not as judgmental as he believed her to be. But the truth was, he was right—to a point. She had always believed the worst of him and then been proven wrong.

She thought she'd married a debauched, drunk womanizer who might be a traitor to his queen. Instead, her husband was a rather bookish, sober gentleman who was fighting a war against corruption within his own ranks.

"I'm sorry I hurt your feelings."

"Bah." He brushed aside her guilt with his free hand. "I have very few to hurt. Just ask any woman in any random ballroom."

She did not believe him for a second. "Jasper."

"You wounded my pride more than anything." He finally glanced her way and squeezed her fingers. "You do not need to carry guilt for that. It's a stumbling block that's led me into my own rash behavior."

"Like not telling me you ripped your wound open?" She raised an eyebrow as she met his stare. "Claudette asked if you were worse *again*. Why didn't Stapleton send for me?"

She could see Kit leaving her clueless about her husband's health, but she'd thought the butler liked her.

Jasper's grimace made her gasp. "You sat there arguing with me while you were bleeding and didn't say anything?" she said. "You let me *leave the house...*" That realization was almost worse than finding him outside Claudette's door. Claudette, whose husband had died while they had been separated. Who hadn't had a chance to say goodbye. "Why?"

"I was angry," he said. "I wanted you to choose to stay and listen to me."

Annabel fought his tight hold. "Do you realize what could have happened to you? That I would have been halfway across the city with no idea that you were..." She corralled her thoughts before they ran away with her tongue. "You should have told me, Jasper."

"I should have, yes. But if you had stayed with me, Rachel would be betrothed to some liver-spotted man three times her age. It all worked out in the end."

Her sister would be ecstatically happy, but her husband would have bled to death without her. "That is not a fair trade."

The orchestra signaled the end of intermission.

"Neither of us are saints." He lifted her hand to his lips. "That seems to be something else we have in common."

The list grew longer with every day. "Not to mention our fierce tempers."

"That, too." His gaze held hers, and his smile crinkled the corners of his deep blue eyes. "In the grand scheme, this is nothing but a rock in the road. We cannot let it distract us from what is most important."

The gaslights sputtered as they dimmed until the stage was the only focus.

"My mother always insisted the theatre was scandalous." Annabel scanned the stage and the crowd. "I wonder why she thought that."

He adjusted his chair, coming close enough that their knees touched. "Sex."

A shiver went through her, ending with her hard nipples pressed against her corset. Every breath wound them tighter. "There's none of that in this play."

"Not in the play. In the building." His husky laugh heated her to her toes. "Why do you think boxes are so popular?"

The actors returned for the second act, and the crowd quieted. Within minutes, Annabel was once again lost in the story.

"Look up three boxes and two boxes to your right," Jasper whispered.

Curiosity compelled her to look through her glasses in the direction he indicated. A lady she didn't recognize was alone in her box, though her knee was against the rail in a most unladylike pose. She seemed focused on the play, but her mouth was open in a gasp that had nothing to do with the action on the stage.

"Her lover is on his knees under her skirt." Jasper traced a finger across her bare skin along the back of her dress.

Annabel pressed her thighs together, embarrassed by the heat flooding through her at the memory of Jasper doing the same thing. "How does she stay quiet?"

"Practice." Jasper made the word sound like sin itself. "The thrill of illicit sex is the possibility of getting caught, but no one *really* wants to be caught."

Cheeks hot, Annabel took one last glance at the lady in the throes of passion, her bare hand over her mouth to muffle her cries. An odd sympathy bloomed in her chest. She had to use a pillow to hide her wails as Jasper tormented her with his tongue, and she still wasn't certain the whole household couldn't hear her.

A small trickle of dread followed in the wake of Jasper's finger on her skin. "Is that why you like coming to the theatre?" While she enjoyed sex with her husband, she couldn't imagine having it where people could look up and see them in the act.

"It can be fun to watch if the play is boring, but otherwise no." His palm was warm on her shoulder, reassuring. "There is a difference between an eagerness to be together and a fetish."

Laughter from the crowd drew Annabel's attention back to the stage, but after a moment she found herself scanning the boxes opposite them. Jasper's soft laughter raised gooseflesh on her arms.

"Fourth row up, to your left," he whispered. "Find the box that looks empty."

Annabel lifted her glasses and found the box without a problem, noting that one of the chairs was turned away from the stage. The longer she watched, the more the details came into focus. Fingers curved around the seat of the chair; the lady's skirts clung to the legs.

Her companion was a shadow behind her, though his buff trousers occasionally caught the light from the stage. The chair rocked in a familiar, intimate rhythm.

Another round of laughter took Annabel by surprise, and she dropped her glasses into her lap. Everything inside her ached with an emptiness that began at her center. Her clothing tormented her too-sensitive skin. Jasper's solid thigh was her only anchor, but she couldn't remember having reached for him.

His stare glittered in the dim light.

Embarrassed by her display, Annabel withdrew.

"Leave it." Jasper pulled her back and curled his fingers around her palm. "Please. I like it there."

She liked it there too. But every shift of his muscles reminded her of the man across the way. It made it difficult to focus on the stage, but she managed. It helped that she'd read Shakespeare so often she could recite it with the actors.

As the play ended, they stood with the other audience members for an ovation. Her hand was cool without Jasper's, but anticipation hummed beneath her skin.

Once in the hallway, they moved with the crowd toward the doors. Frederick stayed on their heels. They reached the way out, and the crowd separated, everyone looking for the shortest route to fresh air. All but two men, off to the side, who were in a heated argument. Reginald Spencer and Charles Melton, the Marquess of Graydon.

"Jasper."

"I see them. Keep moving so we don't draw attention to ourselves."

Once outside, they hurried to their coach. Jasper helped her inside. "Take the long way home, please, Lawrence. Through the park."

He closed the door and extinguished two of the lanterns, throwing them into near darkness.

"Spencer and Graydon." Annabel tempered her glee at the key discovery. Jasper had hoped the marquess wasn't involved in this scheme. Bits and pieces of collected information shuffled in her brain.

They stuttered to a stop when Jasper's mouth claimed hers in a hot, deep kiss. She returned it eagerly, hungry for him in a way that would have shocked her only a few months earlier. She had missed the thick silk of his hair under her fingers and the sweet, wild scent of his skin.

His greedy hands roamed her body, stoking the fire between them.

He pulled away, his chest heaving with every breath in a most complimentary way. "I promise we'll pick through every detail, but I won't be able to concentrate until I've had you trembling beneath my hands." He delivered another shocking kiss. "At least once."

He removed his gloves with a violence that should have ripped them to pieces and then struggled from his coat. His broad shoulders and strong arms stretched the fabric, reminding Annabel of how he'd felt under her hands and the pleasure they'd given each other.

She loved this man. If they separated after their mission was concluded, she would still love him. It made her ten times a fool, and considering sex with him doubled it.

Despite all that, Annabel peeled off her gloves. Excitement coursed through her, pooling at her center. It was foolish, yes, but she'd have memories like none other. "Travis said you shouldn't exert yourself."

"He has no imagination." Jasper sat back on the opposite seat and swept his gaze around the carriage, as though he'd never seen it before. After a moment, he refocused on her. Her favorite wicked smile spread over his face. "I'm about to scandalize you."

Yes, please. Cool night air brushed her ankles.

He ran his tongue along his bottom lip. "Stand up and turn around."

Annabel obeyed his whispered command, pitching unsteadily with each roll of the carriage wheels. Then, mimicking the lady from the box, she bent at the waist until her elbows were on the seat and she was clutching the edge of the upholstery. She had to spread her legs to keep from toppling forward.

Her corset stays dug into her breasts and her waist, making her wish she was naked. In a coach, rocking down the streets of London, where one shift of the curtains could expose her to the *ton*. It should have been shocking, but all she could think of was the man behind her and his touch on her skin. How eager she was to have him.

"You never cease to amaze me," Jasper said as he ran his hands under her skirts, gathering them as he went. The air chilled her knees, then her thighs, and finally her behind, but his fingers left trails of heat in their wake.

It was nothing compared to his hot breath over her hip before the rasp of his teeth and the wet flick of his tongue.

"Spread wider, love. I'll need more room."

The action pushed her breasts against the cushion and her behind higher in the air. It would be horribly embarrassing if she stopped to think about it, but she had no time to consider it.

Jasper stood behind her. His trousers teased her thighs as his knuckles brushed her hip. In this close space, she felt his buttons give way. Then he was there, prodding her center. She bit her lip to muffle her needy whimper.

A thud against the wall of the carriage startled her.

"Just me," Jasper rasped. "This damn thing wasn't made to stand up in."

He pulled her to him with one hand and filled her deeply. Annabel's groan of relief ended in a smile as she heard him echo it.

He withdrew and returned with greater force, hitting a spot that shattered her relief and replaced it with hot, shivering pleasure. She buried her face in the upholstery to muffle her scream.

It continued stroke after stroke, again and again, the same cushion rescuing them from discovery tormented her breasts with delicious pressure. Her nipples were likely wearing a hole in her corset. Her head nudged the wall, and Annabel braced her hands there, pushing away to avoid breaking her neck. The result brought him deeper and ripped a cry from her throat as her toes curled in her shoes.

"God yes, like that," Jasper growled. "Take me, Annabel."

She did, answering every delightfully brutal stroke with one of her own, coming apart as her husband snarled and swore above her. Her throat was raw, her dry tongue stuck to the velvet, and her shoulders trembled from exertion. She'd be on the floor if not for Jasper's bruising hold as he poured himself into her.

It was incredible.

"Did I hurt you?"

Jasper found it difficult to do more than whisper as they rode through Hyde Park, piled together as though they were in bed. He was sated, exhausted, and more than a little in awe of his wife.

She brushed his cheek with a kiss. "I may have a bruise or two, but it was worth it."

He'd have a crick in his back for days—and he'd smile with every twinge.

"How did you know?" she asked.

"I watched you in the theatre." He'd almost taken her then, sent Frederick to fetch the carriage and pulled Annabel into the shadows against the wall. But he didn't like public sex, and she would have had to be quiet. Neither of them would have enjoyed that.

She was as honest about her enjoyment as she was with everything else. Just thinking about it made him want her again.

"I'll admit I thought it would be easier to do than it was." He looked to the dimly lit walls and inconveniently low ceiling. "We need a larger coach."

Annabel snuggled against his chest and pulled the blanket to her chin, which only worked to expose her feet. "We need a longer blanket first."

We. The word warmed him from the center outward in a way he'd never expected. Jasper pulled her closer and pressed a kiss to her disheveled hair. As much as he liked her perfume, he enjoyed the scent of the real her, crisp and slightly sweet, with just enough salt to remind him of a few moments ago. "Certainly."

When he'd thought about marriage, which wasn't often, he'd always considered it a necessary thing in a longer line of necessary things. Title. House. Lords. Wife. Children. Done. He'd had a vague idea of what he expected from a wife. Pretty enough to catch attention, smart enough to not be embarrassing, and good enough at running the household. They'd see each other enough to create a peaceful home and go out enough to be interesting.

Good enough. He'd have had a life that was *good enough.*

Annabel had saved him from that.

His chest tightened, making it difficult to breathe, much less speak. "Dearest?"

"I know you'd hoped Graydon wasn't involved," she said at the same time. "I'm sorry."

He shrugged as best he could while reclined against a seat with his arms full of his wife. "I just didn't figure him for paying the queen's money to his friends."

"They aren't friends."

"Just because they were arguing? I hate to tell you, but male friends argue more than they have civil conversations. We save civility for other people." He and Kit fought like devils at times. Perhaps that was because they were related.

"Spencer doesn't have friends, Jasper. He has chess pieces." She eased from his hold and straightened, putting them eye to eye. "Not all of us are pawns."

She was no one's pawn. He traced a finger down her cheek to the point of her chin. "You believe Spencer has something on Graydon."

"I know he does."

Her intelligence and her certainty excited him, but he envied her ability to form coherent thoughts. His brain was still after-sex fuzzy. "What do you know?"

"Jocelyn Fletcher threw Viscount Raines out of her...house for assaulting a girl."

He liked Jocelyn Fletcher, trusted her, but she was as tenacious about protecting her staff as she was about ensuring her information was accurate. "Annabel, the ladies at the White Rose are paid for sex however their customers want it, within reason. If Raines got heavy-handed—"

"Not a lady, Jasper. A *girl.*" She put her finger to his chest.

"And it shouldn't matter who it is. Women have the right to be safe and respected in their own homes, whether they are paid for or bartered off for their dowry."

The flash in her eyes reminded him of the night she'd scolded him at his own party. He'd suspected even then that, given the chance, she would fly. A smile stretched slowly across his tired face. "Yes, Lady Ramsbury."

"Don't patronize me over this. Under the super-fine and the horses, he is a brute and a bully, and—"

He pressed his fingers to her lips, and her breath warmed his fingers. "Tell me what you've learned."

"Spencer was there when Jocelyn banned Raines."

The road beneath them changed from the park's gravel to city cobbles, rattling Jasper's teeth and clattering through his head. He pushed himself upright.

"So he knows what happened." His mind began to spin. "And he was already backing Graydon's bid for lord high treasurer."

"But he was appointed to the Exchequer instead," Annabel said, continuing the story. "Because the queen wanted the ability to dismiss him if need be."

God love a woman who understands Parliament. "That position carries a great deal of honor. A scandal could tarnish it." He thought for a moment before shaking his head. "Getting barred from a brothel is still a weak excuse for blackmail."

"Not if it ruined his son's chance to choose the diamond of the Season and her lucrative dowry," Annabel countered as she angled to face him.

"Which it hasn't." Jasper squared off against her, rising to the battle.

"They aren't married yet," Annabel said. "She may surprise you."

A shadow crossed her eyes, merely a flicker but enough to raise questions. "Annabel?"

She shook her head. "We will not use this story in our scheme."

The carriage slowed for the turn into the rear lane and then eased to a stop. "Home, sir."

"Thank you, Lawrence," Jasper called up. He stared at Annabel for a moment, taking in her half-down hair, loose pins, and wrinkled gown. "Ask Frederick to stay atop, please. I'll see us into the house."

Jasper lowered the stairs and stepped down before offering his hand to Annabel. As she reached the middle step, he met her gaze. "Then we'll find a way to stop him."

They were at the base of the stairs when Jasper decided to share his last piece of the puzzle. "The queen and the prime minister suspect embezzlement because funds are not available for improvement projects she had promised."

"But only in the poorest districts," Annabel said. "At least, that's what I've read in the news."

"You've read correctly. The prime minister has investigated every supplier and contractor." He snorted a laugh. "It's likely the only time someone has hoped for graft."

"Which only leaves the treasury," Annabel said as they entered his room.

Jasper paused at the door and watched her move about his space as though she'd never left it.

"Taxes." She looked in the mirror and gasped. "Why did you let me walk through the house like this? If your mother had seen me..." She filled the basin with water and set to work cleaning her face.

If Mother had seen you, she'd have been relieved that I'm trying everything I know to save my marriage. Not to mention his country and his queen.

Annabel had found a purpose in the capture of Collins, Spencer, and Raines. That shared challenge had let the two of them form an easy truce. They were friends. They always had been. Good marriages were born out of worse.

She dried her face and began fumbling through her ruined curls to find the pearl-headed pins that caught light whenever she moved. "Reports say so many shillings are flowing into the queen's coffers that it's difficult to count them all."

Jasper pushed away from the wall. "We've thought the same thing." He tugged an overlooked pin free and offered it to her. "But we've looked at the books and can't find a discrepancy."

The laces at her back gave way under his fingers, revealing his favorite corset. Satin stitched peonies winked at him, their delicate pink matching the marks under her shoulder blades. They'd be bruises by morning.

"You said I didn't hurt you," he whispered as he traced the undergarment's unyielding curve. Her shiver made his mouth water, and he prayed she didn't stop talking and remember where she was.

"You didn't." The shy look she gave him over her shoulder bested the flirtations of any experienced mistress.

Friends would never be enough. A *good* marriage would be a betrayal of everything he knew was possible with her. Jasper unbuttoned his waistcoat and shrugged free of it. Then he hooked his thumbs under his braces.

Annabel lifted his hairbrush and tugged it through her thick hair. It stopped halfway down, barricaded by a mass of tangles. "This will take forever. Whose receipts are you using?"

He gave her his comb. Anything to keep her from going to the dressing table in her room. "Everyone in Lords has—"

She looked at him like he was the slow boy in maths class. "Jasper, he's not going to skim from anyone who has the right to review his ledgers." She smoothed one section of hair and moved onto another. "We need to find a different group."

"A shilling here and a sixpence there?" He tossed his shirt aside. "It would take forever."

Her touch stopped him in mid-reach for his trousers. Her fingers traced what would be a permanent reminder of how much danger he'd placed her in.

"See?" He met her warm brown gaze and thanked whatever Fate had placed her in his path. "Perfectly fine."

Annabel untied her corset as he unbuttoned his trousers. Her shift fell to the floor as he extinguished his candle and slid between the warm sheets. She joined him a moment later and curled against him in the dark. Her hand against his chest was as comforting as the fire in the grate.

Her toes brushed his calf, and his breath left his body in a sigh that emptied him to his heels.

"We need a group of business owners who pay significant amounts but whom Graydon doesn't know." She yawned. "I believe I know who to ask."

"Of course you do." He kissed her forehead and smiled as her breath fanned over his skin at an even, slow pace. His hand shaped to the curve of her hip, as the firelight turned her hair a warm gold.

His wife was a rare treasure, and he wasn't giving her up without a fight.

CHAPTER TWENTY-FIVE

THE RAMSBURY COACH came to a stop at the end of a line of carriages waiting outside Tavie Foster's home.

"It looks like a ball instead of a tea." Frederick looked out the window before opening the door. "We should walk from here to avoid being late, my lady."

"Thank you, Frederick." The crowd both pleased and unnerved her. She had worried that a hastily called emergency meeting would mean low attendance, but the Circle had proven her wrong. However, now she'd have to address a large crowd.

You can do this.

Jasper's last words before she'd left the house, and his warm kiss, gave her courage as she took her footman's arm. "I could reach the door on my own, you know."

"His lordship made me promise not to let you out of my sight." Frederick smiled. "He was right peeved you wouldn't let him come."

"No other husbands accompany their wives." She didn't count Drake Fletcher, since he and Jocelyn worked together. "I'm not certain they're allowed." And, despite his promises, Jasper would never *meekly stay in the drawing room.*

Martin, the dashing butler, welcomed them at the door. "Lady Ramsbury, please allow me to take your coat and hat." He nodded to Frederick. "Albert will take you to the kitchen, sir."

"With all respect, sir, I'm to stay at the door." Frederick's eyes widened at the crowd of ladies. "I'd prefer inside, but I can wait on the steps if it would be easier."

"Frederick is under orders from Lord Ramsbury." Annabel came to her guard's defense lest he be branded as an uppity footman. Lord only knew what Martin would do if he learned the young man had a pistol strapped to his ribs. "I'm sorry, Martin."

"Not at all, your ladyship. He can help with the door." He called a young, red-headed man forward and delivered Annabel's hat and coat. "You can help me here while Frederick minds the door."

Annabel gained a bit of courage from settling one negotiation before she even entered the boardroom. It doubled when Thea greeted her with a mischievous smile. "My first emergency meeting seems to be a success."

"Thank you so much for doing this." Annabel looked past her to the table, which was already filling with attendees.

"My pleasure." Thea winked. "We haven't had any skullduggery all Season. Come with me to the head of the table."

She sat to Tavie's right, and motioned Annabel to the chair to her left. Mr. Fletcher joined them, taking the chair behind Thea. He was handsome, but Annabel imagined him to be the example of what her favorite novelists labeled as *brooding*.

Jocelyn took the chair to his right, her lilac silk dress in stark contrast to the man beside her. "Hello, Annabel. I'm glad to see you joined us."

"It may be just the once." Annabel felt the need to mitigate expectations. She really had no idea what business she could offer, and Jasper didn't operate one. At least, not a proper one with a sign above the door or a product with his name on a label.

The Marquess of Ramsbury, Spy. That would cause quite a stir.

He would love it.

"We'll see," Jocelyn said. "May I present my husband, Drake?"

He looked up from his notes and nodded with a smile that

was almost unnoticeable. "Lady Ramsbury."

"Mr. Fletcher."

They are a most unusual couple, Annabel thought as she faced forward. Then again, Society would say the same about her and Jasper unless they saw them at home.

Jasper. Couple. Home. Her marriage, no matter how it had begun, now felt very real.

All sorts of emotions came with that admission, threatening to swamp her at the worst possible time. Annabel seized on two and let the others swim past. She would not disappoint Jasper and give Kit Yarwood a chance to gloat over her failure, and she would not lose. Not now, when she was so close to such an important goal.

Tavie tapped her gavel. "Ladies. Come to order."

A thrill went down Annabel's spine. This was her part in their *grand scheme,* her idea for how to trap an embezzler, so they could trap a traitor, so they could trap a murderer.

Once the crowd had settled, Tavie swept her gaze and smile around the room. "It is good to see each of you for our first ever emergency meeting. I will cede the floor to the Marchioness of Ramsbury, who has a request for us to consider."

Annabel went to the podium and smoothed out the foolscap covered with Jasper's neat, bold strokes. She'd expected sentences to read. He'd given her one. *Don't be angry at me. Use your own words.*

"Thank you for giving me an audience today." She drew a shaky breath. "I've come to ask for your assistance, but first I would like to tell you a story. It begins with a soldier from Wales and the daughter of a French diplomat who met in Cairo during the Second Ottoman War."

She continued weaving Gareth and Claudette's tale in broad strokes as she walked inside the circular table, meeting each member's eye. Giving no names to the players, she tied the threads from Gareth to Collins to Spencer to Graydon.

"If you will help by allowing me to compare your business's

tax receipts to the treasury records, I believe we can stop a grave injustice to a family who misses their son, a wife who wishes to properly grieve her husband, and to the people of England who put their faith in their queen."

The room was quiet as her audience stared at each other, wondering who would begin the questions.

"You seek to oust Graydon, then?" one matron asked.

Damn. Annabel hadn't masked the players as well as she'd thought.

"No, ma'am, not if his records are accurate and his behavior is honorable. We have been tasked with finding why tax money collected from you is not reaching the people and the projects as the Crown has promised. There may be any number of reasons that do not deal with the death in Wales. It may also be a clerk in the Exchequer rather than the man himself."

"And you guarantee our anonymity?" a younger woman asked. Her gaze was direct, and her honey-blonde hair was pulled into a severe, simple style.

"I do," Annabel said. "Just as I hope you will guarantee ours. Our objective, our lives, are in danger if our opponents know we are coming."

"If I may." Mr. Fletcher came to her side. "Your men of business will give the names of companies and receipt amounts to me. I will deliver them to Lady Ramsbury. She will not know which of you owns what company, or anything about your businesses, unless you wish to tell her."

Once she was certain no questions remained, Annabel ceded the floor. "Thank you, ladies. Tavie."

"Thank you for joining us, Lady Ramsbury. If you'll wait in the drawing room, we'll cast our votes."

Annabel left the room, praying she'd done enough.

"There is tea waiting, your ladyship." Martin ushered her to the drawing room and held the chair nearest the table. "Plus a few cakes we held back in case you need the strength." His smile took years from his face. "Mrs. Foster can be a handful on her own, but get them all together…" He gave a mock shiver as he left the room.

"Would you care for something, Frederick?" Annabel asked.

Her bodyguard glanced from the window, but only for a moment. "No, my lady. Thank you. I'll wait until we're home."

With every bite and each sip, Annabel remembered pieces of the story that would have been better than what she had chosen. She thought of evidence she had used and hoped she hadn't used too much or let her tongue slip on a name.

The boardroom door opened, and Thea hurried across the dark tiled floor. Her smile was wide. "All of them are excited about being spies and helping those who live in their counties. Many of us began our endeavors to help our own villages." The fire in her eyes hinted at a temper to match her red hair. "To suspect that someone has stolen from us, and therefore from them, is distressing."

"Thank you." Annabel squeezed Thea's hand before turning toward the door. She couldn't wait to get home and tell Jasper how well she'd done. She didn't need to check to know Frederick was two steps behind.

"Drake and Jocelyn will be in touch soon," Thea said, following her to the hallway mirror. "Likely this afternoon. Drake understands the urgency better than the others."

Annabel pinned her hat before taking her reticule from Martin. "I don't know how I can repay your support and encouragement, Thea."

"I'm sure something will come up," the duchess said with a smile. "Go. Give our best to Jasper."

CHAPTER TWENTY-SIX

INKY BLACK FILLED the carriage, so deep Annabel wouldn't know Jasper was there if his lips weren't at her ear.

"As much as this plan worries me, I must say I approve of the disguise."

His fingers traced from her knee up the inside of her thigh, following her inseam.

His warm breath and clear intent made her shiver until she was boneless. "You're distracting me."

"What's sauce for the goose…" He nipped her earlobe and soothed the sting with his tongue. "You should see your arse in a mirror."

"I don't believe this is why Jocelyn sent me trousers." Annabel gathered all her determination and moved away enough to kiss him hard on the mouth. She kept her hand on his jaw. "And we don't have the time, anyway."

"Promise me you'll be careful." His fingers curved around her wrist, his black glove matching hers. "No stubborn risks, Annabel."

The cab rocked to rest close enough to see Westminster, but at enough distance that the driver wouldn't make the connection. "It's a bit late for that, I think."

The gas lamps gilded his hair and leached the color from his face. His blue eyes glittered like stars. "Promise me."

"Of course." She'd spent enough time with him that she could adopt his breezy confidence with ease. The door opened behind her, and the cab shifted with the weight of a new passenger. "And you do exactly as Drake tells you. Save the adventure for later, Jasper."

"Don't worry, Annabel." Drake's deep voice filled the shadows between them. "He's on lookout duty. No skulking allowed."

"Most boring job on the crew," Jocelyn quipped as she held the door. "We're going to have much more fun."

Annabel climbed from the cab and joined her co-conspirator, who was dressed almost identically.

"Trousers?" Annabel looked down her body and wiggled her toes in her soft-soled boots. "Why?"

"They're easier for movement and make less noise than skirts. Think of them like scratchy drawers." Jocelyn began walking across the street, leaving Annabel to follow.

"I've never worn those either," Annabel said as she caught up easily. Trousers were also lighter than skirts, and she'd be lying if she said she missed her hobnailed boots.

"They're more trouble than they're worth, honestly. Wouldn't recommend them."

Annabel tugged her waistcoat. "Like these things." No wonder Jasper stripped to his shirt sleeves the minute he was home.

"They're not made for breasts." Jocelyn crossed into the shadows cast by the hulking castle. It was quiet enough to hear the Thames whisper past. "Watch for bobbies," she said as she knelt in front of an inconspicuous wooden door.

Annabel's nerves jangled as she swept her gaze back and forth, straining to see any movement in the shadows. *Mad Marchioness Breaks into Parliament* was not a headline she wanted her mother, or Jasper's, to read over their morning tea.

The latch clicked. "Come along," Jocelyn whispered.

They entered a dim, narrow stairwell. Annabel grew dizzy as she followed its path. Jocelyn was already halfway up the first flight, her steps all but silent.

Annabel followed her, refusing to look down as they climbed. By the time they stopped, she was breathless. "How do you know where we're going?"

"You'd be surprised what a tenner can buy." Jocelyn put her finger to her lips before opening the door and checking the hallway beyond. "Let's go. Mind the carpet."

The immaculate red carpet.

"We're in the palace." Annabel clapped her hand over her mouth to muffle her whisper.

"Only just." Jocelyn clicked her watch closed. "And right on time."

Though Annabel followed her down the corridor, she couldn't help but stare over her shoulder and wonder what she'd find around the far corner.

"We can explore that way next time." Jocelyn chuckled as she tugged her forward. Their target was a door at the end of the hall. It was flanked by a glass window with a shade drawn over it.

They'd reached the Exchequer office. Jocelyn tried the latch and sighed as it gave under her hand. "Her Highness should really be more suspicious of insiders."

"I'll tell Jasper to let her know," Annabel quipped. It was easier to do this if she didn't take it too seriously.

The outer office was almost the length of a dining room, crowded with desks and closed cabinets. A tray of neatly stacked pages was squared into the corner of each desk. Pens lay in their rests aligned in front of black glass ink pots.

Annabel's faith in her plan wavered. This was not an office that was designed to conceal theft. These weren't men who worked in shadows.

Jocelyn led her to the back, to a room dominated by a desk almost the size of Jasper's bed. Ledges lined the shelves behind it. She pulled a candle from her pocket and lit it with a match from the jar on the desk. "The guards will be by soon. I'll watch the door."

Annabel nodded, already focused on the gold letters on each ledger's spine.

She pulled her list of Circle members from her pocket and smoothed it out on the desk. After that, she wrestled the first giant ledger free and laid it open on the desk. She had hoped for alphabetical records, but instead she found numerical. Thank goodness Drake had asked for dates as well as amounts.

"What made you think he would have these in his office?" She sorted her list into date order.

Jocelyn was keeping an eye on the outside office. "No one would keep theft in plain view."

"My father did." Annabel used Graydon's pen and ink to write the first figures on her list, halfway down the Circle members.

"Your father was hiding from his wife, not the queen." Jocelyn straightened. "Hush."

Annabel knelt and used her body to shield the glow from the candle. The weight of this mission hit home. She and Jocelyn had sneaked into the queen's former home, even if just for a moment. They were now in a courtier's office, using his things.

After a moment, Jocelyn relaxed. "They're gone. Keep going."

We need out of here without delay. "Come help." Annabel pulled the second ledger from its place on the shelf and turned it to the middle. "April should be here. Check the dates and estimate two months per book."

From that point forward, Jocelyn found ledgers and Annabel searched for entries. Each stroke of the pen was messier than the last. She hoped she could read it when she got home. "Finished."

Annabel capped the ink and then cleaned the pen using her shirt sleeve. She put it back on its rest, just like the others she'd seen. By the time she'd finished, the ink had dried on her list.

"Ready?" It was a rhetorical question. Jocelyn was already at the door.

JASPER STRETCHED THE length of the sofa and used the rolled arm as a pillow. It was a poor substitute, but it allowed him to see Annabel at his desk, where she'd been since she'd returned from the Exchequer office.

The oil lamp created an island of light with her at the center, the black night creating a frame, head bent over a blank ledger sheet as she compared the figures she'd stolen to the ones she'd been given. She also had the totals the prime minister had given to him and Kit, and another book she'd retrieved from her library at Ramsbury House.

A plate of uneaten biscuits sat at her elbow. "Are you going to eat at all?" Jasper asked.

"Are you going to sleep?" she countered. "It's late, and you had an eventful day."

It had been both impressive and terrifying to watch Fletcher break into Spencer's home, to see him blend into the shadows and emerge victorious with what seemed to be alarming speed. No wonder Kit roamed the house at all hours, checking the doors and windows. "So did you."

Annabel looked up from her work. She was still in her trousers, and she had ink on her nose.

If anything had happened to her, he'd have had Fletcher's head mounted on the wall. No matter how much he liked the man.

A yawn stretched his mouth as his eyelids drooped. Fighting exhaustion, he rose from the couch and went to the desk.

"Don't distract me," she mumbled. "I almost have this worked out."

He lifted a biscuit from the plate and broke it in half. The pages spread before her were lists after lists of numbers, calculations, and totals. His eyes crossed. He pulled a chair near her and handed her half the biscuit. "What are you doing?"

"In a moment," Annabel said as she chewed. She trailed the fingers of one hand down the column on her sheet and the other down the list Fletcher had copied from Spencer, checking her work. A census book lay open at her elbow. The cap that had been part of her disguise peeked from underneath.

"How did you come across a census book?" he asked as he offered another treat.

She took it. "Father bought one from a library that received two. I always liked seeing Chilworth on the list. It made us part of something larger than ourselves."

She drummed her fingers on the desk as she stared at her work, reminding him of hoofbeats in a race. Finally, she nodded. Hesitantly at first, then with more certainty.

"You have it?" He sat straighter, staring again at the inked figures. "How?"

"The difference between our friends' receipts and the number in the ledgers is one percent from each, which makes sense. It is easier to keep track of a single calculation. But it's also more difficult to explain away as an error."

She pointed to a total. "This is how much they paid." To another. "This is what the ledger says they paid."

It was a large amount, but from a damned small sample. "What does this prove?"

"It gives us a basis for an estimate. Taxes are only assessed on those with an income over one hundred and fifty pounds per year. That's not going to be a large number of people in agricultural counties." She indicated one list. "I took only twenty-five percent of their population at the minimum income threshold. Three percent taxes, multiplied by one percent."

It was a halfpence for each. "That's not a large amount."

"It is when you add them all together." She pointed at a second total. "And then for counties with industry, ports, or other trade—like Bath. I've estimated half the population would pay taxes to equal this." She indicated a third sum.

London was its own category. She had increased the estimate to sixty percent of the population at the same halfpence.

"That doesn't take businesses into account, or those that make more than the minimum threshold. If we use our comparisons, he's taking three shillings for every five hundred pounds."

All totaled, her estimate was nearly one thousand pounds.

"If he's taking that same amount from tariffs or any other fund, and there's no reason to believe he isn't, the amount could double. Perhaps triple."

She tapped Fletcher's scrawled figures. "This is what Spencer has taken."

It was more than one thousand, but less than three. "Why did he write it down?"

"Force of habit, perhaps." She dropped back in the chair. "A trophy, maybe. Proof of what he'd been able to do." She stared beyond the light that encircled them. "I could understand that."

Jasper stared at her work, formulating the presentation to the prime minister and then the battle for Graydon's confession. Ruining Charles Melton's reputation would be distasteful, but inevitable if they were to put an end to Spencer's manipulations.

To make Parliament honest.

To make Annabel safe.

She was still checking her work, as he'd done before submitting exams. Everything she'd been through since their marriage had been a test. It had been months of new dresses, hateful gossip, running the household, treacherous ballrooms, and wrecked gardens. Not to mention thieving men of business, murderous highwaymen, and a bloody husband.

Now she'd invaded Westminster and come away with the last piece of their puzzle.

Jasper put a finger under her chin and lifted her face until he could see her weary eyes. "You are extraordinary, Annabel."

Every time he kissed her, it was different. Tonight it was a slow exploration by two exhausted partners, the sweetness on her tongue augmented by a boldness he'd never tasted before. It ended when her stomach rumbled.

Jasper pulled away, laughing. "I knew you were hungry." He stood and pulled her with him. "Let's see if Cook left anything in the kitchen."

CHAPTER TWENTY-SEVEN

"Y OU MIGHT ATTEMPT to *not* look so happy with yourself," Kit said.

Jasper wasn't pleased with the job he had to do, but he *was* happy. They were writing the end of this chapter, and he could begin a new one.

Hopefully with his wife, whom he'd left sleeping.

"Lord Ramsbury? Lord Warwick? The prime minister will see you now."

Kit stood and adjusted his coat and cravat. "It's strange not to be in uniform."

It was likely best that he didn't have a saber at his hip. "We need you as a peer today, not a soldier."

They followed the usher to Lord John's inner office, where Lord Graydon and his son, Viscount Raines, were already waiting.

"What is the meaning of this?" the younger man asked. "We understood our meeting to be how *our* family could be of service to Her Majesty." He flicked a glance at Kit. "To have the Chitester family included as well is—"

His father's hand on his shoulder silenced him.

It also made him flinch.

"Please be seated, gentlemen," the prime minister continued as though Raines had not spoken. "And we'll begin."

They followed his directions, sitting on opposite sides of the table. Jasper kept Annabel's figures out of sight, waiting for the proper time.

"Lord Graydon." The prime minister turned to the Melton side of the table first. "As treasurer, I believe you should be aware of a grave matter." He paused. "The queen believes there is a thief in your office."

The man's reaction was limited to a twitch and a gulp. "Thank you for bringing the matter to my attention. I will begin an investigation immediately."

"There is no need. We asked Lord Ramsbury and Lord Warwick to undertake it on our behalf." Lord John switched his attention to Jasper. "And they have completed their review."

Jasper removed Annabel's work from his pocket and unfolded the sharply creased sheets. "In this tax year alone, someone in your office has stolen over one thousand pounds from the Crown."

"That is impossible," Graydon bellowed. "How did you arrive at that figure?"

Jasper focused on the head of the table, on the man who had trusted him to find the truth, as he summarized Annabel's conclusions. He only hoped that he remembered everything that was important.

"Prime minister, this is a fiction," Graydon said. "Where did the marquess obtain any evidence for these wild numbers?"

"From the ledgers in your office, Lord Graydon, which are being removed as we speak." Jasper kept his tone even, saving his wrath for the others in this scheme, the murderers and manipulators. "This is too consistent, too widespread, to be the work of multiple clerks, unless the whole of the Exchequer is involved." Disappointment and sadness left a sour taste. "You, Charles."

"It is ironic that Lord Ramsbury claims to have found a thief by being a thief himself," Viscount Raines said. "Perhaps he has also become a forger to advance his political—"

Again, his father stopped him. Again, he flinched.

Kit drew a sharp inhale and leaned forward in his chair. His knuckles grew white.

"Charles," Jasper began. "We have known each other for a long time. This may be your doing, but it isn't you. Someone is behind this."

He had the answer in his other pocket, but he wanted Graydon to have a chance at redemption.

The older man ran a hand down his face. As he reached his chin, his shoulders lost their shape. "Reginald Spencer learned of one of Philip's…indiscretions. One that, should it be revealed, might limit his marriage opportunities."

"And I told you that no father would overlook a title because of a girl in a brothel," Raines said.

A deep sadness fell over Graydon. "Any responsible father offering a worthy dowry would want his daughter married to a man with a flawless reputation."

Jasper would. He suspected Raines's presumed father-in-law would as well. Annabel's argument after the theatre whispered through his memory. *Raines is a brute and a bully.*

Of course, she could have simply been fighting for this same girl, but Jasper doubted it. A brute and a bully was always a brute and a bully, no matter the rank of the victim.

He'd need to speak with Bainbridge about Charlotte.

"Back to Spencer," Kit said. "Lord Graydon, did Spencer demand money in return for his secrecy?"

Graydon nodded, head down. "With the amounts coming into the treasury, I fooled myself into believing no one would miss it."

"If we hadn't needed money for the bridge in Cumberland, we likely would have." The prime minister tapped his ring against the table. "Lord Graydon, we must discuss the extent of your punishment, but know that it will begin with your immediate removal from office."

"I understand, sir."

Solving the puzzle with Annabel had been exciting, as was

closing in on Collins. Jasper was already anticipating the satisfaction of stopping Spencer and getting justice for Gareth. But this? Sitting across from an honorable man as he watched his life crumble around him? This was the ugly side of those successes.

"Your cooperation in the capture of Mr. Spencer may weigh in your favor when deciding further repercussions," the prime minister said as he stacked the papers and closed the file.

The matter was closed. Jasper put his hands on the chair, eager to push himself away from the table and leave the room.

"If I may, sir?" Kit asked, but then continued without waiting for permission. "Viscount Raines, how did you injure your arm?"

The young man's face went blank. "My horse threw me."

Jasper frowned. Melton's horse master had earned the title—the family's stable was well trained. Not to mention, Raines was celebrated for his skill in the saddle.

"You weren't grabbed from behind while running through Green Park?"

"What? No." The young man's voice rose, both in pitch and volume. "Why would I be *running* anywhere?"

"Because the Ramsbury footman was chasing you," Kit said. "While Jasper was bleeding in his family coach."

Graydon stared open-mouthed at his son. "Philip?"

"I told you no one would care, but you didn't listen." Raines's face twisted. "You know what would ruin our family? Embezzlement."

"What did you do?" Graydon demanded. "Philip! What did you *do*?"

"Spencer said if I stopped Ramsbury's investigation, the threat to you—to us—would disappear. There was only one way to end it."

"You shot at me during the hunting party?" Jasper asked, wanting to be certain what *stopped* meant.

Raines bobbed his chin in the barest of nods.

"And again on the highway?"

"I had a blade. Collins had the pistol," he sneered. "He lost his bottle when you fired on us."

They had come on either side. "You were after Annabel as well."

"Spencer reasoned that we should hedge our bets. If you were gone, we would have time to straighten matters before she or Warwick resumed pursuit. If she was gone, you'd lose your heart for it."

By now, Graydon had his head in his hands. It would take just a quick flick to shove his fingers in his ears.

Jasper had a white-knuckled grip on his chair, so tight that the curved wood gouged a trench in his palm. "And here in London?"

"She knew too much." Raines's eyes were hollow. "You got in the way."

Jasper launched himself from the chair and reached the other side of the table in four long strides. Raines was in his hands, his face under Jasper's fist in the space of two breaths. He didn't know he was roaring until Kit wrestled him away.

"Take a breath." Kit thumped his chest to urge compliance. "Breathe. Again. Again."

Raines was a whimpering, bloody mess. Graydon was in tears. While the prime minister was still seated, his eyes were wide.

"My apologies, Lord John. Lord Graydon." Jasper would not apologize to Raines. Ever. The whelp should be grateful to walk.

"Thank you, Jasper." The prime minister didn't smile, though there may have been a gleam in his eye. "Perhaps you should go home to your wife. I can manage the rest."

CHAPTER TWENTY-EIGHT

"LADY RAMSBURY?"

Annabel looked up from Jasper's correspondence, grateful for the respite. After yesterday, she was tired of numbers and thinking. "Yes, Stapleton?"

"There is a lady here insisting to see his lordship." Stapleton looked over his shoulder as though expecting to see the guest waiting. "She is quite insistent on waiting."

Something in his demeanor, perhaps the way he said *lady*, made her cap the ink pot and stand. "Speak plainly, Stapleton. Please."

"She is not the sort who should be in polite company, and I think she should be gone before Lady Lambourn and the young misses return home."

No matter what he thought, the visitor had already gotten her bluff in. Tongues would wag until dinner if they were seen shoving a reluctant woman out of the house and down the front stairs. "Ask her to wait in the drawing room. I'll be just a moment."

Stapleton nodded and left her to check her appearance in the mirror. The dark circles under her eyes were the only remainders from her late night bent over figures. It would be easy to assume they were from a night spent dancing or at a midnight supper.

Society was the perfect disguise. No wonder Jasper chose it.

Annabel descended the stairs and went to the drawing room. Waiting there was a red-headed young lady wearing far too much rouge for an afternoon in Mayfair, and a dress more suited for evenings in scandalous parts of the city.

"Good afternoon. I'm Lady Ramsbury. How can I help you?"

"Sally Howard, your ladyship." After a curtsy, Sally handed over a calling card. "The marquess left this with me if I should ever need it."

The card carried Jasper's name but Sally's perfume. Annabel recognized the scent. He'd kissed her but come home smelling of Sally. The servants had laughed.

Annabel drew a deep breath of rose-scented air. "Would you care for tea, Miss Howard?"

"No, ma'am, but thank you." Sally clutched her reticule on her lap. The velvet was worn slick in places. "They'll miss me soon."

"All right, then." Annabel sat opposite her. "Lord Ramsbury is with the prime minister this morning, and I'm unsure of when he'll return. Is there something I can do to help, or should I give him a message?"

"He was down at the docks when we met, following a lout from Wales."

Collins.

"He's a nasty piece of work, that one, but he's only in a few times a month. *When his ship comes in,* he says." Sally leaned forward. "But he's here today, and he's got a gleam in his eye I don't like. All us girls are staying well clear of him, but he don't seem to notice."

Collins is in London.

"When I went to the bar for drinks, I overheard him muttering into his whiskey about teaching a *jumped-up queen's man to keep his titled nose out of Wales.*" Sally looked past Annabel to the window. "The more he drinks, the surlier he gets, your ladyship. Sends a chill down my back. Always has done."

That description could be Kit as easily as it could be Jasper. If they were lucky, it might even mean Spencer himself.

"I got busy with work." Sally's gaze flicked down to her lap. "Begging your pardon, your ladyship. And when I looked up, he was gone. I knew, just knew, I needed to come warn the marquess."

Annabel looked past the cosmetics and the low neckline and into Sally's eyes. It would be easy to think all sorts of things. The most obvious was that the girl was devoted to Jasper for a more sordid reason, but Annabel trusted her husband.

He had never given her a reason not to.

There was also the possibility that Sally was in league with Collins and was helping him set a trap. She had Jasper's card, after all. "Why?"

The look in Sally's eyes hinted at hard-won wisdom of a world Annabel knew very little about. "His lordship treated me like a lady with a brain in my head. That may not be rare for you, but it is for me."

"It is rarer than you might think." No one had seen her worth, perhaps not even Annabel herself, like Jasper. Perhaps she and Sally knew more of the same world than Annabel had supposed. "Thank you for warning us."

She escorted Sally into the hallway, near the table where calling cards went and where they kept money for messengers who came to the door. "Let me—"

"No, your ladyship. The marquess paid me plenty before. I won't take more, especially not from you." Sally leaned forward to whisper, "Your butler thinks I'm here to bring trouble. I don't want him spreading gossip that there's a secret you're paying me to keep."

Annabel pressed her lips together to keep from laughing over the image of Stapleton gossiping. "I thank you for that."

She walked toward the front door, but Sally walked toward the back of the house. Annabel caught up to her and escorted her through the hall. Questions bubbled on her tongue, but there was no time to ask them. Perhaps after matters were settled, she could shock Society by inviting Sally to tea.

She opened the door and took Sally's hand. "Thank you again, Miss Howard. Please look after yourself."

"And you, your ladyship." Sally squeezed her fingers. "Men like that won't be choosy about who they hurt."

Annabel watched until she left, her eyes on the red dress that had seen better days, but her mind on Sally's last words. There was a possibility that Collins was in London to find Kit, but Kit had no one else in his life. A man intent on harm would search for the largest number of targets.

Or an easy one.

Lady Lambourn, Jane, and Johanna were due home within the hour. If Collins waited out front, he could injure or snatch one of them and disappear into London before anyone was the wiser.

Or he could push his way into the house and lie in wait for Jasper and Kit to return. After all, Frederick and Lawrence had gone with Jasper this morning. That left only Travis and Stapleton here.

Or he could carry out his plan and let Jasper come home to chaos. The best outcome would be chaos. The worst was unthinkable.

He needed to be away from the house.

Annabel hurried to her room and unboxed the first hat she set hands on. She took time to find a matching coat, ensuring she would look presentable and calm, at least from a distance. It took two attempts to find the correct gloves.

Returning downstairs, she struggled into her coat. Her fingers trembled as she pinned her hat.

"Your ladyship, is this wise?" Stapleton said from the stairs. The man had an unnatural way of simply appearing. "If you'll wait, Lady Lambourn will return with the barouche after tea."

"I'll walk." Annabel fixed him with the glare that was her own unique gift. "You and Travis will be here when Lady Lambourn and the girls return, and you will stay here until Lord Ramsbury instructs otherwise. When he arrives, tell him…"

Her brain whirred. If she said too much, Stapleton would delay her departure or try to prevent it altogether. If she said too little, Jasper would never find her at all.

"Tell him he can find me at home."

She looked in her reticule to check for the key. It would never do to get to Ramsbury House only to be stranded on the street where Jasper had almost died.

"My lady?" Stapleton opened the door for her. "Please be careful."

She squeezed his arm as she passed. "It's nothing but a walk."

The street was almost empty, given that it was teatime. It would have been the perfect time to get a look at Collins, but Annabel didn't dare. This only worked if he thought her oblivious.

She quickened her pace. It was also important that he didn't grab her close to home.

Her breath came easier when she put Grosvenor Square at her back and marched toward Piccadilly. The streets were busier; shops were full of people. Hyde Park was to her right.

Annabel couldn't see the park and not think of Jasper and the first time he'd kissed her, and their delightfully scandalous ride after the theatre. He'd helped her be brave, time and again. He'd given her the courage to do this.

Though he'd never see it that way. He was going to be furious.

At Piccadilly, she entered the sea of people on the thoroughfare. People shouted to be heard over the near-constant rattle of passing carriages.

Annabel stayed close to the brightly painted and decorated storefronts, dodging patrons as they came and went. Bits of music floated through the doors, teasing her to stop and listen. Food smells, both sweet and savory, set her stomach grumbling over missing tea.

She reached St. James Street deafened and dizzy, yet determined to revisit Piccadilly when she could enjoy it.

The tree-lined street in front of her made her smile, despite the chilling memories of their last visit. The old marquess, Jasper's grandfather, had meant it to be a place to work away from the social bustle of Mayfair. Jasper wanted to make it a home.

In the distance, the new giant clock at the end of Westminster Palace looked like a toy. Parliament.

Jasper. Annabel's toes twitched. If she kept walking, if she quickened her pace, she could reach him. She could lead Collins straight to him.

Or the man could catch her in between, leave her dead body in the gutter, and still have time to return to Mayfair to kill her husband.

The traffic here centered on Green Park. Barouches and gigs passed her, the women frowning at her choice to walk alone while the men touched their hats in greeting. The few pedestrians comprised couples and families.

Annabel stood out. As did the triple step of a man with a cane walking behind her. *Clip. Clop. Tap.*

Clip. Clop. TAP.

Clip. Clop. BANG.

She quickened her steps, one hand in her reticule and panic building as the house key eluded her. When she found it, she clung to it like a lifeline.

There was no stopping to admire the front door or the flowers under the windows. There was only the keyhole and her heart hammering in her ears.

She was inside in a breath. The dark, quiet house wasn't as welcoming as she'd hoped, and a chill crawled up her back as she struggled to lock the door.

It flew open, shoving her backward as Collins shouldered his way into the hall, a pistol in his hand.

"Hello, Lady Ramsbury."

Annabel had never been certain what to expect of the man,

but it certainly wasn't someone who could have passed for a Society grandfather. His eyes, though, were hard—like bright stones in a shallow pool, and his leer was just as cold. Looking closer, years of heavy drinking had left a map of broken veins and ruddy splotches across his face. His red and swollen nose looked painful to touch.

"Get out of my home, Mr. Collins."

He advanced. She retreated, never taking her eyes from his. She found the library by touch and then, continuing backward, the stand where the bust of Plato rested.

She twisted and lifted the plaster likeness. Earlier in life, she had been disappointed to discover the cheapness of the reproduction. Now, as she lifted it over her head and hurled it at her stalker, she was thankful.

It hit him on the chest and shoulder, just enough to push him against the wall in a daze. His pistol hit the floor and fired in a thunderous roar. Annabel shrieked and leapt backward as the balls thudded into the opposite wall, burying themselves in the newly painted plaster.

She made for the back of the house and the servants' stairs.

Her hat blocked her view, and its wide brim and bright color made her a moving target. She unpinned it and tossed it aside, wincing as the pin pricked her thumb. Blood bloomed across her glove.

She reached the landing and dithered over which direction to go. Collins's heavy steps on the front stairs made the decision for her.

Hiding the hatpin in the folds of her skirt, Annabel turned toward the rooms at the end of the hall in search of a place to hide until help arrived.

"WHY DIDN'T YOU stop her?" Jasper asked as he tightened his grip on his pistol.

Stapleton, a shotgun in his lap, gave a long-suffering sigh. "Sir. I could hardly lock her in her room like a child."

Jasper didn't blame the man for his impertinence. He'd asked the same question at least twice since they'd all climbed into the carriage, not to mention shouting it while standing in the hall.

"Tell me again." Anything to keep his mind from what could happen to Annabel as they crept down Piccadilly toward St. James Street.

"The…lady knocked on the back door, brandishing your card and demanding to wait until you returned. Since your mother and sisters were expected home, I thought it best to ask Lady Ramsbury for assistance."

So he'd asked Annabel to meet with Sally in the drawing room, which still smelled of cloying roses.

"After a few moments, she showed the visitor out the way she'd come. I thought the meeting had gone well—they both seemed in good spirits, as much as I could tell—but then your wife went upstairs for her hat and coat."

And said she was *going home.*

It was easy to believe she'd been upset after meeting a doxy from the docks who bore his calling card. He'd spent precious moments raging that she'd assumed the worst of him—again.

But then he'd calmed and seen past the superficial. Sally wouldn't have come to Mayfair on a lark, and the only connection they had was a knowledge of Collins.

If Kit's campaign to split Collins and Spencer had worked, it would be predictable for the man to travel from Wales to London and confront his partner in crime.

And it would be equally predictable for Spencer, who by now knew his scheme was collapsing, to set Collins loose on his enemies.

Considering those points, if Annabel was fleeing from Collins, she would never return to her family home and risk them. After all, she'd fled Lambourn House rather than risk Mother and the girls. Going to Chilworth Manor or Kennet Hall would require a public coach and waiting for the day of travel.

There was only one home remaining, though it was empty of anything but dust and shrouds. Jasper found himself hoping she considered Ramsbury House *her* home but praying she hadn't gone there alone.

"I could run faster than this," he grumbled as he looked out the window.

"That would be a fine news story. *Armed Marquess Dashes through Piccadilly with Bastard Cousin in Frantic Pursuit.*" Kit touched the barrel of Jasper's pistol, encouraging him to lower it. "We also shouldn't brandish our weapons out the windows."

Jasper set the gun on the seat between him and Travis and dropped his elbows to his knees. Maybe they would move faster if he didn't watch. And, indeed, it did sound as though the horses began to make better speed.

If Collins had followed Annabel to St. James Street, God only knew what they would find. If he had caught her before she'd reached the house, they might not find her at all.

Travis put a hand on his arm, which sent his heels to the floor. The clip-clopping steps ceased.

Three sympathetic, yet irritated, faces stared at him.

"Apologies," he mumbled.

They made the turn from Piccadilly onto St. James, and Lawrence pulled the team to a stop. Kit put a hand to Jasper's chest, making him wait until last to exit.

"Grown man," he grumbled.

"Frantic husband," Kit shot back.

It was a fair warning. As worried as Jasper was about Annabel, he had to keep his wits.

Their small group gathered a great deal of attention. Part of it was likely due to the coach, which was far too grand for a day in the park. Most of it, however, could be attributed to six armed men in the middle of the street.

"Travis and I will go through the back and up the servants'

stairs," Stapleton said. He took the key Jasper offered—his mother's spare. "Frederick and Lawrence, you're responsible for keeping their lordships safe."

It wasn't lost on Jasper that his butler had resumed the role of commander and put himself between Collins and escape.

The older man put a hand on his shoulder. "She will be fine, sir. And he will not get past us."

The remaining four waited until Travis had rounded the corner and disappeared down the alley. Then they walked at a painfully slow pace toward the house in the middle of the row.

As they drew nearer, Jasper grew transfixed by the spot in the pavement where he'd been standing as Raines approached, bent on harming Annabel. His still-soft scar itched under his shirt.

To their left, the door to Ramsbury House stood open. Kit put himself in front of Jasper and stepped forward. Lawrence stopped him, allowing Frederick to take the lead.

"Serves you right, Lord Warwick." Jasper chuckled.

"Still in front of you." Kit looked over his shoulder, a cocksure grin on his face.

Lawrence fell in behind, and the long barrel of his rifle floated into Jasper's peripheral vision. "I know you're worried about her, sir. But if I say *fall*, you do it."

Jasper nodded and drew a deep breath as he stepped over the threshold.

A pistol lay on the floor between the library and the stairs, surrounded by a sprawl of rubble that had once been the bust of Plato. A large, bloody handprint circled the walnut orb at the base of the baluster.

Annabel had put up a fight. Jasper exhaled and smiled. Of course she had. "Stepping over the mess would have slowed her," he said. "She went up the back stairs."

"She did at that." The voice came from above.

Collins wasn't much taller than Annabel, which made her the perfect shield. Rather than a pistol at her head, he held his thick black cane across her throat.

She looked ready to chew nails. Her hands were fists at her side.

Jasper worked his tongue against his teeth to moisten his dry throat. Nothing would be helped if his command cracked in the middle. "Mr. Collins, release my wife."

"I need you to listen," the man shouted back, his words slurred. "And I think you're more likely to do what I want if I have your lady wife with me."

He weaved on his feet. Jasper wasn't sure if was due to a day in the pub or the blow to his head, which left a bloody trail through his graying hair.

All Jasper needed to do was keep him occupied so he didn't hear Stapleton and Travis on the back stairs.

And keep him from harming Annabel.

"All right." Jasper tightened his hold on his pistol. "What do you want?"

"I want that bastard there out of Wales and leaving me alone." He nodded toward Kit. "And he needs to take that French bitch with him."

"You need to watch your language in front of the lady," Jasper said. This was his home and his wife. He wasn't going to cower and comply. "But tell me why, out of everything you could ask, you want that."

"I had a good scheme there. No one was getting hurt, and we weren't causing trouble for anyone but Her Royal Highness in whichever castle she wants. Men were able to feed their families and have a few quid in their pockets."

"Until you blow the mine." Kit's words landed like stones.

"Closing an empty hole won't do nobody harm," Collins sneered. "We'll have a few weeks on a picket line and maybe come out the better for it."

Annabel flinched every time he spoke, which only served to make Collins tighten his hold.

"A mine is never empty, Abel," Kit said. "You know that. And you also know that death adds legitimacy to any strike and urgency to any negotiations. Are you certain Spencer means to keep this bloodless?"

Collins blinked at them.

How long will it take Stapleton and Travis to get up the stairs? How will I know when they are there?

"He's not a man to trust, Abel." Kit sounded calm, but his hands were shaking.

"Says the man who wants to stretch my neck for murder." Collins lifted Annabel's chin to a height that made Jasper lose his breath.

Something in her fist caught the light, like jewels under a chandelier in a ballroom. That made no sense. The only jewels she kept at home were her wedding ring and her hatpin.

"Dear God," Lawrence muttered. "She wouldn't."

She would, if pressed. The only option was to keep everyone, including Annabel, calm.

"I want to see you get a fair trial for something everyone in Cardiff believes you did, given the stories we've heard." Jasper spoke to Collins but focused on his wife, willing her to wait. "Spencer will weave a tale that lays everything at your feet."

"Either path, I hang." Collins used his body and the pressure from his cane to steer Annabel toward the stairs. "So you and the bastard earl are going to let me out of this house and out of London, and I'll leave her ladyship at the Welsh border."

"Or you can tell the prime minister about Spencer's plan to create a coal shortage and hold the country hostage."

Collins paused halfway down the stairs. "You have been busy."

I have a brilliant wife.

Jasper kept his face to Collins, using the turn of the stairs to move closer, even by the smallest step. This situation was deteriorating. "There are alternatives to hanging."

He was certain he was wrong. He hoped he was lying to the man. What was more, he hoped Collins didn't know he was lying.

The man's mouth flattened into a thin line, and his eyes hardened. His knuckles grew white.

And then he was screaming and shoving Annabel away, reaching for both his arm and his foot at the same time. Annabel was a waterfall of blue muslin tumbling down the stairs. The crack as she struck the banister echoed through Jasper.

The hatpin was still vibrating in Collins's shoulder as he raised his cane and roared, signaling a charge down the stairs. Stapleton and Travis came into the upstairs hallway, weapons at their shoulders. Lawrence and Frederick raised their guns from below.

Jasper rushed to Annabel's side. On his knees, he put his arm up to block the blow, should it arrive.

"Alive!" Kit shouted as he put himself between their private army and the man they'd hunted for months. "We need him alive."

There was a thunder of steps and shouts on the stairs. Collins thudded against the plaster more than once, spewing profanity. Jasper didn't care about any of it.

Annabel wasn't moving.

CHAPTER TWENTY-NINE

NNABEL SAT ON the front row of the gallery, her hands clutching her reticule to keep them from reaching for her throbbing head. The rail was the only thing blocking her view of the chamber below.

Reginald Spencer was being led away. His wife and daughter had stayed in Bath.

"Will he go to the same prison as…the other man?" Claudette asked. She flatly refused to say Abel Collins's name.

"Likely not. He'll have better food and fewer rats." Below them, Jasper was deep in discussion with Drake Fletcher. "But he'll be there longer."

Is he searching for a new man of business? A proper one? Annabel bit her cheek to quell her smile. *Proper* would make Jocelyn laugh.

"Though I went to war with Gareth, I never considered myself a warrior, never thought of myself as hostile." Claudette drew a deep breath. "I am most definitely hostile."

Annabel's neck was still stiff from her tumble down the stairs. "I'll go with you to the hanging."

Jasper looked up at them. His smile was too thin for a victory this large.

Their mission was over. "Let's go down now that the crowd has thinned," she said.

Collins might as well be taking her to the gallows with him.

Jasper met them at the bottom of the stairs. Exhaustion had remapped his face, leaving heartbreaking lines and shadows. He caught Claudette in his arms as she embraced him. Friendship and Frenchness made things so much easier.

"I shall leave you both," the young widow said as she kissed Annabel's cheeks. "Gareth's family is waiting to say goodbye before they sail."

Her absence left nothing but silence. Jasper offered his arm. "Shall we go?"

It was over. Spencer's corruption was contained. Collins was going to hang. Mr. Christian had fled for parts unknown, taking his investors' cash with him—and none of it belonged to her father.

"Bainbridge has canceled Charlotte's engagement." Jasper's words were soft and slow, more evidence of his exhaustion. "He's using the Melton family's midnight flight as the reason."

"Thank God," Annabel breathed. She would rest easier knowing Viscount Raines wouldn't be around the corner in the park or behind a fern in a ballroom.

"I wanted so badly to stop this corner of government corruption, to find Gareth's killer, and I have." He shot her a quick smile. "We have. But there is a path of devastation in our wake…"

Annabel stopped him in the middle of the great hall and stared into his fathomless gaze. "Which none of us anticipated. And which is none of our doing. You did not make Raines a villain, or Graydon a thief, or Collins a murderer. And Spencer was a greedy, manipulative bastard long before we came along."

His smile wasn't as sad this time. "You've taken to swearing quite well, Lady Ramsbury."

"Something else we have in common." She loved this man and the life they'd created. She'd fight for it, even if it terrified her.

His eyes searched her face. "If I had lost you on those stairs…"

"Then it would have been my own fault for haring off and putting myself in that position." She knew she'd made a mistake the moment she'd taken the turn onto Piccadilly. "But I was genuinely worried for your mother and the girls."

"I know." He chuckled. "Though I cursed your stubborn nature for most of the night while I watched you breathe." He reached for his side, where his skin was still knitting together. "Something else I think we have in common." He offered her his arm again, and cursed when she limped forward. "Stay here and let me fetch the coach."

Annabel tightened her hold. She was tired of coaches and guards. She wanted to talk to her husband. "I don't think you should hire Drake." Her words echoed back to her.

Jasper stopped in mid-stride. "I believe he limits his talents to blackguards worse than me."

Tears flooded her eyes, and his frown wavered in front of her. His gentle touch melted her until she was sobbing against his shoulder.

"You told me you didn't want to marry me, and I talked you into it for all the wrong reasons." Jasper cradled her against him, and his words tickled her ear. "You've been shot at, almost stabbed, practically a widow, chased through Piccadilly, and thrown down the stairs."

She took the handkerchief he offered and blotted her tears before she backed away. "And broken into Westminster, helped catch an embezzler, a violent thug, a murderer." She didn't want to consider what her life would have been like without him. "I've also found my freedom, my voice, and a husband who values my unique contributions to a marriage Society trapped him into."

"I love you, Annabel," Jasper whispered against her lips.

"Something else we have in common." She tunneled her fingers into his thick hair. "I love you."

It was a long time before she thought of anything but how his body felt under her hands and how his mouth felt on her skin, but when Jasper finally raised his head, the light had returned to his eyes.

"We'll need a man of business temporarily," he said as they resumed their walk. Sunshine greeted them as they emerged onto the noisy street. "We really should have a wedding trip."

"Paris would be lovely in this time of year." Annabel said it because every Society couple went to the Continent. It was quick and easy, and just scandalous enough to be entertaining. "Though I'll need to talk to Jocelyn before we go. She's asked for my help on a business matter of some sort."

Frederick saw them approaching and leapt from Lawrence's side. It was a relief to see him unarmed. Just another footman.

"Has she really?" Jasper maneuvered her through the crowd. "That will work fine. I need to make my presentation in Lords before we go."

Pride swelled in Annabel's chest. They had been working on his speech for veterans' rights for the past week. He now woke at midnight to think rather than worry.

"Would you mind if we didn't do Paris?" He cast a sly look her way. "There's a ship leaving port in two weeks, sailing for St. Kitts. In the Caribbean."

Annabel stopped in the street, her mouth open in a most unladylike fashion. An island. An honest-to-God adventure.

"I thought we might enjoy seeing real sharks." He put his hand on her back to urge her to resume their walk. "And whatever exotic thing we might find."

They reached the coach, and he helped her inside. She dropped against the cushions with a sigh.

Jasper sat beside her and lifted her foot to his lap to remove her boot and massage her swollen ankle. "The queen has asked us to look in on some of her property while we're there. Perhaps poke around in the caretaker's records."

No titled lady in London, or elsewhere for that matter, should get a thrill from the idea of breaking into someone's private chambers. They certainly shouldn't wonder if they could learn to pick a lock in two weeks' time.

"Maybe we could tour a sugar plantation or two," Annabel added. "There might be a good opportunity there."

"There might indeed." His fingers left her ankle to travel up her calf. The carriage rocked forward with a jolt.

Annabel pulled the pins from her hair. "How exciting."

"I warn you." He caressed her knee. "Sailing means narrow beds and thin walls." His fingers curved to the shape of her thigh. "We won't have a great deal of privacy."

"Then we'll have to be quiet." Annabel undid the buttons on his waistcoat. His broad chest was warm and solid under his fine cotton shirt. His shoulders gave easily as she pulled him down for a kiss.

She pulled away to gasp as his fingers reached her center. The smile on his face was wickedly glorious. "I think we should practice."

The End

ABOUT THE AUTHOR

Peri Maxwell has lost herself in reading romances all her life. She began writing as a challenge to herself and wrote her first historical romance on a dare, and now she's hooked. She prefers to write heroines who can stand toe-to-toe with a hero, challenge society's rules for good reasons, and find love with heroes who admire an equal (even if it's a little reluctantly).

She enjoys history, humor, and a good mystery. An armchair historian, she also has a background in women's studies.

Peri lives in Arkansas with her husband and the two cats who rescued them. When she's not writing or reading, she's working her day job or spending time with her family and friends (the same ones who dared her to write a historical romance).